The Guardship

Also by James L. Nelson

The Revolution at Sea Saga
By Force of Arms
The Maddest Idea
The Continental Risque
Lords of the Ocean

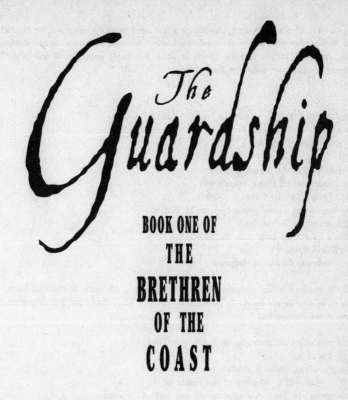

The Guardship

BOOK ONE OF
THE
BRETHREN
OF THE
COAST

James L. Nelson

POST
ROAD
PRESS

AN AVON BOOK

AVON BOOKS, INC.
1350 Avenue of the Americas
New York, New York 10019

Copyright © 2000 by James L. Nelson
Cover illustration by Frank Schoonover
Interior illustrations by James L. Nelson
Inside back cover author photo by Lisa M. Nelson
Interior design by Kellan Peck
Published by arrangement with the author
ISBN: 0-380-80452-2
www.avonbooks.com/postroadpress

Library of Congress Cataloging in Publication Data:
Nelson, James L.
    The guardship / James L. Nelson.
        p.   cm.—(The brethren of the coast ; bk. 1)
    1. Virginia—History—Colonial period, ca. 1600–1775 Fiction.
I. Title. II. Series: Nelson, James L. Brethren of the coast ; bk. 1
PS3564.E4646G83   2000   99-39239
813'.54—dc21   CIP

First Post Road Press Printing: January 2000

POST ROAD PRESS TRADEMARK REG. U.S. PAT. OFF. AND IN OTHER COUNTRIES, MARCA
REGISTRADA, HECHO EN U.S.A.

Printed in the U.S.A.

OPM   10   9   8   7   6   5   4   3   2

To Lisa,
my beloved wife

Acknowledgments

My thanks to Stephen S. Power, Captain-General of Post Road Press, for his help and enthusiasm with this new series. As ever, thank you to Nat Sobel, Judith Weber, and all the fine people in their office. And thanks to Tish Clark for the just desserts.

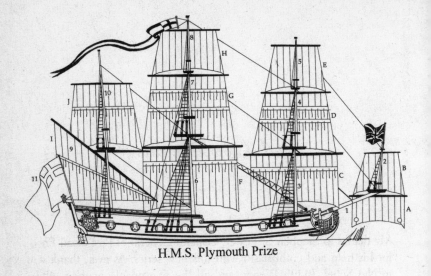

H.M.S. Plymouth Prize

A. Spritsail
B. Spritsail Topsail
C. Foresail or Fore Course
D. Fore Topsail
E. Fore Topgallant Sail
F. Mainsail or Main Course
G. Main Topsail
H. Main Topgallant Sail
I. Mizzen Sail
J. Mizzen Topsail

1. Bowsprit
2. Spritsail Topmast
3. Fore Mast
4. Fore Topmast
5. Fore Topgallant Mast
6. Main Mast
7. Main Topmast
8. Main Topgallant Mast
9. Mizzen Mast
10. Mizzen Topmast
11. Ensign and Staff

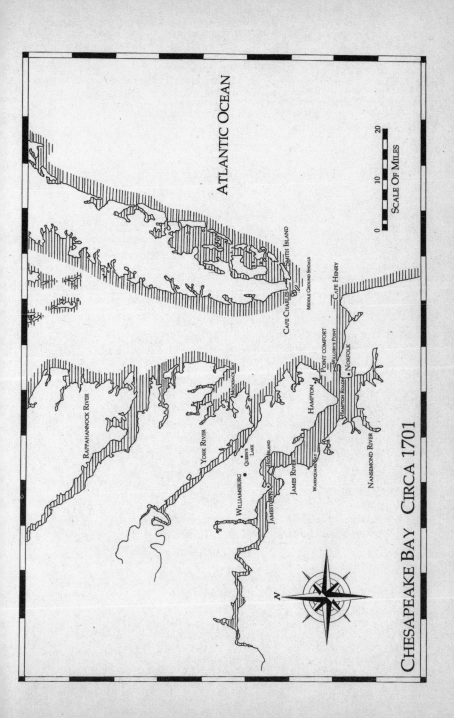

ATLANTIC OCEAN

SCALE OF MILES

0   10   20

SMITH ISLAND

CAPE CHARLES

MIDDLE GROUND SHOALS

CAPE HENRY

POINT COMFORT

WILLOW'S POINT

HAMPTON ROADS

NORFOLK

HAMPTON

MOCKIACK BAY

RAPPAHANNOCK RIVER

YORK RIVER

QUEEN'S LAKE

WILLIAMSBURG

JAMESTOWN

HOG ISLAND

JAMES RIVER

WARIOQUAKE BAY

NANSEMOND RIVER

N

CHESAPEAKE BAY CIRCA 1701

The Guardship

Chapter 1

PUBLICK TIMES in Williamsburg. April the fifth, the Year of Our Lord 1701. The night before Marlowe killed young Wilkenson. The night Marlowe was asked to command the guardship.

The colony of Virginia was a wild place then, a wilderness of great rivers and creeks and islands and mile after mile of woodland that had never seen a white man's face. Otter and beaver in vast numbers. Enough fish in the water that a man could fill a canoe in half a day. A place where a man could disappear forever, and many did, and not always by their own design.

There were few towns of any note in the tidewater regions. Travel in Virginia and Maryland was made easy by the great Chesapeake Bay. Rather than struggling over decrepit roads the people there used the rivers as their highways, and there was little need for them to bunch up in settlements.

So, they lived in far-flung plantations where, with ax and torch, they beat back the thick forest to make room for tobacco, more and more tobacco, that unfailing cash crop.

And when they did congregate for Publick Times in the capital city of Williamsburg, after their long and unnatural solitude, it was a raucous time indeed. The streets overflowed with people. Men and women, freemen, indentured servants, and slaves moved in throngs from one revelry to the next. Beautiful coaches with matching teams and footmen in fine livery pushed down sandy Duke of Glouchester Street.

As the warm day gave way to the cool of evening, a spirit of good humor prevailed throughout the tightly packed taverns, boyling houses, publick houses, and ordinaries. All men, gentlemen and commoners, were fellows on that day, and planters, tradesmen, farmers, laborers, mechanics, sailors, thieves, and picaroons reveled together in the streets.

Thomas Marlowe stood to one side of the ballroom, the grand ballroom in the governor's house, watching the brilliant silks and velvets, the long white wigs of the gentlemen, and the great piles of hair atop the ladies' heads as they moved across the floor in their elaborate cotillions and minutes.

He could feel the sweat running down his face under his own wig. The weight of his red silk coat with its gold embroidery, the snug-fitting waistcoat, seemed to grow more unbearable with each moment. His shoes pinched intolerably.

The air outside was cool, sweet, and pleasant, but inside the hall, with its great chandeliers and their hundreds of burning candles and the crowd of people all whirling and curtsying across the floor, the atmosphere was thick and all but unbearable.

From a nearby open window Marlowe caught a welcome breath of air, and with it came the muted sounds of gunfire and singing and shouting and laughter. The common people had taken their celebrations to the public square, carrying on in the country manner. It was a very different kind of celebration than the governor's highly civilized affair, and, Marlowe imagined, considerably more fun.

But despite his discomfort he managed to do a tolerable job of appearing to enjoy himself. There was no one there, excepting Francis Bickerstaff, who stood beside him, who might have guessed at how miserable he was.

"I quite fail to understand, Marlowe, why we must subject ourselves to this torment," Bickerstaff said. "I am certain that we are witnessing one of the circles of hell. I should think we will see enough of damnation in the next life that we might forgo it now."

Bickerstaff was the most plainly dressed man in the crowd. This is not to say that his clothing was poor, far from it. He wore a blue silk coat, adorned with only a bit of embroidery, and that blue as well, a simple white waistcoat, and breeches, all of the finest silk, unadorned, a plain cut, subtle and of the highest order.

"Now, Bickerstaff," said Marlowe, "we could hardly decline an invitation to the Governor's Ball. One does not advance in Virginia society by staying at home and ignoring such affairs."

"Why you should be so obsessed with rising in Virginia society is yet another mystery to me."

" 'There are more things in heaven and earth than are dreamt of in your philosophy, Francis Bickerstaff.' " Marlow turned to his friend and smiled. "Is that not what your William Shakespeare said?"

Bickerstaff sniffed. "Something to that effect, though he is hardly 'my' William Shakespeare."

Marlowe was Bickerstaff's junior by about ten years, or so he guessed, but that was only a guess. Bickerstaff would not reveal his age, and Marlowe did not know his own for certainty, but he imagined Bickerstaff was around forty-five. He had a thin frame and the perpetually dour countenance of the serious pedagogue, which indeed he had once been. He was a learned man, skilled in Latin and Greek, mathematics, natural science, and all of those subjects befitting a gentleman.

Marlowe opened his mouth to reply, when his eye caught a parting in the crowd as the dancers drew apart with the precision of soldiers on a parade ground. He turned, and for an instant he could see clear to the far end of the room.

And there he saw her, for the first time that night.

Her hair was the color of fresh straw and made up in a great pile, held in place by a gold comb, which in turn was covered with jewels that glinted in the light from the chandeliers.

Her skin was white and perfect and smooth from her forehead to the tops of her lovely round breasts, pushed up by her bodice. Her waist was tapered down perfectly to the point where her farthingale held silk skirts far out from her sides. She was beautiful, and though Marlowe had made no overtures in her direction, thinking it improper given her circumstance, and indeed had spoken to her but a few times, he was her slave.

Her name was Elizabeth. Elizabeth Tinling. She was twenty-three years of age and already a widow. Her late husband, Joseph, was one of the wealthiest planters in the tidewater. He had died two years before, of heart failure, or so it was generally presumed. There had not been much talk of his passing.

Marlowe had purchased the Tinling plantation from Elizabeth soon after his arrival in the colony. That afternoon when they had closed the deal, and perhaps half a dozen other chance encounters, was all of the intercourse that he had had with her.

From the moment he first saw her he had wanted more, but then, for all his wealth, he had held no place in colonial society, being newly arrived, enigmatic.

Much had changed in the intervening two years, and while he might not be the first man of Virginia, still his star was on the rise. He had seen to that.

He considered those things in the few seconds that he had Elizabeth in sight. Then, like the Red Sea closing on Pharaoh's legions, the crowd came together again and she was lost to his view.

The dance that was now under way was one of the Scotch reels, a dance well within Marlowe's limited ability to perform, and that bolstered his courage.

"Bickerstaff, I do believe I shall ask Mrs. Tinling for the next dance."

"Bravely said, Marlowe, but I think you will be frustrated in that endeavor. Here comes the governor." Bickerstaff nodded to another corner of the room. "And he seems to be making a rhumb line for you." In the past few years Bickerstaff had taken to using nautical jargon.

Marlowe looked in the direction that Bickerstaff had indicated. Governor Nicholson was indeed working his way toward them though the crowd. The long, curly white hair of his wig swished around his collar like a horse's tail as he nodded greetings to his many guests. He was agitated, Marlowe could tell, despite his attempts at gaiety as he pushed his way across the room.

He had reason to be agitated. Marlowe had seen to that as well.

"Marlowe, Marlowe, how the devil are you?" Nicholson asked, plowing through the last of his guests and extending a hand.

"I find I am well, Governor, thank you. And yourself?"

"Fine, fine. As well as can be expected, with what I must endure. Bickerstaff, how are you, sir?"

"Very well, Governor, thank you," said Bickerstaff, giving the governor a shallow bow.

"Listen, Marlowe, I know you did not come here to conduct business, and I must beg your forgiveness for making this request of you, but might we have a word in private?"

Marlowe had quite expected this, but still it was annoying, just at the moment when he was intent on approaching Mrs. Tinling. He looked across the room, but the dancers filled the floor and he could no longer see her. "I would be delighted, Governor."

It took the two men another ten minutes to extract themselves from the ballroom. No one had come to the ball to conduct business, but still it seemed no one could resist the opportunity for a private word with the governor, even if it meant speaking into his ear over the sound of the music.

At last they came to the governor's office, just down the hall from the chief entrance to the building. It was a beautiful room with shelves full of leather-bound books, an enormous desk, and racks of firelocks and pistols. The ceiling was twelve feet high, and one wall was composed almost entirely of windows, which, mercifully, were flung open. The cool air wafted in, as refreshing as a rain shower. Marlowe wanted desperately to shed his wig and coat and enjoy the night air to its fullest, but that would never do in front of the governor.

"Sit, please," Nicholson said, indicating a chair in front of his desk. He sat, and the governor called for his servant to bring a sneaker of punch, which he did, and pipes as well, and soon the governor and Marlowe were enjoying a private glass and a smoke.

"I suspect you know why I wish to speak with you," the governor began.

"If it is about the silver, I pray you put it out of your mind. The fault is entirely my own. I should have expressed more curiously as to its origins. . . ."

"Nonsense. It was in no way your fault, and your returning it thus was a noble gesture," said Nicholson. "A noble gesture."

A noble gesture, thought Marlowe. Indeed.

He had purchased an extensive set of silver tableware from Captain John Allair, captain of His Majesty's Ship *Plymouth Prize*. The *Plymouth Prize* was the Royal Navy guardship on the Virginia Station, sent to enforce the customs laws and protect the colony against pirates. Virginia was the most valuable colony in all of America, but for all that the admiralty still considered the Chesapeake to be something of a backwater, a place to send their most rotten ships and failed captains. In Allair and the *Plymouth Prize* they had quite outdone themselves.

Like most in the long line of inept guardship captains, Allair had a number of businesses on the side, most of them illegal. One such business consisted of confiscating "contraband" goods off of arriving vessels and then selling them himself.

His luck in that venture came to an end on the day that he confiscated what was, unbeknownst to him, Governor Nicholson's personal silver.

Less than a week after he sold the silver to Marlowe, Marlowe invited Governor Nicholson to dine with him. The governor had instantly recognized the tableware that he had ordered from London half a year before. For Nicholson, that was Allair's final, intolerable act.

"I have suffered that rascal quite long enough," the governor said, reaching across his desk for a pile of paper stacked near the edge. "The fact that he holds a commission as captain in the Royal Navy does not impress me. A thief's a thief, no matter what his rank."

Through the open windows Marlowe could hear the unrestrained revelry of the crowd in the square, the sound of which nearly overwhelmed the delicate music drifting in from the ballroom away down the hall.

The wide sleeve of Nicholson's coat floated over the various things on the desktop—ink pots and quills and his glass of punch—as he reached for the papers. Marlowe tensed, waiting for him to knock something over, but he did not.

"See here, Marlowe," Nicholson said, locating the paper he wanted in the stack. "This is a copy of the invoice for my silver."

He handed the paper over, and Marlowe ran his eyes down the list. "One sugar bowl, silver, with king's arms, one punch bowl, ditto," he read. He nodded his head. It was not the first time he had seen that invoice, though Nicholson did not know that. "There is no question, sir, but that this invoice describes the silver I purchased from Captain Allair. By God, I do apologize."

"No apology needed from you, Marlowe." It was an awkward situation, awkward for both men. "As I said, it's none of your fault. It's all on that thief, Allair."

"I am loath to think the worst of a King's officer," Marlowe said, "but I can't imagine how he came to have your silver."

But of course that was not true, not true at all. Marlowe knew perfectly well how Captain John Allair had come by the governor's silver.

He had asked him for it.

Chapter 2

THE DANCERS came together, meshing like the gears of a clock, and blocked Elizabeth Tinling's view of Thomas Marlowe at the far end of the room.

Or, more to the point, they blocked Marlowe's view of her. For Marlowe had been looking, had been bracing himself to ask her for a dance. She recognized the look, the posture, and she would have welcomed the overture.

On the one hand, it would have saved her from having to further endure the vapid young Jamestown fop in the brocade coat who was trying to engage her in conversation.

On the other, it would have saved her from Matthew Wilkenson, who was also eyeing her and was ever so casually approaching, a wolf circling toward an animal too wounded to escape.

Of lesser consideration was the thought that she might do well to become better acquainted with Mr. Thomas Marlowe, might even enjoy his company. But now the open space was filled with dancers and she feared the moment was lost.

"I swear," she replied to whatever the fool from Jamestown had said, "this heat will be the undoing of me. I feel positively faint."

She flashed him a quick smile, cast her eyes over the room.

Governor Nicholson was making his way over toward Marlowe, which would end any chance of Marlowe's rescuing her, but it was an interesting development nonetheless.

". . . and so I said to him, ha, ha, 'Well, sir, if this is the finest horse you have to offer—'" the idiot in the brocade coat was saying.

"Oh, I beg, sir," she interrupted, "but at the banquet table they have an everlasting syllabub for which I absolutely perish. Might I trouble you to fetch me one?"

"But of course. Your servant, ma'am." The young gentleman bowed and grinned, delighted to have some service to perform. He pushed his way through the crowd toward a table that to Elizabeth's certain knowledge contained no syllabub at all, everlasting or otherwise.

She smiled at his back, wondering how long he would search for it. Quite a while, she imagined. He would not wish to come back empty-handed. She felt just the tiniest glimmer of guilt at using him thus, but she could not bear to listen to him for one moment more, and such practical jokes were her secret delight.

And men could be such fools.

She turned back to the endlessly fascinating crowd, social interplays, the feints and attacks and flanking movements of the colony's ruling class. A good deal of surreptitious attention was being paid to the governor, who was leading Marlowe out of the ballroom, a development that piqued her curiosity as well.

Marlowe had been only two years in the colony, but in that short time he had managed to insinuate himself into Virginian society in a way that could only be accomplished through good looks, an affable nature, and a great deal of money, all of which he possessed. He was well liked and well respected.

Elizabeth kept her distance, ignored his obvious interest in her. Elizabeth understood people, had observed the species in all its plumage, understood there was something not quite right about Thomas Marlowe.

She stole a glance to her left. Matthew Wilkenson was making his way toward her, boldly now, his generally haughty and disdainful expression exaggerated by drink, his gait unsteady. If Thomas Marlowe was climbing the colony's social precipice, then the Wilkenson clan stood on its summit, looking down. Matthew Wilkenson was the younger of the two Wilkenson boys, but the one who had inherited the old man's force of personality, the heir apparent to the Wilkenson fortune.

That, along with the Wilkensons' close ties to the Tinlings, and Matthew's insufferable arrogance, had apparently given him the idea that Elizabeth should, by rights, be his. He was becoming less subtle on that point.

She turned and looked at the place where Marlowe had been standing, still hoping for some respite from Matthew Wilkenson, but Marlowe and the Governor had disappeared through the far door.

Thomas Marlowe. She had met him almost two years ago, just after his arrival in the colony. A very bad time in her life. Joseph Tinling had died just a few months before, and she was trying to weather all of the rumors that swirled around about that event.

The house and its contents were not hers, of course. They became the property of William Tinling, Joseph's eldest son, a son by his first marriage, who lived back home in England.

For long months she had fretted over the decision he would make concerning her future.

William had lived in Virginia for some time and was a particular friend of Matthew Wilkenson's. He might have decided to return and take over the plantation. He could have left her penniless if he so chose.

It was a warm day in early spring, the last year of the last century, when the Tinlings' factor, who served as their agent in the colony, arrived with a curt letter from the elder Tinling. The note instructed him to sell the plantation and give Elizabeth one quarter of the proceeds and inform her that doing so would dissolve all ties between herself and the family. The

Tinlings wanted no more to do with Virginia, and no more to do with Elizabeth.

And along with the note, the factor brought a potential buyer.

"My name is Thomas Marlowe," he said, giving a practiced bow, "and my associate is Francis Bickerstaff. We give you condolences on your grief, ma'am, and shall respect your privacy."

"You are new to the colony, sir?" He had a look about him that she had not seen in a long time. He was handsome, to be sure, and cultured and genteel, but he was not a fop. There was something wild behind that facade, like a tiger that has been trained to the house but remains nonetheless a dangerous animal.

"We are new to the colony, yes, ma'am. Mr. Bickerstaff and myself have spent these past four years or so in travel and are looking now to establish ourselves."

"Well, sir, if it is your wont to respect privacy, and to have your own respected, I would suggest that you have come to the wrong land. But forgive me, I am still in some shock over my husband's death and I do not wish to dissuade you from purchasing this fine plantation. Do look around, and perhaps you and Mr. Bickerstaff will join us for dinner?"

Elizabeth spent the next two hours supervising the packing of her clothes and personal belongings. The rest of it—the furniture, the horses, the slaves, even the portraits on the wall— she would sell with the house and never think on them again.

At last Marlowe and Bickerstaff and the factor returned from their tour of the plantation, talking, excited, their fine shoes covered in mud. As Elizabeth seated them around the dinner table she asked, "Tell me, sir, what did you think of this place?"

"Magnificent ma'am, just what we had hoped for," said Marlowe.

"These Virginia plantations are much lauded in England," Bickerstaff said, "and I find the land is all that it is said to be, though to be sure the houses do not in any way compare with those great homes in England."

"They do not, sir," said Elizabeth, and it was true. The most palatial dwelling in Virginia would be considered but a modest country home in England. "This is still a wild land, for all of the pretensions you will find."

They passed the time agreeably, Marlowe animated and amusing, Bickerstaff quiet, pedantic. An odd pair. With gentle prodding Elizabeth was able to establish that Marlowe was from Kent, though he was circumspect about his family, which further engaged her curiosity. Said he had commanded a privateer for many years during the last war, had spent a good deal of his time abroad.

That might explain why his accent was not quite right, she thought. And perhaps why the man himself was so . . . curious. Not in any objectionable sense. There was nothing about him—his looks, his manners—that was objectionable. There was just something out of line. A man to be approached with caution, or not at all.

When the last of the dishes were cleared away, Marlowe clasped his hands in a self-conscious manner, the first such gesture Elizabeth had seen from him, and said, "I do not wish to be rude, but perhaps we should talk about the sale of the plantation."

"You are not rude at all, sir, it is a subject dear to me," said Elizabeth.

"Then perhaps I can make an offer to you, ma'am. Sir?" Marlowe nodded to the factor. "Would, perhaps, five thousand pounds be a fair price?"

Five thousand pounds of tobacco, the coin of the realm in the tidewater. Elizabeth considered that offer. It was fair. Not exorbitant, not even generous, but fair, and she wished to be rid of the place quickly. But, like most people in Virginia, she had little specie, little hard money, and it was money that she needed now, not tobacco that would take this Marlowe half a year to grow.

"Well . . . ," said the factor, not overly impressed with the offer. "We are opening ourselves up to some risk, sir. Crop failure, a drop in the price of tobacco on the market. With that in mind, perhaps it would be better—"

"Perhaps you would consider this, sir," Elizabeth jumped in. Her interests were different from the factor's, quite different. The factor would hold out for the best price, however long it took, while she wished to get at least some hard money and get it quickly. "Might it be possible to make up a part of that in specie, and the rest when the crop is in? I know that that is a great deal to ask, but our circumstances force this condition on me."

The factor scowled at her, but she ignored him, tried to ignore the confusion on Marlowe's face. He glanced over at Bickerstaff, but the older man looked equally confused.

"I am at a loss, ma'am," he said at last. "I have no land now, no crop . . ."

"Of course not," Elizabeth said, growing irritated. "I assumed that the five thousand pounds of tobacco you offer would come from your first crop after purchasing this plantation. I have no objection to that, but for my immediate concerns—"

"Tobacco?" Marlowe interrupted. "Did you think my offer was five thousand pounds of tobacco?"

"Well, certainly," said the factor. "Tobacco is the unit of currency in this colony. What else is there?"

"My offer was five thousand pounds sterling, sir. Gold and silver, if that is acceptable."

It was only with the greatest effort that the factor did not spit his tea all over the table, and even Elizabeth had difficulty in controlling her reaction. Five thousand pounds in gold and silver? It was unheard of in the cash-strapped colony. It was an exorbitant price for the plantation.

"Yes, that would be acceptable," said the factor, recovering quickly. "Will you send to your bank in England?" ·

"There is no need, sir. I have the funds here."

She stared at Marlowe. He had with him five thousand pounds in gold and silver? She would not consider asking how he happened to have five thousand pounds in specie. And she would treat him cautiously. Very cautiously indeed.

But perhaps, she thought, staring at the door through which he and the governor had disappeared, it is time to relax that caution a bit.

The rumors about Marlowe's past ran through the colony: He was the third son of the Duke of Northumberland, he was a former naval captain drummed out of the service, he was a former pirate, he was the bastard son of the old king. She did not believe any of it.

But Marlowe was wealthy and growing in power, and while he made an obvious effort to ingratiate himself with the powerful families of the tidewater, still he did not seem in the least intimidated by them, or anyone, for that matter. He had the governor's ear. Perhaps he was an ally she should cultivate.

But now he was gone, and nothing could save her from the unwanted attention of Matthew Wilkenson.

"Allair has been relieved of his command," Governor Nicholson said, taking the invoice and replacing it on the pile of papers. "I believe as vice admiral it is within my authority to do so, and if not, too damned bad, I say. I'll not suffer a thief to run amok in the guise of an officer of His Majesty's Navy. We have endured fewer insults from the pirates and picaroons than we have from him."

"Well, sir, I am very sorry to have been the instrument of Allair's downfall," Marlowe began, but the governor cut him off.

"Nonsense. It was none of your fault, and frankly I'm glad this has come to light. But look, here's what I wished to speak to you about. The colony cannot be without a guardship. The pirates are swarming about the Capes, and once word of Allair's arrest is spread abroad they'll be amongst us with nothing to fear. Now you, sir, are a former naval officer yourself—"

"Please, Governor," he interrupted, holding up his hand, "I was captain of a privateer, not a naval vessel. I have not held a naval commission, though to be certain I participated in many actions with the navy during the last war."

"Yes, of course, a privateer. But still you have the experience of many a sea fight. And as you are a gentleman of some breeding there can be no question as to your suitability for a naval officer. What I am asking, sir, is will you take command of the *Plymouth Prize?* At least until we have communicated with the admiralty and an official replacement for Allair has been sent?"

Marlowe smiled. "If it would be helpful to my king and my adoptive home, Governor, then I should be delighted to accept."

And delighted he was.

Marlowe had watched Allair's conduct aboard the *Plymouth Prize*, his petty thieving and his robbing honest merchants of trifles, and he found it intolerable. He could not stand to see the guardship used thus, to make pennies. Not when he knew that in his own hands the ship could be made to yield a fortune and at the same time raise in colonial society the name of Marlowe to the heights of Rolfe or Randolph or Wilkenson.

"Perhaps we should return to the ball?" Marlowe suggested, for fear that the governor, once begun on the subject of the guardship, would not be easily stopped. He was still thinking of the lovely Mrs. Tinling, had not lost his resolve to approach her.

"Yes, of course, but, pray, let us make certain we are of one mind on this. You will take command of the *Plymouth Prize* at your earliest convenience?"

"I will."

"Excellent, excellent. If you would like to send a man by tomorrow, I shall have your official orders drawn up, and your commission, and you can then go aboard as soon as ever you are ready."

"Then all is settled, sir," Marlowe said, standing as if to leave.

"Yes, quite, but for one small thing . . ." said the governor, half standing and then sitting again.

"That being?" Marlowe sat as well.

"The fact is, it seems Allair has a mind to keep possession of the ship. I have ordered him to relinquish command and report to me, but he has so far refused and remains on board. . . ."

They sat in silence for a moment, both thinking the same thing: the *Plymouth Prize* would have to be taken by force from her legal commander. What more was there to say? Nothing, or so the governor apparently felt. He stood at last, smiled, and held out his hand, which Marlowe shook.

"Well, we should return to the ball," he said. "I have no doubt that you'll find some means to extract that rogue from the ship. Your king and country are much indebted to you for this."

Indeed, thought Marlowe. But in fact he shared Nicholson's confidence that he could pluck Allair from his ship like a splinter from a thumb, and the thought worried him not in the least.

And as to the debt that the country owed him, he was equally confident that the *Plymouth Prize* could be made to pay that debt many times over.

Chapter 3

"ELIZABETH." MATTHEW Wilkenson, grinning with the cocky air of the confident. "Might I have this dance?"

"Mrs. Tinling."

"Beg your pardon?"

"Address me as 'Mrs. Tinling.' You take great liberties, sir."

"Oh, Mrs. Tinling, is it?" Elizabeth felt her anger and disgust rise in proportion to Wilkenson's widening grin. "Your husband has been gone nearly two years, and you, ma'am, do not look to be in mourning any longer."

"Whether I am in mourning or not, sir, is no cause for you to be discourteous."

"Forgive me, Mrs. Tinling." Wilkenson bowed deep at the waist. "Might I have this dance, Mrs. Tinling?"

"I am faint with the heat, Mr. Wilkenson, and I do not believe I shall dance this next."

Wilkenson straightened, looked her in the eye. His expression was something altogether different from his former arrogant, self-satisfied look. "There is no call for you to continue with this game. I am growing weary of it."

"I do not know what game you refer to, sir. I do not wish to dance."

"And I do, and I think it is in your best interest to cooperate with me."

"Oh, indeed? And do you think because the Tinlings and Wilkensons were such friends that I am beholden to you? Do you think it my duty that I yield to your base whims?"

Wilkenson glared at her for a long moment. "Duty? No, it is not your duty to me. But perhaps to yourself. Your position in this colony is tenuous. You know that. And there is nowhere for you to go. I have had much correspondence with William Tinling since his father's death, you know. He has told me much. So I suggest that you consider . . . accommodating me."

"Or what?"

"Or you might find your position entirely untenable. I should hate to hear tales being spread abroad, and I think perhaps that might be best prevented through an alliance between you and me."

Elizabeth held his hateful gaze. Matthew Wilkenson had started this advance six months before. Back then he had just wanted to bed her, nothing more. She had seen animal desire in all its forms and recognized its countenance.

It was different now. Now it was base urge mixed with thwarted pride and a need to possess that which was denied him. Wilkensons, like Tinlings, were not used to being denied. It drove them to distraction.

And in the end he would win. They both knew it. He could make life unbearable for her in the colony. She could not return to London, and even with the money she had received from the sale of the plantation there was not enough to set up in some other city, as if a single woman, even a widow, could travel on her own. She could fight him, but in the end he would have her, and the longer she held out the more he would make her pay.

"Very well, sir. This one dance," she said through clenched teeth. She held up her arm for him to take.

"Are you enjoying yourself?" Marlowe asked Bickerstaff once he and the governor had returned to the ballroom.

"No."

"Oh, but I think you are."

Bickerstaff sniffed by way of reply. "Your meeting with the governor? It went well?" he asked. He sounded as if he could not care less, but Marlowe knew that he was consumed with curiosity.

"Very well. He has—Is that Matthew Wilkenson with whom Mrs. Tinling is dancing?"

"Yes, I believe it is. Now, what has the governor done?"

"He has relieved Allair of his command and asked me to take charge of the *Plymouth Prize*. I had always supposed there was some kind of animosity between Mrs. Tinling and that young Wilkenson git. Sure she cannot be taken with him?"

"The governor has given you command of the guardship?" Bickerstaff said. His voice incredulous, more so than Marlowe had ever heard. "Relieved a king's officer? Is this over the affair with the silver?"

"That and other things," said Marlowe, his eyes never leaving the dancers. "You'll own that Allair is hardly fit for command of a king's ship. Is this the first dance they've danced?"

"Yes. Nor did Mrs. Tinling seem overly anxious to dance this one, you will no doubt be relieved to know. So are you to have a commission as an officer? A naval captain?"

"Insofar as it is within the governor's power to issue one, yes. It will be temporary, perhaps, but yes, I shall be a commissioned officer."

At this Bickerstaff actually smiled. "Now, this is something of an irony, is it not?"

"I quite fail to see why."

"But tell me, it seems a great coincidence that Nicholson's silver should end up on your table, and a week later the governor is invited to dine. Are you entirely certain it was an accident?"

Marlowe pulled his gaze from the dance floor, met Bickerstaff's eye. Bickerstaff could at times be quite irritating, with his exaggerated sense of nobility. "It was an accident, be assured," he said, leaving it to Bickerstaff to believe that or not.

He turned back to the dance floor. Elizabeth was smiling, though the expression did not look entirely genuine. "Son of a bitch."

"So when do you take command?" Bickerstaff did not press the point about the silver.

"As soon as is convenient." The music stopped, Wilkenson bowed to Elizabeth and Elizabeth in turn curtsied, and then Wilkenson took her arm and led her off the floor. "Son of a bitch," Marlowe muttered again, and then to Bickerstaff said, "There is one small problem."

"What might that be?"

"Allair is apparently unwilling to give over the ship."

"And what will you do?"

"We, sir, we. We shall convince him of the desirability of doing so."

Marlowe's attention was now entirely given to the people across the room. Wilkenson had led Elizabeth over to a knot of his friends, all cut from the same cloth as himself. Well-bred, rich dandies. Families that numbered their time in Virginia by generations.

Marlowe hated the arrogance of that crowd, the disdain they had for all who were not of their class. It was greatly at odds with his own craving for acceptance among the colony's elite. He tried his best not to think on it.

But he could not ignore it now. Wilkenson still had a hold of Elizabeth's arm, and though their movements were subtle and people kept blocking his view, it appeared to Marlowe as if he was holding her despite her desire to be released. She seemed to be tugging, just slightly, against his grasp. Wilkenson and his friends were laughing at some unheard joke. Elizabeth was smiling as well, at whatever had been said. Marlowe was certain that the smile was forced.

"Marlowe," Bickerstaff said softly. "Perhaps we should leave now. I fear the oxtripe I ate is not sitting well with me."

"Bear up a moment more, sir. I would first like to have a word with some friends of mine." Marlowe left him there and made his way across the room. He could see words pass between the people as they saw him approach, giggles and glances in his direction. He was afraid that his cheeks were turning red.

"Sir," he said to Matthew Wilkenson when he arrived at the far end of the ballroom, "you seem to be enjoying some joke, all of you, and I would fain know what amuses you so."

"It is a private joke we are enjoying." Wilkenson looked not at Marlowe but at his companions, who were still giggling like idiots. He was half drunk, smiling his stupid, arrogant smile, his eyes never fully meeting Marlowe's but shifting between him and his tribe.

"And I would know what you are laughing at," Marlowe said. "And you, ma'am," he turned to Elizabeth, "does this gentleman amuse you, or would you wish me to remove his hand from your arm?"

"Pray, sir, it is none of your affair." Elizabeth's voice had a desperate, humiliated tone.

"Yes," said Wilkenson, "it is none of your affair."

"If a lady is suffering an insult, sir, then it is most certainly my affair."

"Oh, you are indeed a noble one." Laughter spewed through Wilkenson's closed lips as if he could not contain himself. "It seems there are many pretensions of nobility tonight." He looked quickly at Marlowe, then back at his friends. They were averting their eyes, as if Marlowe was something shameful.

"I would ask you to explain yourself, sir," Marlowe said. "But first to take your hand from the lady's arm."

"Please, Mr. Marlowe, I am quite well," said Elizabeth. She did not sound well at all.

"I shall attend to my affairs, sir," said Wilkenson, "and I suggest you do the same. Begone, you upstart crow." He turned and grinned at his friends, looking for them to share his delight. But they were nervous now, and rewarded him with no more than half-smiles and muted chuckles.

"I said take your hand from the lady's arm."

Marlowe grabbed Wilkenson's hand in a crushing grip and

removed it from Elizabeth's arm, as easy as taking a toy from a baby's fist.

Wilkenson managed at last to jerk his hand from Marlowe's grasp. "You lay a hand on me, you bastard?"

"I shall lay a boot on your arse, sir, if you do not apologize to the lady."

"Marlowe, please," Elizabeth implored, but it was beyond that now.

Wilkenson was red in the face, lips pressed tight together. He glanced at his friends for support, but they would not meet his eyes, and that seemed to make him angrier still. "You dare to touch me? Do you think you can impress us with your bloody money and your lies of noble birth. I can well guess at the truth about you, sir, easier than you think, and I am not afraid to tell others."

"If you wish to discuss affairs between you and me, then we may do so, but I will not tolerate your insulting a lady."

"Well, this is rich," he said, his voice loud enough to make others turn and listen. "A scoundrel and a liar, an upstart with pretensions of gentle birth, coming to the aid of another one of that ilk, and a slut to boot."

There was an unnatural quiet around them, as if they were not a part of the ball taking place in the rest of the room.

"For the sake of harmony in this colony I might be willing to suffer insult to myself," said Marlowe, "but I cannot tolerate such words spoken about a lady. I must demand satisfaction."

This brought Wilkenson up short, at least for a second. How could the silly bastard have expected anything less? Marlowe wondered. Wilkenson had been too long allowed to do as he wished, his behavior beyond challenge.

"Oh, for the love of God!" Elizabeth glared at Wilkenson and then Marlowe and then stamped off.

Wilkenson watched her go and then turned to Marlowe. He hesitated, and his eyes went wide, then narrow. "Very well, then, you shall have it." The arrogance was gone from his voice, as was the mirth. He had now put himself in the way of real danger. He glanced again at his friends.

"Very good, sir. I shall send my man to meet yours," Marlowe said, then turned and walked back to where Bickerstaff was standing. He did not turn to see what reaction his challenge had received.

"You seem to have thrown them into some great consternation," Bickerstaff said as Marlowe stepped up next to him.

"I should imagine. I have called the pup Wilkenson out."

"Was that wise?"

"Wise or not, I had no choice. Will you be my second?"

"You need not ask."

"I am grateful to you, sir. Now perhaps you would be so kind as to go speak with his man and work out the details of this thing. I shall wait outside."

"I should be delighted. Shall I request a meeting at dawn tomorrow?"

"That would be most agreeable."

"Shall I allow him the choice of weapons?"

"Certainly," Marlowe said. "He will choose pistols, of course. They always do."

The hour before dawn was gray and deep green. A mist like gauze hung in the trees and all but obscured the far end of the field on which they were to meet. The air was cool and fresh and moist. And still, utterly still. From far away a rooster sounded, and then another, but there was no other sound than that. It was the kind of morning, peculiar to the tidewater, that makes it seem the most perfect place on earth, the original garden.

Marlowe and Bickerstaff stood waiting while their horses ran teeth over the lush grass, entirely careless of the drama they were about to witness. The early morning was as comfortable a time of day as one was likely to find in the spring in that country, and Marlowe was thoroughly enjoying the quiet of the place. The brilliant rays of the sun were showing themselves through the thick forest to the east, the light splintering as it worked its way through a thousand leaves, flickering as if the trees themselves were burning.

He had to remind himself of why he was there.

"A lovely morning for a duel," he said, but softly, not willing to break the silence with his normal tone. "I certainly hope we have one."

"I can't imagine we won't." Bickerstaff spoke softly as well.

"You are quite certain they understood the time and the place?"

"Quite. They'll show, depend upon it."

He did not share Bickerstaff's certainty. If Wilkenson chose to ignore his challenge, Marlowe could rightly deem him a coward. But if he and his friends chose to ignore him completely, to view him as not worthy of consideration, it might be an even greater humiliation. All of Marlowe's aspirations of rising like a phoenix in Virginia society would be for naught.

He was starting to grow genuinely concerned when Bickerstaff nodded his head toward the far end of the field.

A coach and four was coming down the road, rattling along, ending the morning quiet. It was a big, yellow painted affair, a coat of arms on the door, and Marlowe recognized it as the Wilkensons' vehicle. He and Bickerstaff watched in silence as it crossed the open space and pulled up ten feet from where they stood.

George Wilkenson, Matthew's older brother and apparently his second, stepped out, followed by Jonathan Small, a doctor of physic, the most prominent in Williamsburg.

"A good thought, to bring a doctor," Bickerstaff said.

"They won't need him," said Marlowe. "They would have done better to bring a priest."

Wilkenson had chosen pistols, which was no surprise to Marlowe. His type, cowards at heart, always did. With swords it was cut and thrust, attack and retreat, a drawn-out affair with too much opportunity for mischief. With pistols it was one shot apiece, honor quickly satisfied and little chance to do harm, and in most cases any harm that was done was slight.

For all that, Matthew Wilkenson was not looking very well that morning. He was quite pale, even waxy, a slight tremor in his hands. He glanced nervously around as Bickerstaff and

George examined the pistols, each choosing one for their man and loading it.

Marlowe watched the young pup twisting his fingers together as his brother performed for him the duties of a second, and he found that strange animal, conscience, gnawing, gnawing.

What beast is this? he thought. He was very much in his rights for demanding this satisfaction, after the insult he had suffered, and more so in defending Elizabeth's honor.

"Bickerstaff," he said with a sigh, "pray go and tell young Wilkenson that if he will retract his statement in front of those who had occasion to hear it, and apologize to Mrs. Tinling and vow never to spread such lies again, I shall consider honor to be satisfied."

Bickerstaff said nothing, just cocked an eyebrow at him, then walked across the damp grass toward the enemy's camp. Marlowe could not hear what was said, but he could see in young Wilkenson's actions that Bickerstaff's words had emboldened him. Did the pup construe his charity for fear, his offer as an attempt to save his own skin? He saw Matthew stand more upright and shake his head. Bickerstaff nodded, turned, walked back.

"He says you shall not escape your mortal danger so easy," Bickerstaff reported, "but if you wish to withdraw the challenge, then, Christian that he is, he will allow you to do so."

"Such nobility. One rarely sees it these days. Does he think me afraid?"

"I believe he does. He took great courage from your attempt to cut and run."

"Very well," Marlowe said. "If he will be a fool to the last, at least he will not die a coward."

The protocol for the affair, as Bickerstaff and George Wilkenson arranged, was for the duelists to stand ten paces apart, backs to each other, turn on the word, and fire. The seconds paced out the distance, and young Wilkenson and Marlowe took their places.

Marlowe stood quite still, his pistol held across his chest, and looked out over the field. How very much one's thoughts are concentrated at a moment such as this, he thought, how very sharp everything seems. The smell of wet grass and the hint of brackish water in the air, the trees, now bathed in orange light, standing over their long shadows, all seemed so very much . . . present. That was not the first time he had had such thoughts. He understood why some men became addicted to dueling.

"Ready!" George Wilkenson called out. Marlowe could hear the strain in his voice. It occurred to him that Matthew Wilkenson might be an excellent shot, that he, Marlowe, might have real reason to be afraid. But he was not.

"Turn and fire!" He turned, gun still held across his chest, faced Wilkenson thirty feet away. Wilkenson turned as well, turned as quickly as he could, bringing his gun up as he did, desperate to fire first. Marlowe saw the puff of smoke in the pan, the muzzle flash as the gun went off.

Wilkenson was a good shot, a very good shot, as it happened. Marlowe felt the bullet pluck at his coat, heard the frightful buzz as the ball flew past. Had Matthew not been in such a panic, Marlowe would have died. But now Marlowe had all the time he needed to fire back.

He brought his gun up at last and leveled it at Wilkenson's head. Wilkenson staggered back a step, then another, quite contrary to the protocol of the thing, experiencing the terror, the absolute terror of pending death. Marlowe had seen it before, in the eyes of more men than he cared to recall. He would not make Wilkenson suffer long.

He lined the end of the barrel up with Matthew Wilkenson's jaw; the slight rise of the ball in flight would put it right through his forehead. His finger caressed the trigger, feeling the resistance of the spring.

And then he changed his mind.

Now what in the hell is happening to me? he thought as he lowered the gun a quarter of an inch and aimed it at Wilkenson's shoulder. If he did not kill the little bastard, there was every chance that the rumors would start again. But still he could not do it. He could not kill him.

I am a fool and I shall regret this, he thought.

It took Marlowe just three seconds to come to that uncharacteristically charitable decision, but that was longer than Wilkenson's courage could hold out.

"No! God, no!" Matthew Wilkenson screamed, twisting, ducking, just as Marlowe pulled the trigger. The ball, carefully aimed at Wilkenson's shoulder, struck him right in the head.

Through the cloud of gray smoke Marlowe saw Wilkenson lift off the ground, literally lift off his feet, and fly back, arms thrust out, the fine mist of blood blown from the back of his head caught in the rays of the early sun. He came to rest flat on his back.

"Oh my God! Oh my God!" George Wilkenson ran over to where his brother lay. Marlowe walked over there as well, at a more leisurely pace, and Bickerstaff joined him.

"He almost bested you," Bickerstaff observed, looking at the rent in Marlowe's sleeve just below the shoulder. Ten inches from his heart.

"Almost."

Matthew Wilkenson was sprawled out on the grass, arms and legs flung out, dead eyes open, staring at the sky. He had left a path where his body had slid through the dew. In his forehead was a hole the size of a doubloon. His head rested in a growing puddle of blood. Dr. Smith leaned over and closed Matthew's eyes. George Wilkenson was on hands and knees, vomiting.

Marlowe shook his head as he looked at the dead man. He was sorry that young Wilkenson had died, he had not intended to kill him. He did not feel remorse; he had seen too many men killed, had killed too many himself, to feel that. He was just sorry.

After a long moment, during which the only sound to be heard was George Wilkenson's retching, Marlowe said, "I believe that honor has been satisfied."

"You bastard, you son of a whore." George Wilkenson

looked up at him, a long thread of vomit hanging from his lips. "You killed him."

"Yes. It is customary in a duel."

"You didn't have to kill him, you son of a bitch. You could have . . . you didn't have to kill him."

"If he had stood like a man, rather than flinching like a coward, then he would still be alive."

"You bastard. Whoreson."

"Now, see here," Marlowe was starting to lose his patience, "perhaps you are accustomed to playacting when it comes to affairs of honor, but I am not. I will suffer only so much abusive language from you. If you think you have been wronged, then I suggest you play the man and do something about it. We have the pistols here. If you care to demand satisfaction, then let us have it out here and now."

Wilkenson said nothing, only glared at Marlowe, his eyes wet.

"There's been quite enough of this for one day," said Dr. Smith.

"I am in agreement, Doctor," said Bickerstaff.

"Very well." Marlowe dropped the pistol to the ground. "But hear me, Wilkenson. Your brother wronged me and he insulted a lady in an unpardonable manner, and still I gave him the chance to apologize and save his life. Now, you can tell your family, and anyone so inclined, that any man spreading malicious gossip about me or insulting a lady with whom I have a friendship had best be prepared to meet me on this field. I will suffer no such insults. Good day, sir."

He turned and walked toward the end of the field to which his horse had retreated. He could hear Bickerstaff's boots on the grass just behind him.

"You lowered your aim, Marlowe. I saw that. Perhaps we shall make a gentleman of you yet."

"And if the Wilkensons are typical of the breed, I'm not so sure I fancy being one. Stupid bastard. I gave him ample opportunity to save his life."

"I think perhaps the gentle people of this colony are not accustomed to duels ending in death."

"Well, if they are going to play at being men, then they had best get accustomed to playing rough."

Perhaps it was best this way, he thought. Half-measures would never do in a case where his very honor was at stake. His honor and that of Elizabeth Tinling.

Had Wilkenson made a public apology, that would have been one thing; Marlowe and Elizabeth would have been vindicated and Wilkenson humiliated, and he would have never mentioned it again.

But if he had lived through a duel, with honor satisfied, then the insults might have come around again, and with more vehemence. Wilkenson would have grown restless under the shame of Marlowe's having allowed him to live. No, insults and innuendo such as the ones Matthew Wilkenson was promoting could not go unanswered. They would spread like the plague if they did, and then Marlowe and Elizabeth would be shunned by the better sort in the colony.

Well, honor is satisfied now, he thought. Matthew Wilkinson was forever silenced, and George Wilkinson was too much of a coward to risk his brother's fate. The rumors had been stopped dead. Stopped, Marlowe hoped, before anyone would guess at the truth of the matter.

Chapter 4

JEAN-PIERRE LEROIS staggered out of his tent, squinting and blinking in the late-morning Caribbean sun. Tears rolled down his cheeks. His head pounded with the onslaught of light. He pulled his battered hat lower over his eyes, took another pull from the whiskey bottle in his hand, and surveyed his domain.

Off to the east, scattered among the green forest, was the small town of Nassau, in reality no more than a few houses, shops, and taverns. The majority of the island's population, some two hundred or so men and perhaps fifty women, were scattered along the half-mile stretch of beach on which Le-Rois's tent was pitched. But they were not, strictly speaking, citizens of New Providence or any other place. They were men on the account. The Brethren of the Coast who had just recently discovered the sparsely inhabited island as a nearly ideal base for their tribe. They were pirates.

The lot of them, the crews of the three decrepit ships at anchor just off the beach, were making their home on the white sand. Sleeping wherever they had passed out, or gambling, or cooking, or eating, or fornicating. And they were all drinking, all those who were still conscious—drinking bitter wine or "kill devil" rum or rumfustian, made of beer, gin, sherry, raw eggs, and whatever else happened to be available.

LeRois scowled. He looked around. His skin was burned so dark, he looked more like an Arab than a Frenchman. Those parts of his face not covered with beard were splattered with dark spots where burned gunpowder had embedded itself in his skin.

He scratched distractedly at his jaw. There was something dried and crusty in his beard, he did not know what. He could smell the stink of his own clothes, his black and faded broad-cloth coat, his wool waistcoat and cotton shirt, all of which had, at one time, been fine apparel. It was his custom twice a year to shed his clothes—coat and waistcoat, his shirt and breeches and stockings, the wide red sash he wore around his waist—and burn them all, replacing them with whatever new clothes he could buy or take.

The new clothing was a mark of his good fortune and his God-given right to command. But their last cruise had not been a success. He had found no clothes worth taking, no money with which to buy new. Another blow to his already waning authority.

He took a long drink from the bottle. The liquor burned as it went down, but it was a reassuring sensation. The edges of his sobriety dulled. The beach, the tents, the blue sky, and the clear aqua sea seemed too sharp, too vivid, too real. He drank again.

He squinted against the harsh glare of the sun on the sand and the water and searched among the bodies for William Darnall, the quartermaster of the *Vengeance*, that much-battered ship that was his command. His command for now. His command as long as those men who sailed her agreed that it should be his command. As long as he could, through success, intimidation, and brutality, make them obey.

It was twenty-five years since LeRois had deserted from the navy of his most Catholic Majesty of France. He had been a very junior master's mate then, but he had been telling people that he had been a *maître*, a master, for so long that he now believed it himself.

For nearly twenty years he had been on the account, an extraordinarily long career for a pirate. His name was well

known among those who used the sea. It carried with it suggestions of the most egregious debauchery and violence. Accurate
suggestions, and much to LeRois's liking.

Six years before, seven years before, no one would have
questioned LeRois's right to the rank of captain. He was one
of those few of the pirate tribe who was strong enough and
mean enough and lucky enough that he could consider himself
the undisputed master of his ship. No voting, no arguing, no
threats to his authority. Such things were the practice aboard
other ships. Not his.

But that was before he had fought young Barrett, and lost.

He scowled as his eyes swept the beach. He paused, squinting at a familiar face. Not Darnall. It took LeRois a few seconds
to place it—the face seemed to shimmer like heat off the
beach—but then he gasped in surprise, staggered back a few
feet in the soft sand.

It was Barrett. He stood not twenty feet away, leaning
against a stack of casks, grinning. Just as LeRois remembered
him all those years before, a frightened young seaman of fifteen
aboard a little English merchantman, a victim of LeRois and
his tribe.

"Son . . . of . . . bitch!" LeRois shouted, the protracted
curse starting as a low rumble in his throat and building to a
scream. He brought the bottle back over his head. The boy
changed into the man as he had last seen him, sword dripping
gore and blood, LeRois's blood, bidding farewell.

LeRois heaved the bottle, and even as he did he realized
that Barrett was no more than a hallucination, another of those
ghostly images that were appearing to him with disturbing
frequency.

The half-full bottle shattered against the stack of casks,
showering the man sleeping in their shade with glass and whiskey. He startled up, looked around, and saw LeRois standing
there, shaking, sword drawn.

"LeRois, you are a goddamned crazy son of a whore. Fucking lunatic," the man growled, pulling himself to his feet and
walking away. LeRois followed him with his eyes. Did not

move. There was a time when no man would have dared to say that to him, no man would have insulted him and then turned his back. That was before he had been bested by the whore's git.

He felt something inside him snapping, breaking with the strain. Like the slow bending crack of a yard springing under the pressure of a sail. Like shoring giving way. The vision of the boy had unnerved him. Now this bastard was ignoring him as if he presented no threat at all. That was too much. Too much by half. Jean-Pierre LeRois was indeed a threat, and it was time to remind the others of that fact.

He had let things slip, but now there was a plan, a plan that would make them all rich, and the means to carry it off. That thought gave him back the confidence he had enjoyed in the early days. It was time to regain his control.

He wiped his sweating hand on his coat, took a fresh grip of his sword. He headed off across the beach, his eyes fixed on the back of the man he had disturbed. His shoes sunk deep in the sand, and he felt the hot grit under his stockings. His footsteps made no noise. He picked up his pace, his breath coming faster, though he had walked no more than a dozen yards.

He was ten feet away when the man sensed the threat, the loom of LeRois's six-foot-two-inch, two-hundred-and-ninety-pound frame coming up behind. He turned fast. His eyes leaped from LeRois's sword to his eyes and back to his sword. He jerked a pistol from a sash around his waist, cocked it, and pointed it, but it had been many years since LeRois was bothered by the sight of a pistol pointed at his gut and his advance did not falter.

LeRois raised the sword over his head. An animal scream began to build in his throat. The lock of the pistol snapped and nothing happened. The man's eyes went wide as he looked up at the gleaming sword that the big man held aloft.

"LeRois!"

LeRois stopped and glanced to one side, then the other. He had heard his name, clear as a pistol shot: "Ler-wah," spo-

ken with that ugly English pronunciation, as if the fucking
Roast-beefs could not work their tongues to create the elegant
French sound.

But had he, really? Or had he just imagined it? There
were men around him, watching him. Were they real? He was
suddenly very uncertain. He could taste the terror in the back
of his throat.

"LeRois!" William Darnall came trudging up. He paused,
reached his hand under his wool shirt, and scratched hard.
Spit a stream of tobacco into the sand. "Reckon we should get
under way today."

LeRois stared at him. Darnall had called his name. His
quartermaster. He had not imagined it at all. "*Oui*, we get
under way."

Darnall squinted at him, and his eyes moved toward the
sword. "What do you reckon to do with that?"

LeRois looked at the sword in his hand as if he had never
seen it before. He remembered the man he was about to kill.

He turned, but the man was gone and he could not see
him anywhere among the pirates and whores who were watching the confrontation. A fight to the death in the pirates' camp
was considered a fine amusement. Like a good cockfight or
bull baiting.

LeRois shrugged and slid the sword back into its scabbard.
"The fucking *cochon*. I let him live," he said to Darnall by
way of explanation.

Darnall took a long and contemplative chew of his tobacco
and then spit another brown stream onto the sand. With the
sleeve of his light blue wool coat, which had once been a dark
blue wool coat, he wiped away that part of the spittle that had
not cleared his long black beard. He resettled the faded, battered, and salt-stained cocked hat on his head.

Like LeRois, he wore a red sash around his waist and under
that a leather belt that supported a cutlass and a brace of pistols.
Rather than breeches he wore the wide-legged trousers of the
common seaman. Flea-bitten calves and ankles protruded from
the frayed ends of his trousers. He was barefoot.

As quartermaster, Darnall was second in command of the *Vengeance*, though in fact, like most pirate quartermasters, he ran the ship, save for those times when they went into a fight.

LeRois squinted at him. Darnall was being very familiar with him, as if they were old friends. More and more the quartermaster had been treating him that way. LeRois did not see in Darnall's manner the hesitancy and the underlying fear that he had once evoked in all men, and that irritated him.

He was swimming up to the surface of the sea from the black depths. He had been bested by Barrett all those years before, and it had dragged him down. But now he could see daylight again, overhead. He would break through. He would see the fear again.

"What say you, Captain? We get under way on the ebb this afternoon?"

LeRois was certain that the men of the *Vengeance* had been discussing this, had indeed already decided. They had finished careening her a week before, had set her rig to rights and loaded stores aboard. She was ready for sea.

He felt the shoring in his mind slipping further, cracking and splintering. Soon there would be no more playacting like this. He would take absolute command again.

"*Oui, farirez plus de voiles*, we make sail at the first of the ebb."

LeRois's eyes moved across the beach to the narrow strip of water between New Providence and Hog Island that constituted Nassau Harbor. The *Vengeance* was riding at a single anchor, her sails drying to a bowline. She looked like a wreck from that distance, hardly good enough for the breaker's yard. It was time for LeRois to change ships, his men's attitude, his own fortunes.

And now there was a plan. A great partnership. Set up through the conduit of his former quartermaster, Ezekiel Ripley. As much of a plan as LeRois's mind was capable of formulating after twenty years of violence and disease, near starvation, and the most abject debauchery.

But that was no matter. The finer points were the purview

of those ashore. He just had to plunder the helpless merchantmen who carried their cargoes throughout the Caribbean. And that he was certainly capable of doing.

It was well past noon when they began to ferry the men out to the *Vengeance*. The longboat had been unwisely hauled up on the beach and left to bake under the tropical sun. The planking had dried and shrunk, opening up the seams and requiring those not pulling an oar to bail.

All save LeRois. He was captain, he would have none of that. He caught the few askance looks thrown aft at him by those of the ship's company who resented his assumption of superiority. Ignored them. They would learn soon enough who was in charge, and those who did not would die.

It took seven trips back and forth before all of the *Vengeance's* men were aboard. The preponderance of them were English and French, but there were Scots and Irishmen too, and Dutchmen and Swedes and Danes. One hundred and twenty-four men all told, three quarters of them white, representing nearly all of the seafaring nations of Europe.

Black men made up the other quarter of the crew. Some were escaped slaves who had learned all there was to know about cruelty on the sugar plantations of the Caribbean. Some had been on their way to the auction houses when they were taken from the Vengeances' victims, brought aboard to do the menial tasks aboard the pirate ship—cooking and manning the pumps, tarring rigging and slushing down masts—and had earned their way into the pirate tribe through hard use in battle.

However the black men had arrived, they were now Brethren of the Coast, full members of the ship's company. The only place in the Old World or the New where black men and white stood side by side as equals.

And they were, all of them, black men and white, heavily laden with weapons. And they were all drunk.

"Ship the capstan bars, rig the swifter," Darnall called from the waist, and the crew of the *Vengeance* shuffled off in various directions to perform those tasks. They could do them just as well drunk as sober. It was how they generally did them.

"Rig the messenger! Nippers, stand ready!"

It was half an hour of shuffling, tossing gear aside, and digging more gear out from the piles of junk that littered the deck before the capstan was rigged for weighing anchor. "Heave away!" Darnall shouted, and the pawls began their steady click click click as the men stamped the capstan around.

In the bow, the nippers lashed the heavy anchor cable to the messenger, shifting their nips as the eight-inch thick rope came inboard and was fed down the hatch.

The job of stowing the wet cable away on the cable tier, wrestling the tons of rope into neat coils, was a hot, filthy, horrible job, and since there were no slaves or captives aboard to do it, it was not done. Rather, the cable was allowed to pile up where it fell, and if it rotted from being stowed wet it was no matter. Every ship had anchor cable aboard. They could always take more.

LeRois stood aft on the quarterdeck, arms folded, watching, saying little. Gave the occasional order to the men on the helm. Darnall was the quartermaster and he was running the evolution, just as he ran all the mundane aspects of the *Vengeance*'s operation.

LeRois had only one thing to do, and that was to give the order for their destination. He wondered how receptive the Vengeances would be. Wondered if he would have to kill anyone to get his orders obeyed. Perhaps it would be best if he did, get things off on the right foot. The incident on the beach had left him anxious for blood.

"Anchor's a-peak!" Darnall called out. "Hands to the sheets and halyards! Come along, you bloody laggards, haul away all!"

The *Vengeance*'s sails had never been stowed, since they were prone to rot when stowed and, more to the point, stowing them was a great effort that would just have had to be undone once it was time to get under way. For that reason the Vengeances had only to sheet topsails home and haul away on the halyards, then heave a pawl on the capstan to break the anchor loose and they were under way.

"Fall off, fall off, meet 'er," LeRois growled at the helmsmen as the bow of the *Vengeace* swung off. Forward, the men at the braces heaved away, trimming sail to the new course with never an order shouted, never the least bit of confusion. Lazy drunkards that they were, the Vengeances were prime seamen to a man, like most pirate crews, and they knew their business.

The *Vengeance* steadied on her course, sailing west out of Nassau Harbor, as more and more canvas was spread to the trade winds: courses, topgallants, the lateen mizzen, the spritsail and spritsail topsail, set and trimmed with all the speed and efficiency an expert though drunken crew could display.

The ship itself was a pathetic sight. Running gear piled in heaps along the waterways and on top of the six pounder guns that lined the weather deck. The long quarterdeck and forecastle that she had sported when LeRois and his men had first taken her had been cut back to give more fighting room in the waist. It had not been neatly done. The jagged edges of hacked-off planks still protruded here and there. The wood on the once-covered areas of the deck was altogether darker then that of exposed places. Great white patches showed in the standing rigging where the tar had worn away. The paint was blistered by the sun and flaking off.

The *Vengeance* needed a great deal of work, a fact that was entirely ignored by the men aboard her.

Once the ship was under way, and sails trimmed, each man claimed for himself a piece of the deck on which to sit and continue the drinking and gambling and sleeping that had been interrupted by the afternoon's work.

LeRois stepped up to the quarterdeck rail. "*Écoutez! Écoutez!* Listen here, you men!"

Men put bottles down. Heads turned aft.

"We're going to the British colonies on the American coast, do you hear?" LeRois said. "I am setting course for there."

The men looked at one another, some nodding agreement, some shaking heads. A low murmur ran across the deck.

The bosun was the first to speak. LeRois had expected as much. He was a sea lawyer. A new man, volunteered from one of their last victims. He would die by LeRois's hand in the next minute if he objected too strongly. Set a good example. "I reckon there's fair pickings down around Panama way, or south of Florida."

"Perhaps," said LeRois, "but we go to the American coast."

Silence swept like a cat's paw across the deck. The bosun coughed, stood up from where he had been leaning on the fife rail around the mainmast. "Reckon we should vote. Says so in the articles."

There was a gentle murmur. "Reckon he's got a right to ask," someone said, just audible.

LeRois stepped forward and down the ladder to the waist, moving slowly. He said nothing. The bosun's face swam before him. He felt the excitement rise as he closed with the man. LeRois the master was back, LeRois the Devil.

"I reckon we should vote, is all I said," the bosun began again. He saw that his words had no effect on LeRois, and that the huge man was still advancing. Reached for the knife in his belt.

LeRois grabbed the knife by the blade just as it cleared the leather, twisted it, cutting his own hand open, and tossed it away. With his other hand he grabbed the bosun's neck under his wispy, uneven beard and squeezed, watching with delight as the man's eyes went wide, his fists striking feebly at LeRois's arm, unable to get past his long reach and strike his face or body. The bosun flailed wildly, growing weaker, growing more frightened and desperate.

"America, Captain, like you said," someone called, and there was a chorus of agreement among those men who knew LeRois well enough to still fear him. LeRois tossed the gasping bosun to the deck. He felt the warm blood running down his palm. Dripping off the tips of his fingers.

"Very good," he said and stamped aft, then to the helmsman said, "Make your course north-northwest, a quarter west."

LeRois did not tell the men about his plans. He had a vague notion that they would not believe him.

But they would soon enough, when he had made them all wealthy men. Once they reached America. Once they were cruising off the Capes. Once they were in the Chesapeake.

Chapter 5

KING JAMES, majordomo of the house, stood in the doorway of Marlowe's now vacant bedchamber. He ran his dark eyes over the room. The house girls had made the bed with military precision. They had cleared away the bottle of rum and the bottle of wine and the half-empty glasses, had swept up the ashes and the sprinkling of tobacco and placed Marlowe's pipe carefully on the mantel.

They had picked up the silk coat and waistcoat from the floor where James knew Marlowe had dropped them, had retrieved the long white wig, worth as much as a laborer might make in half a year, which Marlowe had flung into the corner.

The room was immaculate, but James knew that it would be. If it was not, the house girls would answer to him, and they had no wish to do that. He took pride in the way that he ran things. Pride was something he had not felt in many, many years. Not since he had been taken by the slavers. Not in all the long twenty years of his slavery. Not until Marlowe had come along and freed them all.

It was virtually his first act after buying the Tinling place. He had offered no explanation, just freed all of the slaves that had come with the plantation. Offered them wages, based on the success of the tobacco crop, if they would stay and work the land. Which, of course, they all did. They had nowhere else to go.

James had been a field hand then. Never believed that Marlowe would actually pay them, but the others did, and they doubled their efforts in the fields. Fools, James thought. A white man's trick, another low white man's trick to get more labor out of them.

Which it was. And even though Marlowe had indeed paid them, quite handsomely, it did not change the fact that it was a trick. And it had worked.

The white people in Williamsburg had been stunned, horrified at what Marlowe had done. But now, two years later, the freed slaves still had not run amok, had not cut Marlowe's throat or risen against the white people in the colony. They kept to themselves and grew tobacco, a prodigious output of fine, sweet-scented tobacco. As good as any in the tidewater.

But King James's anger would not be quenched by such a simple thing. Nor had Marlowe's taking him in from the fields and making him majordomo of the household caused that fire to burn less bright.

King James, born a ruler. Now that he was free he would never let a white man find him wanting. For Marlowe that meant that his household was run with perfect efficiency. He seemed to have known that such would be the case.

King James shut the door behind him, stepped over to the big wardrobe. He opened the doors and ran his eyes over the clothes hanging there.

"Lay out my working clothes, James, if you would," Marlowe had said that morning. "You know the ones I mean. I'll be away 'til noon, and when I return we'll be going aboard the *Plymouth Prize* for a while, me and Bickerstaff, so pack up whatever we'll need."

"Yes, Mr. Marlowe."

"You'll be coming as well, so pack a kit for shipboard. You'll be commanding the *Northumberland*."

"Yes, sir." The *Northumberland* was the sea sloop that Marlowe used for transportation and cargo on the Chesapeake Bay and beyond. It had been owned by Joseph Tinling, then called the *Duke of Gloucester*, had come to Marlowe with the sale of the plantation.

Marlowe had renamed it and had trained King James as a deckhand, and then mate and eventually master. James worked hard at the sailor's arts, learned fast, at first just to prove to Marlowe that he could, to prove to himself that he was not afraid. His only other experience with ships had been aboard the slaver, and that had colored his perception of all seagoing craft. But soon, and much to his surprise, he found that he loved the sloop, the freedom of being under way.

"And tell me something, James," Marlowe said. "Can you fight?"

"Fight?"

"In a battle. Hand to hand. Can you use a gun?"

King James smiled, just a hint of a smile. He thought back to a different life, twenty years before, on the other side of the Atlantic Ocean.

He had not been a king, of course, no matter what the other slaves said. He had been a prince, a Malinke prince of Kabu, near the Gambia River, from the House of Mane. Could trace his ancestary back to the great general of Sundiata Keita, Tiramang Traore.

"Yes, sir, I can fight."

James shuffled through the coats hanging in the wardrobe, searching out the "working clothes." He did indeed know the ones that Marlowe meant. They were old and well-worn, had once been repaired with great ungainly patches put in place with a sailmaker's needle before he had had the house girls redo the repairs with their expert hands. They were clothes from some other lifetime of Marlowe's, a lifetime about which James knew nothing but often speculated.

He found first the old blue broadcloth coat. The fabric was bleached a light color save for those places under the collar and on the turnback of the cuffs where the sun had not reached. There the cloth was still a dark blue, the color of the Chesapeake Bay water on a clear autumn day.

He ran his fingers over one of the newly replaced patches, checking the seamstress's work. He could find no cause for complaint. He looked at the inside of the coat, at the hole that was covered by the patch. Made by a pistol shot at close range.

He laid the coat on the bed and with it the silk-embroidered waistcoat, which had once been a fine garment, the canvas breeches, worn as soft as chamois, and the cotton shirt, the only new part of the ensemble. Marlowe's old wool shirt still hung in the wardrobe, but he had no interest in wearing that. Not when he could afford cotton.

His hat was a three-cornered affair, battered, like the rest of the working clothes. It was plain and black. Actually, it was more of a dark gray, bleached out through long exposure to sun and salt air, comfortable in a way that the more dandified things were not.

King James reached into the back of the wardrobe and pulled out Marlowe's boots, old leather knee-high boots that he had shined to the highest polish they would take. He reached in again and pulled out Marlowe's sword.

Marlowe had a number of swords, most of them the kind of silly, frail, ornamental weapons that the white gentlemen wore; gentlemen who did not need a sword and would not know what to do with one if they did. But this sword was a killing machine. The sword Marlowe used for the work that a sword was meant to do.

It was a great clumsy thing, poorly balanced, ugly. King James grabbed it by the grip and slowly pulled it from the scabbard, enjoying the feel of the cold wire-bound handgrip, enjoying the weight and the gleam of the late-morning light coming in through the window as it glinted off the straight, double-edged blade. He rarely had the chance to hold a weapon in the twenty years that he had been a slave. It felt good to do so. It felt natural for a prince of warriors.

He dropped the scabbard to the floor and held the great sword in the manner he had been taught by the fighting men of the Malinke who saw to the education of princes. They had not had such fine steel, of course, but great iron swords, half again as heavy as Marlowe's. Marlowe's big sword felt like a stilletto in his hands.

His boyhood seemed unreal to him now. Magical. Like the Christian heaven he had heard so much about. Once he had had slaves and others to serve him, and he answered to no man save his father. A long time ago. Another lifetime. After all of the years, all of the hatred and anger, the agony and terror, he had little more than wisps of memory of the Guinea Coast.

The Guinea Coast. He was using the white man's name now. Could no longer recall the Kabu Malinke name for his own home.

He lunged at an imaginary enemy. Thought of his father, as he had every day since the time the Bijago slave raiders had ambushed their hunting party, bursting into the camp at dawn with swords, spears, muskets given them by the white men for exactly that purpose.

His father had fought like an enraged bull, slaying them all, all who came at him, flinging himself at the attackers to save his people. No man who was stronger, fiercer than his father, not even the deadly Bijago islanders, no man that was his match. But his father was no match for a musket ball.

"Tell me, James, can you fight?" Marlowe had asked. Yes. Side by side with his father that morning. Killed five men for certain, probably more.

But slavers did not murder valuable young men of fifteen. They waited their chance. Hit him on the side of the head. When he woke he was in chains, and in chains he had been ever since.

There had not been one day since that James did not wish he had been killed at his father's side.

He picked up the scabbard and thrust the sword back into its sheath. The weapon was too heavy to be comfortably worn on a belt. Instead the scabbard was attached to a frog on a buff leather shoulder strap, which Marlowe wore over his right shoulder. Over the left went another strap with loops to hold a brace of pistols.

James had seen him wearing those weapons only on the few occasions he had been asked by the neighbors to help hunt down fugitives. Whatever it was that Marlowe once did—captaining a privateer, presumably—whatever it was that required him to be so heavily armed, he did no longer.

James placed the big sword on the bed beside the other things, ran his eyes over the entire ensemble to make certain everything was in order. Considered what of his own he would take. He did not know where they were going, but wherever it was it apparently would involve fighting.

King James felt the pleasure of anticipation, a feeling he could not recall having had once in his adult life. Marlowe had given back much of what the other white men had taken away. He had to admit as much, however grudgingly. Marlowe had given him back some semblance of leadership. He had given him back his pride and his freedom. And now Marlowe would give him back his warrior's soul.

The old man was in a rage, an absolute rage. George Wilkenson had never seen the like. Twenty-four hours after the death of his second son, his favored son, he was still in a fury, as if possessed by Satan himself.

Jacob Wilkenson paused for a moment in his tirade, catching his breath. The two men were in the library in the big Wilkenson plantation house, the finest library in the colony. Walls lined with massive oak shelves supporting the hundreds of books that the old man had purchased over the years. Which George, alone of all the Wilkenson clan, had actually read.

Above the books and circling the room, portraits of Wilkensons dating back to those who had fought against Cromwell and his Puritans, and lost, and a few even earlier than that. They seemed to George to be glaring down on their two living descendants, waiting with scant patience for them to do something to avenge the great wrong done their family.

Jacob, whose thoughts were no doubt running along the same lines, was standing by the massive fireplace that made up a majority of one wall of the room. He picked up a poker from the rack by the fireplace and jabbed at the burning logs within the brick confine. Then the rage swept over him again.

"God damn his black soul to hell!" he screamed, turning and flinging the poker across the room. It smashed into the etched glass front of a cabinet containing the family's Restoration chinaware, shattering the glass and the plates within.

George Wilkenson flinched at the sound of the destruction, but his father seemed not to notice. George had seen the old man in fits before, but he had never seen anything like this. He would have expected mourning, sorrow, weeping at the death of his son. But Jacob had done none of that. He had only raged.

"If you didn't have the courage to kill him, why in God's name did you not have the whore's son arrested for murder?" Jacob Wilkenson turned on his son. "Arrest him, have him strung up in public. I want you to send word to Sheriff Witsen. It ain't too late, your lethargy aside."

George Wilkenson held his father's eyes. He was growing weary of this. "Matthew was called out, Father. It was an affair of honor." He felt a profound grief at his brother's death. Unlike the old man. But he knew that Matthew could be a hothead. He hated Marlowe for what he had done, but he could not see the crime in it.

"Honor? What does that son of a bitch Marlowe know of honor? Tell Witsen to arrest him. I own that bastard's soul, he'll do as I say."

"I have no doubt that he'll do as you say, but no jury will convict Marlowe of murder, and then we'll look the fools for having tried to attack him thus."

Jacob Wilkenson glared at his son, white eyebrows coming together across his freckled and wrinkled forehead. "You've got no spine, boy."

"Perhaps not, but at least I have retained my wits." The logical thing, of course, was for George to call Marlowe out to avenge his brother's death. The very thought made him sick to his stomach. He imagined himself on that wet grass, his own blood running out from under his lifeless body. He prayed that his father would not suggest it.

"Your brother was the one with spine, and you're the one with wits," Jacob spat. "Are you telling me that the governor won't back us up against this bastard Marlowe? The Wilkensons are the first family of Virginia. Are you saying that Nicholson would stand behind this upstart?"

"This upstart seems to have the governor's ear, and his confidence. He is doing Nicholson a great turn with the guardship, and Nicholson will be in his debt."

"What do you mean, 'with the guardship'?"

"Nicholson has stripped Allair of command and has asked Marlowe to take over the ship."

At that Jacob Wilkenson stopped his pacing and his arm-waving. Stared at George as if his son had told him the colony was sinking into the sea.

"Apparently, Marlowe was some kind of privateer captain in the last war," George continued. "In any event, he has accepted the governor's offer. Had you not heard?"

"Marlowe . . . is taking command of the guardship?"

"As I understand it. And I reckon if he does anything at all well, then he shall have his way with the governor."

The elder Wilkenson was silent for a long moment. George shifted uncomfortably under his gaze. Then the old man turned and stared into the fire.

"This will not do," he said at last. "This will not do at all. That little bastard will not murder my son and then become some kind of hero in this colony. Never!" He turned and faced his remaining son. "You *will* do something about this, is that clear?"

"Well, Father, what I can do—"

"Oh, don't shit yourself, I'm not suggesting you call Marlowe out. If he could kill Matthew, then he sure as hell could kill you, and that would do me precious little good. I want Marlowe disgraced, arrested, hung like the goddamned cur he is."

"But how—"

"Do it! Think of something!" Jacob Wilkenson roared, flipping over a small table as his rage overcame him once more. A porcelain vase shattered on the hearth. "You're the one with the wits, pray, do not forget!"

Chapter 6

ELIZABETH TINLING sat at her dressing table and regarded Lucy's reflection in the mirror. She was a lovely girl, sixteen or seventeen years old, skin the color of hot chocolate with cream, soft brown curly hair tumbling out from under her mobcap and falling over her shoulders. Even if that pig Joseph Tinling had not actually bedded her, Elizabeth was in no doubt that he had thought about it. Had probably tried.

Lucy was one of only three servants Elizabeth had taken with her from the Tinling House. The only one she truly loved, genuinely trusted. A kindred spirit, more than Lucy or anyone would ever know. She would never part with Lucy.

The young slave was standing in the doorway to the bedchamber. Elizabeth's eyes moved from the face in the mirror to the white card in Lucy's hand. She had heard the knock on the door, the muted conversation belowstairs.

"Gentleman here to see you, ma'am," Lucy said.

A gentleman caller. Just the day before, a gentleman caller would have meant Matthew Wilkenson and his unwanted courting, if such it could be called. But Matthew Wilkenson would not be calling on anyone today, save his maker, and for the sake of his immortal soul Elizabeth hoped he was less obnoxious in that interview than he had been with her.

It could be George Wilkenson. She was expecting him. She had no doubt that he would come calling at some point, and wish to discuss with her just what had taken place.

Elizabeth swivelled around and reached out her hand, and Lucy handed her the card. Printed in a bold copperplate was the name Mr. Thomas Marlowe, Esq. No more.

That was the other caller she had expected.

She stared at the name for a moment, considered having Lucy tell him that she was out for the day or too faint to receive callers or abed with vapors or some such thing that effects highborn ladies. Instead she sighed.

"Very well. Show Mr. Marlowe into the sitting room and tell him that I shall be down directly." She could not put this off forever.

She had been thinking about Marlowe all that morning, which was hardly a surprise. He was now the chief topic of conversation in Williamsburg, and to her annoyance her name was now linked with his. Marlowe the enigma.

Killing Matthew Wilkenson had been a wild and reckless act. It would bring down on his head all of the vengeance of the Wilkenson family, and that could be considerable, given their wealth and standing in Virginia society.

And she would feel it as well, for he had ostensibly killed the little git to defend her honor.

There were only two possibilities. The first, the most likely, was that Marlowe was too stupid to understand the implications of what he had done, too foolish to consider the consequences. That thought made her furious. Had he, through his own idiocy, brought her even more trouble?

The other possibility was that he entirely understood what he had done and did not care. She did not know Marlowe well, but from what she had seen there was a reckless quality about him that one did not often see among highborn men. Had he not freed all of his slaves? That was sheer madness, but he had done it, and now the old Tinling place was one of the most successful plantations in the tidewater, the only one where they did not live in constant fear of a slave revolt. If he did understand what he had done and was not afraid of the consequences, then he was a fool or a very bold man indeed.

There was one thing, however, of which she was quite certain: Marlowe would expect something from her. Men did not risk their lives in a duel strictly for honor, no matter what the world liked to believe. Just as Matthew Wilkenson had expected payment for his discretion, so Marlowe would want payment for his chivalry, and Elizabeth knew in what coin he would wish to be paid. She was tired of it. She was angry.

She stood up and looked at herself in the mirror, smoothing out her dress and adjusting her long blond hair so that it fell just so across her shoulders. It was time to go and see what kind of a man this Thomas Marlowe was, a hero or a fool. It was time to find out what he would demand of her.

Marlowe fiddled with the hilt of his sword as he listened for any sounds from abovestairs. He was nervous, an emotion to which he was not accustomed, and it was making him irritable. He was nervous because he had no notion of what kind of a reception he might get from Elizabeth Tinling. If indeed he was received at all, which was far from certain.

By killing Matthew Wilkenson in defense of her honor he had involved her in what might become a protracted feud, quite against her will. She might be grateful for his defending her thus, or she might be furious with him for involving her and making the two of them the chief subject of all the gossipers of Williamsburg.

He looked up at the sound of light footfalls on the stairs, but it was only Lucy returning from presenting his card. He braced himself for some excuse; she was out or abed with vapors or some nonsense.

"Mrs. Tinling says will you please wait and she'll be down directly."

Lucy led Marlowe into the sitting room. "Pray, sir," she asked, "how does King James do?"

"Very well, Lucy. As well as ever."

"I'm pleased to hear it, sir. Might I trouble you, sir, to give him my regards?"

"I should be delighted."

Lucy curtsied and gave Marlowe her charming smile and then left him alone. He looked around the room, trying to distract himself.

It was a comfortable little house, built of wood, clapboard style, and situated on the wide Duke of Gloucester Street, just a few blocks from where the new capital building was rising from the turned earth. Plastered walls freshly painted in a light blue, furniture simple but elegant and well made. All of it was new; Elizabeth had taken nothing from the Tinling House when she left.

Marlowe had paid a good price for the old Tinling home, but he did not know what percentage of that money had gone to Elizabeth. It must have been a fair amount, for her new home was not inexpensive, particularly not when one considered the stable and the coach she maintained. He imagined that for the sake of appearances she had no choice but to continue to live in the manner she had previously enjoyed.

He stared out of the window to the street beyond. The celebrations were over and the revelers had gone back to being blacksmiths and coopers and farmers. But the town was still crowded with the activity of Publick Times, the courts and assemblies in session.

He could hear the sounds of the work taking place on the new capitol building. Soon Nicholson would begin construction of a governor's palace as well, and Williamsburg would begin to look like a proper capital city for the most prosperous colony in English America. But at present there were just a few shops and houses lining the broad street, the beginnings of the capital at one end and the College of William and Mary at the other.

He could not distract himself for long, and his thoughts wandered back to his most immediate problems.

That morning at breakfast Bickerstaff had observed, "There's much talk abroad about the duel. As best as I can tell, public opinion seems quite split as to your being a great man or a murderer. I suppose such opinions turn on whether or not the speaker owes money to the Wilkensons."

It occurred to Marlowe that in the two years that he had lived in that country he had never heard of a man being killed in a duel. He had seen noble wounds, the odd arm hung in a sling, but never a one of them killed. He wondered, with not a little consternation, if he had committed some grave social blunder.

Well, he thought, if I have, there is nothing for it now. He hoped that Elizabeth would be as sanguine.

"Good morning, Mr. Marlowe."

Her voice nearly made him jump. He had not heard her come down the stairs.

He turned and faced her. She stood in a shaft of sunlight coming in through the window, her yellow hair almost white where a few wisps hung loose under her mobcap and shining like gold as it spilled down the front of her dress, framing the flawless skin of her face and long neck. He was taken again by her beauty, and he found it a bit disconcerting. But not half as disconcerting as the look on her face.

Her fine, full lips were pressed together, and they were not smiling. There was a hint of a wrinkle on her forehead as she knitted her eyebrows ever so slightly. Her eyes, the color of the sky on a clear autumn day, flashed in the light.

"Ah, good morning to you, Mrs. Tinling," Marlowe said, bowing awkwardly. He straightened, and met her eyes. The silence in the room was oppressive. This was not going as Marlowe had hoped.

"What do you want, Mr. Marlowe?"

"Want?" Marlowe felt embarrassed and a bit angry all at once. "I want . . . merely to pay you a visit. A social call."

There was silence again, a long silence. "Indeed?" Elizabeth said at last. "You suppose that I owe you that much at least, after defending my honor?"

"Owe? You owe me nothing."

Now he saw from which quarter the wind was blowing.

She thought he was here to demand favor for services rendered, here to take up where the dead Wilkenson git had left off. Well, if he had wanted her thus he would have taken her, and Wilkenson be damned. The old Marlowe would have, in any event.

But he was a gentleman now, and would not have her in such a manner. He would not have her at all, if she was not interested in giving her affections freely, and he would not look a fool, sniffing around where he was not wanted.

"I see how it is with you, ma'am," he said. "I will leave you now. Good day."

Thomas took a step toward the door, actually more of a stomp, so angry was he that Elizabeth had misconstrued his motives in calling on her, his motives in fighting Wilkenson.

"Wait, Mr. Marlowe," she said, and her tone was more contrite, but not by much. "Won't you sit?"

Marlowe paused and looked at her again, and then without a word he sat in the chair she indicated.

"Forgive me, sir. I am much put out by the events of the past days. I would never wish to see bloodshed on my account."

"There was nothing for it, ma'am. That Wilkenson pup's abuse could not be suffered. I should be less than a man if I let it pass. And lest you think that I called him out just to curry your favor, let me remind you that he insulted me as well."

"I don't know if you appreciate the trouble that you might have caused. For you and me."

"I hope none are so foolish as to give you any more trouble. It pleases me to think that the example I made of Matthew Wilkenson should be enough to discourage that. As for me, I am unconcerned. I have seen trouble, ma'am, much worse than any that the Wilkensons or their ilk can create, and I shall serve out to them double what they give to me."

They were quiet again, but there was none of the animosity that attended their earlier silence. Elizabeth regarded Marlowe, sizing him up, he imagined, getting the measure of his sincerity, his bravery, and his foolhardiness.

"You know, Mr. Marlowe, I do believe you will. Would you care for some tea, or chocolate, perhaps?"

They spent the next hour in enjoyable and relaxed conversation, talking about nothing in particular, and most certainly not talking about the death of Matthew Wilkenson and the possible repercussions for both of them. At last, and with some great reluctance, Marlowe said, "Forgive me, ma'am, but I must away. As unfashionable as it might be, I have some work I must do today."

"I understand from others, sir, that you will be commanding the guardship."

"That's true, in faith. Governor Nicholson has asked me to take command until a replacement is sent out from home. I should think it will be six months or so."

"That horrid Captain Allair has resigned?"

"No. The governor has seen fit to replace him. I shall have to go out to the *Plymouth Prize* today and see if he will relinquish his command."

"And if he will not?"

"Then I shall show him how it is in his best interest to do so."

"The way you showed Matthew Wilkenson that it was in his best interest to behave himself?" Elizabeth gave a half-smile, slightly wicked and conspiratorial.

"Perhaps. Let us hope that Captain Allair is a better student than Wilkenson was." Marlowe smiled as well. He felt something pass between them, some understanding.

"Do I take it that you were a naval officer before coming to this colony?"

Hardly, Marlowe thought, but he said, "Not a naval officer, ma'am. I was captain of a privateer in the last war."

"Oh, indeed." Elizabeth did not sound entirely convinced, and for a moment Marlowe was thrown off balance. She would toss him aside with disdain if she thought he was not of the most gentle birth. How could she do otherwise? The widow of Joseph Tinling, one of the great aristocrats of the tidewater.

He would not have married any woman who was not of the finest pedigree.

"You are a brave man, Captain Marlowe," Elizabeth continued, "putting yourself in the way of those pirates that cruise the bay. I have heard the most horrible stories about them. But I shall not keep you from your duty, though I fear for your safety. I know how you men are about duty." She stood, and Marlowe stood as well.

"I thank you, ma'am, though I'm sure I shall be in no great danger."

"One more thing, Mr. Marlowe. Or, let me say, Captain Marlowe." She hesitated, as if searching for the right words. "I thank you, sir, for defending my honor as you did. I am much in your debt."

Marlowe took a step closer to her. "You are not in my debt, not at all. I did only what a gentleman should do."

"Still, Captain, I am grateful." She looked down, then met his eyes once more. "I am not accustomed to having my honor defended thus. And I think perhaps the world is a better place for having one less Wilkenson in it."

"I believe you are right, ma'am. And it is I who am grateful for the chance to perform some little service for you."

He bid her good day and walked out to where he had left his horse hitched to a rail. He mounted, and from that vantage point, looked around the capital city of Williamsburg, which seemed to be rising from the green earth at the command of Governor Nicholson. It was lovely, just lovely.

The next thing he realized, he was home. So wrapped up was he in thoughts of Elizabeth Tinling that he could not recall one incident, not one moment of the five-mile ride back from her house.

Chapter 7

CAPTAIN ALLAIR, as it turned out, was not just reluctant to turn over the command of the *Plymouth Prize*, he was nearly rabid on the point. Had he been a dog, Marlowe would have shot him. As it was, he nearly did.

Thomas rode up to the big house to find Bickerstaff and King James waiting on the wide front porch. Next to them, a pile of equipment: muskets, pistols, his sea chest and Bickerstaff's, various bundles that King James had apparently decided they could not do without.

Bickerstaff was calm and philosophical as ever, the slightly eccentric schoolmaster. But Marlowe had seen him in no-quarters combat, knew that he was unflinching and deadly in a fight. King James stood like a tree to the side and behind where Bickerstaff sat.

Seeing the two men filled Marlowe with optimism. Far more so than the sight of the company of Virginia militia loitering on the lawn.

There were about two dozen men in the company. As he rode up, the lieutenant, who was not above twenty years in age, called an order and the men shuffled to attention.

Marlowe pulled his horse to a stop where the company was drawn up, dismounted, and handed the reins to the waiting boy. He had requested the troops of Governor Nicholson for the purpose of taking the *Plymouth Prize* from Allair, there being an off chance that Allair's crew would help him defend his command. And while Marlowe did not believe that that drunken fool could actually engender enough loyalty in his men that they would risk even the slightest injury for him, he reckoned it was a good job to be prepared. Hence the militia.

There was little about them that was uniform, including their uniforms. Their regimentals had started out red, but they were more of a pink hue now, save for the lieutenant, whose coat, either newer or of better quality, was still a respectable color. Their waistcoats were either white, red, or blue, as were their breeches. Their ages ranged from seventeen to fifty years or more, and the same was true of their weapons.

In all they were not an inspiring sight, and it was only when Marlowe thought of the morose, despondent crew of the *Plymouth Prize*, against whom they would have to fight, if it came to that, that he felt his old confidence return.

"Lieutenant . . . ?"

"Burnaby, sir. Lieutenant Burnaby, Virginia Militia." The young lieutenant swept off his hat and gave a shallow bow.

"Lieutenant Burnaby, thank you for your promptness," Marlowe said, extending his hand. "With any luck I shall dismiss you men by nightfall tomorrow."

"Oh. Do you not think we shall have to fight?"

"I don't think so, no."

"Oh." The lieutenant seemed disappointed.

"But I'm not saying it can't happen. We could have a bloody day on our hands," Marlowe added, and this seemed to brighten Burnaby up some. "Now, pray, give me a few moments to shift clothes and we'll be off."

He found that King James had laid his clothes out on his bed, as he had asked: the long blue broadcloth coat, the silk waistcoat, the canvas breeches, the tall leather boots. Garments from another lifetime, come back. Except that now they were clean and pressed and mended to perfection, and the boots were shined so bright they reflected back the light from the open window.

With relish he stripped off the clothes he had worn to call on Mrs. Tinling, starting first with the accursed wig, which he flung into the corner like a dead, longhaired white cat. Next the silk coat and waistcoat, which he unceremoniously dropped on the floor. He unbuckled his silly gold-hilted sword with the jewels mounted on the pommel and dropped that on the pile at his feet.

King James, who had accompanied Marlowe into his bedchamber, unbidden though he was, picked up the discarded clothing as fast as Marlowe could shed it.

"Lucy begs me give you her regards," Marlowe said as he pulled on the old breeches. "If I am not entirely mistaken, I think she is fairly smitten with you."

"Hmmph," said James, placing the wig on a table stand. "Lucy is just a foolish girl."

"Indeed, nor do I think much of her taste in men, but you might be well advised to take advantage of her poor judgment."

"Hmmph," James said again.

Marlowe grinned at James but could not get a rise out of him, so he sat on his bed and allowed James to help him into his good, honest wool stockings and knee-high boots. He ran his arms into the loose-fitting cotton shirt and then the waistcoat.

He picked up his old sword, drew the blade from the scabbard. It was a murderous-looking thing, with a wire-bound grip, a brass hand guard, and a straight, heavy double-edged blade over forty inches from hilt to tip. It felt as natural in his hand as his hand felt at the end of his arm.

And he thought, How very odd this life can be. He thought of the times standing on the channel of some decrepit vessel, screaming like a lost soul, closing, inexorably closing on some terrified victim. He thought of the steel that that blade had beaten back, the gore he had wiped from its edge.

He shook the memories away, pushed the sword back into the scabbard. He draped the shoulder strap over his shoulder and adjusted it until the sword hung just right. He draped the other shoulder strap, the one that would hold his pistols, over his left shoulder so the two of them made an X across his chest. Like a target.

"You look quite the villainous rogue," Bickerstaff said as Marlowe stepped out onto the porch. There was nothing in his tone to indicate that he was joking, though Marlowe knew he was.

"And you look like some damned Puritan." Bickerstaff was dressed almost entirely in black—old clothes, like Marlowe's. "Very well, then, let us go and take command of a man-of-war."

They were like an army in miniature as they marched south to Jamestown, where the *Northumberland* waited to take them to the *Plymouth Prize*. At the head were the officers, Marlowe and Burnaby, and Bickerstaff, who might have passed for the army chaplain. Behind them marched the main body, twenty-five men strong, and behind the troops came the baggage train, which consisted of one dray piled with the things that King James had packed. Last came the camp followers, half a dozen servants to function as cabin stewards, cook, and the like.

They arrived in Jamestown late in the day. Marlowe found it a dismal place, even more so than he remembered, with fetid swamps on every hand. The charred ruins of the old capitol building still stood, two years after the fire that had sealed the decision to move the capital to Williamsburg. The town was quickly falling to ruin as more and more people abandoned it with each passing year.

The *Northumberland* was tied to one of the sturdier docks that jutted out into the James River. She was around seventy tons burden, fifty feet long on deck and eighteen at the beam. Massachusetts Bay–built and only ten years old when Marlowe bought her as part of the Tinling estate. A quick and lovely vessel.

He had rerigged her to his own taste, stepping the single mast aft a bit and giving her a longer topmast and increasing the size of her square topsail. Besides that sail she carried a huge gaff-headed mainsail and three headsails. She was fast and weatherly. Marlowe generally used her for commerce on the Chesapeake, but now he intended to make her a tender to the *Plymouth Prize*.

They slept aboard that night, Marlowe, Bickerstaff, and Burnaby in the tiny cabin aft, the militia and the servants sprawled out on the deck above.

The next morning they got under way, with the five men of the *Northumberland*'s crew elbowing their way through the crowd of militiamen, farmers to a man, to get at the sheets and halyards. Useless as they might be as sailors, the militia was good at least for brute force, and Marlowe gave his people a rest by putting the soldiers on the halyards.

In short order they had mainsail, topsail, staysail, and jib set, and with that canvas showing they wafted off the dock in the light morning breeze. King James stood at the tiller, keeping the vessel near the middle of the river as they cut their way through the muddy water downstream to where the guardship swung on her best bower.

It was no great difficulty to find the *Plymouth Prize*. After Allair's brief foray into extortion and piracy, stopping those vessels engaged in honest trade and carefully avoiding any that might give him trouble, he had all but worn himself out and had not moved the ship for a month at least. She lay at anchor about fifteen miles down the James River, in a place calculated to be inconvenient for anyone—Governor Nicholson or any of the members of the Council, for instance—to get to.

They dropped the *Northumberland*'s anchor about half a cable upriver from the *Prize*. Once the hook was secure, the two longboats they had been towing astern were hauled alongside and the militia clambered into them.

"Your men have their weapons loaded?" Marlowe asked Lieutenant Burnaby.

"Yes, sir." He did not look as eager for a fight as he had the day before. Marlowe smiled, thinking of the first time that he himself had gone into a real fight. Like the young lieutenant, he had not been so anxious for it when faced with the reality of the thing.

"Good. No one is to fire unless I give the command. I should prefer to bring this off without bloodshed."

"That would be preferable, sir, I agree."

The longboat bearing the militia pulled away from the *Northumberland* and the sailors rested at their oars, waiting for Marlowe and Bickerstaff and Burnaby to take their places in the other boat and lead the way. A moment later the two boats, rowing in line ahead, dropped downriver toward the *Plymouth Prize*.

The guardship was a sorry sight, her sails hanging half out of their gaskets, her yards askew and her standing rigging slack. Great patches of white rope showed through where the tar had worn away from her shrouds and stays.

The ship's quarters and stern section were adorned with lovely and intricate carvings, but these, too, were suffering much from neglect. The paint and gilt had mostly flaked away, and the wood underneath was dry and cracked. Three of the carved wreaths that highlighted the ship's side had fallen off, leaving circles of bare wood around the gunports. A mermaid under the taffrail was missing her head, and the great lion of England had suffered a double amputation.

The crew of the man-of-war numbered about fifty men, and they were well armed with cutlasses, pistols, pikes, and muskets. Some were sleeping, some playing at cards or cross and pile, some just staring blankly at the approaching boats, their state of readiness notwithstanding. No one raised an alarm.

Marlowe had been aboard English men-of-war on a few occasions, and he had seen enough of them in his time to appreciate the taut discipline and fastidious attention to detail that characterized the service. He could not believe that the *Plymouth Prize* belonged to the same navy that had sailed the mighty *Royal Sovereign*.

But he did know that what he was seeing was the natural result of a careless and stupid captain on a backwater station far from the eyes of the admiralty. He had never seen a group of slaves on any plantation that looked more sullen, listless, and poorly dressed than the crew of the *Plymouth Prize*.

He was about to hail the ship, to inquire if Captain Allair was aboard, when the quiet was shattered by a scream, a female scream, which started low and built to a high-pitched shriek and ended with the words "You miserable godforsaken son of a bitch!"

This at last caused some stirring of interest among the men, though not nearly as much as Marlowe would have thought appropriate. Heads turned in the direction of the after cabin, the place from which the scream had come. Several of the men who were closest to the doorway stood up and walked out of the way.

No sooner had they done so than the door flew open and Allair stormed out, head bent, shoulders hunched, while from the darkness of the cabin the filthy insults continued unabated. A fat, red-faced, enraged woman appeared suddenly at the door, holding a bucket over her head. "Get back here, you miserable cockroach!" she screamed, and flung the bucket at Allair's back.

Allair seemed not to notice. He was raging drunk, Thomas could tell, even from that distance. Had the wind not been contrary, he imagined that he could have smelled the captain's breath.

Allair paused, seeing the longboats making for his command. "Marlowe? Is that you, Marlowe, you sheep-biting whoreson villain?" he screamed. "I say, come on aboard and I'll give you the warm welcome you deserve!"

"What are we to do, sir?" Burnaby asked.

"We'll go aboard and take the ship." The coxswain gave the tiller a nudge to bring the boat around in a sweeping arc alongside the guardship. Marlowe could see the lieutenant gawking at him as if he were some kind of fearless wonder, walking straight into that kind of danger. But Marlowe had seen enough of Allair's type to know that the danger was slight.

The longboat came alongside the *Plymouth Prize* and the

bowman hooked the mainchains with the boat hook. Marlowe grabbed on to the boarding steps and made his way up to the deck, Bickerstaff at his heels.

"Marlowe, you son of a whore!" Allair roared. He had retreated to the great cabin and fetched a pistol, which he now held in his hand. "Think you can play me for a fool? Bloody bastard, come asking me to find you a silver table setting! How'd you know that bloody Nicholson's silver was due in, eh? How'd you know?"

As it happened, Marlowe had noticed the invoice for the silver lying on Nicholson's desk one afternoon while meeting with the governor on some other unrelated business, had devised the entire scheme in those few seconds, but to Allair he said, "I have no notion of what you are talking about, Captain Allair, but as I am now legally in command of this ship let me suggest—"

Standing in the doorway twenty-five feet away, Allair aimed the pistol at Marlowe's head and pulled the trigger. The gun went off with a great bang, Allair having apparently used twice the amount of powder needed. Marlowe felt the rush of air, heard the scream of the ball passing by his head.

It was close, though not as close as young Wilkenson had come. Still, it occurred to Marlowe that he should get out of the habit of allowing others to shoot at him. But now the gun was discharged, and Allair had only his sword with which to fight.

"Cock your firelocks!" he heard Lieutenant Burnaby shout from the boat below. What he intended, Marlowe did not know. He leaned through the entry port and shouted, "Belay that! Weapons on half-cock, all of you," and happily they obeyed before someone was hurt.

"Now, up on deck." One by one the militiamen climbed awkwardly up the side of the ship and fell into line with firelocks shouldered. To Marlowe's great relief, none of the Plymouth Prizes made a move to resist.

"Captain Allair, I have orders from Governor Nicholson, Vice Admiral of the Virginia Station," Marlowe began.

"Vice Admiral, my arse! He's got no authority over me, not to remove me from command!"

"Oh, but I say he does."

"You do? And who are you, whore's git? Black villain. You knew about that bastard's silver, you tricked me."

"Perhaps, but that's behind us now. I shall ask you to remove yourself from my ship." He held up the orders that Nicholson had written out.

"Sod off."

He did not take his eyes from Allair, but he could hear more militia coming aboard and fanning out behind him, and beyond Allair he could see the uncertain looks on the faces of the *Plymouth Prize*'s men. As unimposing as the militia may have looked on Marlowe's lawn, they were commanding quite a bit of respect now, among men even less disciplined and less anxious to fight. It seemed as if Allair was the only one interested in defending the *Plymouth Prize*.

"I should prefer it if you were to leave now," Marlowe said, as reasonably as he was able. "You may take your gig and your gig crew. Anything of yours that will not go in the gig I shall be pleased to send along forthwith."

"Oh, you're a cool one, you bastard," Allair spit, "but you'll not use me like you done that Wilkenson git. Come, Monsieur Privateer, see what you can effect against a king's officer!" Allair drew his sword with some difficulty and took a drunken step toward Marlowe.

Marlowe looked at Bickerstaff, and Bickerstaff gave him a raised eyebrow. This was ridiculous. Allair could never best him with a sword, even if he was stone sober.

"Draw your sword, you coward!" Allair roared, gaining courage from Marlowe's sideways glance at Bickerstaff.

So Marlowe drew his sword. He wielded the weapon with great authority, so accustomed was he to its heft and size, and though the past two years of leisure had somewhat weakened his strength of arm, it was not so much that any but Marlowe himself would notice.

That fact, and the size of the straight blade, did not escape

Allair's drunken gaze. He faltered a bit in his advance, scowled, then summoned up all of the courage that the copious rum in his stomach afforded him and came at Marlowe again.

"I'm for you, God damn you!" he shouted, and charged, slashing down with his blade. Marlowe met the attack with the flat of his own sword, stopping Allair's blade as if he had struck a rock and knocking it aside.

Allair was full open, his chest quite exposed and wanting only a quick thrust to end it all, but Marlowe could not. He took a step back. Allair lifted his sword again and slashed away, and Marlowe again turned the attack aside. They went on like that down the deck, one step at a time, attack and parry, attack and parry, with Allair's breath coming faster and his sword coming slower with each advance.

Marlowe heard a firelock cock and heard Bickerstaff say, "No, no." The militia parted as they moved down the deck, the Plymouth Prizes and the soldiers watching the drama as if it were staged for their amusement. But Marlowe did not want them to interfere. As long as the fight was just between Allair and him, no one would get hurt.

At last his heel touched on the base of the fife rail around the foremast and he knew he could go no farther back. Allair managed something like a smile, apparently thinking that he had his enemy on the run and now he was trapped.

He brought his sword down, and Marlowe turned it aside once more. Then Marlowe held his own blade down, point on the deck, his head fully exposed. Allair drew his sword back like an ax and slashed down, intending to cleave Marlowe's head in two.

He would have, too, had he connected, for he put all the strength he had left into that last final blow. But Marlowe stepped aside at the very second that Allair was committed to the blow. The blade came down on an oak belaying pin and split that, rather than Marlowe's skull, and there it stayed.

Allair struggled and cursed and tried to wrench the sword free from the pin, but it would not budge. He looked desperately over at Marlowe, waiting to be finished off, but Marlowe only stared back, waiting for Allair to free his sword or collapse in fear and exhaustion.

"Very well, Marlowe," he panted, falling against the fife rail. "Kill me."

"Never in life, sir, a king's officer. I ask only that you obey Governor Nicholson's legal orders and turn the *Plymouth Prize* over to my command."

Allair glared at him for a second more, then shuffled aft, leaving his sword wedged in the belaying pin. The militiamen stared at him, as did the men of the *Plymouth Prize*.

Another tale of my great daring, Marlowe thought, to be carried back to Williamsburg. A tale of how Marlowe spared the life of the man who tried to kill him. Such the gentleman, they will say, such a man of noble birth.

Only he and Bickerstaff and Allair understood that killing the man would have been the more merciful act.

"Now, men," Marlowe addressed the crew of the *Plymouth Prize*, "I beg of you, lay down your weapons."

Fifty muskets fell clattering to the deck.

An hour later the captain's gig disappeared around a bend in the river, heading upstream to Jamestown. Along with Captain Allair went his great beast of a wife, who had happily decided to remain in the cabin during the confrontation. Had she been on deck, Marlowe would have actually been frightened.

As it was, her presence in the gig left little room for the Allairs' personal belongings, which Marlowe assured them he would send back with the militia the next day. With the former captain properly disposed of, he took his place on the quarterdeck and summoned the crew aft.

"Good afternoon, men," he said in as cheerful a tone as he could manage. "I am sorry for the little altercation that I had with your former captain, but I have no doubt it gave you some pleasant diversion."

There were a few smiles at this, weak smiles. No one laughed. "My name is Captain Thomas Marlowe, and I have here orders from Governor Nicholson instructing me to take command of the *Plymouth Prize*." He quickly read through the orders, added some banal thing about attending to duty, and then dismissed them.

"Pray, sir," one of the men spoke up, "but what shall we be doing now?"

Marlowe smiled. "We'll be doing what the *Plymouth Prize* was sent here to do," he said. "We shall be going forth and hunting down those roguish pirates."

Chapter 8

A SHIP is a vegetable affair. Every part of it, save for those little bits of metalwork, was once a plant of some description. The frames and planks and decking, the hanging knees and clamps and wales, the very fabric of the vessel, all once were living oak, fir, longleaf yellow pine.

It is wood that holds the great mass together—pegs called tree nails, driven into holes bored through plank and frame and hammered home with great force. Then, between these wood planks, are pounded dried plant fibers in the form of oakum to render the hull watertight. And between the planks of the deck is poured the melted pitch of pine trees.

The masts rise from the deck like the great trees they once were. Their roots go down through weather deck, gun deck, and berthing deck to where they terminate in the dark hold, set into a notch in the keelson called a step.

But these roots are not so substantial that the mast can stand on its own, not with the tremendous pressure of sail it must carry. So the masts are set up with rigging: shrouds and stays, unwieldy lengths of cordage that are themselves woven from bits of dried plants and coated with tar distilled from the trunks of pine.

The shrouds come down to deadeyes, nicely worked, round

pieces of wood pierced with three holes through which are rove smaller lines called lanyards. The lanyards in turn are held fast by thin and insubstantial lines called marlin, bound up in an elaborate knot called a seizings. Thus the whole machine, from the great bulk of the mainmast to the tiny seizings on the spritsail topmast shrouds, all work in consort to move this thing called a ship to wherever its masters deem it should go.

And every bit of it, from keel to truck, started its life as a living plant. And like all things that were once alive, it is all prone to rot.

And such was the state of the *Plymouth Prize*.

One look at the anchor cable and Marlowe knew the reason for this condition. From the point where it left the hawse hole to where it plunged into the river, that six-inch-thick rope was as dry and white as a bone, so long had it been exposed to the sun.

Just below the water's surface a great mass of weed and scum held fast to the cable and streamed away in the current. The anchor had not been off the bottom, and the ship had not moved in quite some time. When a ship does not move, and her people do not look after her, she begins her quick return to a state of nature.

Had Marlowe understood the true condition of the *Plymouth Prize*, he might not have been so active in securing her command for himself. As it was, no sooner had Captain Allair disappeared upriver than the carpenter, who, like most of the men, was quick to accept the change of command, came to him and said, "Beggin' your pardon, sir, but might we have some men for the pumps?"

"Certainly," said Marlowe. "How much water is there in the well?"

"Three feet, sir, and rising."

"Three feet? When was she last pumped?"

"This morning watch, sir. Pumped dry."

Marlowe's mouth hung open at this news, despite himself. She had been pumped dry that morning, and already there was three feet of water in the hold, and this while riding at anchor with no strain to speak of on her hull. In a seaway she would leak much worse, and in a gale she would not last an hour. But this was not the worst of it.

The mainmast had a great nasty section of black wood where the rot was eating away at it. The standing rigging was slack and in desperate need of fresh tar. A fine white powder fell from whatever piece of the running gear Marlowe took up and twisted open, a sure sign that the rope was rotten and would not bear any strain.

After sending half the men to the pumps, Marlowe sent the other half aloft to shake out the sails, it being his intention to let the canvas dry to a bowline. They climbed with great care, taking each step slowly, lest the rope on which they stood break and they fall to deck.

On the fore topsail yard he saw a man put his foot clean through the rotten fabric of the sail.

Another man, loosening off the main topsail, was halfway out the yard when the footrope on which he stood gave out under him and he fell screaming from that great height. All about the ship men froze, aghast, as the unhappy soul bounced off the main top, hit the main yard with a thump that sent him spinning, and plunged into the river. But despite all that, they fished him out, fully alive but shaken, and after a few cups of rum he was quite set up again.

It was a prodigious amount of work that the *Plymouth Prize* needed to put her in fighting trim, if, indeed, she could ever again hope to achieve that exalted state. And Marlowe understood that if she could not, then he, Bickerstaff, and all of the Prizes might well be dead within the week.

This much and more Marlowe discussed with Bickerstaff as they trudged across the western beach of Smith Island toward the low grassy hills and clusters of trees in the middle of that place.

It was late afternoon, the day after he had taken command of the *Plymouth Prize*. The guardship was still where they had found her, being readied for sea by First Lieutenant William Rakestraw, whom Marlowe hoped, after a lengthy interview, was at heart an able officer, grown dull under Allair's lethargy.

Behind them, riding at anchor in the shallow bay, was the sloop *Northumberland*. Marlowe had left her small crew aboard, had taken only Bickerstaff and King James with him. No one else needed to know what they were about. He trusted no one else to walk with him into the lion's den.

"Admit it, Tom, she's worse off than you had imagined," said Bickerstaff. "Even I can see that. She needs prodigious work. And not a sort of tidying up, either, blacking down the rig and sweeping up the decks and that sort of thing. No, she needs careening, she needs a new mainmast, she needs new running gear rove off, a new suit of sails."

"Honestly, Francis, how you go on. You would think the ship is sinking under our feet."

"She is not now. Now we are on dry land. Yesterday she was, and when we are aboard her she shall be again."

"Very well, she is sinking. But we cannot, you see, go to the governor complaining about the need for repair. That was Allair's excuse, and I reckon the governor has had a belly full of it. No, I fain would accomplish something before we suggest heaving her down. And if we meet with success in our current venture we shall earn our own keep, and then some."

"That is another matter." Bickerstaff stopped, forced Marlowe to meet his eye. "This seems a very selfless thing you are doing, taking command of the guardship. Now, you have your qualities, to be sure, but selflessness is not high among them."

Marlowe held his gaze, that wonderful gaze. There was nothing condescending, nothing judgmental in his look. Had there been, Marlowe would have run him through long ago, or died trying. He looked as he always did, as if he wanted only for Marlowe to be true to himself.

But that, of course, was irritating in its own right.

"Francis," he said, "you alone understand the circumstances that led me . . . us . . . here. What better way for us to take our place in society than to save society from these evil pirates?"

"Save them? What you have in mind—what I believe you have in mind—smacks of the sweet trade itself."

At this Marlowe grinned. "Well, now, you must know that old saying 'set a thief to catch a thief'?"

"I do. But you are a gentleman, Tom. You are not a thief, and you are not a pirate."

"You can't expect me to ask these villains to leave of their own accord. And you can't expect those lazy sods on the *Plymouth Prize* to fight like they mean it without they have some compensation for their troubles."

Bickerstaff looked at him for a moment more. "You are very near the edge, my friend." He turned and resumed walking.

They pressed on, side by side. King James scouted ahead, moving with animal stealth, recalling those lessons he learned as a boy in his native Africa. Now and again he would show himself, give the two men a sign that all was clear.

Smith Island was an odd-shaped spot of land about five miles long and, where they were crossing, thankfully less than a mile wide. It was actually in the Atlantic Ocean, less than half a mile east of Cape Charles, just north of the entrance to the Chesapeake Bay, part of the string of barrier islands that stood like a rampart along the coast. It was secluded and had on either side good sheltered harbors. It was perfect for ships prowling between the Capes, awaiting a rich prize. It was a popular spot among the pirate tribes.

And there were a lot of them. King William's War had ended two years before, and all of the major powers of Europe had returned to their usual uneasy peace. During that war, like any war, those of a piratical bent were employed as privateers, plundering enemy ships under their monarch's letter of marque. It was perfectly legal, even patriotic, to do so.

But with the signing of peace in Casco the privateers did not always quit their lucrative trade. Many of them just carried on raiding merchant ships. But now it was called piracy, and ships of any nationality were game. And those that looked to capture the rich tobacco ships outbound from Virginia and Maryland, and the richer merchantmen coming from England with English goods, all congregated at Smith Island.

Allair knew that, which was why he had so carefully avoided the place. Bickerstaff and Marlowe knew that as well, and that was why they were there.

It took them two hours to work their way up the hilly interior of the island, moving slowly, watching for signals from King James and seeking cover lest there be a lookout watching that side of the island. By the time they approached the far ridges that looked down into the harbor, the sun was setting at their backs. Anyone looking in their direction would be looking right into its rays, effectively hiding them from view.

"Not so many as I would have thought," Marlowe said to Bickerstaff. They were lying on their bellies amid tall grass and a small stand of oak, looking down at the harbor three hundred yards away. There was only one ship at anchor there, her topmast and topgallants glowing orange in the evening light.

She was a big one, several hundred tons by Marlowe's guess, and pierced for twenty great guns. There was no flag flying from her ensign staff, but neither man needed a flag to tell them what she was.

She might have been a man-of-war, for all her arms and men, but a man-of-war would not have her yards all askew and her deck piled with rubbish and her sails hanging like laundry hastily taken in before the rain. Marlowe and Bickerstaff knew pirates, and everything about her indicated that such she was.

Most of the beach was in shadow, but not so dark that they could not see the activity there. There were one hundred men at least, fully occupied. Some were ferrying stores and loot and guns from the anchored ship and piling them on the sand. Others were stacking up wood for the great bonfire around which they would later roast their dinner and perform their drunken rituals.

"I believe they are going to careen her," Marlowe said.

"It would appear so. Observe, not half her great guns are still aboard."

"I see. That's good. I can't imagine they'll bother erecting batteries on shore. I doubt they know that I am now in command of the guardship."

"And when they discover it, I doubt they'll be greatly concerned."

"I'll grant you that," Marlowe said.

"In any event, it appears that they will be here for some time. A week at least, I should think, before they voyage again."

"And when they do voyage again," said Marlowe, "it will be, for most of them, that great and final voyage, the one we all must take."

"Why, Marlowe, you are becoming positively poetic. Now let me suggest you leave off before you further embarrass yourself."

Marlowe smiled, his face nearly lost in the deep shadows. "Quite," he said, and suddenly he felt another presence, a person directly behind him. He rolled over, grabbed for a pistol. King James was crouching there. They had not heard him approach.

"There is a lookout about one hundred yard that way," King James pointed north, "and another on that far ridge. But they both drunk."

"Very good." Marlowe paused for a moment, waiting for his heartbeat to return to normal. "Now let us talk some strategy and then quit this place."

When at last the *Plymouth Prize* was put under way, Marlowe could only thank the Lord that they did not have to take her out on the open sea.

He and Bickerstaff had returned the day after their scouting foray to find that Lieutenant Rakestraw had made a great effort and had pushed the men to do likewise. The lower shrouds were set up for a full due, though gently, so as not to further wound the rotten masts, and blacked down afresh. The ship was scrubbed fore and aft, and what spare sails she carried were bent on, at least those that were not in even worse shape than the first. There was no spare cordage to replace the running gear, but much of it at least had been turned end for end.

"I reckon that's about all we can do, sir, with what we got aboard," Rakestraw reported, standing beside his new captain on the quarterdeck as the banks of the James River slipped by. "I don't care to say so, sir, and I fain would make an excuse, but she does need careening something fierce."

His clothing, Marlowe noticed, was neater than it had been before. He was wearing a new jacket and cocked hat. He seemed to be standing straighter.

"Don't be afraid to say so, Lieutenant. You are quite right in that, and we shall heave her down just as soon as we are able. Allair's mistake was that he made demands without giving anything in return. Soon we shall prove to the colony that they cannot do without us, and then we shall have whatever we require."

"Yes, sir," he said. "But please, sir, what are we doing?"

"In due time, Lieutenant, in due time." Marlowe did not need to have word of his plans reaching the lower deck. It would do the men below no good to spend the next two days in mortal fear.

Marlowe knew about mortal fear. He knew the fear that the pirates could engender, and knew better than most how legitimate that fear was. He had seen mouths stuffed full of burning oakum, living men carved up with broken bottles, women raped to death.

But it was not the drunken rascals on Smith Island who had done that. It was another man, at another time, and he put it out of his mind. He might fear that man, but that man was not the one he would be facing.

And that was fortunate. He realized how fortunate it was that very morning as he watched the Plymouth Prizes, the men upon whom he would rely during the upcoming, bloody fight, struggling just to raise the anchor from the bottom. It took some twenty-three minutes just to rig the capstan with messenger, bars and swifter, the men wandering around, staring as if they were seeing the *Plymouth Prize* for the first time. It was beyond belief.

At length, and with much trouble and much broken gear, they won the anchor and made the *Plymouth Prize* move from that spot on the James River where she had become such a fixture.

The pumps had not stopped once from that minute, nor did they the entire time they were under way.

And for all of the thirty hours it took them to close with Smith Island, Marlowe could think of only one thing: I am taking this ruin of a ship, and these men, against a band of brigands who outnumbered us two to one. A band to whom killing is as much a part of life as is sloth and complaining to the men of the *Plymouth Prize*.

Chapter 9

GEORGE WILKENSON stood in the shadow of Mrs. Sullivan's ordinary, half hidden around the edge of the building, trying to look as if he were not hiding. But in fact he was. He was keeping a close eye on Elizabeth Tinling as she and Lucy wound their way through the Market Day booths on the far side of Duke of Gloucester Street.

It was a perfect spring day, with random white clouds sailing across the blue sky and a cooling breeze blowing off the bay, blowing away the heat and the stink and the flies. The weather seemed to affect everyone who had business in Williamsburg. The joviality, smiles, laughter, and general bonhomie all served to make Wilkenson that much more miserable.

He had been shadowing them for the past hour, since they left the house and walked down the crowded street to do their marketing. This type of skulking was not at all to his liking. He was, after all, one of the most powerful men in the colony, the one who ran the vast Wilkenson holdings of ships and tobacco and slaves. Their increasingly lucrative import business as well: cloth, silver, furniture, firearms, and sundry equipment from England that were so much in demand.

Their father might have favored his bold and ostentatious younger brother, but George knew that it was he, the quiet, methodical one, the man of thought rather than action, who was responsible for turning the small Wilkenson fortune into the still-expanding Wilkenson empire.

He was waiting for the chance to speak with Elizabeth alone, but Lucy was still following her like a puppy.

He let his eyes wander over the young slave.

Lovely. Light brown skin that spoke of some illicit liaison between master and slave somewhere in her forgotten family history. A pleasure to look at, and George could well imagine that old Tinling had not been able to keep his hands off of her, even with a wife like Elizabeth.

It was common knowledge that Lucy was in love with King James, Tinling's surly, vicious, rebellious field hand. Marlowe's majordomo. George knew about those Africans and their insatiable carnal desires. His mind wandered to images of James having his way with Lucy, her firm brown body writhing under him, head thrown back, screaming, heels dug into the sharply defined muscles in the small of his back, his powerful hands gripping her waist.

He shook himself from his reverie, which was only serving to titillate and distract him, and concentrated on his quarry. He watched Elizabeth step around a pie cart, then turn to Lucy and say something that he could not hear. Lucy nodded and walked away, off on some errand, and Elizabeth was alone.

Wilkenson stepped out of the shadow of the ordinary and hurried across the street, shouldering past the crowds, men and women out strolling in their fine clothes, laborers in the aprons of their trade, ragged slaves sent to town on their masters' business.

He approached, considered what he would say and how he would say it.

Here again, he thought, is the difference between Matthew and myself.

Matthew had been bold and stupid, blundering into a fight that he should have known he could not win. George, on the other hand, was more cunning. Like a cannon fired from a great distance, he would kill Marlowe before he even saw it coming. The bastard would be dead before he heard the shot. Wished that his father could see the advantage of his ways over Matthew's.

He sidled up beside Elizabeth, fell in with her step. "Good morning, Mrs. Tinling." He tried to sound like a man in control.

"Good morning, Mr. Wilkenson," Elizabeth said without looking at him. "Are you quite done hankering around after me, lurking in the shadows like some pickpocket?" She turned to him and smiled.

Wilkenson scowled, said nothing. Her beauty always made him a bit unsteady, and her sharp tongue could bowl him over. He was always awed and jealous of Matthew's ability to approach her. He had secretly felt, after her husband's death, that she should have been his, but he never had the courage to act.

"Now see here, Mrs. Tinling, we have a few things that we must discuss," Wilkenson managed at last. He pictured in his mind the great estate that he controlled, the hundred and fifty slaves who lived and died by his command, and that gave him a renewed confidence.

He waited for Elizabeth to speak, but she did not, so he continued. "As you are no doubt aware, that villain Marlowe killed my brother. Killed him for your sake, in fact."

"I do not know why Mr. Marlowe killed your brother, sir. I suggest you ask him."

"The 'why' really does matter. He did, and now he must pay."

"He killed your brother in a duel. If he cheated in some manner, then it was your duty, as Matthew's second, to prevent it."

Wilkenson stared into her blue eyes. It was pure nonsense to suggest Marlowe had done anything illegal or immoral. He had known it from the start, knew that Elizabeth did as well. He had already decided that he would not argue the point.

"Regardless," Wilkenson said, "he must pay."

"Why do you not simply call Marlowe out and kill him in a fair fight? As he did to your brother. It is what any man would do." She put just the slightest emphasis on the word "man."

"I have in mind something far more painful than a bullet. I wish to see Marlowe disgraced before he dies. You are going to help see that happens."

"And if I refuse?" Elizabeth asked, her eyes flashing, her face set in a hateful scowl. She looked more beautiful than ever. Wilkenson felt himself becoming aroused, despite himself.

"I think you know that I can make things most uncomfortable for you in this colony."

Elizabeth's expression did not change. She just stared at him with a hateful look. Wilkenson imagined that she had expected the threat. He hoped that she would not call him on it, for then she would realize that it was a threat that he could not carry out.

When she did not respond, George continued. "Matthew kept no secrets from me. I know everything that William Tinling told him about you. We both know that it could ruin you in this colony. Pray, do not make me say it out loud."

In fact, he hoped very much that she would not, for he did not really know what Matthew's secret was. His brother had been a close friend of William Tinling, and William had told him something about his father's young bride, but Matthew had kept it to himself and had taken it to the grave.

Elizabeth, apparently, did not know that. And judging from her expression, whatever the secret was, it was damning indeed.

"Very well," she said at last. "What is it you want of me?"

"You have become close with Marlowe, I understand."

"He called on me once. Is that 'close'?"

"Nonetheless, he has an eye for you," Wilkenson continued, "and we shall use that to our advantage. You will go to his house at some time that he is there and . . . seduce him into some illicit liaison. I shall arrive, prepared to issue a challenge, and when I do you shall scream that you are being violated, at which point I will burst in and catch him in flagrante delicto. We shall arrest him for rape and see him tried and convicted. You, of course, shall testify against him."

Even as he said it Wilkenson realized how utterly craven

a plan it was. But in order to see Marlowe hanged he had to catch him in a provable crime, and this was the easiest and most humiliating that he could manufacture.

Elizabeth shook her head, disgusted. "That is the most cowardly, pathetic thing that I have ever heard."

"Perhaps. But you will do it nonetheless." Wilkenson felt his cheeks burning with embarrassment. Maybe when this was all over he would show her what it was really like to be taken by force. Show her that he was not the timid little man she thought he was.

He shook those thoughts aside. "I will expect a note from you by week's end indicating when you will be at Marlowe's house and the exact moment that I am to arrive. If I do not receive word by then . . ."

"Pray, don't say it." Elizabeth's tone was equal parts weariness and contempt. "You have been none too subtle with your threats already."

"Then we understand each other?"

Elizabeth glared at him, her lips pressed together. "Yes, yes, whatever you wish. I have no choice, it seems, but to be part of your pathetic plan."

"Quite true." He had applied the stick, and she had moved in the right direction. Now he would show her the carrot. "Incidentally, that new home of yours is very nice. Very nice indeed. It could not be inexpensive."

She looked hard at him, wary. "It is not, but it is within my means."

"Unless, of course, the note of hand should be called in. Then I imagine you would exhaust your funds paying it off."

"Perhaps. But the note is held by Mr. David Nelson, who is a man of honor, and who assures me he will not call it in." She could see what was coming. Clever little slut, Wilkenson thought.

"Ah, but that is no longer the case, you see, because I purchased the note from Mr. Nelson, along with several others, and now it is mine to call in whenever I so choose. If I have your cooperation in this matter, I may well be persuaded to tear up the note, and you will own your home, free and clear. If not, then I fear you shall be bankrupt paying it off, once I call it in."

He let the words hang in the air. George Wilkenson knew a great deal about persuasion.

"If I . . . I shall have my house, free and clear, if I do this?"

"Indeed."

"Very well, then. I shall do as you wish." She seemed to deflate in resignation.

"Good. I shall bid you good day." He gave her a curt bow, turned on his heel, and turned back again. "You will send a note, then, by week's end?"

"Yes, yes. I said yes."

"Good." He turned again and strode away. He could feel his cheeks burning, and his neck and palms were covered with sweat.

Still, it was a good plan, because the crime would be perfectly believable. It would take no art to show that, after killing Matthew Wilkenson for her honor, Marlowe came to expect certain favors from Elizabeth, and when they were not forthcoming he tried to take them.

It was perfectly believable that George should go to Marlowe's house to issue a challenge. His claiming that he was doing so would quiet those people who were asking abroad why George did not call Marlowe out, while at once assuring Marlowe's death by hanging and saving George from having to fight the rogue. Perfect.

Nor would it be any great effort to get the others to do his bidding: Sheriff Witsen and the jury and even Governor Nicholson.

George was careful never to put the family into debt, not to their agent in London or to anyone in the tidewater. Owing money meant owing allegiance, and George Wilkenson would owe allegiance to no one.

Instead he accrued the allegiance of others through his generous lending of money to any who asked with the proper humility, and he never demanded that it be repaid on any schedule.

But he understood, and his debtors understood, that the entire sum was always due in full upon demand, even if it meant the debtor's ruination. In this way George Wilkenson exercised control over half of the population of Williamsburg.

He suddenly felt a desperate need for this all to be over, for Marlowe to be hanged and buried so that he could get on with his business.

I am not Achilles, he thought. No, I'm not the warrior. I am Odysseus, the clever one.

George Wilkenson took some comfort from that notion.

Chapter 10

IT TOOK twenty hours, dropping down the James River, then standing east-northeast with an average eight knots of breeze over the starboard quarter for the *Plymouth Prize* to cover the sixty miles from her former anchorage to Smith Island. They had all sail set, including the little spritsail topsail that set on the spritsail topmast at the far end of the bowsprit. The great lumbering guardship pushed along, seemingly as reluctant as her men to go into battle. But like her men, go she must, and one by one Marlowe pricked the miles off the chart.

In all it was a fine sail. The weather in Virginia, when it is good, is the best in the world. And those two days were good, with the warm breeze making cat's paws on the blue water of the bay. The sky from horizon to horizon was a fine clear blue, just a little lighter in color than the water.

Off the starboard beam, framed by Cape Charles to the north and Cape Henry to the south, the Atlantic Ocean stretched away, glittering and flashing and melding at last with the pale blue sky on the indeterminate horizon. In their wake was the low green coast of Virginia's mainland, and forward the long peninsula that ended at Cape Charles. Overhead a variety of birds wheeled around the trucks of the masts, and under their keel the bay rolled with barely perceptible swells.

A good thing, for the *Plymouth Prize* might well have sunk in anything worse.

One hundred yards off the larboard quarter the *Northumberland* kept station. It was only with much difficulty that King James was able to sail slowly enough so as not to headreach on the *Plymouth Prize*.

There is so much to do, Marlowe thought, so very much to do. The Plymouth Prizes were tolerable seamen, but they had grown lethargic and unmotivated under Allair's command. Nor was their seamanship his immediate concern. More pressing was their training for combat, so that they could acquit themselves well, or at least so that he and Bickerstaff and King James would not die as a result of their incompetence.

"First position," he heard Bickerstaff call out, and the fifty men drawn up in a line in the waist moved into the first position for sword work: feet at right angles, left hand behind their backs, cutlass held before them. They were as graceful as pelicans waddling on shore, and just as intimidating.

"Second position," Bickerstaff called, and fifty right feet came forward, ready to lunge or parry. It was all very pretty and nice, and a few years before Marlowe would have thought it a waste of time. Fancy drills had nothing to do with the bloody, desperate hack and slash of a real fight. But he trusted Bickerstaff, and Bickerstaff had convinced him of the importance of learning the fine points first, and then later the grim reality of the thing.

"Extension in three motions," he called, and fifty men lunged at an imaginary enemy. Two of them stumbled while attempting this, fell to the deck. Marlowe turned and stared out at the blue water and the wooded shoreline far away. The time had come to reconsider his strategy.

It was three hours past sunset when the *Plymouth Prize* made her ponderous way around the east shore of Smith Island. The moon was almost full, and in that silver light Marlowe had a clear view of the bay and the pirate ship still at anchor. A huge fire was burning on the beach, and sounds of the distant bacchanal drifted over the water. Everything was as perfect as he dared hope.

They had parted company with the *Northumberland* at sunset after ferrying over Francis Bickerstaff and a force of ten of the best men the *Plymouth Prize* had to offer. Lieutenant Middleton, second officer aboard the *Plymouth Prize*, was sent to take command of the sloop and King James was returned to the guardship. The black man was not happy about that development, Marlowe knew, but there was no choice. He needed King James by his side.

"Sir?" Lieutenant Rakestraw stepped up to Marlowe and spoke in a conspiratorial whisper, glancing over to the leeward side of the quarterdeck where King James stood.

"Yes, Lieutenant?"

"Sir, it's . . . ah . . . about the nigger, sir? King James?"

Marlowe glanced over at the man in question. He looked a dangerous sight, to be sure. A bright red rag was tied around his head, and he wore nothing but a waistcoat, unbuttoned, a loose cotton shirt, and baggy trousers. A cutlass and two braces of pistols were hanging from crossed shoulder belts, pressing the cloth of his shirt down and revealing the powerful chest beneath. His right hand rested on the quarterdeck rail, his left on the hilt of his cutlass. The muscles of his arms rippled with the slightest movement.

"Yes, what of him?"

"Well, sir, is it wise to arm a nigger that way? I mean, to give him guns? I don't think it's legal, sir."

"Perhaps you're right," Marlowe said. "Why don't you go take them away from him?"

"Sir?"

"Go disarm the man, Lieutenant. I daren't."

"Oh. Well." Rakestraw apparently did not think it so important, under those conditions, that King James be disarmed.

"See here, Mr. Rakestraw, I know this is irregular, but King James is a vital part of the thing, and I reckon he'll be a good man to have at our side when the fighting starts."

"Well, if you say so, sir . . ." Rakestraw said, and said no more.

Marlowe stepped down off of the quarterdeck and into the waist, where the men were gathered. Each held a musket cradled in his arms and two pistols in his belt and a cutlass dangling from a shoulder strap.

They were a motley and ragged bunch, and Marlowe had no fear that they would be recognized as a man-of-war's men. Nor was it likely that the pirates would guess the *Plymouth Prize* was one of His Majesty's proud vessels. There was nothing more he needed to do to give the ship an appearance of piratical neglect.

"Now listen up, you men," he said. "I've gone over the plan sufficiently, so I won't bore you with it again. You've worked hard, and so I'm going to give you all a cup of rum, by way of thanks."

This met with a murmur of approval. He dispatched two men to fetch up a breaker while he continued. "This fight could be a hard one, but hear me and take heart. The pirates will be taken quite by surprise. What's more, I'll wager they are all drunk as lords and in no condition to resist."

That was half true. He had no doubt that they were drunk, but he also knew that being drunk would only make them more fearsome in a scrape. Ardent spirits did that, which was the real reason he was giving them to his own men.

"So remember, all of you, stand fast, do your duty, obey orders, and tomorrow you shall be heroes. And rich, to boot." At that last he saw a few heads turn, a few glances exchanged.

These shortsighted wool-gatherers haven't considered the prospect of booty, Marlowe thought. But now they would, and it would make them that much more cooperative.

He turned and headed back for the quarterdeck as the breaker of rum made its appearance. His presence would have only dampened the men's enjoyment of the moment and prevented them from speculating about possible riches.

They rounded the easternmost tip of the island and turned westerly, coming close-hauled with larboard tacks aboard. The wind held steady, and the *Plymouth Prize* was making three knots at least, heeling just a bit to starboard. The moonlight and the huge fire on the beach glinted off the little waves in the bay, flickering and dancing. The far-off revelry and the crackling of the flames seemed unnaturally loud in a night otherwise silent. The dark silhouette of the anchored ship stood out sharp against the fire and the reflections on the water.

"Stand by to let go the anchor," Marlowe called forward, and Lieutenant Rakestraw, just visible by the cathead, called back, "Aye!", leaving out the "sir" as Marlowe had instructed. Things were working out well, the way that he had hoped.

They stood in past the anchored ship. She was indeed a big one, bigger than the *Plymouth Prize* and more heavily armed, though now she was a flute, her gunports empty and her heavy guns ashore. It would have been no great difficulty to board her and carry her off, but she was not what Marlowe was after. What he wanted was ashore—the pirates and their ill-gotten merchandise.

"Who's that?" called a voice from the pirate ship, heavy with drink, loud with surprise. The fellow left aboard to keep watch, no doubt, Marlowe thought, and a fine watch he is keeping. The *Plymouth Prize* was already alongside and no more than fifty yards away before he spotted her. "What ship is that?" the watchman added.

"*Vengeance*," shouted Marlowe.

"And where do you hail from?"

"Out of the sea!" It was the usual pirate response to that question, defiant, mocking all seagoing etiquette and protocol.

There followed a brief silence, and then: "What do you want?"

"I'll tell you, but it's no business of yours. We need a harbor, we're leaking like an unstanched wench. D'ya not hear our pumps going?"

There came a grunt by way of reply. "Very well, then, but keep your goddamned distance, hear me? And if you'd beach her, then just stand on, there be a bar of but one fathom deep just ahead."

Marlowe heard his words but gave them no thought. The watchman had not raised an alarm. His mind was now occupied with the beach. If they stood in another cable length or so, he figured, then they could land in the dark. Those pirates encircling the inferno would be blinded by their own fire and silhouetted against the flames. Yes, it would be a handsome thing.

And then he thought of what the watchman had said. He turned to King James.

"Did that villain say 'If we'd beach her . . .' " he began, but got no further. The *Plymouth Prize* lurched to a stop. Marlowe staggered forward, thrown off balance. The grinding sound of her bow running up on the sandbar was carried back through the fabric of the ship.

"Son of a bitch," he said out loud. They were hard aground. The ship began to swing, pivoting on her bow as the stern was blown downwind. Overhead he heard the flap of canvas as the sails luffed, and then they fell silent as they came aback.

Just as Marlowe was assuring himself that there was no harm done—they were only on sand—he heard a creaking, a horrible creaking and snapping of wood, a groan of cordage and the sharp pop pop pop of ropes coming under great strain.

He looked up. The mainmast was leaning to starboard and aft. He could see the wood coming apart, actually see it splintering, where the mast had rotted at the base. The sails were full aback and pushing the whole thing over the side.

"Clew up the topsails! Clew up the mainsail!" he shouted. "Just cut the damned sheets away! Just cut them away!" What he hoped to accomplish he did not know, nor did it matter. The men just stood there, staring dumbly aloft, as if his orders were directed at some other crew.

The mast leaned farther and farther. One shroud, then another and another, snapped and flew across the deck as the mast went by the board. The mainstay was stretched taut as a harp string and groaned under the load. He could hear the fibers popping as that rotten rope tried to hold the entire weight of the mast.

"You there, in the waist," he called to a knot of men standing just beneath the stay, "stand clear. . . ."

Then the mainstay lanyards parted and the heart, a great block of oak made fast to the end of the mainstay, whipped through the gang in the waist. One man turned at the sound and caught the block full in the face. It carried him along as it knocked the others about the deck, like a cannonball blasting them apart.

Vigilance, vigilance, and no standing about, Marlowe thought, taking some small satisfaction in seeing the sluggards pay thus for their somnambulism.

The mast hesitated, as if making one last effort to remain upright, then toppled over the side. Mainmast, main top, main topmast, main topgallant, flagstaff, fore topgallant and flagstaff, and half a ton of rigging all collapsed into the harbor.

"Drop the damn anchor," he called forward, heard the anchor splash down.

He looked over the water toward the beach. A hundred of the pirate revelers were standing in the surf, watching the fun as the Prize's mast collapsed. That was the last thing that the mast had taken with it—their chance at surprise.

He stepped down into the waist, spoke in a sharp whisper. "Get those boats alongside. Load your weapons, and remember, I'll flog the man to death who fires before I give the word."

"We're still going ashore?" someone croaked.

"Yes. And I'll flog to death the next man who questions my orders." And by God he meant it, too.

The two big boats were pulled alongside, and one by one the men clambered down the boarding steps and took their places at the thwarts, their muskets laid down amidships. Marlowe stood at the gangway, looking down. White, expectant faces looking back at him. He had intended to land the men at the dark end of the beach, but now that was out of the question. The pirates would think such a move was an attempt to flank them, which indeed it was.

"Oh, to hell with it," he said out loud. If the villains on shore thought the Prizes to be fellow Brethren of the Coast then they wouldn't be surprised to see the men come ashore heavily armed. It was what that type did.

"Listen up, you men," he said in a loud whisper. "We're going right at them. When we beach, just pull the boats up and step ashore, easy as you please. Keep your mouths shut, only I talk. Then, when I give the word, jump into formation and prepare to fire a volley. Is that clear?"

He heard murmured acknowledgment floating up from the boats, but he felt no great confidence that his orders had been understood, or if they had, that they wold be obeyed. Well, he thought, there's nothing for it now.

He climbed down into the first boat and sat himself in the stern sheets, and without a word King James followed, taking up the tiller. The former slave seemed oblivious to the dirty looks shot aft by the Plymouth Prizes, who apparently did not fancy the idea of a black man as coxswain.

But what they did not understand, as Marlowe did, was that it was the perfect touch for their disguise. Nowhere outside that rude democracy of the pirate world would one find a black man on such an equal footing with whites.

Lieutenant Rakestraw, dressed much like his men and looking in no way like a British naval officer, took command of the second boat, and with a word the oars came down and the boat crews pulled for shore.

In the moonlight Marlowe could see the faces of the men at the oars. They were tight lipped and grim, and their skin appeared pale and waxy. Beads of sweat stood out on foreheads, more so than was warranted by the temperature or the exertion.

They were a very frightened bunch. Marlowe caught a whiff of something that suggested someone had not been able to hold his bowels, but that smell could well have come from another source. At least their backs were to the beach, and the waiting pirates would not see the terror in their faces, only the calm visages of himself and King James.

They closed with the beach, one hundred yards, fifty yards.

He could see the pirates massed there, waiting for their arrival. There were over a hundred of them, and not above forty Prizes. That would also help the pirates feel secure, though it did nothing for Marlowe. He thought of what he would say, how he would hold their attention while his men formed up.

He could smell the fire now, and the roasted pig and the rum and the discharged powder, all those familiar smells of a pirate encampment. The boats ground up on the sand, and the men of the *Plymouth Prize*, the stupid sheep, just sat there, oars dangling in the water.

"Get out and pull us up on the beach," he growled, and reluctantly the men left the familiar boat and stepped ashore at the feet of their enemy.

Marlowe stood and swaggered forward to the bow of the boat and hopped down onto the sand with King James a few feet behind.

"Who the fuck are you, then?" asked one of the crowd. They were twenty feet away, pushing forward to get a look at the newcomers, and they looked every inch the pirate mob. Most wore no shoes or stockings. Some wore breeches, but most wore the baggy trousers favored by sailors the world over. At least half of them wore sashes around their waists, red, generally, into which were thrust pistols and cutlasses. Others wore pistols hung around their neck on slings of bright-colored ribbon.

Some had long coats and cocked hats, much like Marlowe's, and others had bright-colored rags tied about their heads. All wore beards of some description, and their hair was long and generally unkept. The smell of rum could not have been stronger had there been a distillery right on the beach. They were a murderous, ugly bunch.

"My name is Sam Blaine," Marlowe announced, "which ain't of no importance. But hear me. The guardship here has a new captain, and he ain't afraid to fight. You seen my mainmast go by the board? I was in a scrape with him yesterday, fought it out for three hours before I could draw off, the bastard. He done for my mast. Goddamned miracle it stood this long. And he's bound for this place, to the devil with his black soul."

This news gave some pause to the crowd of brigands, enough that Marlowe could glance over his shoulder at his own men. The second boat had pulled up. Rakestraw hopped ashore and stepped cross the sand to Marlowe's side. All but a few of the Prizes were now on the beach, and most were reaching for their muskets. That would not go unnoticed.

He looked back at the pirates. There was not a man among them who was not armed. Cutlasses were much in evidence, though only a few were drawn, and pistols as well, though with any luck none were loaded.

"Here, what's the meaning with all them firelocks?" another of the pirates asked. Marlowe heard a murmur running through the gang, and a few more cutlasses were drawn. He heard the lock of a pistol snap into place.

A minute more, he needed but a minute more for his men to be in place and then he could demand their surrender. "Listen to me," he said, "I just finished telling ye—"

Then one of the Plymouth Prizes broke, succumbed to his terror, unable to endure the tension of standing face-to-face with this fearsome enemy. He screamed "Bloody whoreson bastards!" and a gun went off like a cannon right in Marlowe's ear. He felt the rush of air, heard the frightful whine as the ball passed by and struck the pirate just in front of him in the throat, tossing him back into the sand.

"God damn it!" He whirled around and shoved James down in the sand, no easy task, and fell on top of him as his panic-crazed men raised their muskets and blasted the pirates with a wall of lead. He felt bits of flaming wadding land on his hands and face and burn like stinging insects, heard men scream in terror and agony. The Prizes could not miss; they were firing from fifteen feet away into a solid crowd of men.

Marlowe scampered over James and crawled on hands and knees out of the way. He could hear more screams and curses, and gunfire being returned.

At last he leapt to his feet, Rakestraw beside him and James scrambling behind. Fifteen or so pirates lay thrashing on the sand and the other eighty were shouting, drawing weapons, charging at his men.

His men, in turn, had thrown their muskets away, as they had been instructed, but rather than drawing their pistols and firing again—the second part of Marlowe's plan—they turned their backs and rushed into the surf, ignoring even the boats in their panicked flight.

Marlowe pulled his sword with his right hand and a pistol with his left and shot down the pirate leading the rush on the Prizes, then charged into the surf after his own fleeing crew.

"Your pistols! Your pistols! Turn and fire!" he shouted. He reached the man leading the retreat, up to his knees in the water and running hard with high, exaggerated steps. Where he thought he was going Marlowe could not imagine. He smacked the man hard with the flat of his sword.

One pirate fired, then another and another, and the Prizes began to fall. "Turn and fire!" he shouted again, and this time he was joined by Rakestraw, who had also hurled himself into the mass of fleeing men. It was Marlowe's plan to kill as many of the villains as they could with musket and pistol. He never had a hope of his men standing up to the pirates in swordplay, fighting hand to hand.

They were all in the surf now, and the pirates were on top of the rearmost of Marlowe's men and hacking them to pieces. He could smell the blood, like warm copper. That smell and the screams of men dying badly were all ghosts from a past he thought he had left behind.

He pulled another of his pistols, fired it into the face of one of the pirates, threw it aside, and pulled another. Rakestraw and King James had disposed of all their pistols and left five dead men at their feet, and now they were standing in front of the onrushing pirates, cutting them down as they came.

Marlowe fired his last pistol and missed, and the man beside him pulled his gun and fired as well, then one after another of the Prizes turned and fired and the onrush of pirates faltered. Marlowe saw pistols whip through the air as they were thrown at the attackers and men reached for their second guns. The spirit of resistance seemed to sweep over his men as fast as had the panic, and now they stood fast in the surf and fired.

Holes appeared in the rush of attackers as the brigands died where they stood. One took a step back, then another, and soon they were all backing away from the Prizes, but they did not break and run, and Marlowe knew they would not. These men were no strangers to this kind of fight and this kind of carnage. There was no grief for lost comrades, and each of them knew that surrender meant hanging.

"At them, men!" he shouted, waving his sword over his head, and thirty cutlasses were drawn and the Plymouth Prizes screamed and charged.

They did not get far. The pirates might not stand up to gunfire with no weapons of their own loaded, but now the Prizes' guns were spent and it was steel on steel, and in that contest the pirates would not be bested. The rogue horde screamed as well and fell on the man-of-war's men as the two bands came together in a crash of blades.

Marlowe charged through the press of Plymouth Prizes. Before him was a monster of a brigand, as big as a bear, a long black beard, matted hair, blood smeared on his face. And between them was one of Marlowe's own men, trying to fend off the pirate's flashing blade.

Marlowe put a hand on his man's shoulder, tried to push him aside, when the pirate's sword erupted through his back, skewering the man and pushing through so far as to prick Marlowe in the chest. Marlowe met the pirate's eyes and the villain smiled at him, actually smiled, while Marlowe's man shrieked and puked blood, squirming on the sword.

Marlowe smiled as well and drew his sword back. The pirate screamed a curse and struggled to free his weapon from the dying man, but he could not. Marlowe drove his sword right through the pirate's face, just below his left eye, and pulled it free as the pirate fell, still screaming, now in rage and pain, into the shallow water.

He pushed the pirate's victim aside—if he was not dead,

then he soon would be—and met a blade coming down on him, turned it aside, and thrust. He looked around. He was all but alone, save for King James, slashing and hacking by his side.

The black man's face was set in an expression of utter fury, and he screamed out words that Marlowe could not understand. His teeth flashing and his skin glowing under a sheen of sweat as he worked his blade back and forth, cutting, stabbing, parrying, striking down all comers.

But they were surrounded by the pirates, and his own men were once again inching back into the surf.

"To me!" he shouted, but he did not think they heard him over the chilling shrieks of the pirates, and even if they did he did not think they would have obeyed. Two days of drill could not give those men the mettle to stand and fight skilled and desperate killers.

He slapped James on the shoulder to make certain he noticed, then took a step back, and then another. To his right Rakestraw was fully engaged, but on seeing his new captain step back the lieutenant did likewise.

They were outnumbered and nearly surrounded, and no doubt soon would die. He slashed right to parry a cutlass, but not fast enough. The blade cut through his sleeve and rent his flesh. He felt the warm blood running down his arm and knew from past experience that he would not feel the pain until later, if he lived that long. How had he let himself be trapped thus, with no means of escape?

He had not. Of course he had not. In the very instant he remembered, he was greeted with a volley of gunfire, the sweetest sound he ever heard. It came from behind the wall of pirates, flashing in the night and lighting them up from behind.

In the few seconds of light from the muzzle flashes he saw bloody, hideous faces, cutlasses dripping gore, bodies floating in the surf, and ten of the pirates fell, dropped by the careful aim of Bickerstaff's men.

Bickerstaff. Marlowe had forgotten, completely forgotten about him, though all along he was the only hope they really had of victory. He had made it across the island, had come up behind the enemy. Just in time.

The pirates half turned, not willing to show their backs to Marlowe's men but frightened by this attack from behind. As well they might be.

Bickerstaff's small band fired again, pistols this time, then flung themselves at the startled brigands, hacking with their cutlasses, Bickerstaff himself at their head. It was a horrible sight, horrible at least for the pirates who fell under their blades.

"To me!" Marlowe shouted to the men at his back, some of whom were already waist deep in the water, and with a cry they charged as well.

And that was too much for the pirates. With many a curse and a damning of the victors' black souls, they flung their weapons in the water and threw their hands over their head. Marlowe had seen it before, the moment when a halter around the neck sometime in the future became a better option than the certainty of a sword thrust in the next few seconds.

They stood there for a moment, King's men and pirates, listening to the moans and screams of the wounded, the heavy breathing of frightened and exhausted men, the lap of water around their ankles.

Marlowe looked up at Bickerstaff, standing on the other side of the gang of prisoners. He looked as calm as he ever did. Beside him, breathing hard, the point of his sword resting in the sand, was Lieutenant Middleton. The light from the distant fire illuminated half of his face and glinted off of the blood on his sword blade.

"Bickerstaff," he said at last, "how very glad I am to see you."

Chapter 11

"SILENCE! SILENCE!" LeRois roared, and one by one the pirate horde, frenzied, drunk, crazed with wanton debauchery and the madness of tearing apart a captive ship, fell quiet.

"Silence! Sons of bitches!" LeRois roared again, and the last of the pirates was quiet and all that LeRois could hear was the groaning of the merchantman's captain, lying on the deck by his feet, rocking side to side in agony.

"Silence, *cochon!*" LeRois kicked the man hard in the ribs. The captain gasped. LeRois kicked him again, and the man was silent.

And then someone started screaming, a long, drawn-out shriek like some damned soul cast down. Made the hair on the back of LeRois's neck stand up. "Who is screaming, son of bitch!? Who is that, I will kill them. . . ." He looked around at the Vengeances standing on the deck. Their faces told him it was no one, the screaming was in his head, and even as he realized it, the sound died away.

He cocked his ear to the north. They were a league south of Cape Charles, having just that afternoon arrived at the wide mouth of the Chesapeake Bay. And no sooner had they raised the Capes than the small merchantman, which they were at that moment plundering, had skirted the dangerous Middle Ground Shoal and sailed right into their arms.

For the first time in ten hours the pirates were silent, straining to hear whatever it was that LeRois was listening to. The only sound was the water slapping the hulls of the two ships, the slatting of sails and rigging and the occasional cracking as the two vessels, bound together by grappling hooks, rolled against each other.

Then LeRois heard it, just the faintest hint of sound carried on the offshore breeze.

Gunfire. Small arms going off in volleys.

He frowned and concentrated on the sound. Yes, it was small arms. The pirate's hearing had always been extraordinary, and years of listening for that sound had conditioned him to pick it out even through the most primal din. He was certain that he heard it. But of late he had been hearing more and more things that no one else did.

He turned to William Darnall, who was standing beside him, ear cocked in the same direction. "Sounds like firelocks," Darnall said, to LeRois's vast relief. "Lot of 'em."

"Smith Island, *oui?*" LeRois said, jerking his head in the direction of the muted gunfire.

"I reckon," Darnall agreed. "That's where she bears."

LeRois listened for a moment more and then shrugged. "It is of no matter," he said, and then, like men who could hold their breath no longer, the pirates resumed their shouting, their cursing, and their raucous destruction.

LeRois kicked the captain once more for good measure and then walked aft, using his sword as a walking stick, gouging it into the deck and jerking it free as he walked. The men of the *Vengeance* had torn open the liquor stores and the captain's private reserve and were consuming it all as fast as they could. They were making great sport of terrorizing the few passengers on board, forcing them to drink great quantities of rum, making them curse the king and the governor and damn their own souls to hell.

The pirates would have their fun in that manner, but they

would do no more harm than that. The merchantman had surrendered without a shot, surrendered at the first sight of LeRois's black flag. By way of reward, the people aboard her would not be tortured and they would not be killed.

The merchantman's crew had been compelled to break open the ship's hatches and were swaying out all that was in the hold: tobacco, mostly, but also some fine cloth that had made its way up from the Spanish Main, as well as barrels of wine that would bring a fair price if not consumed by the Vengeances first. Along with that, the pirates would take the spare sails, some coils of rope, and the anchor cable to replace their own rotted one.

There had been gold as well, doubloons that had no doubt come up the coast with the Spanish cloth. Not many, but enough to share out among the men.

The captain, foolishly, had refused at first to reveal where the coin was hidden, but a few thumps with the flat of LeRois's sword and a length of burning match tied between his fingers had ultimately rendered him quite vocal on the subject.

Even after they had the gold in hand, the pirates kept at the old man, burning the pieces of match down the full length of his fingers. They jeered as their victim, lashed to a ringbolt on the deck, had twisted and screamed and cursed. The man needed to be punished for his reticence. His example had assured the future cooperation of the people on board.

LeRois made his way over to where the passengers stood huddled against the rail, shrinking back from their tormenters. The few women among them were shielded by their husbands, as if that would do any good at all if the pirates chose to have them.

The Vengeances were screaming and running up and down the deck, dancing, firing off guns, drinking, cursing, banging drums, urinating, and hacking to pieces any part of the ship or rig within reach of their cutlasses.

LeRois was as drunk as any of them, and the weird images swam in front of him, lit up in frozen scenes by the flash of pistols. The screams seemed to come in layers, each building on the other, building to a cacophony of anguish and terror. He found it harder and harder to tell if the images around him were a reality or a nightmare, if he was awake or asleep or dead and in hell.

He took another long drink from the bottle of rum in his hand, savoring the burn of the liquor going down his throat, the earthy reality of the pain. He looked over the passengers who were providing his men with so much amusement. They all looked wealthy enough, and he reckoned that any would do for the business he had in mind. Any that were married.

He grabbed the first couple he came to, a gentlemanly sort of fellow of middling age and his pretty wife whom he was shielding from the screaming tribe. He grabbed them both by their clothing and jerked them away from the rail and shoved them into the open deck. Before the gentleman could utter a word, LeRois pulled a pistol from his belt and pressed it against the woman's forehead.

"Where are you from, *cochon*?" he asked the man, but the man remained silent, scowling at LeRois.

LeRois felt the snapping in his brain. He began to tremble. He cocked the lock of the pistol and jammed the muzzle against the woman's head, pushing her back with the force. "Where are you from?" he screamed.

"Williamsburg."

"You know many people, live in Williamsburg?"

The man hesitated. "Yes," he said at last.

"*Bien, bien*, you fucking pig. You know a poxed son of a whore named Malachias Barrett?"

"No."

"You certain, you son of a bitch?" He pressed the gun into the woman's head. She shut her eyes and grimaced, her lip trembling as she waited for the end.

"No," her husband said with finality.

"Very well," said LeRois at last. "I have a message for you to deliver, and if you do, the *belle femme* she is okay, and if you don't, then I take her first, then I give 'er to the crew, you understand?"

The man hesitated again, no doubt envisioning what his wife's final days on earth would be like if he did not understand and obey. "Yes, I understand."

LeRois squinted at him, trying to assess his sincerity. It was hard to think. He wished the screaming would stop, just for a moment.

Yes, he decided, the man would do as he said.

A shadow of a movement caught his eye, like a dark ghost overhead. He looked up, shot through with fear, but it was only his flag, his own flag, stirring in the breeze. It flogged and collapsed, the black flag with the grinning death's-head and the cutlasses crossed below, an hourglass at the bottom to show that time was running out.

It was a flag that had already caused terror across the Caribbean and the Spanish Main, a flag for which the Royal Navy had been hunting for nearly twenty years.

And when he was done with the Chesapeake, he vowed, the people there would shit themselves just at the sight of it.

Elizabeth Tinling sat at the small desk in her sitting room. She stared at the blank paper. Stared up at the ceiling. Twirled the quill between finger and thumb and then began to write.

G,

Have just received word that Marlowe has Changed his Plans at the last instant and will not be home tonight so I shall not venture to his home. I pray this Note reaches you in Time. I will send word to you again when I am Certain of his being home.

E.

She stared at the note for a moment, her thoughts elsewhere. When she saw the ink was dry she folded it, sealed it with wax, and wrote "George Wilkenson" across the front.

She stood and smoothed out her skirts and tugged her short riding jacket into place. On her head, pinned securely in place, was a small, round riding hat, and on her feet Morocco half-boots.

"Lucy," she called, and the servant, who was hovering just beyond the door, appeared instantly, giving a shallow curtsy.

"I shall be off now," Elizabeth said. "You are certain that Caesar quite understood?"

"Yes, ma'am."

"Good. I have one more thing for you to do. Take this note. Once it is near dark I want you to go to the Wilkenson plantation. Conceal yourself just off the main road and keep a lookout. When you see George Wilkenson leaving, wait another twenty minutes or so and then deliver this note to the house. Is that clear?"

"Yes, ma'am." If Lucy was at all curious about these instructions she did not let on, and Elizabeth was grateful for that. Lucy had never questioned the part she played in any of Elizabeth's plans. She was a wily girl hidden beneath a veneer of innocent beauty. Elizabeth thought them two of a kind, Lucy a dusky reflection of herself.

Elizabeth called for the boy to bring her horse around. She swung herself up onto the saddle and headed off down Duke of Gloucester Street and the long ride to Marlowe's home.

To her old home.

Home? No, she thought. House, perhaps. The word *home* implied a certain tenderness that she had never associated with the Tinling Plantation.

Indeed, she could not recall any dwelling that she might have called a home. Not the clapboard, waterfront house in the poorer section of Plymouth where she had lived till the age of fourteen with a brutal father and a mother too utterly cowed even to protect herself. Certainly not the house in London where she had met Joseph Tinling.

The town of Williamsburg yielded to the countryside of Virginia as Elizabeth rode down the long, brown-earth rolling road, worn hard and smooth by the hogsheads of tobacco that were yearly rolled down that way to be loaded aboard sloops and barges at Jamestown. The rolling road was lined on either side by split-rail fences, and beyond those stretched the wide green fields of tobacco that seemed to hold the far woods at bay.

She thought about Marlowe. Marlowe with his hoards of gold, his fine manners and eccentric ways, his apparent disregard for any danger, physical or social. In London he would be shunned. He was too wild by half for that society. But Williamsburg was not London, and the colony of Virginia was not Old England.

It was a new land, a land where a transported criminal could, through his cunning and strength of arm, rise to a position of prominence. It was a place like no other on earth, and a new place needed a new kind of man. She thought that Marlowe was such a man. And she was staking a great deal on her being right.

She came at last to the big white house, just as the sun was becoming tangled in the trees at the far end of the tobacco fields. She handed her horse to the stable boy, mounted the steps as she had done so many times before, and stepped through the big front door.

"Hello, Mrs. Tinling." Caesar was there to greet her, with his ingenious smile, his dark, kind, wrinkled face. His eyes were permanently squinted from many, many years in the sun, and his forehead and cheeks still bore the vague traces of some pagan design with which his skin had been scarred, half a century before on the Gold Coast.

She had never seen Caesar wearing anything but rags, but again she had not seen him since Marlowe had bought the plantation and set them all free. Five years before, Caesar had been too old to work in the fields, but Joseph Tinling had kept him at it nonetheless. It was the most prudent thing to do, economically, working the old slave to death.

But after freeing him, Marlowe had asked him to work in the house, second to King James, who gave the old man light duty. Now he wore a clean white cotton shirt and a linen waistcoat. Bare brown calves and wide, splayed feet projected from the legs of white breeches—Caesar could never become accustomed to shoes. "How does it go on here, Caesar?"

"It's as close to heaven as we's likely to see, us poor souls, Mrs. Tinling. Master Marlowe, he set us free, just like he said he would."

Elizabeth knew all this, of course. Lucy kept her well informed of what Marlowe was about, and Lucy still had many friends among her former fellow slaves. But she let Caesar continue and feigned surprise and delight.

"Now we works for wages," Caesar was saying, "and we puts our money together and Mr. Bickerstaff buys us what we need. Them old slave quarters, Tinling-town we used . . ." Caesar's voice trailed off in embarrassment.

"Don't concern yourself. I know that my husband was not well loved, nor should he have been."

"Bless you, ma'am, it ain't nothing about you. You know we all was fond of you. Couldn't abide to see how that son of a bitch used you so, beg pardon. Like I was saying, them old slave quarters are fixed up proper now. It's like we got our own little town there now. Little houses all whitewashed . . ."

"I long to see it. Perhaps later," Elizabeth said. She could hear the pride in the man's voice, and it made her feel good. He deserved no less after a lifetime of bondage.

She despised slavery, for she understood about involuntary servitude, and it was only because she so feared being an outcast that she kept her opinions to herself and did not give her own few slaves their freedom. "Now, come along and show me Master Marlowe's sleeping chamber."

"Ah, yes, ma'am." Caesar was not so certain about that request. "Miss Lucy didn't say nothing about that."

"Oh, it's no great concern. Just a little fun I wish to have. Mr. Marlowe would never mind. You trust me, do you not?"

"Ah, well, I reckon."

They walked up the wide stairway, Caesar leading the way. The gloom of twilight settled on the house and the colors of the walls and the patterns in the carpets became less distinct in the light of that juncture between day and night. Elizabeth followed behind, as if she were a stranger in that house, and indeed she felt like one.

Little had changed in the two years since she had been there; it seemed at once so familiar and so strange. The house filled her with a vague dread. There were ghosts lurking in all the corners. Little good had happened there.

She hoped that Marlowe had not chosen the master bedroom as his own. It was not a room that she cared to see. But, of course, he had. There was no reason for him not to do so. Caesar stopped and opened the door, and Elizabeth stepped into the room.

It was almost exactly as she had left it: the big canopy bed in the same place, the wardrobe, the winged chair, and the trunk. All that was missing was her dressing table, and all that was added was a gun rack. Other than that it was the same.

Caesar stood in respectful silence as she ran her eyes over the rooms. She let the ghosts rise up; she knew that they would in any event. Like recalling a play she had seen a long time ago. She envisioned the beatings, the brutal sex forced upon her. Even when she was willing to give herself voluntarily, he had forced her. Joseph Tinling's type liked it that way. They liked to see a little blood.

She ran her eyes over the big bed. Did Marlowe ever imagine what had taken place there? She let the ghost of Joseph Tinling appear again, the image of his mortal remains as she had found them.

He had been stretched out on that very bed, his breeches down around his ankles, Lucy, half naked, her clothes torn, cowering in the corner, screaming, incoherent. Elizabeth and Sheriff Witsen, with whom she had been speaking belowstairs, had burst in to witness that depraved scene.

She shook her head and turned toward Caesar and met his dark, watery eyes, and an understanding passed between them.

"Here, let me take a look at Mr. Marlowe's wardrobe," she said, forcing brightness into her voice. She stepped across the room and pulled the doors open. There were a dozen coats there, all lovely. She pulled out one made of red silk with gold

on the pockets and cuffs. It was the same coat that Marlowe
had worn to the Governor's Ball the night this had all begun.

She held it up to Caesar's chest. "Goodness, this would
look fine on you, Caesar."

"Oh, no, ma'am. That's a gentleman's coat, that ain't for
me."

"Well, let us just see. Pray, try it on."

"Try it on? But, ma'am, that's Mr. Marlowe's coat! I got
no business tryin' on Mr. Marlowe clothes!"

"Oh, come along, now," Elizabeth said, holding the sleeve
up and practically shoving it over Caesar's arm. "Remember. I
am a particular friend of Mr. Marlowe's, and I am here to
help him."

"I don't see how this is helping him . . ." Caesar muttered
as he struggled into the coat, which was in fact a good fit, if
a bit big. He straightened and tugged the front in place, then
ran his eyes along the garment, clearly not displeased with the
way it looked.

"Very good, Caesar. Now . . ." Elizabeth looked around
the room. In the dressing room adjoining the sleeping chamber
she saw four wigs carefully placed on wooden heads, their long
white curling locks hanging down past the edge of the table.

"There we are." She fetched one of the wigs and made as
if to put it on Caesar's head, but the old man balked, shielding
his head with his hands.

"Now what you doing? I ain't gonna be seen wearing Mr.
Marlowe's wig! Bad enough I's wearing his coat."

"Now, come along, Caesar, you know I wouldn't do anything to get you in trouble. This is all for Mr. Marlowe's good."

It took five minutes of her most persuasive arguing before
Caesar grudgingly placed the wig on his head and followed
her down the stairs. She paused outside of the sitting room
that faced the lawn bordering the front of the house. It was
dark now. The bright painted walls and the rugs and books
and furniture were all turned shades of gray and black.

"You have some others here?"

"Yes, ma'am. William and Isaiah is in the back room."

Caesar called for them, and they appeared in the hall. They were both field hands, big men in their twenties and strong as any man was likely to be. Isaiah carried a musket. It looked like a stick in his hand. Elizabeth noticed that their clothes were clean and newly made. Apparently they could now afford a suit for working and another for special occasions. Amazing.

"William, pray go and light the lamps in the sitting room," Elizabeth said.

William, who along with Isaiah had been staring open-mouthed at Caesar, adorned as he was with Marlowe's coat and wig, pulled his eyes away and said, "Yes, ma'am." He fetched a candle and proceeded to light the lamps, making the room brighter and brighter with each one lit.

There were ghosts there as well.

It was in that room that he had first struck her, knocked her to the floor just by the settee, and in that one stroke had forced her to face all of the things she had suspected about him but had not allowed herself to believe, or even consider. All of the rooms there had their memories, all were stages upon which had been played the tragedy that was her relationship with Joseph Tinling.

William stepped back into the hall, and he and Isaiah retreated to the back room.

"Hold here a moment, Caesar," Elizabeth said. She stepped over to the edge of the window, the curtains still pulled back. "Caesar, I want you to stand right here, but with your back to the window. Do you understand? Under no circumstances are you to turn and face out the window."

"Yes, Mrs. Tinling." There was a note of resignation in his voice now, as he gave in to the nonsensical wishes of this woman.

Elizabeth turned away from the window, and with her back to him she said, "Very well, Caesar, please take your place." She turned and watched the old man move carefully across the room, and then, with his back turned, edge into the place where she had stood. She hoped that the move did not look too awkward.

She glanced up briefly at the window, but from the brightly lit room she could see nothing but darkness through the glass. But she knew that he would be there.

He might trust her. He might think that she would not dare betray him, after his threats and his promises, but he would not take her word alone. He would need more proof than her assurance before he burst into Marlowe's house. He would want to see for himself that she was there and Marlowe was there. He would be watching. George Wilkenson liked to watch.

He stood half concealed behind the big oak that grew in the Tinlings' yard. Marlowe's yard, he thought, and the realization that the big house now belonged to that bastard Marlowe, and not his friend Joseph Tinling, was enough to spark his anger again.

George felt his horse tug nervously on the reins and said some soothing words. He was not hiding, he told himself. Hiding would have been too nefarious, too sneaky. He was just standing by the tree, sort of behind the tree, and looking at the dark house. He did not know who he was trying to fool with his feigned disinterest. There was no one around, and if there had been he would not have taken that place by the oak.

It was all but dark now. Wilkenson guessed that it was somewhere close to eight-thirty, and still the house was dark. He felt a growing concern.

It was not possible that the bitch had betrayed him. He could ruin her. By that time tomorrow he could see her disgraced and homeless. She could not be so stupid as to think that Marlowe could protect her from his wrath. No one in Virginia could protect her from the Wilkensons' wrath.

And then he saw the flame of a candle move in the sitting room. A lamp was lit. Wilkenson could see a servant going around and lighting the others. So he is home, he thought. She had better be there with him.

At last the sitting room was brightly lit, and though he was over two hundred feet away Wilkenson could make out the

book-lined walls, the paintings, the furniture, just as it was
when Joseph had been alive. For all his wealth, Marlowe did
not seem to have much in the way of personal possessions.

Then Elizabeth was there, partially hidden by the curtain,
her blond hair lit from behind by the lanterns. She was too far
for him to see the details of her face, but he was certain it was
she. Who else could it be? She looked out of the window and
then turned; he had only a fleeting glance at her face, but it
was enough. He smiled. Felt his former fears and doubts dissipate. He rested his hand on the butt of his pistol.

She crossed the room, and in her place stood Marlowe.
Wilkenson recognized the red silk coat, the same as he had
worn to the Governor's Ball, and the long white wig with its
tight ringlets. He stood with his back to the window, apparently
engaged in conversation.

He watched them for some time, he did not know how
long, and then Marlowe stepped from his view and Elizabeth
followed. He pulled his watch from his pocket and squinted at
the face. The light from the moon and the few stars was
enough for him to read the time. Five minutes to nine. He
replaced the watch, pulled his pistol from his belt, and checked
the priming. Time to go.

He led his horse up to the front of the house, tied it to a
hitching post. Felt his palm sweating under the wooden grip
of the pistol. It occurred to him that it might look suspicious,
having the gun already drawn, but he could not bring himself
to tuck it away. I won't go in until I hear a scream, and that
will be reason enough to have a gun out, he thought.

He stepped slowly up onto the porch, glanced through the
window into the sitting room. He could see the big clock on
the mantel, and just as he looked at the hands he heard it
chiming out nine o'clock, the sound of the bells muffled by
the glass. He braced himself, ready to charge down the hall
and into the drawing room. Arrest that villain Marlowe for
trying to violate the poor widow Tinling.

His heart was pounding, his palms wet. He felt his fingertips tingling with excitement. He waited.

And nothing happened.

The excitement and the heightened awareness began to dissipate as he waited, waited for some sound from within. He looked up at the clock. Five minutes past nine. God damn you, he thought, scream. What are you about, you silly bitch?

He waited. Ten minutes past nine. It seemed as if he had been standing there for an hour. This would never do. He renewed the grip on his pistol and stepped over to the door. Perhaps something had gone wrong. Perhaps that bastard Marlowe had gagged her.

He twisted the handle, slowly pushed the door open. The light from the sitting room spilled into the hall, illuminating the foyer, the far end of the hall still in darkness. Wilkenson took a hesitant step forward. He stopped and listened. Felt the sweat trickle down the side of his face. He took another step, and then another. Nothing. No sound, no muffled cry, no indication of a struggle. Had she betrayed him after all?

"Don't move! Who the hell are you?" The voice came from behind him, loud and sharp, like a master sergeant's, and Wilkenson felt his whole body jolt in surprise. It was only by a miracle that he did not discharge his pistol. He spun around, found himself looking into the barrel of a musket. At the far end was an old black man, dressed like a house servant, save for the bare calves and feet.

The black man squinted his eyes and cocked his head to one side. "You Mr. Wilkenson, ain't you? The Wilkenson that Mr. Marlowe didn't kill?"

Wilkenson straightened and glanced around. Took stock of the situation now that his shock had subsided. There were two more men behind the old man with the gun, both black. There were no white men, just the slaves. He felt the smallest sense of relief.

"I said, ain't you Mr. Wilkenson?" the old one repeated. He had an arrogant tone to his voice. Not a hint of subservience. Wilkenson would not tolerate that, not from a nigger.

"I am Mr. Wilkenson. Now, put down that gun, boy."

"Don't you 'boy' me, I's the one with the gun. Boy."

"How dare you? No slave will point a gun at me and—"

"We ain't slaves. We free men. And you sneaking around our home with a pistol and we wants to know why."

"Ah . . ." Wilkenson stammered. This situation was unlike anything he had encountered. He would not tolerate such abuse from slaves, or former slaves, or whatever they were. But there were three of them, and if they would not obey him, then what could he do? "I . . . ah . . . heard a noise."

The old man looked back at the other two, and they just shook their heads. Shrugged. Wilkenson could see that they were younger and looked as strong as horses. What little calm he had found now deserted him.

"We didn't hear no noise."

"Well, I did, so you will just have to take my word for it. Now, if you have this situation in hand, then I shall leave you to . . ." He took a step toward the door, but the round hole on the musket barrel followed him, blocked his way.

"Hold up, there. You come sneakin' in here at night, with a pistol in your hand, after Mr. Marlowe done killed your brother, some fool story about hearin' a noise, like you was just passin' by, and you think we's going to let you go? No, sir. I think we best call the sheriff."

"Sheriff! Now, you look here, boy, I've had all of this non-sense as I can take. You stand aside and—"

"Go sit in the sitting room, Mr. Wilkenson, while I send William to get the sheriff, and we'll straighten this out."

"How dare you!"

"Mr. Wilkenson, if you don't sit, we going to have to tie you up."

Wilkenson looked from one dark, expressionless face to another. It was the last word in humiliation, being caught here and held at gunpoint by these niggers.

No, that was not true. The last word in humiliation would be for them to tie him up and let the sheriff find him that way. And they would do it, he could see that, and there was no one there to stop them. What would he do? Appeal to Marlowe?

He felt his stomach convulse with panic, felt the sweat on his palms and forehead. Wouldn't they summon Marlowe? Would Marlowe find him, pistol in hand, held at gunpoint by the house servants? It was too horrible to consider. Would Marlowe charge him with attempted murder? His carefully conceived plan could turn into a nightmare beyond belief.

As if in a dream, he let the old man take the pistol from him. He stepped into the sitting room and sat on the edge of the settee. The old man with the gun sat as well, facing him from across the room, the round eye of the musket staring at him.

The next hour and a half was the worst in all of George Wilkenson's thirty-seven years. He sat unmoving, red-faced, as a servant, a *nigger*, stared at him, held him prisoner while another stood in the doorway, arms folded, staring at him as well.

It was utterly humiliating, and all the while his stomach churned with dread, waiting, knowing that any minute Marlowe would walk through the door, led by some other servant, who would point and say, "There he is, Mr. Marlowe," and Marlowe would start and say "Wilkenson, what the devil? This is mighty irregular."

He clamped his teeth together and took comfort in the one thought that could provide him with comfort—the thought of what he would do to Marlowe, and what he would do to that bitch.

Sheriff Witsen came at last, breathing hard, his round face red and lathered in sweat, his stockings falling down. He had clearly dressed in a hurry. If he had not, then Wilkenson would have crushed him like a bug.

"Mr. Wilkenson, what have they done?" he huffed.

"Nothing. It was all a mistake," Wilkenson said, and said nothing more. With the sheriff there, the servants could hold him no longer. He did not meet Witsen's eyes, or the black men's, as he stormed out of the house, more frightened than ever that Marlowe would make an appearance.

George Wilkenson had never been more humiliated in his

life. Not while being flogged as a boy by his father and his tutor, not after puking at his brother's death and shrinking from Marlowe's threats, not from Jacob Wilkenson's insinuations of his inadequacy. Never. Had never understood the concept of blind rage. Until now.

And he swore that Marlowe would pay for that humiliation. He would pay. Not just for what he himself had done. For what they all had done.

Elizabeth Tinling stood behind the big oak, unquestionably hiding, and watched George Wilkenson and Sheriff Witsen, illuminated by the lights from the house, as they stepped across the porch and down onto the lawn. Wilkenson was practically running. The sheriff, one of Wilkenson's foremost lickspittles, was racing to catch up with him, though Wilkenson seemed to be ignoring him.

She put her hand over her mouth. She could not let herself laugh out loud. Her note telling Wilkenson not to come, which he would find upon returning to his home, along with her protests that she had not gone to Marlowe's that night, would create enough doubt in his mind that she might not get the full brunt of his wrath. But if he discovered her hiding behind the tree, she would be undone.

She shook her head as she watched him swing himself up in his saddle and thunder blindly past. She wondered what perverse aspect of her personality drove her to play such tricks, even when she knew that she would pay for them later.

But it was more than that, and she knew it. It was war now, war between Marlowe and the Wilkensons, and she could not hope to be a neutral party. She had to choose sides, and she had chosen the side that she thought was the stronger. The decision had not been arrived at lightly.

She had immediately dismissed any hope of Wilkenson tearing up the note of hand. He would never do that, not when he realized the power he wielded over her as long as he held it.

Nor would he call in the note. Ruining her would do him no good. No, he would hold her in limbo, as he did with all his debtors. Make use of her. Demand her help in tricking some poor bastard one night. Demand a quick fuck the next.

But Marlowe was also a force to be considered. He had already killed one of the Wilkensons. He commanded the guardship, had the governor's ear, and the governor probably would not care to see his choice of captains hanged. If she bore false witness against him, and he was not hanged, then she would suffer his vengeance.

But it was more than just that. She had chosen Marlowe for more than mere pragmatic reasons. Marlowe seemed a decent man, and what Wilkenson proposed to do to him was despicable, and Elizabeth Tinling was sick of doing despicable things. She had chosen to side with Marlowe because she liked him, and that actually surprised her.

She hoped that she had chosen well.

Chapter 12

IN THE end Marlowe did not flog to death the man who had fired the first shot. It was not that he did not want to, he simply could not discover who he was. It seemed none of the dozen men standing shoulder to shoulder noticed him, or at least they would not give him up. In any event, Marlowe probably would have let him off with no more than two or three dozen lashes, just as a lesson and an example of his charitable nature.

They spent a nervous night on Smith Island, or at least the men of the *Plymouth Prize* did. Those pirates still alive were rounded up and deposited near the fire, bound hand and foot, a circle of armed Prizes around them. Marlowe scrutinized each man, anxious to see if he recognized any of them. If he had, Marlowe would have killed the brigand on the spot and not bothered to explain. But as fortune had it, there were none that he knew.

Bickerstaff, Middleton, and his men went out to the pirate ship and took possession of the five rogues aboard her, who, having witnessed the capture of their fellows and having no boats or any means of escape, had become insensibly drunk. They were rounded up, lowered into a boat by way of a gantline, and taken ashore to join their captured brethren.

All the hands stood guard all night. This was not by Marlowe's orders, but simply because the men were too agitated by the fight and too wary of the pirate captives to think of sleep. Marlowe, Rakestraw, and Middleton stood watch with them by turns, just to make certain nothing went amiss.

"It was a good fight, was it not?" Marlowe said to Bickerstaff as he rose to take his watch. Bickerstaff had been sitting up all that time, away from the men, in contemplative silence. The fire was burning down, and the circle of light had retreated to just a few fathoms out from the red glowing logs. Bickerstaff's face seemed to glow, light and shadow dancing across it as the fire flared and subsided. Marlowe could see his weariness and his satisfaction.

"It was a good fight, Tom," he said. "You were born to this kind of command. This honest command. I know of no other that could have made these men stand and fight."

"I am grateful to you for saying so, sir," Marlowe said, and he meant it, because he knew that Bickerstaff did. Idle flattery had never polluted Bickerstaff's lips. "Nonetheless, it was no Agincourt. Had you not shown up when you did, I think we must have been routed by the rogues."

"But you held your ground. Or your surf, as the case might be."

They stood there for a few moments in silence, staring into the fire. Enjoying their comradeship. They had been together for six years, six years as friends, shipmates, pupil and tutor. They had seen a great deal together, but they were still, after all of it, very different men.

"Well, good night, Francis," Marlowe said at last.

"Good night, Tom." He smiled and ambled off into the dark.

The sight that greeted them in the morning was grotesque, the hellish aftermath of a battle. The bodies of two dozen men at least, Prizes and pirates, lay on the beach or floating in the shallow water. They were black with dried blood, and bloated so their clothing seemed ill-fitting. A swarm of birds clambered over them, tearing at their flesh.

Those corpses in the water seemed as if they were making

some halfhearted effort to shoo the scavengers away, their arms waving slightly as the small surf rocked them back and forth. There were dozens of crabs. It was a ghastly sight, and one or two of the Prizes had to race into the dune grass to be sick.

But the rest seemed quite unmoved by the sight, at least after they began to poke around the great piles of booty that had been deposited on the beach. Much of it consisted of manufactured goods taken from English merchantmen: crockery, plate, silks, linen, barrel hoops, great piles of clothing. It was an unusually rich haul.

The pirates had had a successful cruise, were no doubt ready to sell their prodigious capture. In Charleston and Savannah there were plenty of merchants, strangled as they were by the government's policy toward importation, that were eager to purchase such things. They would not ask embarrassing questions about bills of lading and such.

There was also a tolerable amount of gold and silver, as well as an abundance of weapons: swords, pistols, beautiful muskets. There was a most piratical gleam in the eye of many of the Plymouth Prizes as they fingered the goods, Marlowe's insinuation about their potential rewards having apparently found an attentive audience.

"Mr. Rakestraw," he called out to the first officer, who was poking through a crate of muskets. He set aside the gun he was holding, a beautiful musket, and with a sheepish look on his face, as if he had been caught in some indiscretion, he came over to the captain.

"Mr. Rakestraw, here is what I would have you do. Divide the gold and silver in half. One half shall be for the governor. Then count up how many of our men are still living and divide the other half of the gold and silver into equal shares. Two shares for the officers. And those that suffered wounds, the ones you believe will recover, are to get two shares as well, so figure that in. Never mind those you reckon are done for. Then we shall draw numbers and each man by number will be allowed to choose a new suit of clothes and a sword and pistol. Officers first."

"Yes, sir," Rakestraw said, but he seemed to hesitate. "But, sir, you know that all of this, rightly speaking, sir, is prizes of the Crown. This . . . ah . . . what you're doing here, sir, it ain't regular." Rakestraw's protests were weakened, Marlowe thought, by the fact that he kept glancing over at the gun he had been holding, and seemed near panic when someone else picked it up and examined it.

"You, there," Marlowe called to the man holding the musket, "bring that over here."

Grudgingly the man shuffled over and handed him the gun. It was indeed beautiful, not the kind of crude weapon turned out by second-rate gunsmiths in dark and tiny back alley shops, but a custom-made piece with beautiful engravings on the lock plate and an ivory inlay on the bird's-eye walnut stock. If Rakestraw was to be led into temptation, Marlowe was pleased to see that he would not settle for second best.

He handed the gun to the lieutenant.

"Mr. Rakestraw, you fought well last night, damn well, we should have been bested without you. And you have done a good job of getting the ship in fighting order," he said, which was no lie. "I wish you to have this gun."

"Oh, thank you, sir. But, sir . . ."

"Listen, Lieutenant. Each of the officers and men are entitled to prize money, are they not? We all have a legal claim to a portion of what has been captured. But we both know that it will take a year at least to see any of it, assuming the Lords of Admiralty don't find some means of cheating us of our share. All I wish to do is see that the men get what is rightfully theirs, without having to wait an age for it. I'm just cutting through red tape, no more."

"Oh, I see, sir," said Rakestraw, and he did see, largely because he wanted to. With that fine gun in his hand and the piles of gold and silver ten feet away, he was quite willing to ignore the more dubious parts of Marlowe's justification, such as the fact that the men were getting far more than they ever would in prize money, and that what the captain was doing would be considered no more than pilfering if it was found out.

But it would not be found out. Both men knew that it would not. The pirates were unlikely to tell, nor was anyone likely to believe them. And Marlowe would see that they were locked down in a dark hold before the division of loot began.

The Plymouth Prizes, who in the next hour would make more money than they had in their entire lives up until that moment, were even less likely to tell. What Marlowe was doing for them was only just, after their ill usage by the navy, and must be kept secret. At least that was how they would see it.

Rakestraw, with his new musket tucked under his arm, hurried off to order the prisoners ferried out to the *Plymouth Prize* and to oversee the dividing up of the booty.

"Yonder comes the *Northumberland*," said Bickerstaff, stepping up beside Marlowe and nodding toward the harbor. The little sloop was standing into the bay under mainsail, jib, and topsail, the canvas white in the morning sun. They stood there for a moment, watching the small ship sail into the harbor on the quartering breeze.

"Excellent," Marlowe said at last. "Now, I need you to —"

"Marlowe, pray, what is Lieutenant Rakestraw about?"

He turned and looked in the direction that Bickerstaff was looking. Rakestraw had all of the specie and gold and silver plate piled up on a couple of chests, and an impressive pile it was. He was counting it out into numerous small piles and placing them like chess pieces on the second chest.

"Well," Marlowe said, "he is counting out the specie, you see. Just getting a fair accounting of it for the inventory."

"Indeed? It looks very much to me as if he was dividing it up like plunder. In order that each man might be called up to receive a share."

"Oh, well, I had a notion that the men, lacking as they are in the most basic things, might at least get a shift of clothing out of all this, and perhaps decent weapons to aid in future fighting."

Bickerstaff turned, looked him in the eye. Marlowe wondered why he was unwilling to simply tell Bickerstaff the truth, that he was indeed giving each man a share of the take. Because Bickerstaff would disapprove, deeply disapprove, and he would make it worse by keeping his disapproval to himself. He would think that it smacked of a life that Marlowe had forsworn.

"See here," Marlowe said, "I know that this is not quite in line with the rules of the admiralty, but look at these poor bastards. They're in rags, and the navy has done nothing to better their lot. You think if I ask Nicholson for new clothing for these men he'd do anything but laugh? They fought well. The least I can do is give them some reward."

"They deserve decent clothing, I'll grant you that—" Bickerstaff said, and Marlowe cut him off before he could continue.

"Exactly. Now I need you to go out to the pirate ship and begin an inventory of what is aboard. See if you can discover her original name, owners, what have you. If there is not aboard as far as records, I suppose she can be considered our prize. Perhaps we shall name her the *Plymouth Prize Prize*, eh?"

Bickerstaff did not laugh, did not even smile. "Very well, then, I shall be off." He called out for the boat crew.

It took only an hour to purge from the men the last vestige of despondency that Allair had built up in his four years of command. That was the hour that it took to call each man up and put in his hands a little pile of gold and silver, then to draw numbers and allow each man a choice of weapon and a shift of clothing. Just as Marlowe had done so many, many times before. It made him a bit uneasy for just that reason.

Soon the beach was littered with discarded rags and the men were prancing around in their new garments, sashes tied around waists, pistols and cutlasses thrust in place. They were a happy tribe, a band of brothers ready for more fighting and more booty. And they would not be disappointed.

Marlowe viewed with some satisfaction the scene on the beach. In less than a week he had turned these men around, fought a desperate battle, captured a band of vicious pirates, and in the next hour would greatly increase his own worth. Once word got back to Williamsburg he would be the great hero of the age, his star rising fast in the firmament of the Virginia aristocracy. He would be a gentleman of note, and Elizabeth Tinling, for one, would be impressed. And he had only just begun.

"Mr. Rakestraw," he called. The lieutenant picked up his new musket and hurried over. "I fear we are most vulnerable here, spread out over the beach. If another of these pirates were to sail in, we should be undone. I want to get as much of this prize cargo to safety as soon as we can."

He looked out at the *Plymouth Prize*, pretending to consider his options. "The *Prize* will need a jury mainmast before she sails. Here's what we shall do. Let us load as much as we can aboard the *Northumberland*, just to get it out of here, and the rest can go on the guardship once she's ready."

Then, with Rakestraw in tow, he went through the piles of booty, indicating what among them should be loaded aboard the *Northumberland*. There were three trunks of ladies' clothes, and he found among them a gold cross on a tiny gold chain, as thin as a spider's web. The cross itself had a diamond in the center, and a delicate swirling pattern was etched in the gold, so fine that one might miss it. It was a beautiful piece, and he tucked it in his coat pocket. "Put these trunks of ladies' things aboard the *Plymouth Prize*," he instructed, "and the rest of this aboard the sloop."

It was only natural, of course, that the most valuable things should be sent off first, and it was those things that the men set to loading aboard the sloop. Neither Lieutenant Rakestraw nor any of the officers or men was in a mood to question Marlowe's decision or his motives. Not after what he had done for them.

And King James did not object, did not even raise an eyebrow, when Marlowe told him to carry the cargo of pirate treasure to his little-used warehouse in Jamestown and unload it there, placing it in a discreet corner with barrels of tobacco piled in front of it. "Yes, sir" was all he said, and twenty minutes later the *Northumberland* was standing out of the harbor, carrying Marlowe's part of the take.

It would take him a month, perhaps more, to convert those sundry things to hard money, but they would, in the end, greatly augment his already considerable wealth. He knew who those merchants were, in Charleston and Savannah, as well as any buccaneer.

He had to smile as he watched his little sloop pass from sight around the headland.

What a great frolic, he thought, thieving from the most notorious thieves on earth! Why did I not think of this years ago?

Bickerstaff stood on the quarterdeck of the captured pirate ship and watched the *Northumberland* standing clear of the harbor. Forward, and in the cabin below, he could hear the half-dozen men he had brought with him searching the ship with great gusto, looking for anything worth carrying off.

The pirate ship has been taken, he thought, but there are pirates aboard her still.

He was worried. Worried about Marlowe. Did Marlowe actually think he had kept his pillaging a secret? he wondered. Did he think that he, Bickerstaff, was not aware of the great piles of stolen goods that had been loaded aboard the sloop, bound away, no doubt, for the smaller warehouse in Jamestown?

In his six-year association with Marlowe, Bickerstaff had been careful to avoid doing anything that went contrary to his moral grain, difficult as that was in the circumstances. He had stayed with Marlowe at first because he had no choice, and then because he had become curious, and at last because he had come to like the man.

And he had come to believe that Marlowe was, ultimately, a good and moral man who for all of his life had been deprived of solid instruction in honor and Christian decency.

They had come to Virginia to start over. For Bickerstaff that meant finally becoming more than a half-starved peda-gogue who for all of his learning was still regarded as some kind of inferior because he had Latin and Greek but no money.

For Marlowe it meant taking his place in society, real society, society where one's worth was not measured by ability with a sword or accuracy with a pistol.

But what measure did this colonial society use to gauge a man's worth? His money? The number of acres he had under cultivation, the number of slaves doing his work? Bickerstaff found himself wondering if this society was indeed better than the brutal but utterly egalitarian world of the pirates.

Bickerstaff shook his head and turned to the task to which he had been assigned. He could not be Marlowe's moral compass forever; at a certain point Marlowe would have to find his own way.

He walked to the break of the quarterdeck and then down into the waist. The pirate ship, he saw, was in fact a former merchantman, as they generally were. She had been taken by the brigands at some time and converted, in the pirate way, to a blackguard's man-of-war.

There were half a dozen new gunports pierced through her bulwark. Bickerstaff thought of them as gunports, having no other term for them, but in reality they were little more than holes chopped out with an ax and adorned on either side with eyebolts for the breeching.

There had once been a quarterdeck and a forecastle, but the pirates had taken a saw or an adze and hacked them off, leaving the vessel flush-decked fore and aft. The white and weathered deck planking ended abruptly where the bulkhead had once stood and turned to a darker, less worn wood that had until recently been shielded from the weather. It looked like the high-tide line on a beach.

The gangways had been torn down and most of the fine trim was gone, with only bare patches of wood to indicate where it once had been. The original figurehead was gone as well, replaced by some pirate's carving. Bickerstaff could not venture a guess as to what the new head was supposed to be.

He heard the creak of oars in tholes, and looking over the side saw the *Prize's* gig pulling out, Marlowe in the stern sheets. A moment later, he stepped through the gangway.

"Ah, Marlowe," he called, "I have yet to write out the inventory, but there's little aboard. They were going to careen, as we reckoned, so most everything is on the beach."

"Have you discovered what ship this is? Or was?"

"Yes. Come see this."

Bickerstaff led the way aft to what was once the great cabin but was now the quarterdeck. The entire weather deck, bow to stern, was littered with empty wine bottles, some broken, and various articles of clothing, discarded bones, and the odd cutlass or pistol. Just to starboard of the binnacle box was a small cask of gunpowder, a pile of bullets, and another pile of made cartridges. Beside that was a leather-bound journal from which the pirate who was making up the cartridges was tearing paper for that purpose. Bickerstaff picked it up and handed it to Marlowe.

"As it happens, this is the ship's log. The villain started from the back, so the name of the ship and crew remain."

Marlowe flipped open the cover, holding it so both men could read. There in a neat hand was written "Journal of the ship *Patricia Clark*, Boston. Mr. Paul McKeown, Master." He flipped to the back. The last twenty or so pages were gone. The last entry read "Winds light from the SSE. Up topgallant yards, set topgallant sails." No indication of what had become of the crew of the *Patricia Clark*.

No doubt some of them had thrown in with the pirates, and were now in irons in the *Plymouth Prize*'s hold or being torn apart by crows on the beach. As to the others, Bickerstaff hoped that they had got off as easy, but he reckoned they had not.

God have mercy on their souls, he thought. The sea was a dangerous place, he knew that all too well. A dangerous place for thieves and honest men alike.

Chapter 13

LeRois staggered down the middle of the dust-and gravel-covered street that constituted most of the town of Norfolk. The waning moon and the few stars visible through the thin haze were enough to reveal the half-dozen new buildings that had been put up since his last visit to that port, over a year before. Norfolk was growing quickly, for though it was in the colony of Virginia, it served as the entrepôt for the blossoming trade of North Carolina, a colony with no natural harbor save for distant Charleston.

The air was filled with the sounds of a late night in a port city—drunken laughter from any of several taverns, muted behind closed doors, arguments, the occasional scream, pistol shots. And behind it all was the constant buzz of the insects, frogs, and birds that lived in the swampy regions that surrounded the place.

The *Vengeance* was anchored off Willoby's Point, just beyond Cape Henry and the entrance to the Chesapeake Bay. It had taken the gentleman whose wife LeRois had detained aboard no more than two days to journey to Williamsburg, deliver LeRois's message, and return. His haste was motivated no doubt by the thought of what was happening to his wife during his absence, what would happen to her if he did not return.

During those two days the man's lovely young wife had been locked in the caboose of the great cabin, where her weeping and praying and carrying on had nearly driven LeRois to distraction. When he could take no more he would pound on the door and scream *"La ferme! La ferme!"* and that would quiet her down for an hour or so, and then it would begin again.

In the past LeRois would have had his way with her, just as a matter of principle, his promise to her husband notwithstanding. But it had been several years since he had felt sufficient arousal to lie with a woman. That concerned him, put him in a black mood when he thought on it, but he blamed it on the drink and knew there was nothing he could do.

He did not give her to the crew. He had to have something left when her husband returned. What was more, the pirates found it amusing to see her husband's great surprise at finding her unharmed and his even greater surprise at their being released, just as had been promised.

LeRois came at last to the Royal Arms Tavern, a low, dark building opening onto an alley rather than the main street. One of the least regal-looking establishments in the New World. He pushed the door open and stepped inside. His hat brushed against the rough-hewn beams overhead. There was a haze of smoke hanging like a fog over the upper third of the room. Beyond the dim light of the three lanterns that illuminated the place there seemed to be no colors other than grays and blacks and browns.

The Royal Arms was a rough establishment, the refuge of those sailors and laborers who were not welcome in the other public houses and whores too old or ugly to attract a more genteel clientele. It was also one of the older taverns in the town, a place that LeRois knew well and frequented when in that part of the world. No one in the Royal Arms was in the least bit curious about anyone else's business. He liked that about the place.

He stood stock-still, ran his eyes over the room. He was sweating with abandon and felt a vague terror in his gut, afraid that his carefully laid plan would fall apart, afraid that the screaming would start again.

A curse was forming on his lips just as he caught sight of the man for whom he was searching.

The man was Ezekiel Ripley. He sat hunched over a table, small and ratlike, with a big nose and protruding teeth, dark eyes darting about, and a pipe thrust in his mouth.

Ripley was the former quartermaster for the *Vengeance*. He had sailed with LeRois for years, and had advanced to quartermaster after Barrett had left. Just looking at the man brought back images of that day, of Barrett trying to take his leave, of Ripley calling him coward, of the fight that followed. LeRois shuddered, pushed the memory aside.

Now Ripley was in command of a small river sloop, a legitimate transport vessel that plied the Chesapeake. The fact that a man like Ripley could secure such employment bespoke the dire shortage of experienced sailors in the tidewater.

They had met again by accident in that very tavern a year before, and over numerous bowls of punch had concocted the plan that would make them all rich: LeRois, Ripley, the men of the *Vengeance*.

It was not much of a plan, really, but it addressed one of the biggest obstacles faced by the men on the account. While the most sought-after commodity aboard a plundered vessel was specie, gold and silver in any form, it was the least often found. More frequently the pirates took cargo—tobacco, cloth, manu-factured goods, barrel hoops—all of which had to be sold to do the pirates any good.

The merchants in Charleston and Savannah were a ready market, but they had little money and a surfeit of stolen goods. They would give only a fraction of the cargo's worth, which was their fee for not asking questions.

But Ripley reckoned himself a visionary who could see opportunity, counted himself a big man. Saw a new way of importing goods for sale into a wealthy colony hungry for them. Had the ears of important men ashore, could make things happen.

It was *merde*, of course; Ripley was a lying pig, a little rat fluffing himself up. LeRois knew it, but that did not matter as long as he really could sell the *Vengeance*'s plunder for gold. And he said he could, and he was too smart and too much the coward to cross LeRois.

That was the plan in its entirety. The cargoes plundered by the *Vengeance* would be funneled to market through Ripley, and Ripley would pay the pirates in gold. LeRois did not know with whom Ripley was working, and he did not care. His own part was simple enough, so simple that he had been able to keep it in his head for the year it had taken to organize. It required the cooperation of only a few parties. The potential for profit was enormous.

LeRois knew that this plan represented his last chance. The crew of the *Vengeance* were grumbling, and they would vote him out of his captaincy soon if he did not prove his worth in that office. Before he would step down he would kill as many of them as he could, and then they would kill him, and that would be an end to it.

He crossed to the table. Ripley's rodent eyes darted up at him. "LeRois," he said.

"Uhh, *bonsoir*, quartermaster," LeRois grunted. He had never been able to pronounce Ripley's name. He looked down at the other man at the table. He had never met him, but he knew who he was.

"Take a seat, *Capitain*," Ripley said, obsequious yet trying to take control.

"Come, we use the room in the back," LeRois said, indicating the way with a jerk of his head.

He pushed through the crowd and the smoke, down a narrow hall leading to the back of the building where a small room was available for anyone with private business. As it happened, the room was occupied at the moment by a whore and her customer, engaged in some very private business indeed. LeRois pushed the door open. The dim light of the hallway fell on the startled man and his lady.

"What in all hell, shut that goddamned door!" the man

roared, but his voice trailed off as he got a better look at LeRois, whose bulk filled the doorway.

"Get out," LeRois said. The man hesitated, looked down at the whore lying supine on the table, looked again at LeRois, then fled for the door, pulling his breeches up as he ran.

The woman followed more slowly, smoothing out her dress and shooting LeRois a filthy look, but LeRois paid no attention. The business that he was on was more important than the feelings or monetary considerations of some whore. He stepped into the now vacant room, Ripley and the second man behind him. Ripley shut the door.

LeRois turned to his former quartermaster. "Have you seen Barrett?"

"Barrett's dead."

"How do you know?"

"Last I heard, his men killed him. I ain't heard another word about him in three years. If he was around, I'd know."

"Bah!" LeRois spit on the floor. "He is not dead. There is no one who can kill him but me."

"I don't know who you're talking about," said the man with Ripley, "and I don't care. Reckon we got more important things to talk about here."

LeRois squinted at the man. He was fat, and his shirt and waistcoat were stained and filthy. He was visibly drunk, and he needed a shave. He did not look like a man who would be in the position that he was in.

"You are *capitain* of the guardship?" LeRois asked.

Ripley and the man exchanged a glance. "This here is Captain Allair," Ripley said. "He was the captain of the guardship. He ain't anymore. Governor appointed some other son of a bitch, name of Marlowe, as captain."

"What!?" LeRois roared. "What the goddamned hell is this?" The plan hinged on the cooperation of the guardship's captain for the free movement of the *Vengeance* on the bay. Ripley had assured him that this Allair could be bought, and cheaply. But now there was someone else in command of the man-of-war.

He felt his hands begin to tremble. Something snapping inside his head.

Captain Allair cleared his throat and worked the spittle around in his mouth. He met LeRois's eyes. "Son of a whore Marlowe set me up like he was playing nine-pins. Comes out to the ship for a visit, he says. Tells me he's looking to buy a silver table set, and if I happen across one he'll buy it, for a hell of a lot more than it was worth.

"Well, I found one, aboard a ship in from London, and I took it and it was the goddamned governor's silver, and next thing I know that bastard has my ship! I don't know how he knew, but he did, the son of a bitch."

LeRois stared at Allair as if he were some type of animal he did not recognize. He turned to Ripley. "What the fuck is this? Who is this Marlowe, eh? He will work with us?"

Before Ripley could answer, Allair said, "Sod Marlowe, the sheep-biting whoreson. If you want to move on the Bay, you best see I get back my legitimate command! You work with me, or you don't work, understand?"

He leaned closer to LeRois, head back, so that their faces were just a few inches apart.

LeRois squinted harder, as if trying to make out Allair's face through a fog. He jerked a pistol out of his sash, cocked the lock, thrust it into Allair's stomach. Pulled the trigger.

The blast of the gun was muffled by the fat around Allair's waist, but the former guardship captain's shriek filled the tiny room as he fell.

"Don't scream! Don't scream, you son of a whore!" LeRois shouted at Allair, but his commands did no good. Allair lay on his back, holding his stomach as blood ran out between his fingers, screaming, gasping, rocking side to side.

"Don't scream!" LeRois ordered again, and then as if he had forgotten all about Allair he turned to Ripley and said, "Who is this Marlowe?"

Ripley also ignored the man at their feet. He shrugged and said, "Don't know. Never seen him. I don't go ashore much.

Don't need to be recognized by no one, and me in my position."

"Who is this Marlowe!?" LeRois shouted. He kicked Allair, who was still screaming and gasping. "Shut your gob!" A trickle of blood ran out of the dying man's mouth.

"Some gentleman," Ripley continued. "Used to be a privateer, I hear. Rumor is he just did for a bunch of pirates on Smith Island, not three nights ago."

Smith Island. LeRois was certain he had heard something about Smith Island not long ago. He could not recall what it was.

"Oh, goddamn your soul, goddamn you," Allair whimpered between gasps for breath. "Goddamn you, I'm dying! I'm dying!"

LeRois pulled his second pistol from his sash.

"No, no," Allair pleaded, his eyes wide, a dark line of blood running down his face. LeRois put the gun against his head, pulled back the lock, and fired. Through the smoke he could see Allair's body give a satisfying jerk, and as the smoke cleared he could see the dark wet spot spread over the pine boards. In the middle of the black pool rested the remains of the captain's head.

"There, *cochon*, you are not dying anymore." He looked up at Ripley. He could see fear in his rodent eyes. That was good. Ripley must know that *Capitain* Jean-Pierre LeRois was again a man to be feared. Everyone must know it.

"Will this Marlowe work with us?" LeRois's voice was calm now that the screaming had stopped.

"He'll work with us. He will, I have no doubt," Ripley said quickly. "And if he don't, it's no matter. We don't need him, and if he's a problem we'll see him gone. I gots connections, I ain't to be fucked with."

LeRois nodded. That was what he wanted to hear. There would be no change in their plans. Because even though Ripley was a lying worm, there was nobody more powerful than Jean-Pierre LeRois.

Chapter 14

MARLOWE WAS prepared for a reception befitting a returning
and conquering hero. Indeed, he had laid the groundwork for
it himself, instructing King James that the crew of the *Northumberland* were to be given a run ashore after they had quietly,
and in the early hours of the morning, stowed away the most
valuable of the pirate's booty in the secondary warehouse in
Jamestown.

Once given their leave, the crew of the sloop descended
on Williamsburg's public houses, eagerly telling the story of
their exploits, as Marlowe knew they would. Embellished somewhat, as sailors were wont to do, but even in its rawest form
the tale was a remarkable one.

The story swept like a gale over the town and the surrounding plantations, with such force that even Marlowe could
not have anticipated the degree of excitement that greeted the
Plymouth Prize when at last she limped into Jamestown.

They arrived three days after the fight, after a day and a
half of working their way slowly upriver, the *Plymouth Prize* in
the lead, the captured pirate vessel in their wake. Hundreds of
people lining the shore and the docks, cheering like Romans
welcoming the triumphant Caesar into the city.

The *Prize* looked every inch the old campaigner, with her

pumps going nonstop and her generally battered appearance and her stump of a jury-rigged mainmast. It never occurred to anyone that she might look that way due to neglect rather than hard use, or that the mast might have fallen of its own accord rather than being shot away in a desperate fight. It never occurred to Marlowe or any of his men to disabuse them of that notion.

But even the missing mast was not half as exciting to the people as the sight of the dangerous-looking crew of the *Plymouth Prize* stepping ashore. They were a swaggering bunch, with the air of the victorious about them. Their clothes were new, and they were heavily armed, with swords and cutlasses and pistols hanging from ribbons around their necks.

At their head strode Captain Marlowe with the ease of a natural leader, the learned Bickerstaff beside him. And surrounded by the men of the *Plymouth Prize*, as well as the militia who had turned out, came the prisoners, a band of pirates shackled hand and foot, murderers and cutthroats all. It was great theater, and the crowd responded with all the enthusiasm that Marlowe had anticipated.

Governor Nicholson was there, of course, along with the burgesses, all of whom were hoping to reflect some of the brilliant light the Prizes were throwing off. "Marlowe, Marlowe!" the governor exclaimed, shaking Marlowe's hand with both of his. "I give you joy on your victory, sir, I give you joy!"

He was smiling, more happy than Marlowe had ever seen him. The governor had taken no small risk in replacing Allair, a move that might not have been quite legal. If Marlowe had proved to be a failure as well, it would have been most awkward for him.

Well, Marlowe thought, he is vindicated now. And what is more, he is the most important man in Virginia society, and he is in my debt.

"Pray, Marlowe, Bickerstaff, won't you come to my house and dine with me and give me the particulars of your exploits?" Nicholson asked. The burgesses were surrounding them now, and each was taking great pains to be conspicuous, hoping that the governor would ask him to join the party. In the end the governor asked none of them, keeping the heroes all to himself.

They pushed through the crowd, Marlowe and Bickerstaff waving and accepting with humility—in Bickerstaff's case, genuine humility—the thanks and congratulations of the people.

A small coach stood on the edge of the crowd, the coachman brushing the single horse. Looking out from the window, half lost in the shadows, was Elizabeth Tinling. Her blond hair fell down from under her hat, framing her perfect face, her long slender neck, and her shoulders, all but bare with the wide-cut neck of her dress.

Marlowe paused, and their eyes met. She was watching him with a look that he found hard to place: not affection or disdain, a touch of curiosity but not hero worship either, not such as he was getting from the other women in the crowd.

"Forgive me a moment, Governor," he said, and stepped over to the coach, bowing deep at the waist as he did.

"Good day, ma'am."

"Good day, sir. It seems to be your day, indeed."

"Providence has been with me in my fight."

"So it would seem. Though I am hard-pressed to tell, just by looking at your crew, which are the pirates and which the king's men."

Marlowe turned and looked back at his men, who did indeed look very much the buccaneers, with their pistols and sashes and new clothing. "I think, ma'am, you will find that my men are the ones who are smiling."

"I should imagine so," she said. A smile was floating just beneath the surface of her expression, a smile of shared devilment. Marlowe found it most heartening.

"Madam, I have brought you a little trinket, a remembrance of my battle." From out of his pocket he took the gold cross and chain, letting it dangle from his finger for a second, catching the light from the midday sun, and then handed it to her.

"Oh, Mr. Marlowe." She took it from his hands, recognized how fine a piece it was. "Pirate booty, is it? Is this not now the property of the king?"

"I think I am allowed some discretion in these matters. And it's only fair that you should have this, as it was thoughts of you that sustained me through my ordeal."

At this she looked up at him. Her expression was not the one of rapture he had hoped for. "I pray for your sake you are better with your sword than you are with your idle flattery. But in any event, I fear I cannot accept this."

"Please . . . Elizabeth . . . I beg of you," Marlowe stammered, thrown off balance by her unwillingness to accept his present or his silly compliments. "A token of my affection. It shall be our little secret."

She smiled and gave him a conspiratorial raise of the eyebrows, then put the chain around her neck. "Our secret," she said.

"Marlowe, Marlowe, do come along," the governor said as he came huffing up. "Mrs. Tinling," he added with a nod. "Forgive me, but I must take the hero away from you, for the time being, in any event." With that he took Marlowe's arm and guided him away, leaving him to call his farewell over his shoulder. He caught one last glimpse of the tiny cross lying against her pale skin before he had to return his attention to Nicholson.

"Now, I've no doubt that you want to get right back at it, Marlowe," the governor said as they stepped up into his carriage, "but I have to insist that the guardship get some attention. Heaving down, new mast and rigging, the like. I've no doubt the burgesses will approve that. Hell, we'll pay for it with the loot you captured."

"Well, Governor, if you insist."

"And I'm afraid we'll need you at the trial. We have to get these villains tried quick and hanged, by way of example. And I fear you must testify. It's all a bit of a bore, really. Did you have any experience with trials back home?"

"Back home? Oh, yes indeed. I have witnessed quite a few trials back home."

"Good, good," Nicholson said. "Bickerstaff, pray take that seat. I should think we'll get this trial nonsense over in a fortnight, and then back at it, eh, Marlowe? Get the *Plymouth Prize* all tight and yare, eh, just in time for the sailing of the tobacco fleet, I should think."

Elizabeth Tinling fingered the tiny cross around her neck, feeling the irregular surface of the diamond as she watched Marlowe step into the governor's carriage. In three days he had become the most celebrated man in the colony, Virginia's greatest hero.

She reckoned she had indeed chosen well.

There had been no word from George Wilkenson, no solicitors demanding payment of the note of hand. Perhaps he had believed her belated note warning him that Marlowe would not be there. Perhaps he was too afraid that she would tell tales of what he had intended to do. Most likely both. But in any event he seemed to be out of her life, and Marlowe seemed to be in, and as far as she could tell that was a good thing.

It was a few hours before noon the following day when she sat at the window in her bedchamber and watched Marlowe's slow progress down Duke of Gloucester Street toward her house. Judging by the direction from which he was coming, she guessed that he had just left the governor's house, where, it was rumored, he had spent the night.

She had been watching for the better part of an hour, hoping that he would come calling. Now he was a mere two blocks away. She wondered if he would be able to cover that distance by nightfall.

Crowd after crowd of admirers thronged around him as he tried to push down the street. When the circle of people grew too thick to proceed, he would stop and regale them with some story, no doubt a retelling of his exploits on Smith Island. At last the crowd would be satisfied, and with much hand shaking and pounding of his back they would allow him to pass.

He would generally make it about twenty feet before it all started again. At one point he was practically dragged into the

Palmer House Tavern and emerged again a full half an hour later. In this way he came at last to her front door, and Lucy quickly ushered him in.

Elizabeth was so anxious to see him that she did not make him wait above fifteen minutes before going down to the sitting room.

"Mr. Marlowe, you seem to have made quite a stir among the people. Should I have mercy on you, or should I make you give me the entire story of your exploits?"

"I beg you, no. I have told the story so many times now, I scarce believe it myself."

"Indeed? Well, from what I hear it is so heroic that it is scarce to be believed." She smiled at him, and he smiled back.

He was dressed in his fine clothes again, not the rough and weathered apparel he had been wearing when he left the *Plymouth Prize*. He was trim—though one would not call him thin—and his coat and waistcoat hugged his body in a way that did him credit. He had the physique of a man who is not sedentary, and that was notably different from most of the wealthy men of the tidewater. His hand rested on the hilt of his sword with a certain confidence, as if that weapon were an appendage and not a decoration.

He was, Elizabeth admitted, enormously attractive, even without considering his current status. Not a month before, she had looked on him in purely utilitarian terms, a potential bulwark against the Wilkensons. But now her feelings were different. She thought of him in a way that she had not thought of a man in many years. Found herself irresistibly attracted to him.

"Pray, sir, sit." She indicated a chair, and as Marlowe sat she called out, "Lucy, please fetch some chocolate for Mr. Marlowe."

A moment later Lucy appeared with the service, and as she poured Elizabeth said, "Now, tell me, sir, how do you enjoy your celebrity?"

"It wears a bit, I find. This morning has been a trying one. Bickerstaff tells me that the conquering heroes of Rome, as they drove through the streets, would have a slave standing behind them whispering in their ear that fame was fleeting."

"Well, Mr. Marlowe—"

"Please . . . Thomas."

"Very well, I shall call you Thomas if you will address me as Elizabeth. I was going to say that if you had not freed your slaves, you would be able to do the same."

"I don't need a slave for that, Elizabeth. I have Bickerstaff, who acts wonderfully as my conscience. Though I reckon much more of this and I'll think fame ain't fleeting enough."

She smiled at him and sipped her chocolate. His false modesty did not fool her. She could see from the moment he stepped off the *Plymouth Prize* how much he enjoyed the adulation. But that aspect of his personality did not bother her. Quite the opposite. She found that it made him more attractive still. It was the way of all great men, or all men destined for greatness.

"I fear you will have to suffer this hero worship a while longer. The people of this colony live in constant dread of the pirates, and you are practically the first man in living memory to do anything against them."

"You are too kind by half, Elizabeth. But in fact I shall be free of this for a while, at least while we careen the *Plymouth Prize* down by Point Comfort."

"Careen? I fear I do not follow your nautical jargon."

" 'Careening' is how we clean and repair the ship's bottom. It is an onerous task. First we strip the vessel of all of her top hamper—her masts and yards and such—and her great guns as well, and all of the provisions in her hold. Then we run her up on a beach, and as the tide goes out we heave her down— that is to say, we cause her to roll on her side and thus expose the bottom."

"Yes, I've heard how that is done, now that you explain it. But are you to be absent from Williamsburg for a time?" Her voice conveyed far more disappointment than she had intended. She could see that her tone had registered with Marlowe. Giving too much away. It was her intention to be more coy than that.

"I shall be away for a short time. But indeed, I had wished to ask you—and I beg you will not think my proposal in the least bit indecent, for I mean nothing of the kind—but might you be interested in accompanying me? I shall be sailing aboard my own sloop, the *Northumberland*. You are welcome to bring Lucy, if you wish. King James shall be captaining the sloop, and I am certain he would wish to see her, despite his pretensions of indifference. It could be something of a yachting holiday."

"Indeed, sir . . ." The various implications swirled through Elizabeth's mind. Such a trip might be cause for much whispering among the society people. On the other hand, one could do no better at present than to be seen in company with Captain Thomas Marlowe.

". . . to sail off with you, I don't know . . ."

She wanted very much to go, but she was afraid. Not of Marlowe, not at all, though that smoldering, dangerous quality that she had first seen in him had not dissipated in the past two years. She was afraid of what the others might think.

"Just an afternoon's sail, ma'am, no more. We should put out on the morning tide and return that evening."

What in all hell is wrong with me? she wondered. Had she been so long among the silly, pretentious people of Williamsburg that she was becoming one herself? She had never been shy about going after what she wanted. And now she wanted Marlowe, and for once in her life she had reason to hope that the thing she wanted would be hers, and would not be her undoing. No one would raise an eyebrow about a mere afternoon's sailing.

"If that is the case, sir, then I should be delighted to sail with you," she said. It was one of the most truthful statements she had uttered in a long, long time.

Chapter 15

THE LATE-SPRING weather in the tidewater of Virginia was yielding slowly, day by day, to summer.

The winds, always variable in that region, had hauled around from the predominantly north and northwest of the winter months to something approaching south and southeast. And when the wind came from that quarter it brought with it warm air. In later months that air would be hot and moist and miserable, but in those first days of summertime weather it was just perfectly warm, as if there were no temperature at all.

It was just such a day, an hour before slack water, when Marlowe's party came aboard the *Northumberland*. It was not much of a party, consisting only of himself, Elizabeth Tinling, and Lucy, but then, the little sloop did not have the space to accommodate too many more.

Still, King James, now once more in command of the vessel, had prepared for her owner's arrival as if it were the royal yacht. Bunting was flying from the rigging and flags flapped at every high point aloft. The gangplank was freshly painted, with rails set up and strung with rope handholds, made white through the application of pipe clay and finished off with spritsail sheet knots at the bitter ends.

Marlowe stepped aboard first and offered his hand to Elizabeth, helping her over the gangplank. The *Northumberland's* four-man crew, two black men and two white, were dressed out in matching shirts and fresh-scrubbed slop trousers and straw hats. They stood at some semblance of attention as the owner and his guest came aboard, and then with a word James scattered them to the various tasks necessary to get the ship under way.

"Welcome aboard, Elizabeth," Marlowe said.

"Oh, Thomas, it is magnificent!" she said, and she meant it, entirely. With a hand on her wide-brimmed straw hat, she craned her neck to look aloft. The many-colored flags waving in the breeze, the bunting, the white scrubbed decks and varnished rails and black rigging were all too perfect, like a brand-new, brightly painted toy. "It's like something from a storybook."

"Life can be like that, I find," Marlowe said, "if one is able to write one's own story."

They cast off at slack water. The *Northumberland* drifted away from the dock, King James at the helm and Marlowe and Elizabeth standing by the taffrail, enjoying the morning. Forward, the small crew set the sails—jib, staysail, and the big gaff-headed main—with no orders given and none needed. James swung the bow off and the sloop made her way downriver, close-hauled, making a long board to the east until they were almost aground on the northern bank, then tacking across the river and tacking again.

"Your men work very well together," Elizabeth commented as the *Northumberland* settled down for another long run on the starboard tack. "I hear no yelling or confusion, as one often associates with a ship's crew."

"They have been together awhile," Marlowe said.

"They are not the same men as sailed her when my . . . when the sloop was owned by Joseph, I observe."

"No. I let those men go. They were not willing to suffer King James as captain of the vessel."

"They were very foolish, then. King James seems very much the competent master."

"King James is of the type of man who does well whatever he sets his mind to. That is why I did not dare let him remain my slave. He is not the kind of man one needs as an enemy."

"Do you not need him to run your household?"

"He does, when he is not running the sloop. But there is not much to the house. Caesar can run things well enough. It is a waste of James's talent to keep him there."

The *Northumberland* continued on down the river, standing right up to the banks with their strips of sandy beach and meadows of tall grass and patches of woods. Overhead marched a great parade of clouds, flat and gray on their bottoms and swelling up into high mounds of white, sharply defined against the blue of the sky.

They sailed past several plantations, the brown-earth fields stretching down to the water, the slaves moving slowly between the hillocks, preparing the earth to receive the young plants.

The finest of them all was the Wilkensons' home, standing on a hill not one hundred yards from the river, a great white monument to the wealth that family had amassed in just a few generations in the New World. Neither Marlowe nor Elizabeth commented on the place.

It was dinnertime when the *Northumberland* came about after a short tack to the southwest and stood into the wide bay where the Nasemond and Elizabeth join up with the mighty James River. Marlowe's cabin steward appeared on the quarterdeck and set up a small table and chairs, and on the table he laid out a meal of cold roast beef, bread, cheese, nuts, fruit, and wine.

Marlowe helped Elizabeth into her seat.

"Your tobacco crop has come in well, I hope?" Elizabeth asked as Marlowe poured her a glass of wine. Tobacco was never far from the minds of anyone in the tidewater.

"Excellently well, thank you. We've had a prodigious crop, and it is now all but stowed down . . . 'prized,' I believe, is the correct term, into its casks and quite ready for the convoy at the end of May."

"You have learned a great deal about cultivating tobacco in the past few years, it would seem."

"Not a bit of it, not a bit of it. Some of this cheese for you? No, I leave it all up to the people, and they do a fine job. They have forgotten more about the weed than I shall ever know. Bickerstaff takes an academic interest in the cultivation, but I content myself with the odd pipeful and a ride through my fields."

Elizabeth took a sip of her wine. Regarded Marlowe. Such an odd man. "You leave the planting and cultivation up to your Negroes? And they do the work, with never an overseer?"

"Well, of course they do. They are paid a percentage of the crop, do you see? It is in their interest to work just as hard as they can. They are not such fools that they cannot understand that."

Marlowe took a bite and smiled at her as he chewed. There were times when she thought Marlowe might be quite mad. He seemed perfectly willing to consider a Negro as his equal. Indeed, he treated King James more as his fellow than his servant.

Then forward one of the deckhands dropped a hatch cover with a loud bang, like a pistol. Marlowe's head shot in the direction of the sound, his body tensed, and his hand moved automatically to the hilt of his sword. In his eyes that quality like a smoldering flame, the suggestion of a predator. To be sure, the pirates on Smith Island had found out how dangerous he could be. There was not a bit of the mad fool in him then.

He smiled, and his body eased, like a rope when the strain is let off. "Clumsy, clumsy," he said, and poured some more wine.

Once dinner was cleared away they took their place again at the taffrail.

"That is Point Comfort there." Marlowe pointed to a low headland just off the larboard bow.

"And why do they call it Point Comfort?"

"I don't know. I suppose it was a great comfort to see it, after the long voyage from Europe."

"Oh." Elizabeth thought of the time when she and Joseph Tinling had stood on another quarterdeck and viewed that point as their ship stood in from sea. "I can't say that I had that reaction when first I saw it."

"Were you not pleased to see this new land?"

She had never considered that before. There had been so many emotions, whirling like an eddy. "Oh, I suppose I was. My . . . husband was more enthusiastic than I. It was a long voyage, as you say, and a difficult one. I thought one could not—what do you call it?—careen a ship on the Chesapeake."

"That was what Allair would have the governor believe," Marlowe said, and Elizabeth was grateful that he did not remark on her abrupt change of subject. "But he was just too lazy to try. One can careen a ship just about anywhere there is beach and tide enough. Why, I've . . . I've careened ships in some very odd places indeed."

An hour later they passed Point Comfort, rounded up, and dropped anchor a cable from the beach. There on the dark wet sand was the *Plymouth Prize*. She looked sorry and vulnerable, her rig completely gone save for the lower masts: fore, mizzen, and the bright new main. Her guns were gone too, and her gunports stared up at the sky like the hollow eyes of a skull. She was rolled over on her larboard side, and all of her great worm-eaten, weed-covered bottom was exposed to the world. The Plymouth Prizes swarmed around her like ants on a mound of spilled sugar.

"Oh, my goodness," Elizabeth said. It looked as if something had gone terribly wrong. "Is she wrecked? What's happened to her?"

"No, believe it or not, this is what we do. Those fellows with the torches are breeming her, burning all the weed and barnacles and such off of her bottom. Then, once we've made the repairs we need, we'll coat her anew with stuff made from tallow, sulfur, and tar."

"You astonish me, sir, the depth of your knowledge," Elizabeth said. Marlowe was clearly an experienced seaman as well as an experienced fighting man. There was no faking that.

Had he earned all of his wealth at sea? No one became as rich as he was by sailing as an honest merchant captain or naval officer. Was it family money?

He rarely mentioned his personal history prior to arriving in Virginia, and she had the distinct impression that he would rather she didn't ask. She knew so little about him. She found it intriguing and irritating all at once. She could imagine any number of possibilities, many of which she did not care to think about.

Marlowe nodded toward the *Prize*'s long boat, which was pulling toward the sloop, Lieutenant Rakestraw in the stern sheets. "I reckon we'll know soon how much work needs to be done before we can go a-hunting pirates again," Marlowe said.

A minute later Rakestraw climbed up the side, saluted Marlowe, and gave Elizabeth a shallow bow. He was dressed in old clothes, the same as were worn by the sailors, and he was quite filthy.

"Forgive my appearance, I beg, sir, but I have been all day climbing about the hull," he said.

"Please, Lieutenant, don't think on it," Marlowe said. "If you were clean, I should think you weren't seeing to the job properly."

Elizabeth had seen Rakestraw in Williamsburg on several occasions over the past few years. He looked happier now, and more like an officer, than she had ever seen, his dirty, common clothes notwithstanding.

"It appears, sir," Rakestraw continued, "that the chief of the water was coming in where the butts was pulled apart. We found the four on the larboard side, like I reported the other day, and six on the starboard today. There was some soft wood around the sternpost and three planks needs replacing near the turn of the bilge, but the worms haven't got at the bottom nearly as bad as I would have thought."

"No. Allair spent a great deal of time at anchor in the freshes where the water's brackish at best. That might have done for the worms."

"The only constructive thing that Allair has ever done, to

the best of my knowledge," Rakestraw said, the disgust evident in his voice.

"Indeed. Well, Mr. Rakestraw, I do not wish to keep you from your work."

"No, sir. Will you be sailing back tonight, sir?"

"I had intended to do so, but we had slow going coming down and I fear we have missed the tide now. I think we must spend the night here," Marlowe answered, not meeting Elizabeth's eyes but looking instead at Rakestraw, "and wait for the flood tomorrow."

"Oh, quite right, sir, quite. Tide is quite gone," Rakestraw agreed. Had he kept his mouth shut Elizabeth might have believed what Marlowe said, but Rakestraw was not nearly as accomplished a liar as Marlowe.

"I apologize profusely, ma'am, and trust that that will not inconvenience you?" Marlowe turned at last to Elizabeth, looking his most contrite. "You and Lucy shall have my cabin, of course, and I shall take the small cabin. If you wish, I shall send ashore for a coach."

"That will not inconvenience us at all, sir. If we are to be kidnapped by pirates, I am pleased at least that we have found one who is such a gentleman."

"Oh, a former pirate, ma'am. Fear not, I have forsworn that life." He was smiling, but his eyes suggested there might be something deeper, more personal, to his simple joke.

It was one of the possibilities that Elizabeth had considered.

The *Northumberland* was absolutely quiet. All hands were below and asleep, and the sloop rode perfectly still at her anchor, held steady in the soft arms of the current. The only sounds that King James could hear were the occasional call of a night bird from shore, the buzzing of the distant insects, the gentle gurgle of the water.

He crouched over the compass, taking a bearing on Point Comfort and a tall stand of trees just abeam, which he was just able to discern against the background of stars. Once he had taken the bearings he would wait for an hour or so and then take them again and thus make certain the sloop was not dragging her anchor. That was why he was still awake and on deck.

Or at least that was what he told himself. Why he felt the need to fool himself he did not know, especially because he was not. He was perfectly aware of why he was loitering in that place. He was hoping that Lucy would come to him.

He heard the low creak of the after scuttle opening, did not react. It could be anyone—Marlowe or the cabin steward.

But it was not. Lucy stepped hesitatingly on deck, looking forward and then aft. She looked directly at him, but he could see that she was struggling to make out who it was she was looking at.

"Come on back here, girl," he called out softly.

Lucy squinted aft again, then lifted her skirts and climbed up the two short steps to the quarterdeck and came aft. There was just the faintest light on deck, the stars and the dim glow of the covered candle James was using to see the compass, but it was enough for him to see her lovely face, her soft brown hair hanging around her shoulders, her shapely form under her petticoats. Lucy and Elizabeth. They made quite a pair.

She leaned against the rail where King James stood, an inch closer than a casual acquaintance might stand. "What are you doing up at this hour?" she asked.

"I'm seeing to the ship. And you?"

She glanced down at the deck and then looked at him, though not directly. She was not half as shy as she was pretending to be. James knew it. She had learned a great deal working for Elizabeth Tinling. "I just wanted to get some air," she said.

"Good night for it."

They were silent for a moment. He could smell the subtle perfume that Lucy was wearing, the scent of her skin and hair. She was wildly attractive, and he felt emotions rising up that he had not felt in many years. It had been that long since he had felt anything but hatred and anger.

"How is it with you, Lucy?" he asked, surprised by the tenderness in his own voice. "I've seen little of you these past years. How is it in town?"

"It's wonderful, James, truly. There's just that little house, and none of the misery there was at the Tinling place. Best thing that son of a bitch Tinling ever done any of us was to drop dead."

"Hmmph," James said. He could not disagree. "And you're safe enough, because of it."

"What do you mean by that?"

"I mean Mrs. Tinling ain't about to sell you off, 'cause she don't want no one to know how they found old Tinling, breeches around his ankles, his heart burst ripping the clothes off his wife's slave girl."

He stared out into the night, mused on this netherworld of the slaves in the tidewater. An entire society, with a common knowledge and a social structure and their own set of laws about which the white people knew nothing.

And there was not a one who grieved for Joseph Tinling.

Without thinking, James turned and put his hand on Lucy's shoulder. He could barely feel her smooth skin under the calluses of his palm, but he felt her tense up, just a tiny bit, and turn more toward him.

"It's history, Lucy. Don't think on it," he said, as tenderly as he was able. Felt her relax under his hand. Without a word she pressed herself against him and he hugged her, encircling her tiny shoulders in his powerful arms.

"You've changed, James," she said at last. "I . . . I used to be so afraid of you. I wanted you and I was afraid of you, all at once. Now I just feel safe when I'm with you."

"I'm a free man now."

A free man. He pressed Lucy closer, thought about those words. Freedom had meant nothing to him when Marlowe had given it. James had not believed he would really grant it, did not believe anything that a white man said. And even if Marlowe was true to his word, there was nowhere that the former slaves could go. The others had embraced their freedom from the first, but not he. Freedom had come slowly for King James.

It had come with his being taken out of the fields and given a position of authority. It had come with his efficiently running the house, proving to the white men that he was just as able as they. It had come with command of the *Northumberland*. It had come with a restoration of pride. And finally, it had come with being a warrior once again.

"I love you James. I do," Lucy said. She spoke into his chest, and her voice was muffled.

James pressed his lips against her head and kissed her, and buried his face in her lovely hair. There were tears in his eyes, and he would not let her see them. Not her, not anyone.

Marlowe was fast asleep when he heard the soft footstep, the quiet squeak of the door opening. He came instantly awake, and his hand shot out and grabbed the hilt of his sword, and in the same instant he realized that there was probably no one aboard the *Northumberland* who might wish to slay him in his sleep.

The door was at the end of the small cabin and communicated with the great cabin astern. It swung open, ever so slowly. Marlowe released his grip on the sword. Did not dare hope for what might be.

Elizabeth was standing there, wearing nothing but her silk shift. The light from a shuttered lantern in the cabin shone through the gauzy material, silhouetting her slender form beneath the garment.

She stepped into the cabin, reached up, and untied the ribbon holding the shift in place. The shapeless gown slid down her body and piled on the deck, and she stepped out of it and silently climbed into Marlowe's narrow bed.

She was the most beautiful woman that Marlowe had ever seen. He felt a tremor of excitement building in his gut and rushing out to the extremities of his hands and feet. He put his arms around her, running his hands over her skin, smooth, golden, perfect skin. She lay back on his bed and he rolled half on top of her, kissing her, his tongue probing her mouth, finding hers.

She wrapped her arms around his neck, running her fingers through his hair, and wrapped a long leg around his thighs. He ran his lips over her neck and shoulders, covering her with small kisses, cupping a breast in his hands and gently caressing the firm nipple with his lips. She shifted under him and moaned softly, and Marlowe felt his passion building to a dangerous peak.

They spent two hours exploring each other, making love, talking in whispers, holding each other. At last Elizabeth lay still in his arms, and her breath became soft and regular.

Through the half-open door of the cabin he could see the first blue light of dawn. He reached over and grabbed the hilt of his sword, moving carefully so as not to disturb her, quietly drew the blade. He put the sharp point against the door and pushed it closed. He laid the sword on the deck, and together they slept.

Chapter 16

THEY MADE quite an imposing sight, pounding down the rolling road. Jacob Wilkenson at the head on his black stallion, George Wilkenson just behind on his chestnut mare, and behind him Sheriff Witsen and four deputies. They were riding hard. They were all heavily armed.

George Wilkenson concentrated on the motion of the horse under him, his own position in the saddle, the condition of the road underfoot. He was an excellent horseman. Thoughts of his horse and his riding kept his mind from what had just transpired, what was about to happen.

He had said nothing to his father, save to tell him that he had formulated a plan but the plan had not worked out.

He did not dare tell him what the plan was, or mention his own stupidity in relying on the cooperation of Elizabeth Tinling. He did not tell him about the humiliation, or the hard money he had given to Witsen to assure his silence. He said nothing about Elizabeth's note, about his own uncertainty as to her betraying him.

He had mentioned none of those things, but that had not saved him from Jacob's wrath.

His father raged for an hour, cursing him for a fool and reiterating the need to destroy Marlowe. At last he had announced that he would be taking matters into his own hands. They would take the direct route. They would ruin Marlowe financially.

Or, better yet, they would force him into debt. There was no debt in the tidewater that the Wilkensons could not control. And once they had assumed Marlowe's debts, then they would choke him to death, slowly.

Jacob Wilkenson was an unsubtle man. George found his approach to the situation frightening. There was bound to be trouble, perhaps bloodshed, and that frightened him more. The presence of the sheriff and his men did nothing to comfort him.

They turned off the rolling road and raced down the carriage road to the old Tinling house. The tall trees met overhead, their summer leaves mingling together high over the way, giving the approach the feel of a nave in a great cathedral.

At the far end, like an altar, stood the white Tinling house. It would always be the Tinling house to George, no matter who owned it. He thought of the many times he had ridden down that road, happier times.

He felt a vague titillation, as if there was something sexually exciting to look forward to, and he realized that he had come to associate that approach with seeing Elizabeth Tinling, and the thrill he got in just running his eyes over her, watching her as she moved, fantasizing about her.

And once he understood that association the thrill was gone, like plunging into a frozen stream. He felt angry. Humiliated. Impotent.

He hated her, even more than he hated Marlowe, even more because he could not be certain she had betrayed him. It was most convenient that her note had been delivered after he had left to confront Marlowe. He was almost certain he had seen her in the window. Almost, but not entirely. He had been a long way back from the house, and his eyesight was not the best.

She had never been anything more than polite to him. No flirting, no vague overtones of desire in her voice. He was far better looking than that fat pig Joseph Tinling. He was smarter and kinder than his brother, Matthew. But she had ignored him, and now she was off with Marlowe, no doubt making the beast with two backs.

He had not contacted her since that night, had not called in the note of hand. He wanted her to suffer the uncertainty. Perhaps he would use that power over her again, for whatever he wished, and then he would crush her.

He did not have the courage to face her again. From that flowed anger, self-loathing.

His father, he knew, could not care less about Elizabeth Tinling, but she was as much a part of his plans as Marlowe was. He would destroy her just as he and Jacob would destroy Marlowe.

They came at last to the end of the carriage road and bore off to the right, past the big house. A black man came out onto the porch, watched them for a moment, and then ran back inside, but the band on horseback paid him no mind. The only man who might concern them was Marlowe, and they knew for a fact that Marlowe was off on his sloop down by Point Comfort.

They raced down the familiar dirt road that led behind the house, past the gardens and the toolsheds, to the big warehouse where the plantation's crop was stored, ready for shipment.

They pulled their horses to a stop in a swirl of dust, looked around. At the far end of the field George could see the slave quarters. They were newly whitewashed and the roofs were much improved, and they were altogether less dilapidated and less depressing a sight than any other slave quarters he had seen.

But, of course, they were not slave quarters at all. Marlowe had freed his slaves.

At the other end of the field, nearer the warehouse, he could see the patch of woodland that had been cleared for the seedbeds for the next crop. Every spring the new plants were started in beds that had been prepared by clearing and burning virgin woodland. Then, when they were big enough, the young tobacco plants were transferred to the fields.

The seedbeds were already bursting with fine young plants. In the fields, small hillocks had been raised in parallel rows three feet apart, ready to accept the seedlings. And all of that without a white overseer, and, as he understood it, with virtually no supervision from Marlowe at all. He just let the niggers do it, and they did. Incredible.

"Come along," Jacob ordered, and the seven men dismounted. The sheriff's men opened the big warehouse doors. The early-morning sunlight spilled into that cavernous space. It was like any warehouse on a tidewater plantation. It contained an eclectic assortment of things: lumber, empty barrels of various sizes, tools, spare parts for wagons and carriages, coils of rope.

But none of that interested the men. They turned rather to the hogsheads of tobacco stacked against one wall, over one hundred hogsheads filled nearly to bursting. They represented an entire year's worth of work, a year's worth of clearing seedbeds and raising plants, transferring plants, topping, suckering, priming, weeding and worming plants, cutting, bulking, curing, sweating and striping plants, and then bundling them all and prizing them into casks. It was a prodigious amount of labor, and from the number of hogsheads piled against the wall it appeared that Marlowe's crop had been prodigious as well.

"Here, break this one open." Jacob Wilkenson pointed to one of the barrels in the middle of the stack. One of the sheriff's men took an ax and embedded it in the head of the barrel. He jerked it free and struck again, the head of the barrel broke open, and small, tight-packed bundles of tobacco spilled out on the hard earth floor. The air was filled with the scent of fresh cured tobacco, a familiar and wonderful smell to the men of the tidewater.

George Wilkenson looked at the pile of tobacco lying at his feet. He had spent a lifetime in the cultivation of that crop, and there was not much he did not know about it. And he knew that the pile of tobacco in front of him was as fine a sweetscented as was grown anywhere in the colony, cured to perfection and prized into the barrels with no lugs, suckers, or slips. And all done by the Negroes. Amazing.

"Here, what is the meaning of this?"

The seven men whirled around. George flushed in embarrassment and fear, like a boy caught stealing.

Standing in the wide doorway was Francis Bickerstaff. He held a musket in his hand, as did the two black men standing behind him. No one answered him.

"Ah, Wilkenson, is it? Father and son? What do you think you're about, breaking into our warehouse?"

"Nobody's breaking in." Sheriff Witsen stepped forward. He seemed ill at ease, and George imagined that the sheriff did not like what was happening any more than he did. "We're inspecting, and we have the right to do it under the law."

"Tell those niggers to put their guns down or we'll have you arrested!" Jacob Wilkenson ordered. "There are laws against arming niggers."

"There are laws against breaking into another's home."

"This ain't your home, and it ain't your warehouse, is it?" the elder Wilkenson demanded. "No, I thought not. Now, tell them niggers to put their guns down."

All eyes turned to Sheriff Witsen, who cleared his throat and said, "It's against the law, Mr. Bickerstaff, to give them guns."

The warehouse was silent as the men faced off, then Bickerstaff turned and nodded to the two black men behind him. Without a word they leaned their guns against a stack of lumber and resumed their position at Bickerstaff's back.

"As you see, Sheriff, we have no desire to break the law."

"I'm grateful for that, Mr. Bickerstaff."

Jacob Wilkenson turned his back on Bickerstaff and rummaged through the pile of tobacco on the floor, kicking it around with his foot. "Uh-huh, uh-huh," he muttered, and then, turning to the man with the ax, said, "Here, break open another one."

"What on earth do you think you're about?" Bickerstaff

demanded. The ax bit into the head of the barrel Jacob Wilkenson had indicated.

"I told you, we're inspecting the contents of these hogsheads." Jacob did not meet Bickerstaff's eyes but rather focused on the man with the ax.

"They contain tobacco, sir. Whatever did you expect?" Bickerstaff said. "George, what is the meaning of this? Is this some petty revenge for the duel that your brother fought with Marlowe?"

"I . . . ahh . . ." was all that George was able to get out before the second barrel burst open and spilled its contents on the floor and, to his infinite relief, all eyes turned away from him.

"There, are you quite satisfied?" Bickerstaff asked.

Jacob pushed the tobacco around with his toe. "Like I reckoned. It's trash. All trash."

"Trash?" Bickerstaff protested. "That is perfectly good sweetscented, good as anyone might find in the tidewater. It most certainly is not trash."

Jacob turned at last to Bickerstaff. "Know a lot about tobacco, do you? I've been growing tobacco for fifty years, boy and man! You didn't sweat it enough, it's too dry. It'll never last to market."

"That is sheer nonsense. There is not a thing wrong with that tobacco. And even if there were, it is no business of yours."

"Oh, it most certainly is my business. Quality of the tobacco coming out of this colony is the business of every tobacco grower. That's why I brought the sheriff along, in case we had to condemn this lot, which we do." Jacob Wilkenson turned to George and the sheriff's deputies. "All right, men. Take it out and burn it. All of it."

"Burn it! This is an outrage!" Bickerstaff's voice rose for the first time. "This is no more than revenge for Matthew Wilkenson's being killed in what was once considered an affair of honor. Sheriff Witsen, surely you will not suffer this outrage to take place?"

Witsen glanced at Jacob Wilkenson, then down at the

ground, then looked Bickerstaff square in the face. "Mr. Wilkenson's an expert when it comes to tobacco, Mr. Bickerstaff.
If he says it's trash, well, I reckon he knows. And it is his right
to report any tobacco that ain't of proper quality, and it's my
duty to see it's destroyed." He stared at Bickerstaff for a moment, their eyes locked, and then turned back to his men. "Go
on, then, burn it."

The sheriff's men turned to their work. Three hogsheads
were rolled out to a spot clear of the warehouse and smashed
apart. An oil-soaked torch was sparked off with a flintlock, and
soon the whole pile was burning. Then, one after another, the
barrels were rolled out and added to the blaze.

"You could at least not burn the casks," Bickerstaff commented dryly. "Unless they, too, are not up to the standards of
the Royal Colony of Virginia." But his words were ignored. He
said nothing more.

It was two hours before the last of the hogsheads were
added to the flame. By then the fire was so prodigious that the
tobacco had to be flung on from some distance, using shovels
and pitchforks found in Marlowe's warehouse, and the empty
barrels tossed on after them.

From the edge of the flames Bickerstaff and the two black
men watched in silence, and George Wilkenson could see at
the far end of the fields the rest of the former slaves watching
as their year's work was destroyed.

This should be an end to Marlowe, he thought. There
were few planters in the tidewater wealthy enough to survive
the loss of an entire year's crop. He was not even certain that
the Wilkensons could do so. This will ruin the bastard, he
thought, or better yet, put him in our debt.

He concentrated his thoughts on that comforting idea. It
helped to drive away the shame, the utter humiliation he felt
about what they were doing.

Chapter 17

EVIDENCE OF the battle at Smith Island was still visible, though it had been at least two week since the fight.

LeRois scratched at his beard. He thought it had been that long, but now he was not certain. He tried to recall what Ripley had said, but the sand underfoot seemed unusually soft, making walking inordinately tiring, and the sun was beating down on them and he could hear voices talking somewhere, and all those things made it very difficult for him to concentrate.

He took a big drink of gin from the bottle in his hand, held it in his mouth, swallowed it. Looked around the white sand. Off near the dune grass some animal had unearthed one of the poor bastards who had died there, and now a few turkey vultures were taking desultory stabs at what little remained. At first glance LeRois had thought the dead man was Barrett, thought he saw the corpse reaching for a sword, had gasped in fear, but he had been mistaken.

In the surf was the odd pistol or cutlass, half buried in the dark sand. A big blackened circle indicated where the pirate's fire had burned before they had been murdered by the black-heart Marlowe, new captain of the guardship, the one who stood between LeRois and the ultimate fulfillment of his plans.

"Merde alors," LeRois muttered. Drank again.

"He just shot 'em down where they stood," Ripley said. "No call for them to surrender, just shot 'em down, and them that called for quarter is to be hung any day now."

"*Merde.*" Something was giving off a terrible stench. Le-Rois wondered if it was Ripley or himself. Perhaps the poor dead bastard getting picked apart by the birds. "And the ship, the one that was taken, what of the things they had on board?"

"As I hear it, the bastard Marlowe let his men have what they wanted, split it up on a barrelhead and give 'em all a share."

LeRois took another drink, swallowed, and grinned. "This Marlowe, he sound more like a pirate himself than a king's man, no? The son of a bitch. Who is he?"

"Ain't seen him. I keeps away from the towns. Told you. This here's more to my liking."

The little rat was all fluffed up again with self-importance, as if everything that had taken place had been his own doing. LeRois spit in the sand.

The three vessels were riding at anchor above the glassy water of the harbor. The largest of the three was the *Vengeance.* She rode to a single anchor with her gray and much-patched sails hauled out by their bowlines to dry.

Made fast to the *Vengeance*'s starboard side was the small sloop that was the one and only legitimate command of former pirate quartermaster Ezekiel Ripley. On the starboard side of Ripley's sloop was tied a brigantine from New York, which had been northbound a week out of Barbados when she had been spotted from the *Vengeance*'s masthead.

The brigantine had run for all she was worth, which infuriated LeRois. When at last she had been overhauled her crew had fought rather than surrender, which made LeRois lose all semblance of reason.

That was three days before. The last of her crew had just died that morning.

The deck of the brigantine and the deck of the *Vengeance* and the deck of the little sloop were crowded with men. Cargo was coming up from the hold of the pirate—the accumulated

plunder of seven vessels they had taken since leaving New
Providence—and the hold of her eighth and most recent victim, and with stay tackles and yard tackles it was swayed over
to Ripley's sloop and stowed down below.

"If that *cochon* Allair had not lost his ship, we would not
have to sneak around here like frightened puppies," LeRois
growled.

"Yeah, well, you done for him."

"Where is the son of bitch Marlowe now, and his fucking guardship?"

"They're careening the ship by Point Comfort. This past
week Marlowe's been at the trial for them poor bastards they
took here. I reckon they're at the hanging now."

"Careening, eh? Well, why don't we go and blow their
goddamned ship to hell while they are careening?"

"Marlowe set up the great guns on the shore. He ain't that
dumb. I reckon you should just stay clear of him and we'll just
carry on like we are."

LeRois grunted and drank the last of his gin and flung the
bottle into the surf. The hot sun felt good now, and the warm
sand around his shoes was like a heavy blanket. The voices
were gone, and in their place was music, lovely music. LeRois
glanced around the beach, but he could not see where it was
coming from.

There was reason for happiness. The plan that he and
Ripley had devised seemed to be working, despite their not
having the cooperation of the guardship. They had met up at
Smith Island, that familiar haunt, as planned, LeRois with a
hold full of pilfered goods, Ripley with a chest full of hard
money to pay for it. No haggling with bastard shopkeepers in
Charleston or Savannah, who insisted you practically give the
goods away. LeRois could let Ripley pretend he was important
as long as things kept working as smoothly as that.

And just as important, the Vengeances were a happy crew.
The hunting had been good around the Capes. They had been
drinking and pillaging and tormenting victims almost nonstop
since arriving in those waters, and that made for a contented

band of men. And as long as they were contented, there would be no questioning of authority.

It would have been better, of course, if they had not had the guardship to worry about, but the guardship had not bothered them yet. It may have done for the stupid bastards on that beach, but LeRois was not stupid and he would not be caught in that manner.

"The *flotte*, the tobacco convoy, they sail soon, eh?" LeRois asked.

"Yes, a week or so. Gathering now, down by Hampton Roads, but sod the fucking tobacco fleet. We have all the fucking tobacco we needs. There's no call for tobacco around here. It's goods like them"—Ripley thrust his pointed, bristled chin at the barrels soaring out of the *Vengeance*'s hold—"that gots a ready market here. Imports, goods from England, the things what have a high tariff, that's what can be sold here. Besides that, convoy'll have an escort. The guardship, with that Marlowe, what served these bastards out, he'll be there, I reckon."

"Bah, fucking guardship," LeRois grunted. He looked around in the sand, hoping to find a discarded bottle of alcohol of some description, but there was nothing.

Sod tobacco? he thought. I reckon not. Tobacco might not be much in demand in Virginia, but Virginia was not the only market, and he was feeling confident. Tobacco ships had specie aboard them.

He would see about this tobacco fleet.

Marlowe sat, silent and unmoving, and stared out of the aft window of the *Northumberland*'s great cabin. He felt the anger wash over him and then recede, wash and recede, like the surf on the beach. He was aware of the gentle tap of Bickerstaff's foot on the deck, King James's shifting uncomfortably in his seat, but he ignored them until he trusted himself to speak.

"They burned it? All of it? The hogsheads as well?"

"All of it. And the hogsheads. Near the end, when they

were emptying the casks first, I pointed out that they needn't throw the empty casks on the flames, but it did no good."

"Damn their souls to hell," Marlowe said. "Does honor mean nothing in this place? What, pray, is the use of playing the gentleman if we must endure this petty vengeance? And under the guise of the law?"

"As long as Witsen and half of the tidewater is in debt to the Wilkensons," Bickerstaff said, "then the Wilkensons are the law."

"They are the law on land, sir, but now I am the law on the sea."

The law on the sea. He was that, and that very morning the people of Williamsburg had had a very dramatic demonstration of the fact, as fifteen men were marched to the gibbet set up on the tidal flats of the James River and hanged by the neck until dead.

It was just two years before that an Act of Assembly had given the colonies the right to try men for piracy, rather than transport the accused to London, and Nicholson had leapt at that chance, for he hated piracy with a nearly religious zeal. A court of oyer and terminer had been appointed, a jury sworn in, and the men captured on the beach on Smith Island brought up on charges for their crimes.

It had not been a lengthy trial.

From the start of the thing it seemed unlikely that the men would be found innocent, even if the evidence against them had been less overwhelming. But as it happened, there were a few mariners in the tidewater whose ships had been taken and plundered by the accused, and they provided a most damning testimony. That, combined with what Marlowe had to tell and the evidence found aboard the *Patricia Clark*, was more than enough to find them all guilty.

The three youngest among them were given life in prison in consideration of their youth. A fourth managed to convince the jury that he had been forced against his will to join the pirates—a not uncommon occurrence—and he had been set free.

The rest had been sentenced to die.

Sheriff Witsen had his orders. "You are to hang the said Pyrates upon a Gibbet to be executed by you for that purpose up by the neck until they be dead, dead, dead . . ."

And that was what he had done, before an enthralled crowd of four hundred men, women, and children who lined the banks of the James River. It took two hours to kill them all. The people gasped and shook their heads, pointed to the swinging bodies, showed their children what became of those who did not mind their parents.

It had been a high time for Marlowe, who was once more the center of attention. All of the great men of the tidewater made a point to congratulate him again, to be seen in company with him. Governor Nicholson sat by his side for the duration of the thing. The only thing missing to complete his happiness was Elizabeth, but she had told him, in a tone of disgust, that she had no stomach for such things and would not attend.

Bickerstaff had kindly waited until the end of the day to inform him of what had happened to the tobacco crop during his absence.

They sat in silence for a long moment, Marlowe and Bickerstaff and King James. Marlowe could feel the anger receding again, receding for good. In its place, an objective view of the situation. "It's damned awkward, you know," he said at last. "We shall have no profit from the plantation this year. I'll have to pay the hands out of pocket, as well as buy all of our supplies."

Of course, he had taken from the pirates three times what the crop would have fetched, and hoped to do more of the same, but he did not care to tell Bickerstaff as much. Still, he had hoped to use the crop to explain his sudden increase in wealth. Now he would have to be more circumspect about spending the money.

But those considerations were nothing compared to the great insult he had suffered at the Wilkensons' hands. What they did was beyond the pale, and more so because it was dressed in the guise of law enforcement. It could not go unanswered.

"You know, Tom," Bickerstaff looked up from the table, "I'm not one for vengeance—it is the Lord's domain, not ours. Nor do I care to see this thing go on. But setting your people free is one of the most decent things you have ever done, and it was their profit, innocents that they are, that the Wilkensons destroyed, as well as yours. It grieves me to see them get away with such egregious behavior."

"It grieves me as well."

"Yes, well, it occurs to me that in your position as captain of the guardship, your duty is not just to chase pirates. It is also your duty to enforce His Majesty's trade and navigation laws."

That was absolutely true. Marlowe had all but forgotten that part of it, which was no surprise since he had never intended to enforce them. There was no profit in it. Waste of time. What was more, he intended to raise his stock among the planters and aristocrats of the tidewater. Levying fines on those very people, making them obey the law, would accomplish little to that end.

Marlowe stared out the window, pondering Bickerstaff's oblique suggestion. The Wilkensons could work the laws ashore to their own advantage, but he, Marlowe, was the law on the sea.

"You are quite right, Bickerstaff, quite right," Marlowe said at last, and smiled for the first time since hearing the news. "I have been shamefully negligent in my duty. If George and Jacob Wilkenson will keep an eye on the quality of the colony's tobacco, and so selflessly defend the good name of the tidewater planters, then it is only fair that I should do the same."

Chapter 18

ONCE A year the great fleet of merchant ships from England and the colonies assembled in Hampton Roads to take on board the eighty thousand or so hogshead casks containing the year's tobacco crop from Virginia and Maryland. It took nearly one hundred and fifty ships to carry it all, and the duty on that crop, when it was unloaded in England, would yield the government £300,000 sterling.

The government was thus highly motivated to see that it got there.

For that purpose, the *Plymouth Prize*, with her clean and tight bottom, fresh rigging, new sails, and now enthusiastic crew, dropped down from Point Comfort and took up her station, anchored to windward of the fleet. She would escort the tobacco ships one hundred leagues from land, through the cordon of seagoing vultures that hovered around the Capes, and out into the deep water where they would be protected by the vastness of the ocean.

One hundred leagues from Land's End in England, on the other side of the Atlantic, another ship of the Royal Navy would rendezvous with the fleet and escort it to London, protecting it from the dangers lurking in the English Channel. And thus the great wealth rising from the earth of the Crown Colonies poured into Old England, and the taxes on that wealth poured into the government that had organized the whole affair.

And His Majesty's naval representative in the colony, the man who exercised ultimate authority over the fleet once it had passed beyond the purview of Governor Nicholson, was one Thomas Marlowe, Esq., Master of HMS *Plymouth Prize*.

He was all but laughing with anticipation as he clambered up the side of the *Wilkenson Brothers*.

The *Brothers* was the merchant vessel owned by the Wilkensons, one of the few families wealthy enough to ship their tobacco in their own bottom. Few planters owned ships. Most had to contract independent merchantmen to carry their crop.

The *Wilkenson Brothers* was a big ship for a merchantman, and well armed. Indeed, as far as size and firepower was concerned, she was more powerful than the *Plymouth Prize*, and she would have been quite able to see to her own defense if the Wilkensons had shipped enough sailors to simultaneously sail the vessel and fight her.

But they had not, because they did not care to spend that much money, and because they would never have found that many seamen even if they had wanted to. There were precious few qualified mariners to go around, and each vessel had just enough men to sail her, and not one more.

Marlowe stepped through the gangway and onto the deck, stepped aside to make way for Bickerstaff, directly behind him, and the dozen or so armed and dangerous-looking men from the *Plymouth Prize* who were following him.

George Wilkenson was aboard, as was his father, just as Marlowe had hoped they would be. He was staging the show for their benefit. They had been conferring with the master of the vessel up until the moment they spotted the *Plymouth Prize*'s long boat heading toward them. Now the three men stood by the main fife rail, an early frost in their eyes, arms folded, awaiting an explanation of this most unwelcome intrusion.

"What is the meaning of this? You were not invited aboard this ship, sir, and you are not welcome," Jacob Wilkenson said. He looked like he might explode.

"I understand, sir," Marlowe replied, "and I would not presume to call were it not that duty required it."

"Duty? What duty have you here?"

"As captain of the guardship, it is my duty to see the enforcement of His Majesty's laws concerning trade and navigation, and so I am doing my inspection of the fleet."

"The fleet? You are trespassing aboard my vessel, not the fleet. Is this some kind of trick you are playing, some petty harassment?"

"Nothing of the sort. I shall inspect all the vessels, if time allows. I am simply starting with yours. Now, pray, break open the hatches and let us sway out a few hogsheads for inspection."

"Break open . . ." the master sputtered, speaking for the first time. "Why, we've just got everything stowed down, and hatches clapped down and battened."

"Well, sir," Marlowe said, "unbatten and unclap."

"We shall do nothing of the sort," said Wilkenson with finality.

"Very well, then, I shall do it myself." He gestured to the Prizes and they fell to unbattening the hatch, knocking the wedges out to free the tarpaulins.

"No, no, no time for that," Marlowe said. "Ax men, just cut it open. Just cut through the tarpaulins and grating."

The four men in the boarding party whom Marlowe had ordered to carry axes leapt up on the hatch and raised the blades over their heads.

"No, no, belay that!" the master shouted, mere seconds before Marlowe's men destroyed his tarpaulins and hatch gratings. "Boatswain, see the hatches broke open."

The guardship's men stood in silence as the *Brothers* boatswain and his gang undid a morning's worth of work, hauling back tarpaulins and lifting off the gratings. The stay tackle was let off and swung out over the gaping hatch, and three of the Prizes climbed down into the dark hold with slings to go around the casks.

George Wilkenson and his father and the master watched

with sullen expressions, arms folded. They said not a word, but Marlowe knew that their silence would be short-lived.

Twenty minutes later, the Prizes had a half-dozen hogsheads swayed out and standing on the deck. Marlowe looked them over, walking slowly between them, shaking his head. "This does not look good, I fear. Bickerstaff, be so kind as to measure this."

Bickerstaff laid his measuring stick across the top of the cask and then against its side, and he shook his head as well. "Thirty-six inches on the head, fifty-two inches tall."

"Thirty-six . . ." Marlowe said. "Is that true for all of them?"

Bickerstaff moved down the line, measuring each. "Yes, I fear. They are all the same."

"Well, sir," said Marlowe, turning to Wilkenson, "this is a bit of a problem. A legal-sized hogshead is thirty-two inches by forty-eight inches. I might have looked away, you know, had just one or two of these been a bit oversized, but as it is we shall have to measure them all."

George Wilkenson's mouth fell open, Jacob's eyes narrowed with rage. "Measure them all?" George managed to say. "Do you propose that we sway them all out to be measured?"

"I see no other way that it might be done."

"Oh, to hell with you and your petty harassment!" Jacob Wilkenson shouted. "You do not fool me, you are just trying to get back at us for condemning your trash tobacco. Well, it *was* trash, sir, and we were within our legal right to burn it! It was our duty!"

"And I am likewise within my right to inspect your casks, and it is likewise my duty. And from what I have seen so far, you are in violation of the law."

The Wilkensons and the master of their ship stared at Marlowe for a long second but said nothing.

The salient fact—and every man aboard knew it—was that Marlowe was absolutely right. The hogsheads were above the legal size.

What they also knew, though it was hardly worth pointing

out, was that every hogshead in the fleet was above legal size. With duties and handling charges set per the hogshead and not by the pound of tobacco contained within, it was a great savings for the planters to cheat a bit on the size of their casks, and most customs officers, for some small consideration, looked the other way. They all did it, which was how Marlowe knew he would catch Wilkenson in the crime. But their all doing it did not make it any more legal.

"Damn your impudence, who do you think you are?" Jacob Wilkenson broke the silence. "You most certainly will not sway out our entire cargo!"

"Indeed? And who shall stop me?" The Plymouth Prizes were gathered in a semicircle behind their captain, looking every bit the band of bloody cutthroats, with pistols and cutlasses thrust into their sashes, axes and muskets cradled in arms, and their heads bound in bright-colored cloth.

"You do not scare us, you and your band of villainous pirates," the master growled.

"We have no interest of scaring you, sir, only in enforcing the law. And it looks as if there is quite a bit of enforcing that needs doing."

"Look, Marlowe," George Wilkenson spoke. His voice was low, his tone reasonable. "If we are in violation of the law, by some unhappy mistake, then I apologize for that. Levy the fine and we'll pay it and be done with it. After all, the convoy sails in two days."

"The convoy, sir, sails when I say it sails. And as to—"

"I say, Captain Marlowe?" Bickerstaff called up from the hold where he had gone down to inspect. "I say, look here." He emerged from the scuttle, and in his hand was a clump of fragrant brown tobacco.

"Is this bulk tobacco? Surely they are not carrying bulk tobacco?"

"Great mounds of the stuff, crammed into every corner of the ship." Bulk tobacco, tobacco shipped loose and not prized into a hogshead, had been strictly prohibited by act of Parliament since 1698, though, like the oversize casks, it was unlikely that any ship in the convoy was not carrying it, so profitable was it in clandestine sales.

"Why, sir," Marlowe turned to the Wilkensons and the master, "I am shocked, shocked to find this. This is no more than smuggling, damn me, and you one of the leading families in the colony. I am sorry, but I cannot let this go."

"Just levy the damned fine and get off my ship!" Jacob Wilkenson all but shouted.

"This is beyond a fine, sir. Either you will get this tobacco in hogsheads of a legal size, and the bulk as well, or you shall not sail."

"Not sail?" the master growled. "And how do you propose to keep us from sailing?"

"By removing every sail from your ship, sir, if you do not comply. Now I suggest you get to work. You've a great deal to do."

Less than three hours later the *Wilkenson Brothers* looked like a beehive, with workers swarming over her, racing to get the cargo in order before the sailing of the fleet. Even if it had been legal to sail unescorted, which it was not, it would have been suicide, with the pirates that swarmed around the Capes and infested the sea between the coast of America and the Caribbean.

Of course, pirates would not even be an issue after Marlowe took their sails.

Marlowe imagined that the Wilkensons had considered complaining to the governor, but they would have realized that doing so would be folly. What would they say to him? That Marlowe was being unfair in forcing them to obey the law?

Rather, they and their people worked like men possessed to make their cargo legal. They brought new hogsheads down on sloops, from where, Marlowe did not know, and laboriously hoisted each old cask out of the hold and broke it open to reprize its contents into the new, smaller cask.

The tobacco on the Wilkensons' ship, having been prized once already, was much easier to prize again, but still this operation consumed two full days, with the men of the *Plym-*

outh Prize laying odds and making wagers on whether or not they would finish in time. When Marlowe found himself unable to sleep he would take a turn on the guardship's deck, and from there he could see the sailors and the field hands toiling by lantern light in the waist of the *Wilkenson Brothers*, breaking open hogsheads, emptying them, reprizing the tobacco, and storing them down again.

On several occasions the Wilkensons sent a man over to invite Marlowe to inspect their progress, for fear no doubt that he would demand the new casks be brought up again once they were stowed down. He declined these invitations, each time sending his word as a gentleman that he would trust another gentleman to honor his agreement and the law.

Two days later, with the tobacco fleet making ready to sail, the job was done. The Wilkensons' sloop cast off from the ship's side and began to beat northwest up the James River, and from the deck of the *Plymouth Prize* Marlowe could hear the ringing of hammers as the wedges in the battens were driven home. He was impressed. He never thought they would finish in time.

"Boarding party, are you ready?" Marlowe asked. Gathered in the waist was another armed party, much the same as the first, but bigger.

"Ready, sir," said Lieutenant Rakestraw, leading the gang.

"Very good. Into the boat, then."

"Tom," said Bickerstaff, standing at Marlowe's side, "is this entirely necessary? Have we not had vengeance enough?"

"What we put those bastards through was a mere annoyance compared to the damage they have done us. Look here, Francis, you made the point yourself. Burning our crop does little harm to you and me. It's the field hands who suffer. It is more their loss than anyone's."

"You are not doing this for the field hands. This will not restore their crop. I fear we are only prolonging our pointless warfare with the Wilkensons."

"Nonsense. This will put an end to it, and will give us assurance that such will never happen again. I must go." With that Marlowe climbed down into the boat, unwilling to discuss a decision that he had already made.

Once again he climbed up the side of the Wilkensons' ship, an armed band at his back. The ship did not look nearly as tidy and bravely rigged as she had two days before. There were bits of wood, clumps of tobacco, broken barrel staves, and hoops scattered about. Rigging lay in great piles on the deck. The men looked utterly exhausted, as if they had hardly slept in days, which, in fact, they had not.

The Wilkensons were there, Jacob furious at Marlowe's effrontery, George weary and afraid.

"Marlowe, what in all hell is it now?" Jacob Wilkenson demanded. "I was fool enough to accept your word as a gentleman that there would be no more inspections."

"And none there shall be," Marlowe said brightly. "If you say the cargo is legally done, then I am composed of trust. But there is just one more matter."

Wilkenson and the master exchanged glances, a mutual dread of what Marlowe would say next. A well-founded dread, as it happened.

"I am short of men," Marlowe said, "having not replaced my casualties from the battle of Smith Island. I fear I shall need some of the men from your company to man the guardship."

"You think you will press men out of my ship? You can't be serious."

"Oh, but I am. We all must sacrifice, you know, for the good of all. The guardship needs men enough to protect the tobacco fleet."

Jacob Wilkenson took a step forward, his lips pursed, and Marlowe could well imagine what he was about to say, but he never had the chance. The master grabbed him by the arm and pulled him back, and in a tone of weary resignation asked, "How many men do you want, Marlowe?"

"Oh, I should think eight would do it. These men here, for starters." Marlowe indicated the five men who were just lying back to deck after having loosened off topsails and topgallants. The fact that they were working aloft, and working the topsails, told him that they were the foremost hands on the Wilkensons' ship.

"Eight hands!" This announcement shook the master from his resignation. "But that's half my men! I can't sail if you take eight men!"

"Indeed?" The Plymouth Prizes under Rakestraw's direction had already herded the topmen and three others and were standing in a semicircle around this group of exhausted, confused, and increasingly angry men.

"Look here, Marlowe," said George Wilkenson, trying once more to be the voice of reason. "You have taken your revenge for what you perceive as our crime against you. But this is too much. You know full well that we will lose a whole year's crop if we do not sail. There are no more seamen to be found on the Chesapeake."

"I know all too well about the paucity of seamen in these colonies. That is why I must take yours."

"If you need men," said the master, "why d'ya not take one from each of a dozen ships?"

"I could," Marlowe admitted. "But I will not."

"God damn you!" Jacob Wilkenson exploded at last. "You cannot do this! You cannot press men without the governor's consent! You are breaking the law, you blackballing bastard!"

At this Marlowe looked around in dramatic fashion and said, "I see no law here, sir, other than myself."

"Get off my ship."

"Very well. Lieutenant Rakestraw, see these men down into the longboat." Rakestraw, with many a push and strong word, began to file the unfortunate men down the ship's side and into the *Prize*'s longboat.

"Marlowe, you bastard, you whore's son!" Jacob Wilkenson was across the deck in an instant. He grabbed Marlowe by the collar, and before Marlowe could react jerked him close so their faces were inches apart. "You'll not get away with this, you bastard, d'ya hear? You upstart, coming to this place and worming your way into command of the guardship. . . ."

Marlowe said not a word but reached down to his cross-belt, unclipped a pistol, brought it up between them.

"You think you have the governor in your pocket, sir, but let me assure you—" Jacob continued, then stopped as he felt the cold circle of steel, the end of the barrel pressed into the soft flesh under his chin. He faltered in his harangue. Marlowe drew back the cock.

"Please unhand me," Marlowe said. Wilkenson's grip went slack and Marlowe stepped away, easing the cock of his pistol down. "Another of your family had the temerity to insult me thus, and you were witness to his fate. Be thankful I do not demand satisfaction of you. However, if you wish to meet me like a man, you need just tell me. If not, I will thank you to keep your mouth shut."

The Wilkensons stood staring their hatred at him but said nothing. Marlowe knew they would not rise to the bait. Matthew Wilkenson's arrogance might have been marked by bold stupidity, but Jacob Wilkenson was more cunning than that, and George was the kind of coward who would be devious rather than openly aggressive.

"Very well, then," Marlowe said, "let this be an end to it." He bid them both good day and followed Lieutenant Rakestraw down into the crowded longboat.

Let this be an end to it. He might well hope for that. They all might hope for that, but Marlowe knew it would never be, his words to Bickerstaff notwithstanding.

He had seen enough of that kind of conflict, faction against faction, to know that the only way for it to end would be for one or the other side to admit defeat or for one side to finish the other off.

And Marlowe knew that neither he nor the Wilkensons would ever admit defeat.

Chapter 19

It took the *Plymouth Prize* and *Northumberland* and the hundred and fifty ships of the tobacco convoy the better part of a day to up anchor and make sail. They started well before dawn, and by late afternoon the wide rendezvous at Hampton Roads, once crowded with anchored vessels, was entirely empty, save for the forlorn and nearly deserted *Wilkenson Brothers*.

With late afternoon giving way to early evening, convoy and escort filed out of the great Chesapeake Bay. They wound their way past the Middle Ground Shoal that lay like a submarine trap between the welcoming arms of Cape Henry and Cape Charles and stood out for the open sea, where the only thing between them and England was water. Water and pirates.

It was an awesome sight, that great mass of sail, making their easting in two columns, windward and leeward. One hundred and fifty ships bearing the wealth of the New World home to the Old.

Marlowe, standing on the quarterdeck of the *Plymouth Prize*, took a moment to savor the vision. There was a time in his life when he might have regarded such a fleet with rapacious desire, but now he found, much to his surprise, he was filled with paternal concern.

With that thought he moved his gaze beyond the convoy.

He could still make out the *Northumberland*'s topsail, though the sloop was hull down to the east. He had sent her ahead, with King James in command, to keep an eye out for what lay over the horizon. Even that small vessel was faster than the great lumbering merchantmen.

Marlowe understood that the first few days would be the most dangerous. Once the tobacco fleet was well out in the deep water they would be safe from attack, for the trackless ocean was too vast for the pirates to go hunting about.

Instead, the Brethren of the Coast tended to stay close to those harbors where they knew shipping would be found. Marlowe had little doubt that they would meet with some of them in the one hundred leagues for which he would accompany the convoy. It had been only a few years since the conclusion of King William's War, when many legitimate privateers suddenly found themselves out of business and so made the short step to piracy. Now they swarmed like vermin around the Capes.

It was Marlowe's insight into the mind of the pirate that led to the victory on Smith Island, and he hoped that that alone would continue to make him a dangerous enemy, for he had no formal knowledge of how to escort a convoy. Though he had sauntered about and spoke with the masters of the ships with such great confidence that they all took heart in his command of the situation, he was still doing it all quite extemporaneously.

Thus, it was no surprise that his methods were unorthodox, and it was exactly that unorthodoxy that inspired the confidence of the merchant captains.

It did little, however, to inspire those half-dozen young men of the *Plymouth Prize*'s crew who were strutting about the quarterdeck, clad in the silk dresses that Marlowe had commandeered from the pirate booty on Smith Island, parasols held daintily over their heads, shooting foul looks in Marlowe's direction.

They seemed quite put out, though Marlowe had assured them they looked absolutely charming. He had further assured them that they might run into brigands as soon as they cleared the Capes, and they had to be ready in their disguise.

There were a few things that Marlowe knew for certain about any upcoming encounter with pirates. One was that the *Plymouth Prize* could never hope to catch a pirate vessel. She was much faster now, for her clean bottom and new sails and tackling, but she was still no match for a swift enemy, and pirates ships, by their nature, were always swift.

The best he could hope for was to drive them away, but that was not good enough. The brigands would hang about, lurking on the edges of the convoy, waiting to pick off a slow or damaged vessel. They would follow the tobacco fleet all the way to England if need be.

What was more, there was little glory in merely chasing a pirate off, and no profit whatsoever. No, the only thing to do was to engage the enemy, beat him, and take him. And the only way a pirate would engage a man-of-war was if he did not recognize her as such.

"Here, darling, whadda ya say you give a piece of it to your daddy here, eh?" one of the Plymouth Prizes called aft to one of his mates in a low-cut red silk dress, and this, as it always did, brought howls of laughter.

"Stow it, you whore's son bastard, or I'll do it for you," the man in the red dress snarled, apparently offended by the proposition. Marlowe thought of Elizabeth. She would have parried the ribald suggestion with more finesse. She would have looked better in the dress, as well.

"Now, don't let them jab you like that," he said, trying to bolster the man's spirits, but Marlowe was grinning as well, and that tended to diminish his sincerity.

The costumed hands were stamping around, swearing and spitting and making a big show of playing the men, making certain that everyone knew they were not enjoying this. It was too bad they felt the need to do that, Marlowe thought. When pirates used that ruse they saw the fun in it, turned it into a great frolic. Of course, they were generally drunk when they did.

Marlowe did know enough about convoys to know that one would expect an escorting man-of-war to be in the lead and to windward of the ships she was protecting. But that was not where he placed the *Plymouth Prize*. The guardship was halfway back in the line, her gunports shut tight, no bunting flying from her mastheads, and women, or so it appeared, walking about her quarterdeck. As far as anyone could tell, she was just another of the great convoy of merchantmen.

In the man-of-war's station, under the dual command of her master and Lieutenant Rakestraw, was the five-hundred-ton merchantman *Sarah and Kate*. Like most big merchantmen, she was well armed. Her sides were painted a bright yellow to accentuate her gunports, and her rigging was ablaze with all the bunting from the *Prize's* flag locker. She looked every inch the man-of-war.

When the pirates attacked they would know to avoid the *Sarah and Kate*. And they would know to attack the *Plymouth Prize*. Marlowe would see to that.

The masters of the ships in the convoy had wholeheartedly supported this idea.

The Capes were still in sight, low and black, when the sun set behind them and Marlowe allowed his disgruntled men to take off their dresses. He gave them each two extra tots of rum, which did much to mollify them, and settled the ship into her nighttime routine.

They stood on through the dark hours with a fair breeze and Polaris two points off the larboard bow, just one of thousands of stars on the great dome. The convoy spread out to lessen the chance of collision, and the rising sun found the fleet covering many miles of ocean.

Rakestraw in the *Sarah and Kate* and Marlowe in the *Plymouth Prize* spent the chief of the morning getting them back into some kind of order.

"Oh, that stupid son of a bitch!"

Marlowe pounded the rail in exasperation as the merchantman he was trying to herd into line suddenly tacked across the *Prize's* bow, forcing her to fall off to avoid a collision.

It had been that way all morning, and Marlowe had endured about all that he could when the man at the masthead called down a thankful distraction.

"Deck there! *Northumberland*'s in sight, hull down and running with all she can set!"

Indeed, Marlowe thought. King James had orders not to rejoin the convoy for one hundred leagues unless it was to report the presence of some danger, and pirates were the danger they were most likely to encounter. And if he was pushing the sloop that fast, Marlowe reckoned, then pirates it must be, and trying hard to overhaul him.

"Mr. Middleton, a white ensign to the foremast head and a gun to windward, if you please," he called out. That was the signal he had arranged with Lieutenant Rakestraw. It meant that pirates were about, and that he should act his part as man-of-war while the *Plymouth Prize* assumed her own disguise.

The second officer made the signal and it was acknowledged, and Marlowe eased the *Plymouth Prize* closer to the pack of merchantmen, just one more among many.

It took the *Northumberland* an hour or so to run down on the convoy, and per his orders King James hauled up to the *Sarah and Kate* first and reported to Rakestraw before running down to the *Plymouth Prize*.

The sloop passed the guardship's windward side about a hundred feet away, then swooped around like a gull riding a strong breeze and fell in alongside. King James, standing on the quarterdeck, looked like the Moor of Venice with his cutlass and pistols, his head bound in cloth, his loose shirt snapping in the breeze.

"They's pirates, sir," he called, disdaining the use of a speaking trumpet, his voice clear like a musket shot. "Ship rigged, two hundred ton or thereabouts. They come about when they sees us and chases us, cracking on like madmen. I reckon they should be visible now, mebbe hull up!"

At that very moment the lookout aloft reported the strange sail, calling down that topsails and topgallants were visible to the southeast and coming up fast.

"Well done, James," Marlowe said. "And mind you keep clear when the iron starts to fly."

"Aye, sir," he said, clearly intending to do no such thing.

"Very good. Carry on."

King James bowed at the waist and then shouted out an order, and the *Northumberland* sheered off with that grace of motion she always displayed when well handled, like an expert dancer.

Bickerstaff, who had just gained the quarterdeck, watched the *Northumberland* sail off, then turned to Marlowe and said, "Buccaneers, is it?"

"So it would appear. Nothing else would explain their behavior."

Marlowe stepped up to the rail that ran along the break of the quarterdeck. Most of the Plymouth Prizes were on deck, and most looking aft, waiting for word of what would happen next. They were a more confident tribe than the one Marlowe had led to Smith Island, but not so used to a fight that they regarded it with disdain.

"Listen here, you men," he shouted. "You all heard what James had to say. If those are pirates yonder we have to lure them to us, and then give them the greeting they deserve. You know what to do. Let us clew up the sails and get to it."

And get to it they did, for during the time that the *Plymouth Prize* had ridden at her anchor waiting for the convoy to assemble, Marlowe had drilled them again and again until they could carry out his plan with no thought at all, which was all the thought he wanted from them.

They clewed up the sails and the guardship stopped dead in her wake, then they raced forward and aloft. First they struck the spritsail topsail yard, then pulled the little spritsail topmast out of the trestle trees at the far end of the bowsprit and let it hang from a tangle of rigging in a most unsightly fashion.

They did much the same to the fore topgallant mast and yard, and left them both hanging high over the deck in a great mess of rope and spar and canvas. It took less than ten minutes, and in that time they had managed to create an impressive amount of wreckage aloft.

They reset topsails just as the last of the line of tobacco ships passed them, leaving them behind, a damaged vessel unable to keep station, bucking in the small chop churned up by the fleet's passing.

From the deck Marlowe could just make out the *Sarah and Kate* through his glass. Rakestraw had her right on station, a glory of bunting waving in the morning breeze. And to leeward of her, in two great columns, sailing large with all plain sail set, was the tobacco fleet, running their easting down.

But the pirates would not be interested in a close-packed, well-armed and -escorted convoy. Not when there was a single merchantman wallowing astern, her spritsail topmast and fore topgallant mast and yard obviously carried away in some collision in the dark. The convoy and the man-of-war would leave her to her fate; they could not stop for one ship.

"Those gentlemen who are designated ladies, pray get in your dresses," Marlowe called down into the waist.

Bickerstaff was silent as he stared at the wreckage aloft. At last he spoke. "This is a dangerous game you play, Marlowe. Have you thought it well out?"

"I have. I cannot imagine that they will attack an escorted convoy when—"

"No, not that. I mean this game of capturing pirates." He glanced around the quarterdeck. They were alone on the weather side, and only the helmsmen and the quartermaster were to leeward and they were out of earshot. "Have you considered what will happen if one of them should recognize you?"

"I have. I have considered it well," Marlowe lied. The truth was that he had not really considered it at all. He had only some vague thought that anyone who might recognize him would be killed in battle, or put to the sword afterward. "I cannot imagine that anyone would believe the word of a pirate, particularly one with so obvious a reason to want to sully my good name."

"Perhaps. But proof is not always necessary to ruin one's good name. That was true in London, and I find it is doubly true in the colonies. The mere suggestion of something unto-ward is often enough."

"Well, then," Marlowe said with a forced smile, "let us see that any such a person is killed in battle. But recall that it has been some time, and these people do not tend to live so long."

"Perhaps" was all that Bickerstaff said.

For the remainder of the morning and into the afternoon the convoy sailed on and the pirate closed with them. Marlowe took a glass and climbed up into the maintop and from there scanned the horizon and scrutinized the approaching vessel. It was not unusual for a pirate to have two or three ships, but that villain had only one. A big one, to be sure, bigger than average, but still only one.

Once the pirates had closed to within a mile or so of the convoy, Rakestraw crowded sail onto the *Sarah and Kate* and charged after them, an enraged bull going after the dog that had wandered into his field. Ensigns and banners and jacks of all description flew from various parts of her rig and Rakestraw fired great guns right and left, making quite a show of it, though he had no hope of hitting anything. He was not really trying to. He just wanted the pirates to know whom they should avoid.

"Ladies, come along, we need you aft," Marlowe shouted down the scuttle to the half-dozen young men who were quite purposely procrastinating about getting into their dresses. This set the tribe laughing and hollering, as Marlowe knew it would. It was cruel of him to tease them thus, and he knew it, particu-larly as they were only following his orders, but it helped to ease the building tension on the *Prize*'s deck. Besides, Marlowe enjoyed a good laugh as much as any man before the mast.

At last, to many a cheer and off-color suggestion, the six men sauntered aft and the guardship's disguise was complete. Marlowe ordered up the rum.

"On deck! Pirate's sheered off from the convoy!"

"Very good," Marlowe called aloft, then swung his glass outboard. The pirate ship, which had been closing with the convoy, had hauled her wind, running from the great bluster being made by Mr. Rakestraw and the *Sarah and Kate*. "I'll reckon they see easier pickings," he said to Bickerstaff.

"Mr. Middleton," he turned to the acting first officer, "let us have a couple of men out on the bowsprit pretending to repair that spritsail topmast and a few more aloft pretending to work on the topgallant gear."

"Aye, sir."

Marlowe looked around the deck. The Prizes had finished quaffing their liquid courage. "Mr. Bickerstaff, you'll see to our defense?"

"I should be delighted."

Bickerstaff rounded up the men and positioned them in accordance to the plan they had devised. Marlowe found it quite amusing to watch him, in his fussy, pendantic way, enlighten the crew as to how best they could slaughter a murderous enemy. But the men had come to respect Bickerstaff, thanks in part to the fine drills in sword and pistol that he offered, but due mostly to his timely arrival and hard fighting at Smith Island.

As demurely as the schoolchildren with whom Bickerstaff had spent a majority of his adult life, the men of the *Plymouth Prize* loaded pistols and sharpened cutlasses and readied the great guns for that first, crucial broadside. All but two of the cannon, lardboard and starboard, were loaded with grapeshot, and over that was packed nails, broken glass, odd bits of iron, whatever potentially lethal projectile could be found.

In the same manner they loaded the six small cannon, called falconets, mounted on the rail. Then the men squatted down behind the high bulwark, out of sight, and waited to be attacked.

"Listen here," Marlowe shouted down to the men in the waist. "When these sons of bitches come up with us they'll no doubt be making some noise, yelling and banging swords and chanting and such. They call it 'vaporing,' and it can be damn frightening, but it's only noise, d'ya hear? Don't let it unnerve you, because it means they're all crowded on the bulwarks, which is what we want."

Rakestraw hauled his wind and rejoined the convoy ten minutes after the pirate ship had sheered off. A minute after that the pirate wore around and turned his bow toward the *Plymouth Prize*. They looked as if they might tip over for all of the canvas they had aloft, and they closed quickly with their chosen victim.

"Very good, Mr. Bickerstaff. First gun, if you please."

"Aye, sir," Bickerstaff called, and relayed the order to the gun captain of the forwardmost gun on the starboard side. The captain touched off the powder in the touch hole, and the gun went off with a roar.

The pirate ship, though coming up fast, was still out of range of even a long cannon shot, and the ball plunged into the ocean one hundred feet short. Then the gun crew slowly reloaded and fired again, creating the illusion that the *Plymouth Prize* did not have enough men to fire more than one gun at a time, and that none too quickly.

Marlowe smiled and shook his head. The guardship would appear as pathetic and weak as a lost lamb, firing her round shot into the sea. And there was nothing that wolves loved more than a pathetic and weak lost lamb.

A quarter mile away the pirates opened up with as much broadside as would bear. Round shot whistled through the rigging and one or two even slammed into the *Prize*'s hull, but there was little damage done and no one was hurt. The pirates did not want to sink their victim. That was the last thing they wanted. What they hoped to do was frighten their victim into surrender.

And it seemed to be working, for the men crouching behind the bulwarks were starting to get wide-eyed, their fear all the greater for their not being able to see the enemy.

They might even have panicked had it not been for Bickerstaff, strolling casually up and down the deck, giving them word of what was happening and reminding them of their duty.

He would do well to remind them of the riches that they might win, Marlowe thought, but Bickerstaff was not aware of that part of the operation, and Marlowe was not looking forward to his finding out.

The pirates were two cables off when they began their vaporing.

It started soft, one man upon the quarterdeck banging the flat of his sword against the rail in a slow and steady rhythm, then another, and a third with two bones in his hands that he beat together. Soon they were joined by someone with a drum, beating along with the steady thump thump thump thump thump, and then another with a fiddle who sawed the bow across the strings in a series of short, staccato shrieks.

When the ship had closed to a cable length one of the brigands amidships, a big man with a long black beard, began to chant in a voice like a thunderclap, "Death, death, death . . ."

The chant was picked up by the others, who flocked to the rails on the quarterdeck, forecastle, and waist, and clung to the shrouds and the channels, screaming, chanting, beating the sides with swords and cutlasses, steadily increasing the tempo, the whole terrible sound shot through with the bang of pistols and the high-pitched shrieking of the pirates.

Marlowe watched, transfixed, as they came on. He was carried away by that terrifying sound, the mesmerizing, steady rhythm, coming faster and faster, louder and louder, as the pirate ship ran down on them. It was the most frightening sound in the world.

He gripped his sword with a sweating palm, swallowed hard, tried to turn his eyes away, could not. The vaporing carried him off, bringing up old terrors like silt swirled up from the bottom of a deep pool.

He had heard it before, heard it from all sides, knew the great surge of brutal energy it brought to the pirate tribe, knew the resultant horror. He had learned it all, how to be victim and tormentor, had learned it from the devil himself.

It was that devil he feared. It was not rational, he knew.

That devil was just a man, and there were no other men Marlowe feared. He had bested him once. Most likely he was dead. Marlowe assured himself he had no reason to fear that man. But the vaporing brought it all back, and he could not shake it.

At last he tore his eyes from the pirates crowding their rail and looked down into the waist of his own ship. The devil was dead. He had to be. This was not him.

He hoped that his men would not panic, that Bickerstaff could hold them together. But he could see they were being swept up by the terror of the thing. The vaporing. The sound of pending death.

Chapter 20

CAPTAIN JEAN-PIERRE LeRois stood on the quarterdeck rail, sword in his right hand, his left hand on the backstay, steadying himself. And he felt steady, he felt very steady, and completely in command of himself and his ship as the *Vengeance* closed with this poor unfortunate who had had the temerity to fire upon them.

He was all but sober, having drunk just enough to prevent the shaking, to keep the screaming to a minimum.

And his authority, for the moment, was absolute. That was the way it worked in the sweet trade.

The crew of a ship might make decisions by vote during normal times, but when they went into battle the captain's word was law, obeyed without question and without hesitation. Combat was not a time for democracy. As long as they were in a fight, LeRois was in command.

The vaporing was growing louder, building in intensity as they ran down on the crippled merchantman. The entire company of the *Vengeance* was crowded on the larboard side, screaming, pounding, firing pistols, ready to run alongside and pour onto the deck of their victim.

LeRois felt the excitement building, ready to burst out of him, the way he used to feel when he was with a woman. He opened his mouth and joined in the screaming, letting his hoarse voice mix with the layer upon layer of sound that swirled in his head.

They were going to murder these sons of whores, tear them apart. Not only had they failed to strike their flag at the sight of the *Vengeance*, a great effrontery, but they had fired on them as well, which was not to be tolerated.

There were women aboard. LeRois had seen them through his glass. They might provide days of amusement for his men.

"Hoist up the *pavillon de pouppe*, the black ensign, now!" he shouted to the men below him on the quarterdeck who were tending to the huge flag draped over the taffrail. LeRois always waited until the last second to break it out. He knew that the sudden appearance of that flag, with its leering skull and twin swords and hourglass, would wipe out any vestiges of bravery left in his victim's crew, any hint of defiance not quashed by the vaporing.

The men on the quarterdeck hauled away, and the big flag lifted up the ensign staff and snapped out in the breeze. The death's-head seemed to laugh as the cloth twisted and buckled in the wind.

The screaming built toward a crescendo, careening around in LeRois's head, and he opened his mouth and joined in again.

Half a cable length. There were not above a dozen men on the victim's deck. Those working aloft had come back down and, incredibly, were firing at the *Vengeance* with small arms, as if they wanted to inflame the Brethren more, as if they wanted their own deaths to be as horrible as could be imagined.

Fifty yards and LeRois could feel the excitement like a hot wind sweeping across the *Vengeance*'s deck. The chanting had crested and broken into disorganized screaming, and the horrible sound rolled toward the victim like surf as the pirates shouted and fired and tensed for the leap across to the dead men's ship. Halfway up the shrouds men stood on the ratlines, swinging grappling hooks in small arcs, ready to grab the other vessel in a death grip.

Twenty yards away. LeRois squinted and ran his eyes along the quarterdeck, seeking out the merchantman's captain, who would be his own to finish off. There was the helmsman, and the quartermaster, and . . .

LeRois's scream went up and up in a pitch to a shattering wail of anguish. "Son of a bitch! Son of a bitch!" he screamed. He threw his sword aside and snatched up one of the pistols draped around his neck with a ribbon and fired it blindly at the victim's quarterdeck. For there, unmistakably, was Malachias Barrett, sword in hand, pacing fore and aft, giving orders with the gestures, the stride, that LeRois knew so well.

He dropped the pistol and snatched up the next, and as he did he waited for the vision to go away, because that was what it was, he knew, a vision, just like those others that had been plaguing him more and more.

But the vision did not go away. It persisted with a tenacity that the others had not shown. LeRois felt the panic rising up in him, burning in his throat, felt the great confidence he had thus far enjoyed draining off. He screamed again and fired off his second gun, willing the specter to disappear.

The puff of smoke from the pistol obscured his view of the quarterdeck, blocking out the unholy vision, and in that instant LeRois realized that the tenor of the *Vengeance's* screaming had changed, that the vaporing had turned into something else—anger and fear and defiance.

He shifted his eyes down to the victim's waist, not fifteen yards off. The gunports were open and the great guns were running out, all at once, run out by what must have been a great many men hiding behind the bulwark.

"*Merde* . . . ," LeRois said, and then their prize seemed to explode in a blast of cannon fire. All eight guns erupted at once, blowing columns of flame across the water and filling the air with an unearthly shrieking such that not even the pirates could match.

The big guns fired straight into the densely packed pirates

along the rail and the channels, men who had no cover and nowhere to run, and they tore those men to pieces. LeRois saw bodies flung back on the deck and hanging limp in the rigging and draped over the *Vengeance*'s unmanned cannon.

"God damn you to hell! God damn you!" LeRois screamed, frenzied. A piece of langrage had cut through his sleeve and blood was dripping out of the rent. And more blood, great quantities, was running in red lines down the side of the ship, but that only made him madder still.

"Back in place! Back in place, you sons of whores!" he shouted at his men, and the dazed, stunned pirates, those who could still move, climbed back up on the rail, ready for the leap onto the enemy and the murderous sweep across his decks.

The cloud of smoke rolled away, revealing the unscathed enemy now closer still. The impact of the broadside had slowed the *Vengeance*'s momentum, but it was building again, sweeping the pirate ship down on her victim.

LeRois could see them desperately reloading the guns, leaning into the gun tackles, hauling them out. Along the rail more men—there seemed to be hundreds of them—took up the curved wooden handles of the falconets and swiveled them around, finding where the Vengeances had bunched together and blasting them with deadly fire.

And Barrett was still there.

"No, no, no! Son of a bastard, no!" LeRois screamed. He felt the hands of despair clasping his throat, choking off his words. He could not be there. He had to go. The vision had to go, to be taken up by the thin air like the times before. He fired on it again, but still it floated in front of him, pale, like a ghost, but moving with that animal intensity that he remembered, could never forget.

"No!"

The big guns fired again, from ten yards away, tearing great sections out of the *Vengeance*'s rails and rigging, killing more of his men, sending them running, leaping off the rails to the protection of the bulwarks. None of them would run below, for anyone who did would be put to death by the pirate tribe, but neither would they remain on the rail. Better to die shoulder to shoulder with one's brethren, and better still not to die at all.

There was no more than five yards between the two ships. Aboard their enemy, the wolf in sheep's clothing, the men were standing on the rail, screaming, waving cutlasses, ready to board the Vengeance, just as the pirates had been ready to board them a moment before. A grappling hook soared through the air and caught in the shrouds above LeRois's head. LeRois whipped out his dagger, severed the line.

"Fall off, fall off!" LeRois screamed at the helmsmen who had been shielded from the gunfire by the men on the rails, and without hesitation the helmsmen spun the wheel and the Vengeance's bow turned away from their intended victim, turned away from the convoy and turned toward the open sea.

LeRois looked down into the waist of his ship. He had seen carnage before, lots of it, but he had never seen anything like that. Men lying in clumps, men crawling uselessly across the deck, men holding their guts to prevent them from spilling out. The vaporing, the triumphant shouts of a conquering tribe, had been replaced with the sobbing and whimpering and pathetic moans of wounded and dying men.

LeRois glanced quickly over his shoulder. The enemy was setting more sail, but it did not matter. The Vengeance had all her canvas already set, and she was a fast ship. She would get away this time. She would be back.

He shifted his gaze back inboard, quickly, blocking all vision of that death ship from his field of view. He glanced around to see that no one was watching him, then closed his eyes and begged God to never allow the vision of Barrett to appear again.

"Stern chase, Captain Marlowe? Captain Marlowe?"

On hearing his name the second time, Marlowe realized he was being addressed. Turned from the sight of the fleeing pirate ship, met the quartermaster's eye.

"Huh? Beg your pardon?"

"I asked, sir, stern chase? Shall we follow?" The quartermaster jerked his chin in the direction of the battered enemy.

"Oh . . ." Marlowe looked aloft. The foresail and mainsail were cast off, ready for setting. A gang of men were putting the fore topgallant gear to rights, and another was doing the same to the spritsail topsail. There was no other damage done to the *Plymouth Prize* beyond that which they had manufactured themselves.

He glanced again at the pirate. The *Plymouth Prize* could not overhaul them. Nor could they abandon the convoy and go chasing all over the ocean after the bastard. No, they had their duty. They truly did.

"Sir, are you quite all right?" the quartermaster asked with genuine concern.

"Yes, yes, fine, thank you. No, we must rejoin the convoy. Can't go running off to hell and back after him. I reckon we've done for him."

"Aye, sir," the quartermaster said, just the faintest note of disappointment in his voice. They were going to let all the plunder that the pirate might have in her hold sail off beyond their reach.

But Marlowe knew, as the quartermaster did not, that the greatest reward of all would be if that ship were to sail off and never return.

"Marlowe, Marlowe, I give you joy again on a great victory!" Bickerstaff fairly leapt up the stairs leading to the quarterdeck, hand outstretched. Marlowe automatically extended his own, and Bickerstaff pumped it with enthusiasm.

"It all happened just as you predicted, Thomas, I swear, like staging a play! We had one fellow wounded when a gun ran over his foot—the fool could not stand clear of the recoil—and another was unlucky enough to get a pistol ball in the shoulder, but beyond that there was not one casualty, and not the least wounding of the ship. I daresay you did for a good half of that brigand's company. I should think the ship owners will reward you with some recognition of your meritorious service."

Bickerstaff, in the flush of victory, was far more garrulous than was his nature, and Marlowe was relieved to find that he was not being called upon to respond. He seemed to have lost his voice.

"Did you see that villain, King James, circling around in the *Northumberland,* quite ready to board over the unengaged side if we— I say, Marlowe, are you unwell?"

"What? Oh, no, no, I'm fine. I think the great guns have unsteadied me a bit."

"Unsteadied you? You look as if you had seen a ghost."

Marlowe stared over the rail. The pirate ship was a quarter of a mile away at the end of a long, deep wake, and drawing farther away by the minute. But he could still see that black flag snapping at the ensign staff, the horrible death's-head with the twin cutlasses, the hourglass. He had not reckoned on seeing that flag again.

"A ghost?" Marlowe turned to Bickerstaff. "No, Francis, I have not seen a ghost. God help us all, I have seen the very devil himself."

Chapter 21

THEY HAD brought this disaster down upon their own heads. No, not *they*. *Him*. Jacob Wilkenson. And his beloved son Matthew. Those two, the unthinking, reactionary Wilkensons, had brought this plague upon their house.

George Wilkenson found that that realization made him oddly calm, even in the face of what was, for him, the most unthinkable of nightmares: financial ruin, a choice between poverty and tremendous debt.

How many times in the past had his father brushed him aside, cursing his timidity and showing him how the bold move was the right move? And how many times had his father been right? Every time. Until now.

Now Marlowe had done to the Wilkensons just what the Wilkensons had set out to do to Marlowe, and both, apparently, were ruined. Like two men who shoot each other in a duel.

"I have some people scouring Williamsburg and Jamestown, looking for sailors, and I have requested of the governor that he find us some men, as it was his own appointed captain who robbed us, but I despair of it doing us any good," George said.

The two men were seated in the library, the same room that a month before Jacob Wilkenson had torn apart in his rage. Now the old man was sitting in a winged chair, half staring out the window and listening to his son. He seemed utterly calm. George found it somewhat frightening.

"Bah," Jacob Wilkenson said with a wave of his hand. "It's of no use. Even if we manage to get the damned ship to London without it being taken by some bloody pirate, the market for tobacco will have fallen out. The whole goddamned fleet will have arrived two weeks before, and we'd be lucky to pay the cost of the shipping."

George Wilkenson pressed his fingertips together and made an arch of his fingers. They looked like an old-fashioned helmet to him, like the kind one pictured John Smith wearing. "The tobacco won't last until the next convoy. Are you saying, then, that we admit defeat? That Marlowe has beaten us? That we have managed to destroy one another?"

"Marlowe beaten us? Not likely. We have not begun with Marlowe, oh no. We shall crush him. That has not changed."

"Perhaps not," George said sharply. His father seemed not to grasp the gravity of the situation. "But our circumstances most certainly have. The tobacco crop was our year's income, almost. Without it we are not able to secure what we need for next year's crop. We are not able to pay the overseer nor the master of the *Wilkenson Brothers*, nor the masters of the sloops. We have equipment that needs replacing. We shall have to borrow a tremendous amount or sell off land and slaves, but either way it is our ruin. If you paid the slightest attention to the books, you would know that." There was a perverse pleasure in talking to the old man that way, even though it was George's ruin as much as his father's.

Jacob stood up from the chair and began to pace. "We are not ruined, not by any means."

"You have not seen the books—"

"Sod the damn books! I have more kettles on the fire than are shown in the books. Engaged in a business right now that'll make us twice what the damned tobacco would yield."

"What . . . business? Why have you not told me about it?"

"You ain't got the stomach for it, boy. Matthew set it up,

Matthew and me. More in his line. Not the kind of thing for a man who worries about books."

George felt his face flush, felt his calm give way to anger. Humiliated, once again. If there was one thing in which he took pride, it was his responsible handling of the Wilkensons' business affairs. Now here was his father telling him that there was some entire enterprise of which he was not even aware, something more lucrative even than the plantation, as if all the work he did amounted to no more than a side business, some minor amusement. From the grave Matthew had trumped him again.

George sat in silence as he waited for the flush of the humiliation to pass. At last he said, "You are telling me, then, that there is money enough?"

"There is money enough, and there'll be a damn sight more, as well."

"Might you tell me where this money is coming from?"

"No, I will not. It ain't a business for you."

"I take it, then, that it ain't legal, either?"

"That's none of your affair. I'll tell you how much money we got, and you can look in your damn books and tell me what we need for the plantation, and things'll work out just fine. We have no concerns now but to do for Marlowe. We can live with the loss of our crop, but I don't reckon he can. We have to watch close and see if he borrows money, or if he tries to sell the Tinling place."

George Wilkenson balled one hand into a fist and softly, rhythmically, punched it into the palm of his other hand. Everything had changed now. The arrogance, the triumph over his father's failure, gone. Seemed as if the old man had been right again, as if he really had saved the Wilkenson fortune and finished Marlowe all at once.

"Very good, then," George said. He stood up quickly. "Let me know how I may be of assistance." He could not meet his father's eye. He coughed, glanced up, and then turned and strode out of the room. Could not stand to be there another second.

They were all swimming in his head—Marlowe, his father, Matthew, Elizabeth Tinling—as he climbed the wide oak staircase, taking the stairs two at a time. He did not know where he was going, what he was doing. He was just moving by instinct. Getting away from the old man, trying to get away from his thoughts.

At the top of the stairs he stopped and looked down the hallway, flanked on either side by bedroom doors. His room was at the end, and next to it was Matthew's. He walked down the hall, approaching cautiously—why, he did not know. He grabbed the knob and twisted it and stepped inside.

The room had not been altered since Matthew's death, and George doubted that it ever would be. He knew that his father and mother sometimes went in there and sat on Matthew's bed. Sometimes he could hear sobbing. He wondered if his own death would cause so much grief, if his room would be left as some kind of shrine if he was killed.

"I wonder," he said softly, left it at that.

He stepped farther into the room, brushing his hand over the bedpost, the side table, the small secretary. He sat down in the chair in front of the secretary and began to rummage through the contents of the various pigeonholes in the desk. Notes, letters, a number of ribbons given him by young girls anxious to marry into the Wilkenson fortune.

He shook his head as he thought of it. What a miserable husband Matthew would have made, how thoughtless and cruel he would have been. Marriage would not have slowed his frenzied copulation with every girl who would lie down for him. And with all of the lovely, lovely girls in the colony who swooned over him, he was interested only in Elizabeth Tinling. He would have been a worse husband even than Joseph, if that was possible.

He pulled open a drawer and paused, thought about Elizabeth Tinling.

His hatred for her had not abated, nor had his realization that she was the way to Marlowe's downfall. His father may have found a way to ruin Marlowe financially, but George wanted more. He wanted Marlowe humiliated, scorned, and he wanted the same for the slut who was with him.

It had all been her fault, right from the beginning. If George could bring her down, then it might make Marlowe do something stupid. At the very least, it would be another knife thrust in his side.

His calling in the note of hand would be of no use, now that she was so cozy with Marlowe. He could just set her up in another place, and then he would be all the more her hero. She would be indebted to him.

But Matthew had had something on her, some leverage. George had presumed that it had gone to the grave with him, but it occurred to him that perhaps it had not.

He sifted through the contents of the drawer, tossing papers to the floor as he dug down, but there was nothing. He shut the drawer and opened the next, and again there was nothing beyond the mundane evidence of his brother's former life. The third was the same, as were all the pigeonholes and small drawers inside.

Matthew stood up and pulled the uppermost drawer out and dumped its contents on the floor, searching the drawer itself for anything that might be glued on or hidden. There was nothing, so he threw the drawer aside and pulled out the second, then the third, adding their contents to the pile on the floor, but still he found nothing.

Though he had only just thought of it, he was now convinced that Matthew had something, some real evidence hidden somewhere in his room. He tipped the secretary over, searching for some hidden place, but there was nothing out of the ordinary.

He abandoned the desk and its contents in a pile in the middle of the room and turned to the trunk at the foot of the bed. He tipped the trunk over and lifted it enough to dump out the blankets and clothing and old boots stored there into another pile on the floor. He got on hands and knees and rummaged through the pile, throwing sundry things across the floor, but still there was nothing there.

"Oh, son of a bitch, son of a bitch, where is it?" George said, giving his words the full measure of despair he felt. He tipped the night stand over and emptied its drawer out.

His eyes moved to the bureau on one wall and the small shelf of books on the other, and he decided on the books. He grabbed the first and flipped through it, but there was nothing concealed within. He grabbed the second and the third and the fourth, and still nothing, and in his anger he swept the remaining books off the shelf, hoping for something hidden behind, but there was only the wall.

He turned to the bureau and stumbled on the pile of books as he tried to cross the room. He looked down at his feet. There was a black book lying there. A Bible. And three letters half fallen out.

George leaned over and picked the Bible up, slowly, careful not to let the letters drop. He pulled them out from between the pages, slowly, like precious artifacts, and cast the Bible aside.

"Oh, Matthew, what have we here?" he whispered. Each letter was addressed to his late brother. He unfolded the top one. His eyes moved to the bottom of the page to see from whom the letter had come. There in a neat, familiar hand was written "William Tinling, Esq." Joseph Tinling's eldest son. Elizabeth's stepson. Matthew's particular friend. The return address was London.

George moved his eyes back to the top of the letter, but he could not read it because his hands were shaking. He stepped over to the bed and sat down. He closed his eyes and took a deep breath and read.

My Dear Matthew,

It was with great Delight that I read yours of the 23rd and I am pleased that all goes on well in the Colony. We have been much grieved here with the news of my Father's passing, as I have no doubt all have been there, who knew him. But with him now gone from this Life, I think I must set certain things

*straight, if only so there is no Misapprehension between you
and me that would serve to harm our dear friendship. You
may have guessed that I speak of Elizabeth, who fancies herself Elizabeth Tinling and my stepmother, though I suffer the
greatest horror at the very thought of it. . . .*

George read quickly through the letter, then closed his
eyes and forced himself to take several deep breaths and read
it again and again and again.

"Oh, my Lord," he whispered. "Oh, my Lord, my Lord."
It was no mere letter that he held in his hand. It was the first
step toward the ruination of Elizabeth. And when she went
down, Marlowe would not be far behind.

He sat and stared at the pile of books on the floor and
thought about his next move, planning out each step, examin-
ing each possible cause and effect like a chess player, intent
on his game.

The sun was gone and Matthew's bedroom was cast in the
gloom of the early evening when George finally stood up. He
ignored the wreckage that he had created as he crossed the
room and stepped out into the hall. He had no time for a dead
man's room. He had a great deal yet to do.

Chapter 22

THE NORTHUMBERLAND stood in past Cape Henry, beat southwest through Hampton Roads, and reached up the James River with the tide. It was six days after the *Plymouth Prize's* fight with the pirate, and somewhere out on the big ocean Marlowe was about to bid the fleet goodbye.

King James laughed out loud to see the forlorn *Wilkenson Brothers* still at anchor in the Roads, all but abandoned. With the fleet gone there were not enough sailors left in all Virginia or Maryland to get her under way.

In the long shadows of the evening James luffed the sea sloop up to the dock at Jamestown. Two of the Northumberlands leapt onto the wooden platform and the two still aboard tossed them the dock lines. Twenty minutes later, the sloop looked as if it had never gone to sea.

"All right, boys, I reckon you can have a run ashore," James said, and in the gathering dark he could see four heads nodding. "I need you back here noon tomorrow, not one damned second later," James continued. This was greeted with four of the most sincere promises, then the crew of the *Northumberland* scrambled over the side and was gone.

There was no trip to the secret warehouse this time, no hold full of pirate loot to conceal. The quarry had gotten clean away, which was a disappointment to the men of the *Plymouth Prize* as well as those of the *Northumberland*. After the rich haul at Smith Island, none of Marlowe's men were content anymore just to have lived through the fight.

But as it happened, the captains of the merchantmen had given Marlowe a handsome reward as thanks for his good work, and that Marlowe had shared out among the hands. He had split it up on the barrelhead and called each man up in turn, giving each a share, including those aboard the *Northumberland*, and two shares for the ones who had been wounded. That had pleased the Prizes to no end. There was nothing they would not do for Marlowe.

"Thank you, James, for your good work," Marlowe had said as he handed the former slave his gold, two shares, as was befitting an officer.

"Thank you, Captain Marlowe. I reckon a man could get used to this pirating."

King James went below to set the great cabin to rights. Two hours later, with the *Northumberland* in perfect trim fore and aft, keel to truck, he slung his haversack over his shoulder, took one last look around his command, and then hopped on to the dock and headed up the dark road.

The dusty surface of the rolling road was the color of dried bone in the moonlight, and from the woods and swamps on either hand came the sounds of frogs and crickets and a host of other night creatures. James breathed the heavy scented air, smiled to himself, quickened his pace.

Marlowe had sent the *Northumberland* in well ahead of the *Plymouth Prize*. He was worried, or so he had said, about the sloop venturing too far off shore. That was a valid concern, but James knew that it was only part of it. Marlowe also wanted to make certain that the tale of his recent victory was well known in the colony before his return. And with the men of the *Northumberland* turned loose on Williamsburg, money in their pockets, he was assured of the story being told, as much as if he had printed broadsides and pasted them on every building in the tidewater.

It was almost six miles from Jamestown to Williamsburg, but King James was well motivated and he walked quickly. It took him less than two hours to arrive at the outskirts of the capital city, a cluster of civilization amid the wilderness. One moment he was in the dark countryside, all but devoid of houses or people, and the next he was looking down Duke of Gloucester Street, lined with clapboard homes and shops, and at the far end the foundations of the new capitol building, all but lost among the stacks of material and the detritus of construction.

James moved into the shadows of the buildings, stepping slowly, noiselessly, listening to the sounds of the night, just as he had been trained to do as a boy until it had become second nature. Most people in Williamsburg did not believe in the concept of a free black man, Marlowe's words notwithstanding. No one in that city believed a black man had the right to be wandering around the streets late at night, certainly not with a pistol thrust in his belt, a cutlass at his side, such as those James was sporting. Being caught thus would be enough to see him hanged.

He moved cautiously down the street, pausing to listen and then moving again. Once he thought he heard the sound of a heel on gravel. He froze and crouched low by a tree, lost in its shadow, peering around, senses alert, but there was nothing more and he moved on.

He came at last to Elizabeth Tinling's house, the small, cozy, wood-framed home not far from the sight of the Capitol. He glanced up and down the road, and then, satisfied that there was no one there, slipped into the yard past the stable and around to the back of the house.

Lucy's room was on the first floor, in the back, just off the kitchen. It was a tiny room, no bigger than most of the closets in Marlowe's house, but it was a private room and that was a greater kindness than most slaves would ever know.

James snuck up to the window, glanced around again, and then tapped softly on the glass. He shook his head and grinned at the strangeness of the situation. A month before he would never have done this, sneaking around like some criminal just to visit a silly girl. He would have considered it far beneath his dignity.

But now, he reckoned, with all that had happened to him—command of the *Northumberland*, the fight on Smith Island, Lucy's confession of love—he had enough real dignity that he could sacrifice this little bit. And, he imagined, it would be worth the sacrifice.

He knocked again, a little harder, and Lucy appeared in the window, an amorphous form through the darkness and the wavy glass. She pushed the window open. She looked confused, sleepy, a bit annoyed, but when she saw James she smiled wide. The sleep vanished from her eyes.

She was wearing only a cotton shift, and the thin material draped off her body in such a way that it accentuated her breasts and the curve of her waist. She could not have been more enticing if she were wearing nothing at all. Her soft brown hair fell forward over her shoulders and hung in big ringlets around her neck.

"What are you doing, sneaking around, looking like some kind of pirate?" she asked.

"Whatever it is that pirates want, ma'am, that's what I come for." James smiled back at her.

"You best get in here before someone hangs you for a thief." Lucy stepped aside, and James silently hoisted himself through the window. She shut it and turned to him, and he put his hands around her small waist, drew her close, and kissed her.

Lucy put her hands against his chest, so tiny against his bulk, and kissed back, demurely at first and then with a growing passion. She ran her hands over his neck and his hair, and he relished the feel of her thin, strong body, her smooth and perfect skin under the cotton shift.

"Oh, James," she said softly, then put her hands against his chest and pushed away, just slightly, so that James was still able to hold her in his arms. "Tell me that you love me, James. You ain't too proud to say that, are you?"

James looked into her dark eyes, childlike and sincere. Not so long ago he would have been too proud. Not so long ago he would not have been able to love her, or anyone. But a great deal had changed.

"I do love you."

"Will you marry me, if my mistress gives permission?"

James felt a shot of anger go through him at the thought that Lucy would need permission of her mistress, her owner, before she could marry, as if she were some kind of livestock for breeding. And what would marriage mean to them? Would they be able to live together, to sleep together as man and wife?

"James, I'm sorry," Lucy said. "Don't be angry with me. I just . . . I want to be your wife."

James pulled her tight and held her against his chest. "That ain't it. Of course I'll marry you. I'd be proud to marry you," he said. And he meant it, absolutely.

"You think I'm just a silly girl, I know it. But you'd be surprised if you knew all there was to know about me, the things I thought up and done."

Lucy turned her face up to him and kissed him again, even more passionately this time, and he kissed her back with a desperate longing, kissed her mouth and her cheeks and neck.

He scooped her up in his arms—she seemed to weigh nothing at all—and carried her over to the small bed in the corner. He laid her down on the hard mattress and then lay down with her, his feet jutting out over the end. She fumbled with the buttons on his shirt, and he ran his hand along her thigh, underneath the insubstantial cloth for her shift.

They made love quietly, passionately, trying to contain themselves enough that they did not disturb the entire household. It felt to James like the final letting go of all of his hatred, the expulsion of all of his rage, and the embracing of a new life, a life in which he could be his own master. A life where he could again know dignity, love.

Their whispered talk had died away, and they had lain in each other's arms for the better part of an hour when Lucy rolled over and poked James in the chest with her finger. "You best get out of here, mister. My mistress finds you here and there'll be the devil of a time."

"If you insist," James said, reluctantly letting go of her and standing up. He glanced out of the window as he fumbled for his clothes. It was somewhere around three in the morning, black and silent in the city.

He dressed slowly, quietly, then picked up his haversack. Lucy was sitting up in bed, holding the sheet in front of her, smiling in a shy, modest way. James stepped over to her and gave her one last kiss. "I do love you, Lucy. Soon as Marlowe gets back I'll come back here, see you again."

"Next time you best have some ideas of marriage, mister," she said. "Like a date, I mean."

"Next time." James smiled, and then he swung the window open and dropped to the ground outside. He crouched as he hit the lawn and remained in that position, tensed, listening to the night. There was a rustling somewhere, a movement, but it could have been anything, the wind or an animal. He stayed put for a minute more, but there was no other sound, at least none that seemed out of place.

He straightened and moved across the grass. He was careful with each footfall. His steps made no sound. He crossed the lawn, invisible in the shadows, moved down the narrow space between the fence and the small stable. A familiar mix of smells mingled in the air: horses and hay and manure and the slightest hint of leather tack.

James moved down the side of the building and paused before stepping from the shadows onto the road. There was no sound, so he took a cautious step out.

And then there was another scent, not animal but human, unmistakable to one who had spent so much time in close-packed confinement. James whirled around, and his hand moved for his pistol, and as he did he heard the sound of a flintlock snapping into place.

He stopped, like an ebony statue. Not ten feet away, hidden from the lawn by the stable, stood two men. Both had muskets, and both muskets were pointed at James's chest. They were both sworn deputies of Sheriff Witsen.

Finally one of the deputies broke the silence. "What the hell you doing, boy," he asked, "sneaking around here in the dark?"

"Damn my eyes, that ain't a gun in your belt, is it?" the second one added.

For three days the *Vengeance* had drifted, sails clewed up, wheel lashed, while the crew repaired the damage, tended to the wounded as best they could, and tossed the dead overboard.

There was little medicine aboard, save for rum, but at least there was plenty of that, and it was doled out unsparingly to wounded and healthy alike. Those with wounds of their arms and legs that were beyond bandaging were made insensible with drink and then held in place while the carpenter removed the damaged limb with the same tools he used to fix the smashed bulwark. The severed limb was tossed overboard, and in a majority of cases, the rest of the man followed a few days later.

By the fourth day all of those who were sure to die had done so and those likely to live were on their way to recovery. Nearly thirty men were dead or wounded, a quarter of the *Vengeance*'s crew, and with not one bit to show for it. But even with those men gone, there were still ninety of the crew fit for action, and that ninety were hot for blood.

LeRois stood on the quarterdeck watching William Darnall moving around the deck, rounding up the men and sending them aft. It was time to decide what they would do, and that included deciding if LeRois would remain in command. All of the popularity he had gained from all of the wealth his arrangement with Ripley had brought aboard had been nearly negated by the disastrous attack on the tobacco fleet.

The Frenchman ran a sweating palm over the walnut butt of his pistol, thrust in his red sash. He took a long drink from his rum bottle. If anyone presented a serious challenge to his command he would shoot them down, and if the others fell on him and killed him for doing so, then such was his fate. He would rather die on the *Vengeance*'s quarterdeck than lose command of her.

"All right, all right, listen here," Darnall called, and the many conversations fell off and everyone looked aft at the quartermaster and at LeRois. LeRois had decided to remain on the quarterdeck as if he were still in command, rather than join the others on the waist, and he could see the disapproving looks shot aft at him.

"I reckon there's been some high talk about this fight, and what we're about," Darnall continued, "and I reckon we're set to rights enough to get under way, so we had best decide where we're heading."

"We are heading back to the Capes," LeRois announced with what he hoped was finality.

"We ain't taking orders from you, you crazy old man," the boatswain shouted. His face was twisted in anger. He had lost three fingers off his left hand in the fight.

"That is not for you to say."

"Bloody son of a whore, you took us right into a trap!"

LeRois half turned and spit on the deck. "Bah, trap! You did not know it was a trap, *cochon*, none of you did!"

"He ain't fit to be captain, fucking lunatic! He ain't fit, I say!"

LeRois pulled his sword from the scabbard, slowly, eyes locked on the boatswain, and when he spoke his voice was even and terribly sane. "You do not say that to me, eh? You vote on captain, but you do not call me those things. Do you want to fight me now?"

That stopped the boatswain with his mouth hanging open, as LeRois figured it would. LeRois might have been old, and he might have been insane, but he was still the most dangerous man aboard, a skilled fighter, absolutely without mercy and absolutely without fear. That was a fact that no one questioned. He had been bested only once in his life, and that was by Malachias Barrett, and if he ever crossed paths with him he would kill him too.

"I ain't gonna fight you, and my hand half cut off!" the boatswain answered, holding up his bandaged left hand. Unfortunately for that argument the man was right-handed, and everyone aboard the ship knew it, and there was not a thing wrong with his right hand, so with muttered curses he leaned back against the bulwark and dropped his protest.

"This is what we do, eh, what I say we do, and you vote on it now," LeRois said, keeping up the momentum. "We go back to the Chesapeake Bay. That ship we fought, she is gone now, with the convoy, and if she come back she will not fool us again. There is no man-of-war on the bay now and there are many fat prizes anchored there, and many fine *maisons* ashore, no? We teach the fucking *cochon* there a lesson about firing on the *Vengeance?*"

He squinted and looked down at the faces in the waist. Heads were nodding, comments exchanged back and forth.

"Anyone got any other suggestions?" Darnall asked, and that question was followed by a prolonged silence. LeRois knew that that tribe would grumble as sailors always do, but there were few of them who wanted to take the responsibility of making an original suggestion. The boatswain, perhaps, but LeRois had just castrated him.

"I reckon we do like LeRois says," one of the men spoke up, and that was followed by a chorus of "aye"s.

"Anyone here opposed?" Darnall asked, but no one said anything, not even the boatswain, who just glared at the deck.

"Then it's decided," Darnall announced. "The Chesapeake."

"*Oui, oui, bien,*" LeRois grunted, and then called out, "Let us set the sail, then, eh? *Prez et plein,* full and by."

The wind and current had set them north, and it took them nearly two days to recover the distance, two anxious days on a long board out to sea, before coming about and standing in to shore and finally raising Cape Charles and Smith Island fine on the starboard bow.

They hove to that night, not caring to negotiate the passage between Middle Ground Shoals and Cape Charles in the dark.

When the sun came up LeRois hoped to see some unwitting merchantman bound in or out of the bay, but there was nothing save for water and the distant, low-lying capes, so he ordered the yards braced round and turned the *Vengeance's* bow west.

They weathered Cape Charles by late morning and skirted around Middle Ground and stood for Hampton Roads, where he hoped the prey would be abundant. The pumps had been manned an hour per watch, but now as the wind built beyond ten knots and the tired old *Vengeance* worked more in the seaway they were going all but nonstop. What was worse, the men had to work them themselves, having no prisoners or slaves aboard to do it for them.

There was as well a gaping hole in the fore topsail and LeRois expected the sail to blow out at any moment. As the ship heeled and the slop in the bilge was washed around, a most foul odor rose up from the hatches, disgusting even by the pirate's standards. The *Vengeance* would never be able to stand up to a man-of-war. She was just about worn out.

There was no shipping visible as they crossed the mouth of the bay, nothing to the north by the York River and Mocksack Bay, nothing to the southwest by Norfolk. That was not what LeRois had hoped to find, but there was still Hampton Roads, now blocked from their sight by Point Comfort.

LeRois paced back and forth on the quarterdeck, and when his frustration got the better of him he would pull a pistol out of his sash and blow a seagull out of the air, watch it explode in a cloud of blood and feathers, and then resume his pacing.

An hour later they had Point Comfort broad on the starboard bow. "There's a ship in there, up in Hampton Roads!" the man aloft sang out. "Looks like a merchantman, big bastard! Riding to a single anchor!"

LeRois said nothing. He stopped his pacing and waited until the *Vengeance* had drawn abeam of the Point, allowing him to see the wide Roads beyond. It was indeed a ship, a big one, and most likely a merchantman, but he had learned something about appearances as of late.

"We go to quarters, eh!" he called out. "Load the great guns and run them out, we will blow this son of a bitch out of the water if he fire on us!"

There were no arguments from the crew regarding this precaution, and they quickly fell to loading the guns, pulling away the coils of rope and empty butts and personal effects piled on top of them, and tossing it all in a great heap on the main hatch. LeRois brought the bow around until the *Vengeance* was closing with the lone vessel. He swept her deck with a glass. He was close enough to see a few figures moving about, but that was all. It seemed impossible that this could be a trap, but he could not shake that concern.

Merde, he thought. Let it be a trap. I am ready.

They closed to a cable length and still he could see no more than a few men on the deck. He took a long pull of rum, braced himself, and felt his muscles tense as he waited for the image of Malachias Barrett to appear in the lens of his glass. But he could see only a few seamen aboard her, and a stout man who looked like the master, and none of them looked like Barrett. The stout man pointed at the *Vengeance*, turned and spoke a few words to the others, and then they all disappeared from sight.

A moment later they reappeared, this time in a small boat that pulled around the ship's counter and made for the shore and the small town of Hampton. Every man in the boat pulled an oar, including the master, and they quickly left their ship behind.

They have guessed who we are, LeRois thought, and they leave their ship to us.

It was too good to believe.

The *Vengeance* closed to half a cable length and then rounded up with her mainsails aback, heaving to abeam of their victim. LeRois studied the ship, waiting for the hundreds of men to spring up, to run out their guns, but there did not seem to be anyone aboard.

For a long moment there was silence aboard the pirate

ship, silence from the enemy, silence in Hampton Roads, as if the whole world was holding its breath.

"The flag, raise the flag! Run out the guns!" LeRois shouted, and the tension broke like a thunderstorm as the hideous black flag was hoisted up the ensign staff, the great guns were trundled out, and the pirate tribe cheered and shrieked like the host of hell.

And still nothing from the merchantman.

"Give them a gun, one gun!" LeRois ordered, and a single gun went off amidships. Bits of the victim's rail flew into the air, but little damage was done beyond that, for the gun had been loaded with case shot and langrage, meant to kill people, not sink ships.

The blast of the gun echoed around the roads, but still no reaction, no sign of life aboard the other ship one hundred yards away. "Let go and haul on the mainsails! Fall off, there!" LeRois shouted, and the *Vengeance* was under way again, turning toward their prey, running bow-on to them. The men in the waist climbed tentatively up on the rails and into the shrouds. There was no vaporing now. That confidence had been blasted out of them. Now they tensed and waited.

"Round up! Round up!" LeRois shouted to the helmsmen. They spun the wheel, and the *Vengeance* turned into the wind a moment before her spritsail topsail yard would have fouled the other's headrig. The two ships came together with a shuddering crash, and then, and only then, did the pirates begin to scream.

They shouted with all the pent-up fury and tension of the past hour, of the past week, as they poured onto the deck of this most unfortunate ship. They brandished pistols and cutlasses and daggers as they ran fore and aft, and in their blind rage it took them some moments to realize that there was not one person aboard that ship, besides themselves.

They tore open hatches and scuttles and raced below, kicking in cabin doors and searching the 'tween decks and the hold, but there was not one person left aboard. The master and the three men with him had been the last, and they were already to Hampton. The ship was theirs with not the least resistance.

LeRois felt his fortunes changing.

He stepped up onto the merchantman's quarterdeck and from there surveyed all he could see. She was a big one, five hundred tons or thereabouts, and heavily armed. There were twenty guns aboard her, and they looked to be nine-pounders, as well as swivels and arms chests on deck that had yet to be opened. Her rigging was freshly blacked and well set up, and her decks and brightwork and brass bespoke a vessel that was well maintained. He had no way of knowing what shape her bottom was in, but he did know that a master who was so careful about the details was unlikely to let her hull rot away.

"Captain." Darnall came up the ladder to the quarterdeck. He had two bottles in his hand that looked as if they had come from the master's cabin. He handed one to LeRois.

"Ain't a fucking soul on board," the quartermaster reported. "Looks like mostly tobacco in the hold, goddamned lot of tobacco, and worth a fortune. Some money in the master's cabin. Hell of a prize." Darnall took a long pull from his bottle.

"Hell of a prize," LeRois agreed.

"Looked at the logbook. She's the *Wilkenson Brothers.*"

"Uhh," LeRois grunted. His hand was shaking from the fear, fear that he might see the vision. The Vengeances were still screaming, he could hear them, though he could not actually see anyone's mouth moving.

He took a long drink from his bottle, letting the liquid run down his cheeks and beard as he guzzled it. It was red wine, which did not have the same instant numbing effect of rum or gin, so LeRois drank again and again, until he felt the warmth spreading through him. He wiped his mouth with his sleeve.

"You are wrong about the name, quartermaster," he said to Darnall. "Whatever the hell you said she was, she is the *Vengeance* now."

Chapter 23

GEORGE WILKENSON peered into the cell where King James lay, his unconscious body deposited on a pile of hay, the only amenity in the cold, damp stone room in the Williamsburg jail. He was manacled hand and foot, even though he was locked in a cell and did not even look capable of moving. Indeed, he did not even look like he was alive.

They had really beaten him good. Wilkenson winced at the sight of the welts, the swollen eyelids, the dried blood covering his chin and staining his shirt. It was hard to tell, sometimes, with these black fellows, if they had been hurt. But not in this case.

The deputies had taken the opportunity to vent their annoyance at King James's arrogance, and to express, in a physical way, what they thought of a free black man. It was what Witsen had told them to do, of course, and Witsen was doing what George Wilkenson had told *him* to do, though the deputies had gone a bit beyond what George had had in mind.

But it would do the job, assuming they had not killed him. Wilkenson stared for a moment more, until he was certain that the black man was breathing, then turned away.

It was midafternoon. James had been in the cell for half a day. The only light in that dreary place came from a small window high overhead. There were bars across it, even though a child could not squeeze through the space. A stone wall with a single iron door separated the three cells from the other half of the building, where the jailor lived. Wilkenson took one last look at James and then stepped through the door and pulled it shut.

The jailor was not home. Wilkenson had sent him away. He wanted the jail all to himself, a private office for the afternoon. He sat on the battered chair beside the room's single table. Surveyed the crumbs and the dried food and sundry other filth with disgust, then stood and paced back and forth.

He wondered what was causing the delay. Wondered if there was some problem. That thought made his stomach twist with anxiety. He stepped over to the window and peered out from behind the heavy canvas curtain.

Across the wide lawn surrounding the jail he could see the sheriff's men approaching, and between them, half running to match their pace, was Lucy. There did not seem to be any problem. Not for him, in any event.

This was not entirely necessary, of course, this thing that he was about to do. William Tinling's letter alone was enough to humiliate and ostracize Elizabeth, and perhaps even see her charged with some crime. But he had to be certain. He had been fooled before. He would not let it happen again. He wanted confirmation, and no one knew more about Elizabeth Tinling than Lucy.

The door opened, and the sheriff's men all but shoved the young slave girl into the room. She recovered from her stumble, looked up. She saw Wilkenson standing at the far side of the room, and her eyes narrowed.

"Good day, Lucy."

She was silent for a long second, looking at him with contempt, but she was a slave and knew better than to voice that emotion. "Good day, Mister Wilkenson."

"Lucy, I want you to see something." George Wilkenson straightened and crossed the room to the door that opened into the cell block, swung it open, and gestured for her to enter.

She hesitated, glanced around, and then tentatively stepped through the door. Wilkenson followed.

She paused for a moment and looked around in the dim light, and then she gasped and flung herself at the bars of James's cell.

"You killed him, dear Jesus help me, you killed him!" she cried, reaching through the bars, stretching out her hands to the unconscious man ten feet away.

Wilkenson stepped up behind her. "No, he's not dead. Not yet." He put a hand on her shoulder and half turned her toward him. Tears were running down her face. She avoided his eyes. He put a hand under her chin and tilted her face up to his, and their eyes met.

"The sheriff's men caught him sneaking around the town last night. And he had a gun. You understand what that means, Lucy? You understand he can be hanged for that?"

He looked into her dark eyes, wet with tears. She nodded her head, just slightly, acknowledging that she understood.

"Good. Come out here, please." He guided her back into the jailor's quarters. "I wish to talk to you."

He sat her down at the small table and stood opposite her, looking down at her, waiting patiently as she pulled a handkerchief from her sleeve and wiped her eyes.

"I have an idea, Lucy, that you are very much in love with James."

Lucy nodded and the tears came again, and between gasping sobs she said, "We is going to be married."

"That's nice, Lucy. It is. But see here. It has come to my attention that there was something not . . . not quite regular about the situation between your mistress, Elizabeth Tinling, and her late husband. You know that Joseph was a particular friend of mine, and I am anxious to know just what it was that was going on."

Lucy looked up at him, and there was a flash of defiance beneath the fear and the sorrow. "What're you asking me for, Negro girl like me? Ain't no good me telling you anything."

"Oh, you won't be telling me anything I don't know. I

know everything that went on, from an impeccable source. But I would like you to confirm it. I want to hear it all from someone else as well, and I don't reckon there's anything happened at the Tinling place that you don't know about."

Lucy bit her lower lip and looked around the room. The sheriff's men flanked the door, arms folded, watching, expressionless. She was a cornered animal, small and frightened.

Wilkenson put his hands flat on the table and leaned toward her until their faces were only a few inches apart. Lucy drew back and half turned away, but her eyes never left his. "You have a choice to make here, Lucy," Wilkenson said, his voice soft and calm. "I can have King James released, or I can have him hanged. I can do that. You know I can, don't you, Lucy?"

She nodded, her eyes fixed on his, a bird hypnotized by a snake. The tears were flowing with abandon now, and the dull light coming in from around the curtain shone off her wet skin. She stifled a sob and sat more upright and summoned up the strength to speak.

"If you knows what happened, then you know she didn't have nothing to do with it. Mrs. Elizabeth. She didn't even know. Still don't. It was the old woman, the one who did the cooking, it was all her doing, and she's dead this year and more, so there ain't nothing can be done."

Wilkenson frowned, shook his head. "I don't understand—"

"Mr. Tinling . . . he was an animal . . . an animal. Beat my mistress like nothing I ever seen. Beat her worse than a dog, worse than a slave. Almost killed her once, she was in bed for a week, all black and blue. I . . . I . . . don't know why. She never did nothing. He just liked it, liked to hit her. Finally he said he'd kill her, and I swear to the Lord he meant it and he would have done it."

She broke down and put her face in her hands and sobbed.

"Go on, Lucy, it's all right. . . ."

Lucy braced herself again and looked up. "The old woman couldn't stand it no more, she loved Mrs. Elizabeth, we all did. Old woman had the knowledge, poisons and such. She put something in his food, make it look like his heart give out. He dropped dead right in his bedchamber, trying to have his way with me. Ripped my clothes, had himself all hanging out . . . and it weren't the first time . . . and he dropped dead. We all thought his heart give out. Old woman told me the truth of it. Right before she went to her rest, she told me.

"The sheriff, he find the son of a bitch dead that way, breeches all down, and he don't want to talk about it, don't want no one to know how the old bastard died."

She looked around again. Her lower lip was quivering and she was sobbing, but there was a certain defiance about her as well. "It was the old woman killed him, all right, but he would have killed Mrs. Elizabeth if she didn't do for him first. He said so, I heard it, and he meant it, too. He was crazy, the meanest bastard I ever known. I'm glad for what she done."

There was silence in the small room. Wilkenson glanced over at the sheriff's men, noting their wide-eyed surprise, imagined that his own face carried the same expression. He had hoped only to confirm William Tinling's letter, fan the sparks of a rumor, get people talking. But this was another matter, an issue for the law, the courts. Testimony under oath.

"There, is that what you wanted?" Lucy asked.

"Yes . . . yes," George Wilkenson said, but that was not entirely true. It was not really what he had wanted. It was much, much more.

The *Plymouth Prize* dropped her anchor in Hampton Roads to await the flood tide before working up the James River to Jamestown. It would make the trip upriver that much easier, and twelve hours on the hook would allow time for the word to spread about Marlowe's second triumphant return.

The anchorage in the Roads was deserted. Even the *Wilkenson Brothers* was gone. Marlowe wondered how they had mustered enough hands to get her back to her mooring. He pictured George Wilkenson tentatively laying aloft to loosen sail, shaking like a leaf, the old man standing at the wheel bellowing orders, and the thought made him smile.

Marlowe was alone on the quarterdeck, leaning on the taffrail, enjoying the calm of the evening as best he could. The image of that black flag, with its skull and crossed swords, kept swimming in his head.

He was back. LeRois was back. The sight of him was as frightening as it had been the first time, so very long ago, when Marlowe had been no more than a sailor aboard a merchantman. When he had been someone else entirely.

No, that was not true. It was more frightening now. Now he knew what LeRois was capable of, knew what fury LeRois would unleash upon him, given the chance. Pray God he did not get that chance.

Bickerstaff stepped out into the waist. Marlowe hoped he would come aft, distract him from his thoughts, offer him some counsel. His old friend paused and looked to larboard and starboard, taking in the lovely Chesapeake Bay, lighted as it was by the lowering sun, then climbed up the ladder and walked aft. He had a precise, almost delicate way of moving, as if he were dancing, or fencing.

"Good evening, Thomas," he said.

"Good evening."

"It would seem to be as perfect as the original garden, this Virginia."

"Indeed it would, though I seem to recall that the garden had its serpents as well."

"By this awkward and altogether uncharacteristic allusion to Scripture I take it you are making reference to *Monsieur* LeRois?"

"I am."

"Do you think he is here? On the bay?"

"I do not know. He could be. He could be anywhere."

The two men were quiet for a moment, watching a pair of swallows twisting and turning overhead. They looked black in the red and fading light of the day.

"You called him the devil himself," Bickerstaff said at last.

"An exaggeration, perhaps. Not by much."

"I saw him only the one time. Is he much worse than the others?"

"Most of these piratical fellows do not live so long, do you see? A few years, and then they are caught and hanged, or die of some disease, or are cut down by their own men. But Le-Rois, he has managed to survive, as if he was blessed by Satan and cannot be killed.

"He was not so bad, you know, when first I was pressed into his service. But by the time I . . . we took leave of him, he was quite mad. Inhumanly cruel. Drink, I believe, rotted his brain, the drink and the pox and the hard, hard living. And that would not matter so much if he were not so cunning as well, and so able with a sword. At least he was then, and I have to reckon he still is."

"You defeated him in this last fight," Bickerstaff pointed out.

"I drove him off, I did not defeat him," Marlowe corrected. "And that will only serve to make him more dangerous still, because he will be furious over it, and now he will be cautious."

"You bested him once."

"Once. And it was a close thing. I would not like to try that again."

It was first light, with the edge of the sun peaking over Point Comfort, when they won their anchor and made their way upriver under topsails alone. Marlowe had expected word of their return to spread. He had expected boats to greet him, people on the shore to be waving at the mighty guardship, with her bright flags and bunting flowing in the warm breeze. But it seemed as if there was no one there to take notice, as if the very colony had been abandoned.

By midafternoon they had arrived at Jamestown. The *Northumberland* was there, tied up to the dock, deserted, as was the dock itself, save for one black man, who paced and flapped his hands. Marlowe put his glass to his eye. It was Caesar, and he looked as if he could not wait another second for Marlowe to step ashore. Agitation was not in Caesar's nature. It made Marlowe uneasy. Something was not right.

They dropped the anchor and put the longboat over the side, ready to pass the warps to the warping posts and haul the *Prize* up to the dock. Marlowe took his place in the stern sheets, Bickerstaff beside him, and he directed the coxswain to deliver them ashore before the work commenced. Marlowe climbed up the wet wooden rungs onto the dock, Bickerstaff right behind.

"Caesar, what the devil is going on?" he asked. "Has no one heard of our return? Where is everybody? Where is King James?" Where, for that matter, were the governor and the burgesses and all of the admiring multitude he had come to expect?

"I ain't seen King James, Mr. Marlowe, not since he left with you. And the others, I reckon they wants to keep out of your way."

"Whatever for?"

"I reckon folks afraid of you, don't know what you'll do. Some is afraid to be seen with you. It's on account of Mrs. Tinling, sir. Mrs. Tinling's in jail. They done arrested her. Arrested her for playing some part in the killing of her late husband, that son of a bitch, God rest his soul."

Chapter 24

"THIS IS Wilkenson's doing, you know that, of course? Is there any doubt?" Marlowe paced back and forth, bent at the waist to avoid striking his head on the overhead beams of the *Plymouth Prize*'s great cabin. Three lanterns illuminated the area in big patches, leaving the corners in darkness. A swarm of insects swirled around the lights, having come in through the open stern windows. It was hot, despite the slight breeze.

"I have no doubt his hand was in this," Bickerstaff said. He and Rakestraw and Lieutenant Middleton were the only other occupants of the cabin. They were all sitting, watching their captain pace, watching his anger build like a tropical storm. "But we must discover more. We have only the slightest facts of the case, and those at third hand."

"Sod the facts!" Marlowe was surprised by his own anger, a little afraid of it. He had not experienced this intensity in some years. "The goddamn Wilkensons make up facts as they choose, and everyone else just nods their heads and says, 'Yes, sir, whatever in the world you say.' I'll not suffer their lies."

"We will go and speak to the sheriff in the morning, and the governor," Bickerstaff said. His tone was even, his suggestion reasonable, but Marlowe was not in the mood for reason.

"Yes, the sheriff and the governor. Disinterested parties, to be sure. We'll get justice from them, I've no doubt, just as we did when our tobacco was condemned."

"The sheriff is a villain in the Wilkensons' employ, I will grant you that, but the governor has always been fair. . . ."

Marlowe stopped pacing and turned to Bickerstaff and the others. "I'll not wait for morning."

"What do you wish to do, sir?" Rakestraw asked eagerly. The first officer, perhaps more than most aboard the guardship, had embraced his new captain's way of running affairs. He worshiped Marlowe, that was plain.

"I wish to have Elizabeth Tinling out of jail, and so I intend that we shall go and get her out of jail. Pray assemble the men. Cutlasses, pikes, and pistols," he said to Middleton.

A grin and a nod, and the second officer disappeared.

"Thomas, you cannot propose we forcibly remove Elizabeth from jail?"

"I do. Who will stand up to us? The militia? There ain't a force in the colony to reckon with the Plymouth Prizes."

"That is not the point, not the point at all. You are a king's officer now, sir. What you are proposing is against the law."

"Against the law? I *am* the law!"

"You are *not* the law!" Bickerstaff shouted. Slammed his fist down on the table, made Rakestraw jump, so uncharacteristic was the outburst. "It is your duty to uphold the law, not . . . not brush it aside just because you have the power to do so."

"*Merde!* Such talk about law. What law? Wilkenson's law? If they have the right to make up law as they see fit, then so do I!"

"Oh, it is very pretty to think so, isn't it? Thomas, this is a violation of everything that justice and honor mean—"

"Don't lecture me, teacher, I have had quite enough of it."

The two men stared at each other. Through the windows they could hear the clamor of the Plymouth Prizes turning out, the rattle and clash of small arms being issued, the excited buzz of speculative conversation.

"Your army awaits you," Bickerstaff said at last.

"You are goddamned right it does. You may come or stay,

as you wish. I shall not think the worse of you if your misguided conscience will not allow you to accompany us."

"I will come with you, as I did before, after you bested LeRois. But I will not have a hand in what you are about to do. Like our years at sea. I will hope only to dissuade you from this course."

"Hope all you want, pray if you wish, but it will do you no good." Marlowe shed his coat and draped his shoulder belt and sword over his head, then pulled his coat on again. He was silent as he loaded a brace of pistols and clipped them to the leather strap. "They have driven me to this," he said at last, "I did not go willingly." He picked up his hat and stepped out of the great cabin, leaving Bickerstaff alone.

He made his way to the quarterdeck and stood at the top of the ladder, looking down into the waist. The Plymouth Prizes were assembled there. Some had pistols thrust in their belts and sashes, some had boarding axes. Some leaned on long pikes whose bright blades winked in the lantern light, high above the men's heads. They all wore cutlasses. Most had bright-colored cloth tied around their heads and ribbons tied around their arms and legs. Various bits of gold jewelry glinted dull yellow. They were grinning and joking among each other. They were ready to go.

"Listen here, you men," Marlowe shouted, and the buzz on deck dropped off and all heads turned aft. "I reckon you all know what's acting here. There's some might think what I intend ain't right, and I'm not sure they're wrong on that point, so any man here who does not wish to go tonight can stay behind, and there'll be nothing said about it."

He looked out over the upturned faces. No one said a thing, no one moved. And then from somewhere forward a man yelled, "Bugger every one of them fucking Wilkensons!" and the men erupted in a spontaneous cheering, shaking their weapons at the sky, shooting off pistols.

A lantern was opened and a torch thrust in. The cloth-bound end burst into flames, casting a bright and flickering light down on the cheering men, and then another and another was lit until the crowd in the waist took on the aspect of some savage, primeval hunting party.

"Let's go, then!" Marlowe shouted, drawing his sword and leaping down into the waist. The men stood aside as he made his way over the brow and onto the dock, and then, still cheering and shouting, they followed him ashore.

They were a disorderly army, marching up the rolling road to Williamsburg. The cheering dropped off quickly as they fell into the rhythm of the walk, the only sound the steady padding of bare feet on the road and weapons thumping at the men's sides.

Like most sailors, the Plymouth Prizes were powerful men, but they were not much used to walking long distances. Soon they were huffing like a herd of cattle as they trudged along the dusty, hard-packed road, illuminated all around them by the torches held aloft.

An hour into their march Marlowe heard the sound of hooves coming toward them.

"Hold up!" he shouted. He raised his hand, and the footsteps behind him stopped. "Stand ready!" He heard cutlasses draw from their frogs, flintlocks snap back.

The sound of the hooves came closer, and then horse and rider appeared in the circle of light. The man pulled his mount to a stop, half turning on the road, looking down at the villainous band below him. Marlowe did not recognize the rider, just some traveler on the road, and the man did not stop for introductions. His eyes went wide and he said "Dear God . . ." as he wheeled the horse around and charged back up the road, kicking the horse hard with his heels and lying down across its neck, as if fearing he would be shot in the back.

The entire encounter lasted no more than half a minute, and then horse and rider were gone. Marlowe looked back at his men. He could see why the traveler had been so frightened; the Plymouth Prizes must have looked as terrifying to him as Pharaoh's army did to the Children of Israel. And Marlowe knew that they were quite capable of acting as vicious as they looked.

He stepped aside until he could see to the end of the crowd. At the edge of the torchlight Bickerstaff stood patiently, his hand resting on the hilt of his sword. He wished the teacher would step forward and walk with him, but Marlowe knew he would not. Bickerstaff was there, but he was not a participant.

Explain that to the judge when they try to hang us all, Marlowe thought, then waved his men forward again.

It took them another hour and a half to reach Williamsburg, and by then the men were starting to tire, their pronounced step becoming more of a shuffle.

Ten minutes shy of midnight they left the dark fields with their darker patches of trees, the split-rail fences hemming them in, and came at last to the big brick building that housed the College of William and Mary, the western end of the capital city.

Their arrival in Williamsburg seemed to reinvigorate the Prizes. Their steps became more distinct and the light fell in a broader circle as the torches were held higher overhead.

Of their own volition the men holding the long boarding pikes fell into two fairly straight columns and began to march in a regular step at the head of the tribe. Their ordered march, followed by the rag and tag Prizes, with torchbearers fore and aft, rendered the entire procession even more martial, and thus even more frightening, to those citizens who witnessed it.

Marlowe heard shutters and doors open on either side of the wide street and then slam shut again, caught the occasional glimpse of a face peering out at the night raiders. A fluke of the breeze carried the words ". . . but where are the damned bullets?" to his ears, and he smiled. Not all of the people of that city had reason to fear. Some, but not all.

The ad hoc army tramped down the center of the street until at last the jail came into sight. There was light in the windows and spilling out of the door, where three men stood, watching. Marlowe drew his sword and turned off the road, and behind him like the tail of a dragon his men followed. They crossed the grass, stopped in front of the small stone building.

It was Sheriff Witsen, standing by the open door, with two of his men behind him. Just inside, Marlowe could see the jailer, a fat, greasy man dressed in his nightshirt and breeches, obviously trying to keep well clear of any potential danger.

The sheriff and his men carried muskets—three guns against the Plymouth Prizes' hundred or more.

"Good evening, Marlowe," Witsen said, as if they had just met on a country lane. "I heard word from some poor frightened bastard that there were brigands on the road, but of course with the rumor of a pirate being on the bay, everyone hereabouts is fit to be tied. Now, there ain't any such villains abroad tonight, are there?"

Marlowe held his eyes for a moment. Witsen seemed not in the least bit frightened, which was to his credit. The same could not be said for his men, who were nervously shifting the guns in their hands, and the jailer, who was sweating mightily and seemed on the verge of bolting.

"I've seen no villains abroad tonight, sir," said Marlowe.

"I thought perhaps that was why you had turned out."

"I think perhaps you know why we have turned out. I will thank you to step aside."

"That I cannot do."

Then Bickerstaff was there, at Marlowe's side. "Sheriff, you and Marlowe are both men of the law. I can see nothing amiss with giving Marlowe custody of the prisoner until such time as this is all worked out. She would still be in custody, whether it be yours or the admiralty's. And it might well stave off any unpleasantness."

"Perhaps what you say is fair, Mr. Bickerstaff. I ain't a judge, so I don't know. But I can't do that, not until I have orders."

"Orders from whom," Marlowe snapped, "the governor or the Wilkensons? Or will either do? Or perhaps there are others who own shares in your soul?"

He could see that those words had struck home, and he could see the truth in them written on Witsen's face, but still the sheriff did not move.

The jailer stepped forward, his bulk cutting off a good part of the light coming through the door. "Perhaps the captain should read this," he said. He held up a sheet of paper, fluttering like a sail braced to a shiver. "The, ah, confession. From the slave girl."

Marlowe snatched the paper up and read it, then read it again. A transcription of a statement, a story of the old cook murdering Tinling. At the bottom a shaky X, the words "Lucy, her mark." He looked up at the sheriff. "It says nothing here about Elizabeth Tinling's involvement. Quite the opposite, the girl says she had no knowledge of the affair."

"And Mr. Wilkenson says that ain't so, says there's been a murder and the Negro girl is protecting her mistress."

"Oh, this is not to be tolerated. You will release Elizabeth Tinling this instant!"

"I will not. This is none of your affair. I order you to go from this place, Marlowe. I'm prepared to kill whoever I have to, to stop you doing what you're here to do."

"Kill us, will you?" Marlowe said. Turned to his men. "Disarm them."

The Plymouth Prizes swarmed around Marlowe, moving with the nimbleness of men accustomed to working aloft, where nimbleness meant life or death. They grabbed the sheriff's men, jerked the guns from their hands, met virtually no resistance. Six hands snatched Witsen's musket away as the sheriff tried to bring the weapon to bear on Marlowe. Unarmed, humiliated, the governor's men waited on their fate, which was now entirely in Marlowe's hands.

"Get them inside," Marlowe ordered, and the Prizes pushed the three men roughly into the jailhouse. They herded them and the jailer into a corner, held them there at the end of their long boarding pikes. Witsen made no protest about this treatment, no argument concerning his own legal or moral authority. That, too, was much to his credit.

The small, filthy room where the jailer lived was lit by a couple of lanterns hanging from hooks in the wall. Marlowe ran his eyes over the dirty, stained sheets on the bed, the stack of chicken bones on the plate on the table, then saw what he was looking for: a ring of keys hanging beside the door to the cells.

He turned to Rakestraw, who, with Bickerstaff, was standing behind him. "Keep these men here," he indicated the sheriff and his company, "and post some men around the jail. Keep a weather eye out for anyone approaching. They may have turned out the militia, for all that they are worth." He snatched the keys off the nail, grabbed a lantern. "I'll be back in a moment."

Marlowe pushed open the door to the cells in the other half of the small building. He did not want anyone with him. He did not know what he would find, what they might have done to Elizabeth. That thought had crossed his mind several times during the march to Williamsburg, and each time he had chased it away rather than let himself get worked into a frenzy.

But he had thought about it enough to come to a single decision: If they had hurt her, then they would pay. If they had . . . he shuddered to think on it . . . if they had raped her, then they all would die.

He stepped through the door. The light from the lantern illuminated the space, and the bars of the cells threw even lines of shadow across the far wall. He looked into the first cell. There was a black man there, manacled, his back to Marlowe. He moved on. The next cell was empty. He continued down to the last in the line.

Elizabeth was there, half shading her eyes from the light. She looked terrified, seemed to shrink back against the wall, but still there was a quality of pride in her look, and defiance, as if she would kill and die before submitting to any further humiliation. Marlowe felt his love for her welling up, displacing the rage. He wanted to reach out and touch her, caress her, protect her forever.

"What do you want?" she asked, hand in front of her face. Marlowe felt fear displace love. Did she hate him now, for his part in all this?

"Elizabeth . . . I've come for you . . . ," he said.

She straightened and tried to look into the light. "Thomas? Thomas, is that you?" she asked. With the lantern held low as it was, she could not see his face.

"Yes, yes, my love, it's me," Marlowe said, and held the lantern up so that the light fell across his face. He saw Elizabeth's body relax and her grim expression turn into a smile. She ran across the small cell, grabbed hold of the bars, pressed herself toward him.

"Oh, Thomas, you have come for me!" she said.

Marlowe put the lantern on the floor. There was just enough light from the guttering candle for him to see the keys in his hand and find the keyhole in the iron door.

"Are you well?" he asked as he fumbled with the key. "Have they . . . have they hurt you?"

"No, they have done nothing beyond humiliating me."

He inserted the key in the lock—his hands were shaking— and twisted it, and the lock opened with a snap. He swung the door wide and stepped inside and swept Elizabeth up in his arms.

"Oh, my love, my love," Elizabeth murmured, hugging him and then reaching her face up to his and kissing him. He kissed her back, longingly, unable to stop or let her go, unwilling to ever let her out of his sight, out of the sphere of his protection.

At last she pulled back from him, her hands on his chest, and he encircled her with his arms. "Have you seen the governor?" she asked. "How ever have you managed this?"

"The governor? No. I have just come to get you out of here."

"But . . . do you mean to say that you are just taking me out of here? With no authority?"

"I am captain of the guardship, and that gives me the authority. The sixty armed men beyond give me the authority."

She pushed back, breaking his grip on her, and brushed the hair from her face. "Thomas, this is . . . God, can you do this? What kind of trouble shall we have now?" She turned from him, as if seeking some answer in the dark corner of the cell. "What will this mean?" she asked, turning back to him. "I . . . I am not certain what to think. I shall go mad if I spend another minute in here, but . . . the law . . ."

"Sod their damned laws," Marlowe said with finality. "There are no laws in this colony, save for those that the wealthy make up at their own convenience. Well, I am wealthy too, and I have my men, and I shall do as I see fit. They cannot hold you here, not for some nonsense that the Wilkensons have seen fit to concoct."

She met his eyes again, and again there was the defiance, the strength summoned up by a strong woman who has been beaten down but not beaten to death. "Do you know what I stand accused of? The charge that you reckon the Wilkensons have made up?"

"I do. They say you had some hand in murdering your husband."

"He was not my husband!" Elizabeth said, low, through clenched teeth. "I was not his wife, I was his whore! I guess you had better know the truth, Thomas, so you can figure if you really want to do this thing."

She looked up at the ceiling and ran her fingers through her hair. "Oh, dear God," she said, half under her breath, then looked at Marlowe again. "His real wife is back home in England. I reckon she had had enough of the beatings."

Marlowe stared at her, surprised but not shocked. There was little in life that could shock him, after all of it he had seen.

Elizabeth folded her arms across her chest. Her face was set, as if she were challenging Marlowe to reject her, to call her a slut and lock her up again. "He found me in a bawdy house in London," she continued. "Oh, not some low nunnery, selling mutton at a penny a throw—no, it was a fine place, catering to the gentry—but a whore is a whore, isn't she, no matter what the price? Joseph Tinling took me away from there, to be his own mistress, promised me a new beginning, playing at his wife in the new world, and like the stupid tart I am I believed him, and you see what has become of that."

"That was what Matthew Wilkenson knew—"

"Matthew, and now his brother, and soon all of the god-damned colony, I reckon."

They stood there, silent, looking at each other across the cell, Marlowe off balance, Elizabeth planted like an oak, arms still folded, waiting for whatever would come next. "But . . ." Marlowe began, "they have no evidence for the crime of which you are accused. . . ."

She did not move, just held his eyes in that hard stare. "The Wilkensons need no evidence. This isn't about the death of Joseph Tinling, can't you see that? They don't hope to convict me of that. They want only to question me before a judge, make me publicly admit that I am a whore. That will be quite enough to ruin me—and ruin anyone stupid enough to stand beside me."

Marlowe nodded. There was nothing he did not know about desperation, and that was the final act. Elizabeth's ruination, for her sins, and with it his own destruction, for loving her. It was that or sacrifice his manhood by turning his back on her. Elegant, symmetrical, simple vengeance.

He crossed the cell and swept her up again. She resisted at first, pushing him away, but he pulled her toward him with powerful arms and she yielded to him, draping her arms over his shoulders, allowing him to press her close. They stood there like that for a long time, silent, swaying slightly, holding each other.

Here we are, thought Marlowe. Two fallen people, making believe we are something we are not and hoping no one in this new world will ask.

Here we are, outlaws both.

Chapter 25

LeRois pressed the telescope to his eye, watched the river sloop for as long as he could. The image began as a complete thing, one single sloop, and then began to shimmy and divide, until there were two distinct, overlapping vessels, though neither had quite the substance of a solid object. He lowered the glass and shook his head hard, and then, happily, there was one sloop again.

Overhead there came a high-pitched, keening sound, like a gale wind blowing through taut rigging. He looked up in surprise. The day had been calm up until that point. The flags on the two ships, the *Vengeance* and the near wreck that had formerly been the *Vengeance*, were hanging limp, barely moving in the breeze. He did not know what was making that sound.

The two ships were made fast to each other, riding at a single anchor in one of the many small inlets branching off from the Elizabeth River, just north of Norfolk. A deserted place, an area where people generally ignored what others were doing, so the approach of the sloop was cause for some caution. LeRois would not be caught with his breeches around his ankles again. That would be an end to his command.

"Hmmph," he grunted, putting the glass back to his eye.

He licked his dry lips and felt the sweat on his palms slick on the leather covering of the glass. He was afraid of whom he might see on board the sloop. These images of Malachias Barrett were becoming more and more frightening, more real and less apt to dissipate quickly.

Just as the sloop was beginning to divide again he caught sight of Ripley, standing at the helm, holding the sloop on course to luff up alongside the new *Vengeance*.

"*C'est bien, c'est bien*, it is all right, stand down there," he called to the men who were crowded around the great guns and hiding behind the bulwark, small arms in hand. The silence that had held the deck broke into a dozen conversations as the men got back to their drinking, their gambling, their staring at the approaching sloop, and, in some cases, their work.

The new *Vengeance* was in excellent condition, having just been readied for a voyage across the Atlantic, and so there was not very much that needed doing. She was fully provisioned with victuals and water, loaded with tobacco and sundry other things, including a quantity of specie, her bottom clean, her rigging well set up, her sails new. She did not stink belowdecks. There was considerably less vermin aboard. She needed only a little finessing to turn her into the perfect raiding platform.

With the crisis passed, the carpenter and his mates had resumed their part of the finessing. They were hacking off the high forecastle to create more open deck space and expose the great guns in a clean sweep fore and aft. When it came to a bloody fight, they did not need bulkheads and such impeding their movement.

Likewise, the boatswain and his mates were working overhead, turning their new ship into a more manageable barque. She was a big vessel, and while the hundred or so men of LeRois's tribe could have easily handled her, they did not care to expend any more energy than was necessary. Thus the cro'-jack and mizzen topsail yard and all their attendant rigging was struck down to the deck.

Another gang of men were over the side, painting the oiled hull black. Still more were over the transom, cutting away the fashion piece with the vessel's former name carved in it and replacing it with her new, proper name.

The river sloop luffed up and her forward momentum carried her alongside the new *Vengeance*. She came to a stop with a shuddering crash into the hull, and her small crew threw lines aboard the bigger ship, which were caught and made fast.

Ripley stomped across the sloop's deck and scrambled up the side of the ship that had been, until two days before, the *Wilkenson Brothers*.

LeRois took a long drink of rum, wiped his mouth, and regarded the wiry man approaching him. Ripley looked mad about something, but LeRois could not guess what that might be, nor could he care less. They had captured a big ship with a valuable cargo, and without a drop of blood spilled. Ripley's master should be delighted.

"LeRois, you stupid drunk bastard, goddamn your eyes, what do you think you're about?" Ripley called as he stamped aft and up to the quarterdeck.

LeRois squinted at him and chewed at something that had just dislodged from between his teeth. It was not possible that Ripley had just said what he, LeRois, had thought he heard. The shrieking in the rigging grew louder. LeRois dismissed it all as sound, just sound.

"Quartermaster, eh, *qu'est-ce que c'est?*" LeRois spread his arms in an expansive gesture and looked aloft. "The new *Vengeance*, what you think?"

Ripley approached until he was a few feet away and then stopped and spit on the deck. "I think, what the fuck are you about?"

"*Quoi?*"

"What are you doing on the bay, you stupid, drunk son of a whore?"

LeRois squinted at him again. That time he had heard it. Ripley had actually insulted him. He said nothing in reply.

"I told you not to take the tobacco ships, we have all the buggering tobacco we needs! It was general goods inbound,

Spanish stuff, that was what you was after! Are you too dull to remember?"

LeRois shifted uncomfortably. If Ripley went on like this he would have to do something. The quartermaster had apparently forgotten what happened to those who made LeRois angry, such as the old guardship captain in the tavern. "This ship, she is a good one. I can make us richer still with it."

"That ain't the point, you sodden, stupid wretch of a—"

That was it. LeRois's hand shot out, and he grabbed the former quartermaster by the throat and squeezed with the crushing power of a shark's jaws.

Ripley's eyes went wide and he flailed out, trying to pry LeRois's hand away, but with each second he grew weaker, while LeRois's grip did not diminish in the least. After a minute of that, Ripley began to hammer weakly at LeRois's arm. He might as well have been hammering at the mainmast.

After a minute and a half LeRois could see the terror in Ripley's eyes, the terror of pending death, and that was what he had been looking for. He released his grasp and shoved Ripley to the deck, stood over him as he coughed and retched and rubbed his damaged throat.

"You do not talk to me that way, eh?" LeRois said, but Ripley was still far from being able to speak, so LeRois drained his bottle, tossed it over the side, and went forward to hunt up another.

By the time he returned to the quarterdeck Ripley was standing, after a fashion, and leaning against the pinrail, his arm entwined in the mizzen running gear for support. He was still wheezing and coughing in a most pathetic manner.

He looked up at LeRois, and the Frenchman saw fear in his eyes, which was as it should be. LeRois took a pull of his rum and offered the bottle to Ripley. Ripley took it and drank, gagging and coughing but getting the rum down at last. He took another drink and handed the bottle back.

"You listen to me now, quartermaster," LeRois said. Some thoughts had come to him while he had been waiting for Ripley to recover.

Ripley looked at him with watery eyes and nodded.

"We cannot keep on, eh, with the old *Vengeance*. She is too weak, too rotten. With this ship we blow that fucking guardship right to hell."

The mention of the guardship caught the quartermaster's ear.

"Yes . . . ," Ripley croaked, and broke into a fit of coughing. "Yes," he said again when he was done, "you can blow the fucking guardship to hell! That's an idea that will sit well."

"*Bien, bien*," LeRois said, putting a brotherly arm around Ripley's shoulder and leading him forward and down to the waist. "You go tell your friends ashore we make more goddamned money with his ship than they ever dream of, eh?"

"I'll tell them, *Capitain*, I'll tell him," Ripley said, his voice hoarse. "But you are going after the guardship, ain't you, like you said you was?"

"*Oui*, we go after the guardship," LeRois assured him. And meant it. The insult he had suffered at the guardship's hands was not to be endured.

He did not tell Ripley about the trap the old *Vengeance* had sailed into, the slaughter the guardship had caused. Perhaps he would later, after they had murdered every one of those filthy bastards, after he had served that Marlowe out in grand style, but not now. He could not bear to think on it now.

The *Plymouth Prize* was warped back out into the stream and rode there on her best bower. There was a spring rigged from the anchor cable to the capstan so that the vessel could be turned in any direction. The great guns were loaded and run out. Marlowe did not know what to expect, but he certainly would be ready for it.

It had been a long night, a violent, brutal night. When the Prizes had discovered that the beaten black man in the first cell was in fact King James they had not taken it well, for they had come to respect James and look upon him as one of their own.

James would not say who had done that to him, but the Prizes had a pretty good idea, knew the sheriff and his men were involved in some manner. Even if they had not actually done it themselves. That was enough.

They might well have killed the men, and the jailer as well, if Marlowe had not made them stand down.

As it was, the four men were considerably worse off when Marlowe finally locked them in the cell that James had occupied and formed his men up on the lawn outside. A stretcher was fashioned for James. There was talk of finding a chair for Elizabeth, but she assured them that she could walk, and so after much protest they took her at her word.

A small detachment was sent to Elizabeth's home, where Lucy was roused out and told to dress and pack her things, and clothes for Elizabeth as well. They could not remain in Williamsburg, could not remain within the reach of the law. There was no safety for them anywhere in the colony, save for in the midst of the Plymouth Prizes.

Lucy was frightened, nervous, like a deer. Even the assurance that she would be there with King James did not seem to mollify her.

At last Rakestraw drew the men up into two rough lines and marched them out of town, with Elizabeth and Lucy and James on his stretcher sandwiched between them, and at the tail end six men carrying the three big trunks that Lucy had packed.

There was little chance that the alarm would be raised, with the sheriff and the jailer locked away, and little chance that the militia would welcome the opportunity to face this unknown band on the dark road. The march back to Jamestown was uneventful.

They arrived in the early-morning hours, exhausted, and filed back aboard. They warped the vessel away from the dock, anchored, rigged the spring, cleared for action, and collapsed on the deck.

King James was laid out carefully on the upholstered settee

in the great cabin, and there he slept. Lucy curled up next to him and slept as well.

Without a word spoken between them, Elizabeth followed Marlowe into his small cabin. She held his eyes as she took off her hat and kerchief, then reached up and untied the lacing of her bodice and pulled it free.

Her dress and petticoats were torn and dirty from the rough treatment she had suffered, and she shuffled them off and let them fall to the deck. She untied the neck of her shift, as she had done before, and let it drop on top of the other clothing and then slid into Marlowe's bunk.

Marlowe followed her with his eyes, then quickly pulled off his own clothing, pausing only to hang his sword on its hook and place his brace of pistols in their box.

He slid in beside her, wrapped his arms around her, feeling her perfect skin against his, her small shoulders under his big and callused hands. She murmured something he could not understand. He held her tighter.

Five minutes later, they were both asleep. They were far too exhausted, physically and otherwise, for anything beyond that.

The first light of the morning drove Marlowe from their bed, though he could have happily slept another ten hours, waking, perhaps, to make love to the flawless beauty beside him and then sleeping again.

But there were other concerns beyond that, such as what the day would bring, and so he extracted himself from her arms, taking care not to wake her, dressed quickly, and made his way to the deck. Bickerstaff was there, early riser that he was, and he nodded his greeting.

"Good morning, Francis," Marlowe said. Bickerstaff would not lecture him further on the morality of what he had done the night before, plucking Elizabeth from jail. The deed was done. There was nothing more to say.

Rather, Bickerstaff turned to him and said, "I am greatly relieved to see that Mrs. Tinling has not been harmed. I like her very much. I think she may be just the thing to make a gentleman out of you, something I have quite despaired of doing."

"I thank you, Francis," Marlowe said, and he smiled. "Were I you, however, I should not give up on me yet."

"We shall see."

"How does King James do?" Bickerstaff was the closest thing to a physician that the *Plymouth Prize* could boast.

"He was badly beaten. A weaker man might have succumbed by now, but I have great hope of James's recovery. I shall give him a vomit this morning, which I believe will set him up admirably."

It was two hours later that Marlowe and Bickerstaff, along with Elizabeth and Rakestraw, sat down to their breakfast in the great cabin. It was a fine meal, consisting of eggs, hashed beef, cold pigeon, and fritters, fresh food being one of the advantages of sailing within the confines of the bay.

On the other side of the cabin, King James lay propped up while Lucy fed him chicken broth and milk.

They were just enjoying their chocolate when Lieutenant Middleton knocked on the great cabin door.

"Sir, there's a river sloop upbound, about a mile or so."

"Indeed. Hail her and have her heave to and tell her master to come aboard. I would speak with him."

"Marlowe," Bickerstaff said after Middleton was gone, "I urge you not to do anything to further exacerbate this situation."

"Never in life, sir. More chocolate with you?"

Twenty minutes later, they heard Middleton's voice hailing the sloop through a speaking trumpet, then hailing again, and then a great gun went off forward as the sloop's master, apparently, required a less subtle persuasion to heave to and repair on board the guardship.

They listened to the bustle abovedecks, and finally Middleton knocked again and said, "Sloop's master is on the quarterdeck, awaiting your pleasure, sir."

"I shall be up directly," Marlowe said, and then to his company added, "Pray, excuse me. I shall not be long."

He stepped through the scuttle, then around and up to the quarterdeck. The sloop's master had his back to Marlowe, looking upriver at his own vessel. He was a thin, bony man. Dirty clothes, worn shoes. The queue that fell from under his cocked hat looked more like spun yarn than hair. Greasy spun yarn.

And there was something familiar about him, even from behind. Marlowe felt an odd sensation, an alarm in his gut, as if that man did not belong to the present time and place.

"Here, you," said the seaman standing loose guard on the sloop's master, "here's the captain. Show some sodding respect."

The sloop's master turned and faced Marlowe. Their eyes met and held each other, and widened as recognition spread across both their faces.

"Dear God . . . Ripley," Marlowe whispered.

"Barrett . . . it's you, you son of a whore. . . ."

It took both men less than a second to realize the implications of this meeting. Ripley turned and leapt up onto the quarterdeck rail, balancing there, arms flailing. "Grab him! Grab him!" Marlowe shouted, but the stunned guard just watched as Ripley plunged over the side.

"Shoot that son of a bitch! Shoot him when he comes up!" Marlowe shouted next, rushing to the rail, but again the guard was so shocked, and so generally dull, that he did not respond.

"Give me this, you idiot!" Marlowe jerked the musket from his hand and pulled back the lock as he pointed the barrel over the side. Ripley's head appeared above the brown, muddy water. He swiveled around and looked up with wide eyes, then dove again as Marlowe pulled the trigger.

A small spout of water shot up from the place where Ripley's head had been, and Marlowe recalled, with despair, that Ripley was one of those oddities, a sailor who could swim, and swim well.

"Get me another gun, damn your eyes!" Marlowe roared. He saw another of the Prizes rushing aft onto the quarterdeck, drawn by the gunfire, a musket in his hands. Marlowe ran up to him, pulled the weapon from his hands, ran back to the quarterdeck rail.

Ripley was fifty feet away, pulling himself up the sloop's side. Marlowe aimed and fired. The ball punched a small hole in the bulwark beside Ripley, slowed him down not one second.

Ripley tumbled over the side of the sloop, ran aft, calling for his men to cut the cable and set the sails. Marlowe turned forward. "Get some hands to the capstan!" he screamed. "Get the guns to bear on that sloop! I want him blown right to hell, damn you all, blow him right to hell!"

The Prizes moved fast, for there was no equivocation in their captain's voice. They grabbed up the handspikes, thrust them into the capstan, heaved around. The spring lifted out of the river and grew taught, and the *Plymouth Prize* began to turn under the stain, bringing her broadside around.

The river sloop had her jibs up and taut and her mainsail half hoisted when Ripley himself brought an ax down on the cable and cut it in two. The sloop drifted free, drifted downwind, down toward the *Plymouth Prize*, before her sails filled and she began to gather momentum.

"That's well!" Marlowe shouted. The guns would not bear perfectly, but they would bear, and he could not afford to let the sloop get too far away. He saw Bickerstaff and Elizabeth step out onto the waist, look around, then disappear below again, realizing, quite correctly, that they would do best to stay out of the way.

"Hand to the guns! Go!" Marlowe shouted, but the men, anticipating that order, were already training the guns around to bear on the sloop. One by one the guns found their targets and the gun captains brought their match down on the train of powder and the big cannons went off. The water around the sloop was torn up and a few holes appeared in the big mainsail and the low bulwark, but the sloop was not slowed and she was not stopped.

The Prizes leapt to reloading, working like demons to get one more shot off before the sloop disappeared around the bend, upriver. They were frantic to stop the little vessel because they saw Marlowe was frantic to stop it.

Marlowe watched the sloop pulling away. He thought for a moment that she might run aground, but Ripley put her about on a tack that would take them around the bend upriver and beyond the *Plymouth Prize*'s guns.

It was useless to try to pursue. The wind was right over their bow, and the big, square-rigged vessel would barely be able to move in the confines of the river, let alone catch the nimble sloop.

"Secure the guns," he called. Hoped that the despair that he felt was not conveyed by his voice. The sloop's low hull disappeared behind the sandy point, and a moment later her rig was gone as well.

"Marlowe, what the devil was all that about?"

Bickerstaff stepped up onto the quarterdeck with Elizabeth right behind.

"That, my friend, was the sound of my own black history overtaking me." Marlowe turned to Bickerstaff and smiled, a weak effort. "I am undone, sir, quite undone."

Then he looked at Elizabeth, saw the concern in her face. "It seems this is the season for ghosts."

Chapter 26

CURIOSITY. IT was eating at Elizabeth, like vultures, like wolves. Bickerstaff could see that, could see it in her eyes, in the way she watched Marlowe. Curiosity, as natural a part of the female condition as vapors.

At the same time he could see that Marlowe was in such a state of mind as to not invite inquiry even into his present concerns, let alone an examination of the past that so disturbed him. And Elizabeth was sensitive enough to realize this as well.

And so, Bickerstaff knew, she would come to him.

He stepped out onto the deck and strolled forward, avoiding the quarterdeck that so easily communicated with the great cabin. It was dark, being nearly eleven o'clock, but there was light enough from the abundance of stars for him to see all he needed to see.

He wanted to give her the chance to approach him. Did not want her curiosity to drive her to distraction.

He was leaning on the rail and looking up at the stars — or rather, the few planets that he could see — for no more than ten minutes before she stepped through the scuttle. He watched her climb up the quarterdeck ladder and look around, then make her way back to the waist and forward.

"Good evening, Mrs. Tinling," he said, and saw her start.

"Oh, dear," she said, recovering.

"Forgive me," Bickerstaff said, "I did not mean to frighten you."

"It's quite all right. I guess I'm a bit jumpy. And I think perhaps it is time to dispense with the 'Mrs. Tinling' nonsense. Pray call me Elizabeth."

"Delighted, if you will do me the honor of addressing me as Francis."

"The honor is mine, sir."

They stood silent for a moment, their eyes on the stars and their thoughts elsewhere.

"How does King James do?" Elizabeth broke the silence.

"Very well. The vomit has worked admirably. I had intended to bleed him, but I think perhaps it will not be necessary. Any imbalance of the humors seems to have corrected itself, which I observe more often than not it will."

"Are you, sir, a physician? I realize I know so little about you."

And about Marlowe as well, which is doubtless your primary concern, as well it should be, Bickerstaff thought.

"No, I am not. I am . . . I was, a teacher." He turned and met her eyes. She was so lovely, and the simple dress she wore and the plain mobcap with her yellow hair spilling out from under just reinforced that natural beauty. Was it any wonder that she was at the center of this storm? The face that launched a thousand ships, and burned the topless towers of Ilium.

He smiled at the irony of that thought.

It was not two years ago that Malachias Barrett had requested his help in concocting a new name. A new name for a new life.

"How does 'Marlowe' sound?" Bickerstaff had said.

" 'Marlowe'?"

"It is the name of a man who wrote a play about a fellow who sells his soul to the devil for worldly riches."

The former brigand smiled. "It suits me passing well," he said, and at that moment Malachias Barrett died to the world, and Thomas Marlowe was born.

"This morning," Elizabeth said, hesitating, "after the guns went off, Thomas said . . . something about his own history, his own black history, he called it. He said he was undone—"

"He did."

"Oh, Francis, I am so worried. He is so . . . unhappy. What . . ." Her voice trailed off. She did not know how to ask such a question.

"You wish to know what it is in his past? What is his history that plagues him so?"

"Yes." She looked up at him, and her eyes were pleading. "Yes, will you tell me?"

"Thomas's story is his to tell, not mine. But perhaps if I tell you my own, as it relates to him, it will give you some hint of what he was. I think it is my moral right to do so."

"Please, sir, I beg of you."

Bickerstaff looked in her eyes again, dark in the faint light, though he knew them to be blue, like his, but deeper, not the pale blue of a hazy summer sky but the deep blue of the bay. He looked out over the black water.

"I have been a teacher most of my life, in various situations. Greek, Latin, science, philosophy. Fencing, as good fortune would have it. In '95 I was employed by a gentleman of some wealth who was moving his family to Boston. I was given the choice of going with them or finding other employment.

"I had heard so much about America. But of course, you have lived in England, you know the high talk that goes about. I thought it would be just the thing. A new land.

"In any event, five weeks out we were overhauled by another ship, which turned out to be a pirate. We set all the sail we could, ran like a fox, but these piratical fellows are fast, you know, and rarely are they outrun.

"It took them the better part of a day, but at last they came up with us. They were all lining the rail, as I recall, screaming and chanting, beating drums. Vaporing, they call it."

Bickerstaff closed his eyes. He had not thought of this in some time. He had quite purposefully not thought of it.

"We chose to fight. That is no easy decision, for it is a

sentence of death to fight these pirates and lose. There is no quarter for those who do not surrender, but we had a ship full of gentlemen, and oh, they were so brave in the face of it all . . ."

Now the images were swimming in front of him, and he lived it again as he spoke. The profound fear in his gut as that pirate ship ranged alongside, the big black ensign with the grinning death's-head and twin swords snapping in the breeze. He had never been so afraid in his life, before or since.

There were hundreds of them, it seemed, filthy, merciless men clinging to the channels and the shrouds and the rails, howling like one would not expect to hear this side of hell.

The doomed men, crew of the merchant vessel, fired off a few pathetic cannons, but there were not enough men aboard to fire a real broadside, and those who were manning the guns had precious little knowledge of such things. Bickerstaff could see the fury of the pirates building, sweeping through the tribe with each defiant gun.

And then they were on them. Bickerstaff wiped his sweating palms on his coat, took a fresh grip on the sword in his right hand, the long dagger in his left. The pirate ship slammed into the merchantman's side with a horrible shuddering crash and the brigands poured down on the deck, spilled onto the merchant ship like a boarding sea that sweeps the deck fore and aft.

All of the gentlemen's plans, all of their high talk about holding the pirates off, meeting their attack with a solid defense, driving them into a corner, were forgotten in that vicious surge of men. Bickerstaff saw his compatriots cut down, shot down; he saw his employer, the one who had urged them all to stand and fight, flee down a scuttle, his pistol and sword discarded.

And then they were on him, and he had no thought for anything save for the blades that were flashing all around. He felt his sleeve plucked by a pistol ball, felt another tear a gash in his side, but he could do nothing about small arms. He could only fight against the swords.

And that, as it happened, he could do exceptionally well.

He knocked a blade aside as it lunged at him, ran the attacker through, slid his sword free as the man fell and met another, thinking, So this is what it is to kill men in battle.

The pirates were not swordsmen, they were barbarians who could do no more than hack and slash. And they were drunk. They would not best him—as long as he had to fight no more than two or three at a time.

Bickerstaff leapt back as a sword hissed down like an ax, and the brigand missed him completely, stabbing his cutlass into the deck. Bickerstaff stepped on the blade, pinning it down, and stuck the man in the chest with his dagger even as he parried and lunged at another.

He heard cursing, shrieking, screams of agony, defiance, madness all around. It was the inner circle of hell on that merchantman's deck, and he was a poor damned soul who would die on that spot. He was doing no more than putting off that fate for a few seconds more, he knew that, and taking some of the bastards to damnation with him.

Then there was a weird quiet aboard the ship, and Bickerstaff realized that it had been taken, that all of his fellow defenders were dead or, like himself, soon to wish they were. He realized it even as he turned aside the sword of the last of his attackers, knocking the point to the deck, and plunged the dagger into his guts. He watched the man go down, bleeding and clutching at the wound. He stood there, too exhausted to form a rational thought, dumbly watching the man collapse.

Then suddenly his sword was knocked from his hand as another blade slashed down, connecting with his weapon near the hilt. It fell with a clatter to the deck at his feet.

He whirled around, the dagger in his right hand, glued to his palm with drying blood, and leaned against the bulwark, breathing hard. The pirates around him stepped aside. Three feet away stood the man who had knocked his sword from his hand.

"Don't ever drop your guard to look at your handiwork," the pirate said.

Bickerstaff regarded him as the fox, weary from the chase, regards the approaching huntsmen. Young, late twenties, perhaps, tall and lean. He held a big and bloody sword in his right hand. A brace of pistols hung from a long ribbon around his neck. He wore a weathered blue broadcloth coat and wool shirt, canvas slop trousers, battered shoes.

He seemed to regard Bickerstaff with some curiosity, then looked at the five men, dead or dying, at Bickerstaff's feet.

"You done this?" he asked, gesturing toward the dead men with his sword. He seemed not in the least concerned about the fate of his shipmates, bleeding out their lives on the deck.

"I did. I did not see as I had a choice."

"Some hand with a sword, are you?"

"Fencing is a gentlemanly pursuit."

At that the pirate smiled and looked Bickerstaff square in the eye, his intelligent, bemused brown eyes locking with Bickerstaff's pale blue. "And you reckon yourself a gentleman?"

"I instruct gentlemen."

"And what the fuck do you mean by that?"

"I am a teacher. I was taking passage to the colonies to act as instructor to the children of the gentleman who sails with his family aboard this vessel."

"Sailed," the pirate corrected. "He's dead. Run through while he was cowering like the pile of shit he was. Like all them gentlemen. Cowardly bastards. You're the only one that fought worth being called fighting. We lost eight of our men, and you done for five of them."

"You do not seem very distraught over the death of your comrades," Bickerstaff said. It was unreal, like a nightmare, standing there, surrounded by death, death waiting for him, having this conversation with a murdering brigand.

The man shrugged. "A short life, but a merry one. Now come, teacher, cross swords with me." He gestured with the point of his sword for Bickerstaff to retrieve his weapon from the deck. "I'll know who's the better man."

Bickerstaff bent over and picked up his sword, his eyes

fixed on the pirate. Then the pirate gestured for Bickerstaff to move to a clear part of the deck.

"You wish to fence with me?"

"No, I wants to fight with you, and fight I will."

"You are the captain of this villainous bunch?"

"No, I'm the quartermaster. Now, come along."

"I'll fight you, on condition that the children aboard this ship are not hurt."

At that the man laughed out loud. "You'll make no demands, teacher. If you fight and lose, you'll get a better death than them others."

"And if I win?"

"You're no worse off than you are now, and you gets the pleasure of taking another of us to hell with you." At that he raised his sword and slashed down at Bickerstaff, so fast that Bickerstaff just had time to turn the sword away. He lunged, and the quartermaster leapt back, keeping just inches from Bickerstaff's blade, smiling.

They faced off, Bickerstaff holding his sword in the prescribed manner of a gentleman fighting a duel, the pirate gripping his great sword with two hands, like a savage Celt. The pirate attacked, slashing right then left, driving Bickerstaff back with the ferocity of the onslaught, and Bickerstaff worked sword and dagger together to keep him off.

He had no form, no style, but he was incredibly strong, and that gave him speed, and his reflexes were unfailing. Bickerstaff had never before seen such a natural swordsman. He would never have believed that any man as ill-trained as this one could both beat off his attack and put up a formidable attack of his own.

It was pure native ability that saved the pirate's life, saved him from Bickerstaff's accurate, well-trained attacks as the offense and defense shifted back and forth, the two men moving up and down the sticky deck.

At length the pirate stepped back, his sword at his side. Bickerstaff made to lunge, but saw that the man was not defending himself, so he paused as well.

"You should have killed me, teacher," the man said with a grin. "You are one goddamned good swordsman, with all yer fancy moves, but you don't know about real killing."

"I know about honor."

"I reckon you do," the man said, "I reckon you do." He swept off his hat and bowed deep, a mocking gesture. "My name is Malachias Barrett, and I just might have need of you. Come with me."

Barrett led Bickerstaff across the merchantman's deck and onto the pirate ship. None of Barrett's shipmates said anything, none of them even noticed, for they had begun to tear the merchantman apart and have their fun with her people. They were the Vandals sacking Rome, and they had no thought for anything but their own vicious pleasure. Bickerstaff followed— still in that dream state—and he did not even ask where they were going.

Barrett led him down below to the pirate's 'tween deck and then down into the hold. The conditions aboard the merchantman had seemed disgusting to Bickerstaff, but that ship was a palace compared to the dark, wet, reeking confines of the pirate ship. There was gear and personal belongings, empty bottles and half-eaten food flung in every corner, and rats moved boldly across the deck, not even bothering to keep to the shadows.

"Lovely, ain't she? Like the fucking Royal yacht," Barrett said. "I've a mind to leave her."

He opened the door to a small, dark room, then looked down at the sword and dagger that Bickerstaff still clutched in his hands. "I reckon I better take them," he said.

Francis nodded dumbly. The blood had dried on the grips, and he had to peel the weapons from his hands before handing them over. Barrett gently pushed him into the dark room and shut the door. He heard a lock clicking in place, and then there was nothing but darkness and distant, muffled screams.

Bickerstaff opened his eyes. The stars were still there, blinking as the *Plymouth Prize*'s rigging swayed in front of them.

"He saved my life, you see, locking me in that bread room," he explained to Elizabeth. "The pirates killed them all. Killed them in a most horrible manner. All but me and the children, whom Marlowe managed to hide as well."

"Why you? Why the children?"

"As to the children, I do not know. They were of no use to him. Perhaps he decided to honor my condition for fighting him. I like to think it was some spark of humanity that the pirates had not stamped out of him.

"As to why he saved me, well, there was a good reason for that. He had a mind to leave that life on the account, you see. Had been thinking on it for some time.

"These Brethren of the Coast, as they call themselves, sometimes they make quite a bit of money, but generally they gamble it away or drink it away or lose it in some manner. But Marlowe, or I should say Barrett, was smarter than that. He had been hoarding it for some time, years I should think.

"It was his intent to set up in some estate as Lord of the Manor. I can tell you, life aboard one of those pirate ships is no better than a prison in the matter of the food, the conditions. Disease. Marlowe was sensible enough to know he could do better than that."

Elizabeth spoke at last. "But how had he come to be with these men?"

"That is his story, not mine, but I will tell you what I know. He was a sailor, it seems, on a merchant ship. They were taken by this pirate, this Jean-Pierre LeRois, some years before, and Marlowe was pressed into service with them. It is not at all uncommon for those on the account to make others come with them, especially if they have some certain skill or other. I believe Marlowe just took to the life eventually. Embraced it as his own.

"In any event, he had a mind to leave LeRois and so did a number of the others. This LeRois was a madman, it seems, and they had had their fill of him. So after they had plundered the ship I was on, and had their bloody fun, Marlowe announced to this LeRois that he was taking our ship as his own, and taking a good part of the crew with him.

"LeRois, as you can imagine, was quite put out by this. They argued, swore, cursed one another. It seems LeRois had taken Marlowe under his wing, as it were, made him quartermaster, which is a high rank among those people. At last they took to their swords. LeRois was quite a swordsman, I can assure you, and I have told you already how very good Marlowe is. They fought for some time, the whole tribe looking on. Fought 'til each was cut to ribbons and nearly exhausted.

"In the end Marlowe bested LeRois, in large part because LeRois stumbled on a ringbolt in the deck and gave Marlowe that one opening to deliver a serious wound. Thought he had done for him. Left him bleeding on the deck and took the ship, the one we had sailed from England, and me with it."

"But I still fail to see—why save you?"

"Marlowe had all the money to set up as a gentleman, but he had no education, and he knew he could never pass for quality. He thought I could teach him. I told him that he would fool no one in England, but perhaps in the colonies it might be possible.

"I sailed with him for four years, and in that time I went from being his prisoner to his teacher and then his friend. I never participated in any of their raiding and he did not insist, though I can tell you he was never the murderous villain that LeRois was. He had a certain humanity about him. I never saw him murder anyone, nor could I have called him friend if he had.

"At length he had had enough, and had gathered enough wealth to set himself up, so we parted with the others and came to Virginia. The rest, I believe, you know."

"I thought I did, to be certain," Elizabeth said. "But there is still so much about him. . . . Why ever did he free his slaves? Is he such a man of God that he could not bear to own Negroes?"

At that Bickerstaff smiled. "No. I wish I could tell you that he gave them their freedom out of sense of humanity. I should have done so, had they been mine. But with Marlowe it was as much self-preservation.

"There were a number of Africans with the pirates, escaped slaves who had turned to the sweet trade. They could be the meanest of all of them, for there was no chance of anything but death for them if they were caught. And Marlowe had fought side by side with them. I reckon he is the only member of the tidewater gentry to ever consider a black man to be an equal. He has seen the smoldering hatred of men in chains, and he knows how dangerous they can be. He did not care to live with that nagging at him."

"I see."

They were silent for a long time. Finally Elizabeth spoke again. "And so today . . . ?"

"I gather this person who was on the sloop was someone who recognized Marlowe from the days in the sweet trade. He has been living in terror of coming across one of his old fellows."

"And what will this mean?"

"I do not know. But I am so very afraid that we shall lose our Marlowe. That he is becoming Malachias Barrett once again."

Chapter 27

FROM THE quarterdeck of the *Plymouth Prize* they could see them quite clearly, the noble coach and four, the footmen in their livery, the dignitaries in their fine clothing, the boat crew in matching outfits on the thwarts of the launch, oars tossed, made fast at the foot of the ladder below the dock.

"Well," Marlowe said to the company in general—Elizabeth, Bickerstaff, Lieutenant Rakestraw—"this is not entirely unexpected."

"A shot across the bow would keep 'em off, sir," Rakestraw suggested. "Guns are loaded and run out."

Marlowe turned, regarded the first officer. Wondered at how it had come to this, that a naval officer could even suggest such a thing.

"That is the governor, for the love of God," Marlowe said. "I don't think we'll be lobbing round shot at him."

"Beg your pardon, sir," Rakestraw muttered, the outrageousness of that suggestion apparently dawning on him.

Unwilling as he was to fire on Governor Nicholson, still Marlowe was not looking forward to the coming interview. He did not know what to expect, but he did not expect it to be pleasant.

He was no longer sure of his status, his standing with the governor. Nicholson might well be coming to relieve him of command of the guardship. And if he was, Marlowe would have to refuse. The guardship was his sanctuary—or, more to the point, Elizabeth's sanctuary—and the Plymouth Prizes would stand with him. But then he would be no more than a pirate once more, with a stolen government ship to boot.

They watched the governor and his party, three men in all, climb down the ladder and settle themselves in the stern sheets of the launch. One of the men was the governor's secretary. The other, Marlowe was quite certain, even from that distance, was President of His Majesty's Council John Finch, a powerful man in colonial government, a particular friend of the Wilkensons. No, this would not be pleasant at all.

"Mr. Rakestraw, please see to a side party. I wish to have the gentlemen welcomed aboard with all due ceremony."

"Aye, sir," Rakestraw said, still blushing from his suggestion, and hurried off to see to that detail.

"Thomas, I'll not have you jeopardize your position for me," Elizabeth said.

"And I'll not have you used as a pawn any longer," Marlowe said in a tone that did not admit protest.

"Shall I . . . Perhaps it would be best if I did not show myself," Elizabeth suggested.

Marlowe pulled his eyes from the distant boat and looked at her, then reached out and took her hand. "I have no misgivings about taking you from the jail. I will not have you skulking about like a criminal. The crime was in their locking you up. You have been horribly used, and now it is time that you receive some justice, and if they are not inclined to give it then they will answer to me."

He held her hand, held her eyes, until he heard the coxswain yell "Toss oars" and the launch was alongside.

"Come with me," he said. "We must go and meet our guests." He led her down the quarterdeck ladder and across the waist, where a detail of the Plymouth Prizes were formed up in two rows on either side of the gangway, boarding pikes held upright to form a straight if somewhat intimidating corridor for those coming aboard.

Marlowe took his place beside Rakestraw just as the governor's head appeared above the gunwale. Nicholson climbed with some effort and cast a wary eye around as he stepped on deck. It occurred to Marlowe that the governor was no more sure of his status with Marlowe than Marlowe was of his with the governor.

Grand, he thought, we shall be like two drunken blind men flailing at each other.

Nicholson stepped briskly past the line of men, and Marlowe stepped forward to meet him, hand extended. "Governor, how very good to see you again," Marlowe said.

Nicholson took his hand and shook it. "And you, Marlowe," he said. His eyes darted to Marlowe's side. "Mrs. Tinling, I trust you are well."

"Very well, thank you, Governor," Elizabeth said with a curtsy. There were few men more gracious and diplomatic than Governor Nicholson. It was what made him so very good at his job.

The same was not quite so true of President Finch, who stepped up behind Nicholson, gave Elizabeth an unpleasant look, and said, "Marlowe, we have a great deal to discuss."

"I should think so, Mr. President," Marlowe said. Nicholson did not much care for Finch, and Marlowe imagined that the burgesses had foisted the man on him, afraid that left alone Nicholson would be too forgiving with his wayward guardship captain.

He gestured toward the after cabins. "Please, sirs, won't you join me in my cabin, where we shall have a glass and discuss this?"

Five minutes later, the four men—Marlowe, Nicholson, Finch, and the secretary—were seated around the table in the great cabin, brimming glasses of wine before them.

"Well, Marlowe, it seems we have some problems here that need addressing, what?" Nicholson said. "Now, I am aware of your relationship with Mrs. Tinling, but I think you had best understand she has been accused of a capital crime—"

"She has been used horribly, and for some years—first by that pig of a husband, and then by the whole stinking Wilkenson brood, and I shall not have her suffer any further."

"Well, sir," Finch broke in before Nicholson could speak. "As to her marital status, I think we all know the truth in that." He pressed on through the governor's angry look. "That, however, is of minor concern. Of more importance is a charge of murder that has been brought against her— "

"There has been no charge of murder, sir. The charge is of being an accomplice, and to that there is not a bit of evidence. I have read Lucy's statement—she does not implicate Elizabeth in the least. Quite the opposite. This is a sham, brought against her by the bastards Wilkenson, and done so for the sake of vengeance, no more."

"You will not, *not* speak of the leading family in this colony in that manner," Finch said.

"Gentlemen, gentlemen." Nicholas held up his hands, and Marlowe and Finch were quiet. "Please, Captain Marlowe, for all that, Jacob Wilkenson is a member of the House of Burgesses and he has brought charges that can only be cleared in a court of law. I beg you understand that Mrs. Tinling must still be considered a prisoner until her trial."

"I understand that."

"Then you will allow us to take her back into custody?"

"I will not."

"Then, sir," Finch said loudly, "we shall arrest her anyway, and your own base desires be damned."

"And how, sir," Marlowe asked, "do you propose to do that?"

"Now, Marlowe," Nicholson tried to inject civility once again, "this is really harboring a fugitive, you know, and it won't do."

"I understand all of that, Governor."

"And understand as well," Finch broke in, "that your own status is very much in question, very much in question indeed. There is reason to believe that you are not who you say, sir, and might well be wanted by the law, right along with that little tart."

Marlowe shifted his gaze to Finch, and his cold stare stopped the president in mid-bluster. He resettled himself in his seat and cleared his throat.

"Men have died for less than that, sir," Marlowe said. "By my own hand."

"Are you threatening me, sir?"

"Yes."

Finch was at a loss for words, taken aback by the directness of that answer, and Nicholson leapt into the breach.

"Now, gentlemen, I think there is no need for this. We are all of us on the same side, what? Not squabbling like a bunch of Dutchmen. But see here, Marlowe, it is true that there have been questions raised. I should not like to have to relieve you of your command."

"I should not like to have you try."

"Be that as it may . . ." Nicholson was too much of an old campaigner to be thrown off by that implied threat. "I'll own there's no evidence against Mrs. Tinling, that her arrest was all Wilkenson's doing. I think perhaps we can forget all of that, the charges and such, in consideration of the good work you have done, and the service I hope you will continue to perform."

"Now see here, Governor," Finch found his tongue again, "don't you start making promises that you are unable to keep. We said that perhaps we would *consider* overlooking some of this. But this man's attitude is insufferable, and his harboring that—"

"What is this duty you hope I will continue to perform?" Marlowe leaned back in his chair. Nicholson would not have said that if he did not have something specific in mind. He would not be so liberal with his forgiveness if he did not still need Marlowe's services.

"Well." Nicholson cleared his throat, and for the first time he looked uncomfortable. "There are reports abroad that a pirate has been sailing into the bay. I have had some word from down Norfolk way. They're in a state there, I should say, damn near panic. Hampton Roads is all in a fright, sure the pirates will plunder all the country homes, like them villains did up to Tindall's Point back in '82. There is even some thought that they may have taken the *Wilkenson Brothers*—"

"Which, I might add," Finch interjected, "would have been safe with the fleet were it not for you."

"The fleet would not have been safe at all, sir, were it not for me. Jacob Wilkenson should have obeyed the law."

"Jacob Wilkenson, who it pleases you to speak so ill of, is at least seeing to some defense against this villain. He has requisitioned a prodigious amount of military supplies from the militia, he is gathering powder, shot, small arms, and intends to organize his neighbors. I hope, sir, that you can be as helpful."

"Yes, yes," Nicholson said, "now look here, Marlowe, can I count on you to see about this pirate? It would do much to improve your position with the burgesses, which, I have to say, could use a deal of improving."

Marlowe looked at Finch's red and angry face and the governor's blank countenance, the face of a born negotiator.

Here were his choices, laid out for him like dishes on a buffet table. He could resign his captaincy, turn the ship over to Rakestraw, turn Elizabeth over to the sheriff—and turn a gun on himself. He would have no other choice.

Or he could continue back down the path he had come, take the *Plymouth Prize* to the Caribbean, go on the account. Bid farewell to Thomas Marlowe and all he had become. It was the dishonorable route, but at least he would escape with his life.

Or he could go and fight Jean-Pierre LeRois, for he was certain that the pirate spreading terror in the lower bay was indeed LeRois. Vicious, brutal man, his crew probably twice the size of that aboard the *Plymouth Prize*. LeRois would be looking for revenge on the guardship that had fooled him and had so mauled his men. He did not care to think on what would happen once LeRois discovered who was in command of that ship. And he did not think his men could beat LeRois. But that was the honorable route, the route to horrible but honorable death.

Death or disgrace, those were his choices.

"I am still the captain of the guardship, I take it," he said at last, "and so I still have my duty."

Chapter 28

TWO SHIPS were fighting it out, somewhere downriver from Jamestown. Marlowe did not need to see the fight to know it was taking place. The sound told him that. The roll of gunfire echoing off the banks of the James River. The cloud of gray smoke building like a small anvil head on the other side of the long, low peninsula.

They were fighting somewhere past the point of land that terminated in Hog Island, perhaps as far down as Warixquake Bay, but most likely nearer than that.

The sound also told him something of how the fight was going. The two ships were hotly engaged, and had been for close to an hour. One was firing three guns for every one gun the other managed to get off. One had larger guns than the other; the sound was different, which was how he was able to differentiate between them.

The one with the larger guns was the one firing more slowly. Perhaps it was their superiority in weight of metal that accounted for their holding out as long as they had, for the slow rate of fire probably meant a small, poorly trained crew. And that most likely meant the ship was a merchantman, fighting for her life. And if that was the case, he could well imagine what the other ship was.

He looked aloft. On the fore- and mainmast the men were scampering around the uppermost rigging, setting royal sails that had been sent up from the deck. They represented the last bit of canvas the *Plymouth Prize* could spread as Marlowe pushed her hard to join in the fight.

He was desperate to stop the slaughter of the innocents, desperate to be done with LeRois or have LeRois be done with him. He was ready to make his final bid to rejoin Virginia society, or at least prevent his being cast down from it. Ready to fight to maintain the thin and largely worn veneer of respectability that covered him and Elizabeth. He could sit still no longer, letting his fear and paranoia fester.

The day was lovely, with a gentle southwesterly breeze pushing them along. It all seemed so incongruous, the gray sails sharp against the blue, cloudless sky, the green fields rolling down to the wide river, the gentle sound of the water against the hull, and the distant blast of cannon, the chance whiff of expended powder.

Elizabeth was there by his side, a parasol held over her head to shield her fine skin from the sun. They might as well have been aboard the *Northumberland* for a yachting excursion.

But of course they were not, and she was in as great a danger as any of them. Greater, really, for she would not be in the fight and thus could not hope for the quick death that comes with a bullet or a blast of langrage. Marlowe hated to compromise her safety thus, but he had no choice. If he left her ashore she would be in even greater danger from the wrath of the Wilkenson clan.

He wanted to wrap his arms around her, kiss her, tell her he loved her. It did not seem right that in half an hour's time they should be locked in a fight with the most dangerous man Marlowe had ever known.

It did not seem right that he should be so frightened on so perfect a day.

"Helmsman, give that south shore a wide berth, there by Hog Island," Marlowe said, and the helmsman repeated the order and nudged the tiller to starboard. The muddy shallows,

Marlowe knew, extended many yards out from the shore, and he did not relish the thought of putting the *Plymouth Prize* hard aground where she could do no more than wait to be pounded to pieces.

"Sir," Lieutenant Rakestraw appeared on the quarterdeck, "I've the drogue rigged aft and ready to stream, sir."

"Good." The drogue was a sort of canvas cone, two fathoms long, which would slow the *Plymouth Prize* down considerably when towed astern.

"Sir, if I may be so bold . . . ?"

"Why did I have you rig the drogue?"

"Yes, sir."

"It is always nice in these instances to have a surprise or two. If this fellow is the one we met before, then he will surely recognize us, and he will know how many men we have, how many guns and all that. At the very least, we can have a bit of speed held in reserve."

"Yes, sir," said Rakestraw. He sounded doubtful.

It took them another twenty minutes to round Hog Island, and in those twenty minutes the firing beyond the point did not let up for a moment. The poor bastard under attack was apparently holding his own. If he could just live for twenty minutes more, the *Plymouth Prize* would be there to kill the pirates or to die in his place.

The land seemed to inch away as they turned more southerly, and as it did it revealed the two distant ships, like a door swinging slowly open to give a view of the room beyond. They were not so very far away, a mile perhaps, probably less, and there was breeze enough that they were not entirely obscured by the smoke.

Marlowe put his glass to his eye. The merchantman was the closer ship, and she was drawing ahead of her attacker so his view of her was unobstructed. She was a big one, with her merchantman's ensign waving defiantly from her mainmast head. For a moment Marlowe thought she was the *Wilkenson Brothers*, but she was black, not oiled, and rigged as a barque rather than a ship. Her forecastle and quarterdeck were not as long as the *Brothers'*.

She seemed in surprisingly good shape for a ship that had taken the pounding that she had. All of her spars were intact, and he could see little damage to her sails. But of course he could not see the side that was taking the punishment, and the pirates would be looking to kill her men, not ruin their prize.

He shifted his glass to the right. The attacking vessel was more shrouded in smoke, being downwind and firing so many more guns than the other. But he did not have to have a perfect view of the ship to recognize her. He had seen her not so very long ago, when it had been the *Plymouth Prize*, dressed as a merchantman, that she was attacking.

He moved his glass up to the pirate's masthead. There at the mainmast flew the black flag with the death's-head, two crossed swords, and hourglass below. She was LeRois's ship. She would be called the *Vengeance*. Every ship LeRois commanded was called *Vengeance*.

And if LeRois guessed that he, Thomas Marlowe—Malachias Barrett—was commanding the *Prize*, then no other enemy in the world would exist for him.

Marlowe put the telescope down and began pacing back and forth, back and forth, ignoring Rakestraw, Elizabeth, and Bickerstaff, who stood together on the leeward side. He wanted to get on with it. He wanted it to be over, one way or another.

And then the rumble of the guns, which had been their companion for an hour or more, ceased. Marlowe looked up at the ships, now about half a mile distant, and as he did the *Plymouth Prize*'s lookout shouted, "On deck! Ship has sheered off! She's hauling her wind! Wearing around!"

Marlowe could see it clearly from the deck. The pirate, the *Vengeance*, had broken off the engagement and now she was turning away from them. The villains must have seen the *Plymouth Prize* coming.

For a second he harbored the hope that she would turn tail and run, but that was a stupid thing to wish for, in part because it would not happen. LeRois had run from the guardship once. To save face with his men, he could not do it again. What was more, his running would not save the Plymouth Prizes. They would just have to pursue him and fight him sooner or later. They may as well do it now.

And of course, LeRois was not running. The *Vengeance* turned stern toward the *Plymouth Prize* and kept turning, coming around on the other tack so she would be clear of the merchantman and have open water enough to maneuver.

"Mr. Rakestraw, I'll thank you to stream the drogue," Marlowe called.

The merchantman was sailing away, heading upriver, trying to put the *Plymouth Prize* between herself and the pirate ship. Marlowe could see a few figures on her quarterdeck waving their thanks and relief to the guardship. She was a slovenly-looking tub, from what Marlowe could see, but he had no more thought to spare for her. Let her get away. He had a fight think about.

He felt the guardship give a tiny jerk as the drogue filled with water and dragged astern, and her speed was cut nearly in half.

A quarter of a mile away the *Vengeance* began to fire, the round shot dropping all around the *Plymouth Prize*. On occasion they scored a hit, embedding a ball in the side or punching a hole in the sails, but they did no more damage than that.

"Mr. Middleton," Marlowe called down into the waist, "let us hold our fire until we are broadside and a bit closer, and then we shall unleash the furies of hell upon him."

"Furies of hell, aye, sir!" Middleton called back. He was grinning, as were many of the Prizes.

Good God, they are looking forward to this, Marlowe thought.

He turned to address Bickerstaff and was surprised to find Elizabeth still standing there. That would never do.

"Elizabeth, pray, come with me. I will show you the best place to hide yourself when it gets hot."

He led the way down the quarterdeck ladder and through the scuttle, then aft into the great cabin, where Lucy sat huddled in a corner, terrified, like a trapped chipmunk. Marlowe glanced at her and tried to think of some words that might cheer her, but could not.

Instead he pulled two pistols from a case on the sideboard and checked the prime in the pan.

"Elizabeth," he said, handing her the guns. "I want you to take Lucy and retreat down to the cable tier. Take the guns with you. I shall send for you when this is over. But I must be honest with you. We may not win the day, and if we do not, you do not want to be found out."

He felt his voice waver, and he paused and swallowed and then with great effort managed to continue in an all-but-normal tone. "If we are taken, if you are certain we are taken, do not waste these bullets trying to defend yourselves."

Elizabeth took the guns and clasped them to her chest.

"I understand, Thomas. Godspeed."

"Godspeed, Elizabeth. I love you very much." With that he turned and disappeared from the great cabin before he could further embarrass himself.

They had halved the distance to the *Vengeance* by the time Marlowe regained the quarterdeck. The two ships were closing fast, though not as fast as they would have if the *Plymouth Prize* had not been streaming the drogue astern. The wind was off the guardship's starboard quarter and all the canvas to topgallants was straining in the breeze, and Marlowe could feel the sluggishness underfoot as the vessel dragged the canvas cone through the water.

And that was fine. He was in no hurry to plunge into this fight, and the extra time meant more opportunity for the merchantman to escape.

"Stand ready on your starboard broadside," Marlowe called down into the waist.

The Plymouth Prizes were hunched over their guns, watching the target draw closer. It would be a battle with great guns that morning, Marlowe had decided. He could not let the Vengeances board; they would overrun his men in no time. There had to be almost twice the number of pirates as there were guardship's men.

But the pirates would not have the discipline to load and run out, load and run out, keeping up a constant barrage like his own, better-trained men. What was more, the *Vengeance* looked like a tired ship, worn and battered and not able to endure that kind of beating. If the *Plymouth Prize* could just stand off and pound away at them, they would win the day, and the loss of life would be minimal.

The loss of life on the *Prize*, in any event. All of the Vengeances would die. They were Marlowe's past, and they had to be stamped out.

King James climbed up the quarterdeck ladder and walked aft, taking his place behind Marlowe. He looked terrible. His face was battered. He walked with a painful limp, but Marlowe knew better than to try and order him below. He nodded a greeting and James nodded back, and Marlowe turned his attention back to the *Vengeance*.

She was still firing, scoring more hits as the two vessels closed, but still Marlowe held his fire. They were no more than a cable length apart. In less than a minute it would be time to blast them to hell.

He swept the dark hull with his glass. The *Vengeance* was not nearly as battered as he would have thought, after exchanging fire with the merchantman for over an hour. Of course, the merchantman's crew could not be counted on for accurate gunfire, but still they were so close it would seem impossible for them to have missed. And yet the *Vengeance* showed no sign of even having been in a fight.

Marlowe felt that first spark of suspicion flare up and glow in his mind, just as the lookout sang out again.

"On deck! Merchantman's hauled his wind!"

"What in hell is he about?" Rakestraw asked of no one in particular.

The big black merchantman, all but forgotten until that moment, had already completed her turn and was running down on them as fast as she had been running away just a moment before.

"Is he coming to our aid?" Rakestraw asked.

Marlowe laughed, despite himself.

"Not *our* aid, Lieutenant," Bickerstaff supplied. "I believe it is his intention to give succor to the pirate, not us."

"Sir, I don't understand—"

"He fooled us," Marlowe said bitterly. "He lured us right in like the fish we are. The battle was a sham, the brigands have both ships, and now we are trapped betwixt them, goddamn me for an idiot."

Rakestraw's eyes went noticeably wider as he realized their situation. "What shall we do, sir?"

"Die, I should think, if we let them trap us thus. Goddamn me, this is all but exactly what I did to him! How could I be so damned stupid? Mr. Middleton!"

The second officer looked up and waved.

"You shall have time for perhaps two broadsides. Make them count. Fire when you are ready, but soon, if you please."

"Aye, sir! Fire!" Middleton strung the words together, and the gun crews, ready for the past ten minutes, lit off their great guns in one solid wall of smoke and flames and noise.

With some satisfaction Marlowe witnessed the destruction unleashed on the *Vengeance*, the old *Vengeance*, for he had no doubt that the new, big merchantman astern was the newest vessel to bear that hated name. A section of the bulwark was torn away. He saw one gun at least upended, heard the high-pitched shriek of a man trapped under half a ton of hot metal.

The Prizes were reloading under the urgent prompting of Lieutenant Middleton, or seeking out victims over the tops of their falconets, blasting the pirate with muzzle loads of glass and twisted metal. But there were not that many targets to be found, for the old *Vengeance* seemed to be lightly manned.

Just enough on board to make a great show with unshotted guns, Marlowe thought. He felt the anger, the disgust. How could he be so stupid? Would they all die because of his idiocy? Would Elizabeth have the courage to put a bullet in her head, or would the pirates find her, huddled in a dark corner, and . . .

He shook his head, shook it hard, driving the thoughts from his mind. In the waist the Prizes were running out again, firing again. He saw rigging aboard their target swept away like spiderwebs, saw more of the rail collapse. But that was enough of that. He did not want to attack that old and worn-out ship, because that was what LeRois wanted him to do.

"Hands to braces! Starboard your helm!" Marlowe shouted, just able to hear himself through dulled and ringing ears. The *Plymouth Prize* turned northerly, swinging away from the old, damaged pirate.

The black merchantman was bearing down on them now, not two cable lengths away. The brigands were crowding into the bows and head rig, making ready to board. There was many times the number of men aboard her than there was aboard the other ship. Marlowe could picture the bastards huddled down behind the bulwark, snickering at the great deception they were carrying off, fooling the very ship that had fooled them so.

"Damn my eyes, damn my eyes to hell," Marlowe muttered, then called down to Middleton, "Man the larboard battery. Hit 'em as hard as ever you can!"

Middleton had already shifted his men across the deck, and on Marlowe's word he yelled "Fire!" and the larboard guns went off.

The merchantman was coming bow-on, and the *Plymouth Prize*'s guns swept the length of her deck. Marlowe could see some damage wrought by the fire—a cathead blown apart, the spritsail topmast shot in two, perhaps half a dozen of the enemy tossed back on their deck—but he could see nothing beyond that. He had anticipated a duel with the great guns, so the cannon was loaded with round shot, not case shot or langrage. They may have killed a few of the pirates, and that would be a fine thing, but he knew that there were plenty more to take their place.

And then he heard it. The lone voice, deep, slow, chanting, "Death, death, death . . ."

Heads aboard the *Plymouth Prize* looked up, peered over rails and through gunports. The black merchantman was two hundred yards away, a single cable length, and steering to smash into the guardship's side.

"Death, death, death . . ." The voice was joined by another and another, and then the terrible pounding started, and the fiddle and the bones banging together. Most of the pirates were on the merchantman's deck, shielded from the *Prize's* great guns by the bulwark. The men of the *Plymouth Prize* could hear the terrible vaporing, but they could see only a fraction of the enemy, and that made it more terrifying still.

"Fire! Keep firing, damn your eyes!" Middleton shouted.

The men fired again, and the falconets blasted away, and when the noise had subsided and the smoke blown past, it was still there, the black ship coming on, the horrible cacophony, "Death, death, death . . ."

"Sir, shall I stand the men ready to repel boarders?" Rakestraw asked.

"What?" Marlowe was jerked from the horrible vision. "Oh, yes, pray do." He still did not intend for there to be any boarders, but he had already made several atrocious mistakes that day, and there was still time for more.

The pirate, the new *Vengeance*, was one hundred yards from the guardship, her bowsprit pointed right at the *Prize's* waist. Marlowe could picture the sea of pirates breaking over the rail, pouring down on the deck, sweeping all away before them.

Rakestraw was pushing the men to the sides and others back as reserves, ordering them to take up their small arms, telling them to stand fast. But telling them would not do. This was not the drunken lot at Smith Island. This was the crew of the *Vengeance*. This was LeRois.

Fifty yards separated the ships when the flag broke out at the mainmast head, the grinning skull and swords and hourglass in sharp relief against the black field, and the rhythmic vaporing broke down into random screaming and gunshots. Marlowe felt his guts turn liquid.

LeRois is just a man, he thought to himself, but he did not believe that in any way that mattered. He had seen LeRois live despite inhuman wounds, had witnessed him torturing prisoners in ways that could not be countenanced by any creature in possession of a soul. After years in the sweet trade, it remained that Jean-Pierre LeRois was the only man of whom Marlowe was frightened.

He clamped his teeth together, balled his fists.

In his mind he was there again, on the deck of another *Vengeance*, knowing that he had to best LeRois or die the kind of protracted death that only LeRois could arrange. He was there, face-to-face with that madman, sword against sword.

"Oh, damn me to hell," he said. They were thirty yards apart and the *Vengeance* was committed to her course. Marlowe realized he may have left it until it was too late.

"Rakestraw! Rakestraw!" The first officer looked up. "Cut the damned drogue away! Cut it now!"

There was a second's confusion on the man's face, enough for a curse to form on Marlowe's lips, and then he understood and raced aft with all the speed that Marlowe could wish.

The *Vengeance* was twenty yards away, running downwind, turning slightly to keep her bow pointed at the *Plymouth Prize*'s side.

And then, through the screaming and the gunfire and the cheering of his own men Marlowe heard the distinct thump of Rakestraw's ax coming down on the line holding the drogue. He heard it again, and then the *Plymouth Prize* seemed to leap forward under his feet, bounding away like a wild animal set free from a leash.

The *Vengeance*, which had been abeam of them, was suddenly astern. She turned hard, trying to keep on her collision course, but the pirates were gathered in the bow, ready to board, not standing to the braces, and the sails that were set for a downwind run began to flog and collapse as the bow came up.

Marlowe could hear the vaporing dying away, could hear a voice, a voice he recognized—heavy, indistinct, the accent thick—calling the hands to trim the sails.

"Come up, come up!" Marlowe shouted to the helmsmen. They pushed the tiller over and the *Prize* turned further upwind, her bow pointing upriver in the direction from which they had come. "Good, steady as she goes! Make your head to pass Hog Island!" He did not know where he was going, he knew only that he had to get away from that place, away from that ship.

"Permission to fire, sir?" Middleton called from the waist.

Marlowe glanced over at the *Vengeance*. She was almost abeam of them, and they were passing on opposite tacks. "Yes, yes, fire!"

The guns went off in a ragged order, and each shot told on the pirate just forty yards abeam. The *Vengeance* was turning hard, and her yards were swinging as the braces were manned at last, but she had lost a great deal of distance. Now she would be in the *Plymouth Prize's* wake and catching the guardship would be no mean feat.

Marlowe picked up his telescope from the binnacle box and put it to his eye. He felt a wave of terror and fascination all at once, like watching a pack of wolves from what one hopes is a safe distance.

There were any number of the villains on the *Vengeance's* quarterdeck, since a pirate did not observe any of the distinctions of rank found aboard a man-of-war or any other vessel on earth. Some were bare-chested or wore only waistcoats; others were fully dressed in clothes that might have once been fine garments. All were well armed, he could see that, but that was no surprise.

And then he was there, a head taller then the rest, his great mass filling Marlowe's lens as he screamed orders forward. LeRois's face was red and contorted with rage. He was stomping around, slashing at the rail with the sword he held in his hand, gesturing wildly.

The Frenchman would be as furious about the drogue as

Marlowe was about the mock battle. They were pirates both, brigands and villains, and neither of them liked to be played for a fool.

Marlowe saw LeRois pause in his tirade and look over at the guardship. It seemed as if he was looking right down the tube of Marlowe's telescope. Then the pirate picked up his own glass, and as their ships drew apart the two men stared at each other across the water.

Marlowe saw LeRois let his glass fall to his side. He looked frightened and confused, quite in contrast to the LeRois of a few seconds before. The pirate put the glass back up to his eye, and then down again, up and down, three times.

And then LeRois staggered back and pointed the glass up and up until it seemed to Marlowe that he must be staring straight into the sun. And then, a second later, it seemed as if something inside the pirate exploded.

He flung the glass over the side of his ship and pulled a pistol from his belt, cocked it, and fired it straight at Marlowe.

Marlowe jumped in surprise—it was startling, magnified as it was by the glass—but he was quite out of pistol range. LeRois flung the gun down, grabbed another, fired that as well. He was waving his arms, shouting at the men around him, gesturing at the guardship.

He has seen me, Marlowe thought. He has seen me and recognized me, and now he knows it is not just a king's ship he is pursuing, it is Malachias Barrett.

God help me, God help us all, if he runs us down.

Chapter 29

THEY RAN north with the wind abeam and the tide beginning to ebb. The Vengeances continued to shoot their bow chasers, though they had no hope of hitting the guardship since the guns did not point forward enough to bear. The pirates just liked to shoot the guns. Marlowe understood that.

He looked over the taffrail at the big ship in their wake. It *was* the *Wilkenson Brothers*. He realized that once he had taken a good look at her, once they had settled into the chase and thus dealt with their more immediate concerns.

He recalled what Finch had said, about rumors of the merchant ship being taken. The big, powerful merchant ship. Bigger, more powerful even than the *Plymouth Prize*.

He recalled what Finch had said about how she would have been safe from the pirate had it not been for him, Marlowe, taking his revenge on the Wilkensons. Well, that was ironic indeed.

And not only was the *Vengeance* née *Wilkenson Brothers* stronger than the *Plymouth Prize*, she was faster as well, being a bigger vessel with a longer waterline. This might have been a concern if she was handled better, but as it was her sails were not trimmed quite as perfectly as they might be, nor had her new owners set all the canvas that she would bear.

Marlowe imagined that this was due in part to an unfamiliarity with the ship—LeRois could not have had her for more than a week or so—as well as the high probability that all aboard her were drunk and too taken with the excitement of the whole thing to bother with the effort needed to coax another knot or two out of her.

And the Vengeances would realize there was no need to run the *Plymouth Prize* down. They were heading upriver, bound to run out of deep water sooner or later. Then, easy pickings. That had certainly occurred to Marlowe, and from the expressions he saw around him, he guessed others had thought on it as well. The old *Vengeance* was also under way, limping upriver after the two combatants. Two ships on one, with twice the men he had. He did not have a clue as to how he would solve that dilemma.

He was going to lose the *Plymouth Prize*, one way or another. For his present cowardice, running upriver with his tail between his legs, the governor would take the guardship away from him even if LeRois did not. Or he would try, and Marlowe would refuse to give it up, and then he would become as much a criminal as LeRois, all his hopes of a legitimate life pissed away.

"Oh, damn them all," he said out loud. His mind was reeling with the arguments and counterarguments, plans and contingencies. He would just run the damn guardship into the dock at Jamestown and let his men disperse into the countryside, let the governor deal with this problem. If they made it to the dock.

Hog Island was coming abeam of them now. They would have to sail past that point of land and tack and hope they could point high enough to get around the bend in the river with the wind from the quarter that it was.

"Fall off, helmsmen, fall off, damn your eyes!" Marlowe suddenly shouted, panic making his throat tight. They were skirting the point too close. He could see the muddy shoals rising up to grab them, see the dirty water swirling around where their passing had churned up the bottom. If they went aground, they would be dead.

The helmsmen pushed the tiller over and the bow of the *Plymouth Prize* swung away. It was a close thing, and it was Marlowe's fault. He had not been paying attention. He cursed himself, considered apologizing to the helmsmen for cursing them, remained silent.

They stood on, with the north shore growing closer by the second. "Hands, stand ready to come about!" Marlowe shouted, and the men ran to their stations and stood there, grim faced, looking aft for further orders. Each man aboard knew what this meant; if they missed stays, which was easy enough to do in the open ocean, let alone a river with tidal currents to contend with, then the *Vengeance* would be on top of them. The Prizes had figured out what Marlowe already knew: that these pirates would not die as easily as those on Smith Island, that the outcome was likely to be very different indeed.

"Ready . . . helms alee!" Marlowe called, and the bow of the guardship began to turn. There was a fine plantation house on the north shore, a big white house with slave quarters down by the water and fields of young tobacco plants. It seemed to sweep past as the guardship turned.

"Wait for it . . . wait for it . . . ," Marlowe muttered to himself, his eyes on the leeches of the square sails. They held fast, immobile, and then in the next instant they began to flutter and break as the wind came down their edge.

"Mainsail, haul!" Marlowe called, and the main yards were hauled around as the sails on the foremast came aback.

"Turn, turn, turn, you son of a whore . . . ," he heard Rakestraw muttering at his side.

And the *Plymouth Prize was* turning, swinging through the wind with her foresails pressed against the mast. And then they were through and Marlowe called "Let go and haul!" and the foreyards swung around and the guardship settled on the new tack, on the other side of the point. He could feel the tension ease fore and aft, as if the ship itself had been holding her breath.

He turned to look aft, to see if the poorly handled pirate would be able to accomplish that evolution, or if the chase would end there.

He stared at the black ship. There was something amiss, but he could not grasp it.

And then he smiled, and then he laughed out loud and said, "Thank you, Lord! Dear God, thank you!"—for the *Vengeance* was hard aground.

LeRois knew that the drogue was there half a second before it was cut away. He was standing on the new *Vengeance's* quarterdeck, watching with delight and profound satisfaction as his trap closed around the very son of a bitch who had fooled him before, when it occurred to him that something was not quite right.

The breeze was good and the guardship had everything set to topgallants, and yet she seemed to be plodding along, sluggish and dull, though she looked as if she should be quick and handy.

He brought his telescope to his eye and examined the after section of the ship, taking care not to look at the quarterdeck for fear that the vision of Barrett would appear again.

At first he saw nothing. And then, from the window of the great cabin, he noticed the light hawse running down at a sharp angle and disappearing into the water. It had to be a drogue. He had used it himself, many times.

"*Merde alors!* Come up! Come up!" he shouted to Darnall. "The son of bitch—"

He got no farther than that. The line whipped out of the great cabin window, cut from inside, and suddenly the plodding ship that was right under their bows surged ahead, leaving the *Vengeance* pointing at open water.

"*Merde!* Son of bitch! Come up, come up!" LeRois shouted again, but now the helmsman was already pushing the tiller over, trying to keep the bow pointed at the guardship's vulnerable waist.

The vaporing began to die away, and in its place came the sound of flogging canvas.

"*Allez haut le bras! Allez haut le bras, vite, vite!*" he screamed, then screamed it again, and then realized that he was speaking French, could not recall the English words. "Goddamn . . . go to the fucking braces, now!" it came to him, and the Vengeances raced aft, threw the braces off the pins, hauled around to match the sails to the wind.

LeRois looked outboard. The guardship was alongside, heading upriver as the *Vengeance* was heading down. The *Vengeance* was turning in her wake, turning under a hail of gunfire, but the scream of the shot bothered LeRois no more than a swarm of mosquitos. It was a minor annoyance compared to the drogue, compared to the fact that his perfect trap had become a stern chase.

His sword was in his hand, he realized, and as he was shouting orders he was hacking at the rail as if it were the skull of the son of a bitch who was in command of the guardship.

He had to see him. Damn the ghosts. He had to see the son of a whore who had rigged that drogue, wanted to better picture his bloody death.

He squinted and peered across the water. The quarterdeck of the king's ship was not crowded like his own, and it was easy enough to see which of the few there was the master. The bastard had a glass to his eye and was staring at them as the ships passed, watching him, which made LeRois madder still. He sheathed his sword, snatched up his own telescope, trained it on the man he intended to kill.

The image of Malachias Barrett filling his lens, solid, with none of the ephemeral quality it had formerly possessed. He staggered back, stunned. "Son of bitch . . . ," he muttered, and put the glass back to his eye, forcing himself to watch, to watch and wait for the image to go. It had to go.

But it did not. Just like the last time. He put the glass down again and shook his head and then looked once more. It was still there.

He felt his palms go greasy on the telescope, felt the sickness in the pit of his stomach, the desperate need for a numbing shot of rum or gin. What did this mean? Why would it not go?

And then from somewhere in the back reaches of his mind, like the first growling of thunder, building and rolling forward, rumbling and shaking the earth, the thought came that perhaps this was not a vision at all.

Of course. The realization washed over him. Of course. Where else had this son of a bitch learned all these tricks, disguising the ship as a crippled merchantman, the men dressed as women, the drogue? What festering king's officer could be as clever as that?

He could no longer see the guardship, he could not see anything. The whole world was bathed in a bright, white light and there was music, and with the music, more subtle, like something happening on the street outside, was a terrible, agonizing screaming.

"LeRois? LeRois, you all right?" Darnall's voice was like something from a grave. LeRois looked at him, and suddenly the world was back and the music was gone and in its place there was only the screaming, the endless screaming.

And Malachias Barrett, watching him through a telescope. Fifty yards away.

"Ahhhhhhhhh!" LeRois's shriek started low and built in pitch and volume. He threw his telescope overboard and jerked a pistol from his belt. He fired it at Barrett, flung it aside, pulled another, fired that as well.

"Catch him, catch him, catch that son of a bitch!" LeRois screamed. He could feel the tears welling up in his eyes. It was Malachias Barrett. He was getting away.

"I will kill you all, all of you, if you do not catch him!" LeRois shrieked at the men on the quarterdeck.

Darnall spit a stream of tobacco juice on the deck. "I reckon he ain't gonna get away if he's sailing up a fucking river, Captain. Gotta run out of water sometime."

LeRois stared at the quartermaster, trying to make sense of

the words. River. Water. He would run out of water. He would be trapped.

LeRois turned and began to pace, trying to think. To do that he had to talk out loud, for there was no room in his head for thoughts, not with the screaming and the voices, and even then he had to talk loudly enough to hear his own voice over the noise.

Through it all he could hear Darnall issuing orders to the sail trimmers. They were pursuing Barrett as fast as ever they could. If they did not run them down in the next hour, then they certainly would by end of day. The new *Vengeance* was fast and clean, and they were on a river.

LeRois shook his head as he paced. It did not seem possible. It did not seem possible. All those years of hating Barrett for what he had done, all those years, and now Barrett was here, and LeRois would have him soon. He could not imagine how he would kill him. He had thought about it for so long that he hardly knew where to begin.

Big guns were firing. The Vengeances were shooting off the bow chasers. LeRois felt relief at the sight of the smoke, proof that there were indeed real guns firing. He did not want guns going off in his head. That would be too much, too much by half.

He had no sense for how long they had been pursuing. There was something crawling around under his clothes. Bugs of some kind. He could feel them. He scratched and scratched, but they were still there.

He had stopped speaking to himself and had begun to listen to what the voices were telling him, and it was extraordinary. Why had he not just listened to the voices before? Why had he fought them for so long?

They told him all he needed to know to take care of Barrett. They told him how he, LeRois, would have all of the tidewater. It was all to be his. He had been brought there for a reason.

"Here, Captain, look here. Captain?"

LeRois recognized Darnall's voice. He looked up at the quartermaster. *"Oui?"*

"Guardship's coming about. I reckon he misses stays and we'll be right aboard him."

LeRois squinted forward past the bow. The guardship— Barrett's ship—was abeam of a point of land around which she would have to sail to continue upriver. He was coming about, tacking around the shoreline, and once more he was broadside to the *Vengeance* and his speed had dropped off to nothing.

"Run us right aboard of her, eh?" LeRois said. "We don't tack, we just run right into that fucking *cochon*."

"Steady as she goes," Darnall said, and the helmsman held the tiller straight, pointing the *Vengeance*'s bowsprit right at the guardship's waist.

LeRois licked his cracked lips, saw the distance to the king's ship dropping away. Barrett would never get around the point of land in time. They would run the *Vengeance* right into him and then it would be over.

No, then it would just begin.

"Forward, you get ready to board this son of bitch, eh?" LeRois shouted, and once more the Vengeances climbed into the head rig, bolder now after the long chase.

LeRois turned to the man next to him and pulled a pistol from his sash. The man did not object. They were in battle, and that meant that LeRois was in command and his word was sacrosanct. As it should be. As it would be from that moment on, battle or no.

The guardship had made it through the wind and they were hauling their foreyards around, but it was too late for them. The *Vengeance* was no more than a cable length off, closing quickly, the murderous band just starting their slow building chant. LeRois caught a whiff of blood, the smell of fresh spilled blood.

And then the ship jerked under his feet, just slightly, but enough to make him stagger forward. He regained his balance and paused and looked around, then aloft. The sails were still drawing, braced for a larboard tack. He looked over the side. The green fields were no longer slipping past.

The *Vengeance* was hard aground.

"No," LeRois said. It was only a whisper. "No, no . . ."

There was no sound on deck. LeRois knew that everyone was looking at him. He looked forward again, past the unmoving bow. The stern section of the guardship slipped past the far point of land and disappeared.

LeRois staggered back, off balance. The deck of the *Vengeance* seemed to heave like she was in a massive sea. The faces and the rigging and the great guns were swirling around him. He could not make them stop. The screaming grew and grew until LeRois had to hold his hands over his ears and scream himself, but it did no good, he could not block it out.

Then Darnall was standing in front of him. "Captain, Captain, they're still in a fucking river, they can't get past us! Soon as the tide lifts us off, we'll murder them sons of bitches!"

"No! No!" LeRois screamed. He heard the words, but they made no sense. He leveled his pistol at Darnall's head, saw the flash of surprise on the quartermaster's face, pulled the trigger. Darnall was tossed across the deck. He crumpled in the waterways and did not move.

The screaming and the voices were ripping through his head, and through it all came the cracking and popping of that thing carrying away. He staggered back against the bulwark and looked up, and everything was white again. The popping grew louder and became a tearing, a crashing, a rending, and then Jean-Pierre LeRois's last tenuous hold on sanity was gone.

Chapter 30

IT WAS absolutely black on the cable tier, save for the little bit of light thrown off by the lantern Elizabeth had carried below. She sat in a far corner of the tier. Whether she was forward or aft, starboard or larboard, she could not tell, for she was all turned around. She was perched atop a burlap bag filled with bits of old, stiff rope. At least that was what it felt like through her skirts and petticoats and shift.

Lucy sat beside her, all but on top of her, clinging to her and crying bitterly on her shoulder. She could feel the dampness of the girl's tears spreading through the cloth of her dress. Lucy was terrified. Terrified of what the pirates might do to her, terrified of what Marlowe or James or Elizabeth might do to her, terrified at what might happen to them all as a result of her betrayal.

Elizabeth understood. Lucy had just confessed to her what she had done. Or, more correctly, what George Wilkenson had forced her to do. The bastard.

"Oh, Lord, please forgive me, Mrs. Elizabeth, please forgive me . . . ," Lucy wailed, softly, and then fell to sobbing again.

Elizabeth wrapped her arm more tightly around Lucy's shoulders and gave her a reassuring hug. "Don't you fret, sweetheart, there is nothing to forgive. Any woman would have done the same. It wasn't your fault."

At that Lucy wept harder still.

Lucy's hysteria had gone on far longer than was quite justified by the circumstances, or so Elizabeth felt, given that Wilkenson had made her do what she did and that Lucy had in point of fact betrayed no one, save for the dead cook, so Elizabeth turned her attention from the girl to the ship around them.

She stared off into the dark and tried to get a sense for what was happening. The great guns had fired, larboard and starboard, and there had been a great rushing about, but that was some time ago. She had braced for the sound of fighting on deck, but it had not come. Instead things seemed to have settled down. She could still hear gunfire, but it did not seem to be the *Plymouth Prize*'s guns; it seemed too muffled and distant for that.

It seemed as if nothing significant had happened for some time, and Elizabeth found her thoughts drifting back to the murder of her ersatz husband. It had shocked her; she had no idea that the slaves had been capable of such a thing. She pictured the old woman putting the poison in Joseph's food, the smug satisfaction she must have felt serving out death to that bastard.

But the old woman never left the kitchen. She could not have known who would get the poison dish. If Joseph had been the target, then he had to have been poisoned by the person who actually presented him with his plate, which was . . .

Elizabeth leaned back, knitted her eyebrows, took a long look at Lucy, still clinging to her. Hadn't Lucy taken over that duty not a week before Joseph's death?

A question was forming in her mind, her lips shaping around it, when the women were startled by the sound of rushing feet and a man's voice, issuing orders, judging by his tone. It sounded like Thomas, but she could not hear the words.

She felt herself tense. Lucy felt it as well and peeled herself from Elizabeth's shoulder. The faint light of the lantern gleamed on the tears that covered her face. "What's happening now?" she asked, her voice quavering with uncertainty.

"I don't know."

Then the ship, which had been heeling in one direction, came upright on an even keel. The two women looked at each other, but their concentration was directed toward listening to what was taking place on deck. There seemed to be a fair amount of commotion, the kind that Elizabeth had come to associate with sail maneuvers.

And then a moment later the ship began to heel the other way. They felt their whole world tilt back and then stop, and then it was quiet again.

"I believe we have . . . tacked, if I recall the sailor's vernacular," Elizabeth said.

"Is that a good thing?"

"I suppose. At least it means we are still sailing. Lucy . . . ?" Elizabeth continued, but the question was quashed by the sound of feet on the ladder above. Both women tensed. It was the first movement they had heard belowdecks in what seemed an age at least.

"It ain't them pirates, is it?" Lucy whispered.

"Shhh," Elizabeth said, though her thoughts were moving along the same lines. She was certain that the *Plymouth Prize* had not been taken. At least she had been certain a minute before, but now doubt began to creep in. It did not seem as if a fight had taken place, but then, she did not really know what a fight would sound like.

She reached slowly for the pistol on the deck at her feet, wrapped her hand around the butt, and raised it to chest level. She did not know what she would do with it. Marlowe's advice concerning the disposition of the two bullets was clear and sensible, but she did not know if she had the nerve for that. What was worse, she knew that Lucy did not, so for Elizabeth it would be a matter of shooting Lucy first and then herself.

The steps came down another ladder. They could see the loom of a lantern coming closer. Elizabeth drew back the lock of the pistol. The mechanical click was loud in the confines of the cable tier.

The footsteps stopped.

"Mrs. Tinling?" came an uncertain voice. "Mrs. Tinling, it's Lieutenant Middleton, ma'am? You there?"

Elizabeth met Lucy's eyes, and the women smiled. "Yes, Lieutenant, we're here, in the cable tier." She eased the lock back into the half-cock position.

The lantern grew brighter and Lieutenant Middleton appeared. "Ma'am, Captain Marlowe reckons it's safe for you to come out now."

"What of the . . . Have we defeated the pirates? Surely there has not been a battle?"

"No, ma'am. The pirates run aground, and they ain't moving for some time, what with the falling tide and all."

"I see. That is a good thing, is it not?"

It was, in fact. At least it was as far as Lieutenant Middleton was concerned, and he described the morning's events to the women as he led them up and aft to the great cabin, with much talk of drogues and hawsers and draft, tacking and bow chasers and ebbing tides. Elizabeth was able to follow perhaps a third of the monologue. But what she grasped was enough to make her understand that the *Plymouth Prize* had been lured into a trap and had just managed to escape. Apparently it had been a near thing.

Middleton opened the door to the great cabin and Elizabeth entered, nodding her thanks. She was in high spirits, having discovered how narrowly she had just avoided a most unpleasant fate, and she expected that the others would be similarly enthusiastic.

They were not. Elizabeth sensed the mood, tense and volatile, even as she stepped through the great cabin door. The smile faded from her face.

Marlowe was seated behind the table that he used as a desk. Bickerstaff and Rakestraw sat across from him and to either side. King James was in the far corner.

"I give you joy, gentlemen, on your victory," she said. Despite the dearth of joy in the room.

"Thank you. You are well?" Marlowe asked. He was not smiling, did not seem overly concerned about her health—or anyone else's, for that matter.

"Yes, thank you, we are well," Elizabeth replied. "Are you not pleased to have beaten this pirate?"

"We have escaped, ma'am," Bickerstaff supplied, "we have not beaten him."

"And we were goddamned lucky to do that," Marlowe said, and his tone implied that this was the point in contention. "I think we should not press that luck overhard."

"Let me say again, Captain," said Bickerstaff evenly, "that he is stuck on a sandbank. It would be no great difficulty to come about and destroy him where he lies."

"Oh, you presume to tell me what can and cannot be done when it comes to a sea fight? Well, then, since we are repeating ourselves, let *me* say again that he has near one hundred men and two ships. That is twice the men we have and twice the ships, and only one ship is aground.

"And even if both were stuck, there are always his boats. His men could board us from boats, come over the rails from so many points we could never repel them. What is more, those men there are desperate and experienced killers, sir, not the pathetic rabble we call our crew."

"That pathetic rabble was sufficient for you when it came time to remove Elizabeth from jail. They were sufficient to defeat the brigands on Smith Island and to help you carry off what you fancied was your considerable portion of the booty. Yes, I am perfectly aware of that. They will follow you anywhere. My suggestion is that you lead them where you yourself are duty-bound to go."

Marlowe stood suddenly and pounded the desk with his fist, then shook a finger at Bickerstaff. "Do not, do not, presume to tell me my orders. I do not believe the governor had it in mind to have the guardship taken by pirates, have her guns turned against the colony."

They were silent for a moment, glaring at each other.

"Mr. Rakestraw," Marlowe said at last, his eyes never leaving Bickerstaff, "what say you?"

"I will do whatever you order, Captain. I won't question what you say."

"James?"

"Like Mr. Rakestraw says."

"I find this loyalty very refreshing," Marlowe said. "I wish it were more universal."

"And I think," said Bickerstaff, "that I am aware of certain influences coloring your decision that perhaps the others are not. I think perhaps your history leads you to overestimate the abilities of your adversary."

"What are you saying?" Marlowe growled the words. Elizabeth took a step back, had never seen Marlowe like that, furious, smoldering, feral. "Are you saying I am a coward, sir? Is that it? Should you need me to prove that I am afraid of no one, least of all you, I would be delighted to oblige."

"Oh, for the love of God, Thomas . . .," Elizabeth said. This was too much. Bickerstaff was the truest friend any man had ever had.

"Silence!" Marlowe roared, glared at her. His expression was frightening. He swept the room with his eyes. "We shall proceed to Jamestown and lie at anchor with a spring rigged to the cable. We can then perhaps prevent any vessel from coming upriver, protect ourselves from this bastard once the tide floats him free."

Marlowe looked around at the men once more. His eyes settled on Elizabeth. "I would hope that I can still count on some loyalty, that all sense of honor and obligation has not been forgotten."

The words hung in the air. Elizabeth broke the silence. "Oh, for God's sake, Thomas—forgive me . . . Captain Marlowe—this is not the time to turn on those who love you."

"Well, it is refreshing indeed to know that I am loved. But love is not loyalty, is it, ma'am?"

Elizabeth just shook her head. God, but men could be

such idiots, such absolute idiots. She had seen it in all its manifestations. It was absurd to think that Marlowe could rise above it, because he, too, was a man. He could not change that.

She spun around and marched out of the great cabin. If Marlowe was going to be an ass in that uniquely masculine way, then there was nothing she or anyone else could do.

There were about eighty men aboard the new *Vengeance*, dirty, bearded men in long coats, torn and filthy shirts, slop trousers, and old breeches. They wore pistols draped around their necks with fancy bits of ribbon. Some had feathers or more ribbon fastened to their cocked hats, or bright cloth bound around their heads.

They carried cutlasses and swords and axes and daggers, each man according to his preference. They stood in the waist or the quarterdeck or in the rigging or perched on the great guns. They all were watching their master, *Capitain* Jean-Pierre LeRois.

And LeRois was scanning the countryside around the ship, the green fields and the brown river and the blue, blue sky. The whiteness was gone, the blinding white that had seared everything away, and in its place was the world, the earth, all bright and vivid, new, like the first day of creation.

"Rum?" One of the men standing beside him offered him a bottle. LeRois looked at the bottle and then at the man, and then all the men standing there watching him. He had forgotten about them.

"No," he said to the man with the proffered bottle. He did not want rum. Rum just dulled everything. He was finally seeing things clearly, more clearly than he had ever seen them. He did not want the sharpness dulled.

He could no longer feel the bugs under his clothes. The screaming was gone as well, and in its place were the voices, and the voices told him it was time to move.

His eyes locked on a big white house at the far end of the field that ran along the north shore. "We go ashore now!" he shouted to the men. *"La maison,* we take that. We take them all, *oui?"*

Heads turned toward the shore. Whatever he had said seemed to agree with the men. A low murmur ran across the deck and built and built into a chorus of shouting and chanting and vaporing as the men rigged up the stay tackle and yard tackle and swayed the boats out over the side.

LeRois did not know how long it took, minutes, perhaps, or hours, but finally the boats were in the water and the Vengeances were pouring over the rails and down onto the thwarts, filling each boat, then pushing off and making room for the next.

At last there was only LeRois, and he clambered down the cleats and took his place in the stern sheets of the launch. The other boats moved deferentially aside while the launch went first to the far shore.

The boat nudged into the bank and the men leapt out into warm water up to their knees and pulled it farther ashore, then LeRois made his way to the bow and hopped out.

He headed out across the dark brown field. There were row upon row of small dirt hills with plants bursting from the top like little green volcanoes. There were people in the field as well, blacks, starting to move back from the advancing pirates. Some were turning and running. From a cluster of small buildings, the slave quarters, LeRois imagined, more Negroes were fleeing toward the big house.

"Slaves," he said out loud. "They are all slaves."

From the corner of his eye he could see his men spread out in a line behind him as they advanced. People appeared on the porch, white people. One of them had a gun. To defend the place. LeRois could not imagine why. He was an irresistible force. They could do no more than run.

And that was what most of them did, white and black. Fled down the far road in the face of the pirates, clutching a few pathetic possessions.

Let them run. LeRois imagined himself and his men as a great wave, pushing all ahead of it, destroying all in its path until at last those people trying to stay ahead would be trapped and dashed to pieces. There was only so far they could run.

The pirates picked up the pace, stepping faster, then jogging toward that huge house, that repository of comforts and riches. The front door was left open, as if welcoming them in. They swarmed up the small hill on which the house stood and poured across the porch.

A window was smashed and a musket was thrust out—some hero remaining behind to protect his home—and the musket fired into the crowd. A man screamed and dropped, but the pirates did not hesitate in the least, as if they were not even aware of the gunfire.

One of them grabbed up a chair and flung it through a window, leering at the satisfying sound of smashing glass and shattering wood. More chairs were taken up, more windows were broken in.

LeRois caught a glimpse of the hero who had fired the single shot. He was struggling to pull a pistol free from his belt when the horde fell upon him and dragged him through the window and onto the porch, pulling him over the jagged glass he himself had broken. He screamed and disappeared beneath a mass of brigands. There was a brief thrashing, and then he was dead.

The pirates went in through the door and the windows. They tore through the house, wild with the opportunity to loot and destroy. They pulled down curtains and overturned tables, smashed whatever they could smash, just for the sheer delight of it. A bag was located and stuffed with anything that might be of value, and when that one was full another was started.

The family had apparently been at dinner when the Vengeances had interrupted them, for the big dining-room table was spread with turkey and fritters and tripe and asparagus. The pirates swarmed around, grabbing handfuls of whatever struck their fancy and stuffing it into their mouths, smashing the plates on the floor as they emptied them.

They burst into the kitchen. Cooking utensils lay scattered where they had been discarded by the cook as she raced from the house. They ripped through the pantry and the cupboards and feasted on whatever they could find, the freshest food they had had in over two months.

They pulled paintings off the walls and slashed them with their swords and urinated on the faces of the family's ancestors. They raced up the wide stairs and tore the bedrooms apart, hacking the mattresses until blizzards of feathers filled the rooms. They found all of the alcohol in the house. It was mostly wine, which was a disappointment, but there was enough of it at least that each man had two or more bottles to himself.

It was the greatest frolic they had ever had, and the pirates went about their business with a thoroughness and enthusiasm that was rarely seen in men on the account. One by one the rooms were torn apart. Furniture was smashed into cord wood, walls were hacked up, any badge of wealth or privilege was desecrated. Great piles of wreckage filled the place. The screaming and shouting and merriment did not abate for a second.

LeRois walked slowly from room to room, watching his men have their fun. That was fine. There was no harm done. He enjoyed seeing his men so happy.

He had no idea how long they had spent in the house. There was an elegant clock on the mantel in the sitting room, covered with cherubs and birds and such, that seemed to ring and ring until finally LeRois could take it no more and shot it to pieces. They had been there for some time, he decided. Long enough. It was time to go.

"*Allez, allez*, we go, we go!" he shouted, walking through the house and screaming at the men and after some time of this finally getting their attention. "Burn this son of bitch, we go now!" he ordered.

The men glanced at one another. The fools did not want to leave. They wanted to stay here, on this one little spot of land, when there was an entire continent lying at their feet.

"I said, burn this son of bitch! We must go down the road, go to the next house! They are waiting for us there!"

This seemed to motivate the men. A curtain was torn down and gunpowder spilled on it and then ignited with a flintlock. Soon the cloth was blazing and the pirates piled paintings, broken furniture, and books onto the fire. In just a few minutes the entire sitting room was engulfed. The ceiling above began to cave in and the fire found the second floor.

The Vengeances shouted and hooted and swilled from their bottles of wine. They understood now that the destruction had just begun.

Chapter 31

GEORGE WILKENSON was still a good mile from Williamsburg, riding south, when he began to sense that something was wrong.

He had spent the day, a satisfying day, inspecting the family's small plantation on the York River near Queen's Lake. He had found the plantation in good order, with the young plants put in during the last rain and the mill fully repaired and running. It was good to get away from the tense atmosphere at the Wilkenson plantation. To feel like the master of his lands and his people. It was good to get away from his father.

He pulled his horse to a stop, cocked his ear to the south. He could hear bells ringing, clearly, if faintly, a mile or so away. The bells in the city.

He frowned and looked in the direction of the sound. Along the horizon, just above the tree line, he could see a long smudge of smoke, tinted pale red as the sun moved toward the west. Something was burning, something big. Perhaps all of Williamsburg was aflame. But no, the smoke looked farther away than that, farther south. Perhaps the bells were ringing to call people to help extinguish the blaze.

He put his spurs to his horse's flank and continued on. The smoky haze was in the general direction of the Wilkenson plantation, and that caused him some vague worry, but not a great deal. The chance that it was his own home that was on fire was slight, and there were enough people on the plantation that they should be able to deal with any such disaster before it got out of control.

It was twenty minutes later that he saw the first of the terrified citizens streaming north out of the city.

At first it was just a few men who passed him on horseback, riding rather swiftly, and he did not immediately make the connection between them and the ringing bells and the smoke. And while it was odd that they did not stop and exchange a word with him, or even acknowledge his existence, and that there were more riders on the road than one generally saw, still George did not see any cause for concern.

It was when he saw the people following in their wake, common people with wagons piled with possessions, pulled by their pathetic animals, that he realized something was very wrong indeed. Something more than just a plantation on fire. Williamsburg was being abandoned.

"I say . . ." Wilkenson reined his chestnut around and fell in beside a farmer who was leading an old plow horse north along the road. The horse in turn was pulling a dray piled with the farmer's family and a few possessions. From the look of his worldly goods George could not imagine why he had gone to the effort to save them.

"What is this about? Where is everyone going?"

"Anywhere. Away. The devil's in Williamsburg. Tidewater's under attack. Burning all the plantations along the James."

"What? Who? Who is burning the plantations?"

"Don't know. I heard a rumor it's the Dutch again, but it don't really matter, does it?"

To a certain extent the man was right, though George had an idea that it was not the Dutch. In fact, he had a good idea of who it really was, and that idea gave him a sour feeling in his stomach. He had heard it from the master of the *Wilkenson Brothers*. Pirates. Inhuman, savage. A force beyond the pale of human conduct.

He wheeled his horse around again and continued south, riding hard, pounding past the ever-growing stream of people fleeing the capital city.

He came at last to the great pile of earth and material that would soon be the governor's palace and continued on into the heart of Williamsburg. It was absolute chaos, from what he could see, with horses and wagons crowding the street and people rushing out of their houses with armfuls of possessions, piling them on whatever vehicle they had and then hurrying in for more.

He could hear loud, angry shouting, screaming, children crying, the thud of dozens of horses rushing in every direction and the drunken cursing of those of the lower sort who were finding their refuge in a bottle.

He pulled to a stop beside the jailhouse. Sheriff Witsen was rounding up those men who would stand with him. Five, thus far.

"Sheriff, Sheriff!" Wilkenson leapt down from his horse and hurried over to him. "Sheriff, what the devil is going on?"

"It's them goddamned pirates, damn their black souls. Good Lord," Witsen turned to one of his volunteers, "that gun is from the last age, it will blow you to hell should you fire it. Go to the armory and fetch another."

Witsen turned back to George Wilkenson. "They come ashore around noon, just north of Hog Island. Went for the Finch place first. I reckon it was the first one they seen. Most of the family got away, slaves too, but when they were done having their fun they burned it. Moved on to the Nelson plantation and done for that, too. Last I heard, which was about half an hour ago, they was at the Page plantation."

The two men were silent for a moment as the noise and the confusion swirled around them. There was no need to say what both were thinking. The Page house was just up the road from the Wilkensons'.

"What of the militia?" Wilkenson asked.

"Called them out, but most of them are too worried about

getting their own families safe to turn out. I have a man trying to round them up, but I ain't too hopeful."

The pirates were descending on his home, and there was no defense that the colony could offer. George felt as if he were standing there on the green completely naked.

And then another thought occurred to him and he felt himself flush with anger. "But where is the guardship? Where is the great Marlowe and his little precious band? This would seem to be his purview."

"The guardship went down this morning, and they fought it out, him and the pirate, for an hour or so. Don't know what happened, but the guardship is anchored up by Jamestown now. Just sitting there."

"Well, why doesn't someone order them to go and fight these brigands?"

"I suggested the same to the governor. Governor said Marlowe's beyond taking orders from anyone."

"Indeed. Well, we should have expected this. Marlowe is as much a pirate as any of those bastards. No doubt he will be sacking the countryside himself by week's end."

"I've no doubt, if there's anything left to sack. But see here, your father has requisitioned a deal of supplies from the militia—powder, shot, small arms. Guess he thought this might happen. I reckon he's set up for some kind of defense. Once we get some men together here we'll get down to your plantation, and maybe we can hold them off there, or drive 'em back into the river."

"I hope you are right," Wilkenson said as he swung himself up into his saddle. "I shall go to our plantation directly and see what can be done."

It was like riding into battle, trotting down the familiar rolling road from Williamsburg to the Wilkenson plantation. The sun was just below the trees in the west and the southern sky was blotted out by a great cloud of smoke, rising in columns from several locations and tinted red and pink and yellow.

The farthest dark column was the Finch plantation. Wilkenson could tell by the location of the smoke. The next was the Nelsons'. A third he was not so certain of; it might have been the grist mill that was on that road. It did not look as if the Page house was burning, and that most likely meant the pirates had not made it to the Wilkenson plantation. Not yet.

The logic of that did little to relieve the absolute panic that George felt as he hurried toward his home. He was terrified to think of the danger that his family might be facing, with the marauders closing in on them. He was even more terrified of the danger that he himself was in, though he would not acknowledge that.

The acrid smell of the fires became more pronounced as George covered the last half mile to the Wilkenson plantation. He charged down the long road that led to the house, hunched over the neck of his horse, cowering from what, he did not know.

The road was dark, lost in the long shadows of the trees that lined the way. He nearly missed seeing a group of the Wilkensons' slaves, field hands, standing beside a big oak one hundred feet from the house. They each held a cloth with a few things tied in a bundle. They looked very frightened.

He pulled his horse to a stop. "What are you doing here?"

An old man stepped forward. "We afraid to stay in them slave quarters, on account of them pirates, but Master Wilkenson, he say we got to stay on the plantation."

George Wilkenson regarded the pathetic people huddled beneath the tree. He wondered what he should do with them.

His first thought was to arm the Negro men so they could participate in the defense of the plantation, but the idea of an armed slave frightened him even more than the idea of a marauding pirate. There would be nothing to stop the slaves from killing all of the white people in the house and throwing in with the pirates. If they thought about it they would realize that they were better off doing just that.

"You know where the Queen's Lake plantation is? You know how to get there?"

"Yes, Master George."

"Good. I want you to lead all these people there. When

you get there tell the overseer what is happening here. You should be safe, and we'll send for you when this is over."

"Yes, Master. But, Master Jacob—that is . . . your father—says—"

"Never mind that, just go. And remember, I'll be looking for you soon. If you have any thought of running, I will see you all hunted down and punished, depend upon it!"

George found himself shouting the warning at the slaves' backs as the relieved people streamed past him and hurried up the road. He rode a planter's pace the last hundred yards to the house and swung down from the saddle. He looped the reins over the hitching rail—the stable boy was already a quarter mile down the road with the others—and climbed the steps to the front door two at a time.

The scene that greeted him inside the door was much like that he had encountered under the oak, but the faces were white, the clothes were fine, and the few possessions were worth more than the accumulated wealth of every Negro in Virginia. George's mother and his two sisters, his aunt and uncle who had unhappily chosen that month to visit from Maryland, and his maternal grandparents were there in the wide foyer. They were all dressed to travel. They all looked like trapped and frightened animals. He could sense their near panic, and it brought him near to the brink of panic as well.

"What is going on here?" George asked. "Where is Father? Why are you all still here?"

"Your father is in the library," Mrs. Wilkenson said. She drew herself more erect, trying not to look angry or afraid. "He has ordered us to remain, as he thinks we are in no danger."

"No danger . . . ?" George stared, incredulous, at his mother. She could never openly defy her husband, just as George could not defy the man, and that was why they had come to the threshold of fleeing and stopped.

It was no use arguing with her. He turned and raced down the hall to the study.

Jacob Wilkenson was sitting in the winged chair, a book open in his lap. He looked up as George burst into the room.

"Have you forgotten about knocking?" Jacob demanded.

"What in all creation are you doing, sitting here as if you had not a care in the world? Did you not see the smoke? You cannot be ignorant of the brigands that are laying waste to the countryside."

"I am aware of them, and I shall tell them in no uncertain terms that this is not to be tolerated. This was not our agreement. There shall be some penalties, count on it."

"Penalties? What are you talking about?"

"This . . . this brigand, as you style him, is Captain Jean-Pierre LeRois. He works for me. It is the little arrangement which I have mentioned. Matthew and I set it up with that fellow Ripley, who captains our river sloop."

George stared, shook his head. "I do not understand."

Jacob sighed and closed the book on his lap. "I have arranged through Ripley to purchase what this man has to sell. The profit will be tremendous. How do you think we are able to survive with the loss of our year's crop?"

" 'This man'? Surely you do not mean this brigand who has taken the *Wilkenson Brothers*?"

"Of course I do. And here's more news. I spoke with Ripley just this morning, and what do you think? He says that Marlowe is in fact a bastard named Malachias Barrett. A former pirate! A pirate! I knew there was something queer about him, and there it is! Oh, we shall have a merry time with his reputation now!"

It was coming too fast for George, like a heavy rain that the earth cannot absorb. "You have struck a deal with the pirate who has just taken the *Wilkenson Brothers*?"

"And now I shall have him engage the guardship and blow her to hell. The *Brothers* is better armed than the *Plymouth Prize*, LeRois's crew is bigger. He'll do as I say. That's why I have allowed him to keep the vessel. That and the fact that I have every expectation of the underwriter paying us for the loss."

"But . . . the man is a pirate, for God's sake! Did you not

just condemn Marlowe for being a pirate? What are we, that we will put such men in our employ?"

"Goddamn it, George, how are you even able to stand with no backbone at all?" Jacob rose, paced the room. "That is the beauty of the whole thing, do you not see? We send this one pirate up against the other. Marlowe is killed and his memory is blackened by what he has done, what he was. Like plowing the earth with salt. We destroy the man, we destroy his name, his reputation, everything, wiped away. There can be no more complete revenge for your brother's murder."

"And the entire thing hinges on this brigand doing as you wish?"

"He does as I tell him. Ripley informed the man of who is in charge of this affair, I made quite certain of that. Marlowe is killed, and then it is on with our business."

"*Our* business? Your business, sir, not mine. I do not intend to traffic with a pirate."

"Oh, and aren't you the righteous one? These . . . people . . . will rob whether we buy from them or not, to the greater good of those thieves in Savannah or Charleston. If it is going to happen regardless, then it may as well be us who realizes the profit."

"You are mad. You have no control over this animal."

"Of course I do! He works for me."

It was incredible. George Wilkenson shook his head slowly in disbelief. "The sheriff said you had requisitioned supplies from the militia, for some kind of defense?"

"Oh, yes, that." Jacob gave a little wave of the hand. "Yes, that was for the guardship."

"For the guardship? For the use of the guardship?"

"No, you fool, to use against the guardship. I had Ripley bring it out to LeRois so that he might have the stores necessary to blow that bastard Marlowe to hell. And as I hear it, that's just what he did. I told you, he does as I say."

"You . . . you mean to tell me you gave the militia's stores to that pirate?"

"He is not a pirate, goddamn your eyes! He is a privateer.

He works for me!" Jacob Wilkenson stopped pacing, turned on George. His hands were shaking. There were beads of sweat on his forehead. The old man was not as sure of himself as he was acting.

"It's *my* ship they have, *I* let them keep it!" Jacob continued. He stepped quickly across the room and stared out the window at the distant fields. "I got them their ship, their damned powder and small arms, and they know that perfectly well. They do as I say, damn you, they do as I order!"

George did not know what to say. The old man had lost all connection with reality. "Father, I think we had best go," he said softly.

"Don't you talk to me in that patronizing tone, you cowardly little sniveling bastard!" Jacob Wilkenson whirled around and glared at his son. "If you had been considerate enough to be killed in Matthew's place, this would not have happened! Matthew was able to help me keep these people in line, but not you, oh no. I knew you would not soil your lily-white hands with such business! You would think it beneath you!"

"Oh, I have soiled my lily-white hands, so much so that I cannot bear to think on it. But no, I would not have had truck with your illegal and utterly immoral business, not that you ever thought to ask me. Believe me, I am ashamed of what I have done, and even more so of what you and Matthew have done. And I think you are about to reap the crop you have sown."

"Get out! Get out, you sanctimonious coward! Go stand in the hall with the women and the old men!" Jacob screamed, but George's eyes were drawn past his father to the field through the window. A great column of smoke was suddenly visible at the edge of the frame. The glow of a great fire lit the trees that separated the Wilkenson plantation from the Page home three miles away.

"What?" Jacob asked, and turned around to see what George was staring at.

The pirates were pouring into the field by the river, dozens of them, hundreds for all George could tell. They must have taken the road that led along the banks of the James from the Page place to theirs. They were half a mile away at the bottom of the field and closing on the house like a pack of wolves. Even over that distance he could hear their howling and screaming.

The two Wilkensons stared silent for a moment at the coming threat, the wave of death sweeping up from the river.

George swallowed hard, fought the terror down. "Come, we have to go," he said. Surprised by the tone of authority in his voice, despite the fear.

"No," his father said, as if pleading for permission, "no, I must stay and explain to these men—"

"Father, we must go."

"No!" Jacob whirled around, red-faced, remembering who he was. "No! I did not build all this by letting bastards like that LeRois tell me what is what! These men do not tell me what to do, no man tells me what to do, I tell them! Do you hear me? I tell them!"

Incredible. Jacob Wilkenson's pride. His pride was the source of his strength, and his pride would not let him leave, because leaving would be as much as admitting he had done a stupid and horrible thing. Jacob Wilkenson would die before he did that, he would go down insisting that he was right.

George realized all of that, and he also realized that his father would let his family die as well before even tacitly admitting to a mistake.

"We'll be leaving now, Father," George said.

His eyes moved to the window again. Long shadows tugged at the pirates' feet as they charged up the hill. He saw blades glinting in those rays of sun that found their way through the trees. He saw heads bound in cloth, crossed belts holding weapons that slapped against bare chests as the men ran, cocked hats, torn coats, bearded, dirty, blood-streaked faces, grinning faces.

"Yes, yes, good, you go, you goddamned coward, you go and take all those cowards with you, and when this is over don't come back!" Jacob screamed, but George was already out of the room when he finished.

He ran down the hall to the front door. "All of you, come along, hurry!" he ordered, throwing open the door and gesturing with his arm, and the frightened people in the foyer shuffled out the door.

"What about your father? Where is your father?" his mother asked as he half pushed her out the door.

"He will not come, and there is nothing I can do," George said, and his mother made no reply. She would not be surprised. No one knew better than his mother the kind of idiocy of which Jacob Wilkenson was capable.

They hurried down the steps and across the circular drive, and George realized that he did not know what he would do next. The old people could hardly walk. They certainly could not make it to Williamsburg on foot, and there was only his horse nearby.

"Damn it, damn it . . ." George looked around. The shouting and hooting of the pirates seemed to be right on top of him, but they were still on the other side of the house. "All of you, hurry off into those trees," he said, pointing toward a stand of oaks near the end of the drive, fifty yards from the house. "I shall go for a wagon of some sort."

The others were too frightened to protest, for which George was thankful, for he knew it would take only the mildest of arguments for him to change his mind. They hurried off in their awkward, shuffling way, and he turned and rushed around the house toward the stables.

The pirates were swarming over the porch of the house, smashing in windows and kicking in the back door. George paused for a second to watch the destruction, then turned and ran.

He was breathing hard, and his chest ached and burned, when he finally swung open one of the big doors of the dimly lit, whitewashed stable and squeezed through.

The only transportation there was an old dray, pushed toward the back. The family coach was in the coach house, but the horses were there in the stable and he did not care to try to bring them all together under the eyes of the pirates. Rather, he selected one of the draft horses, a great beast of Flemish descent, and led it over to the dray.

He could hear the primal, terrifying sound of the hordes tearing through his home, the shouting and howling punctuated with breaking glass and shattering wood. He did not want to think of what was happening there as he fumbled with the unfamiliar harness of the dray. The horse shifted nervously.

George fitted the bit in the big animal's mouth, slipped the bridle over its head. The slow, intricate work of fitting the horse in the tack had given George's fear the chance to gather again. He was near panic as he stepped across the straw-covered floor and peered out of the door.

There were only a few of the brigands still outside, those who had paused to swill from their bottles before plunging in through a smashed door or window. He could see more of them in the house. They were absolutely frenzied, ripping curtains down, slashing with swords at anything that could be destroyed. He had heard that sharks behaved that way when feeding, but he had never imagined human beings capable of such. He wondered if his father was still alive. Wondered, but did not care.

The Wilkensons had done this to themselves, to the colony. He sucked in a long breath.

His first duty was to get his family safely away. His next was to make some effort to save the tidewater. He knew what that would entail, and the very thought of it made him sick even through the fear.

Slowly, quietly, he pushed the stable doors open and stepped back into the shadows. No one had noticed, but they would not miss the dray rumbling past. He raced back into the stable and climbed up onto the rough seat. He picked up the reins, took another long breath, held it, and then exhaled, yelling "Hey, yah!" and flicking the reins against the horse's neck.

The big horse, already nervous from the noise and from George's unfamiliar hands, burst into a gallop, barely in control. They charged out of the stable—horse, dray, and driver—with stalls, tack, tools, and doors flying past, and raced down the beaten road toward the front of the house. George could hear nothing but the thunder of the heavy hooves, the creaking dray, moving faster than it was ever intended to move, and he was suddenly afraid that the horse would not stop when he needed it to.

Then through the rumble and the pounding he heard a surprised exclamation. A pistol fired and the ball buzzed past. George hunched forward and flicked the reins again, but the horse was running as fast as it could.

They whipped around the front of the house and down the drive. The stand of oaks was a blur as the cart bucked and shook on the dirt road. George pulled back on the reins, shouting, "Whoa, whoa, whoa!" and to his infinite relief the horse slowed and then stopped. It shook its head, whinnied, and shifted nervously on its huge hooves, but it stayed essentially still.

George leapt down from the seat. "Come along, come along, come along!" he shouted, waving his arms at his family huddled in the trees.

His sisters were first, bursting like partridges from the underbrush and leaping onto the filthy cart. Next came his mother, helping her mother and father along, and behind them the aunt and uncle.

"Oh, for the love of God, do hurry," George said. He looked back at the house. A dozen or so of the brigands had left the building and were racing down the road toward the dray.

The thought of dying for the amusement of pirates made George flush with anger even as his stomach convulsed with fear. He stepped forward, scooped his grandmother up in his arms, deposited her on top of his sisters in the back of the wagon. He did the same with his grandfather, helped his mother up, pushed his aunt and uncle in after.

The pirates were twenty yards away, no more. One of them stopped and leveled a pistol and fired. The muzzle flash was brilliant in the fading light.

The ball whizzed by overhead, and just as George was thanking God for sparing his life the horse shrieked in fear and bucked, nearly toppling the cart and spilling the passengers. The animal came down on its four feet and bolted, and George flung himself at the open bed. He grabbed hold of the side rail and pulled himself in as the dray flew down the road. He climbed forward, stepping on someone, he did not know who, and crawled into the seat.

The reins were still lying there, and George took them up, though he did not think the horse would respond to any command from God or man. He could see a streak of blood where the pirate's bullet had grazed its flank.

The crazed beast was charging down the road, quite out of control, but at least it was running in the right direction, away from the house, so George gave it its head. He could hear the shouting and the gunfire at his back, growing farther away as they left the big house behind. He kept his eyes on the road. He hunched over, tensed, bracing for the tear of a bullet through his back. He did not turn around.

Chapter 32

THE VOICES were troubled. They did not think this was good anymore.

LeRois chewed nervously at a long strand of his beard. Something was making the voices upset. It was time to get back to the ship. The ship was safety. This wide-open country was not.

Those thoughts bothered him, but the voices were still soft and soothing, had not reached the point of screaming panic. He walked slowly through the house as if through a museum, glancing at those things that were not yet smashed or stolen. Men ran past, men screamed and beat delicate objects apart with their swords, men guzzled from bottles of wine and rum and whiskey, but LeRois just watched. When they had finished with this house they would go back to the ship. It was time.

At the far end of the hall there was a room that was as yet undisturbed, so he wandered down that way while the men had their fun in the sitting room and the dining room. He could see a wall lined with books, an elegant carpet, a sideboard with bottles. Perhaps he would sit a moment.

He stepped through the door, and his eyes wandered to the windows across the room. A striking view, clear down to the river, a dark band of water in the fading light, running through the fields on either side. It would be lovely, flickering red and orange as it reflected the light from this house, once they had set it on fire.

"LeRois?"

The voice was gruff, demanding. None of his men would speak to him that way. No one who wished to live would speak to him that way. He froze, unsure if his name had really been spoken out loud.

"LeRois!"

He jerked his head around. There was a man sitting in a winged chair, a book open in his lap. LeRois had not even noticed him. And the man knew his name. There was something gnawing at the back of his mind, something troubling, but he could not recall what it was.

"Are you LeRois?" The man stood up and set his book aside.

LeRois squinted at him. *"Oui,"* he said at last.

"Do you know who I am?" the man demanded. "Do you know who I am?"

LeRois just looked at him. The man had shouted. He could not believe it. This man had actually raised his voice in speaking to him.

"I am Jacob Wilkenson! I am the man who employs you! The one who sent Ripley to set this whole deal up, and now look what you have done! This cannot be tolerated!"

LeRois squinted again. The man's hands were trembling. He was sweating. He shifted from one foot to another under LeRois's gaze. LeRois could smell the fear—it was a smell he knew well. The man's bluster was all *merde,* shit, nothing more.

"You work for me!" the man screamed, an edge of hysteria in his voice.

LeRois sensed movement at his back. He turned to find a dozen of his men standing behind him, watching the confrontation, and more filing in. They had paused in their destruction to see what was happening.

"All of you, listen to me," the man was saying. "My name is Jacob Wilkenson. I am the man who has been buying your goods. I am the one who has provided you with specie. We have a good arrangement, and I do not care to see it fall apart now. We can make each other very wealthy, but you must go back to your ship now!"

LeRois could not fathom what the man was talking about, and he concluded that he was insane. There was no other explanation.

The Vengeances began to step around Jacob Wilkenson, to fill the room, to encircle the man. Wilkenson in turn was forcing himself to stand more straight, to meet LeRois's eye, but his bravado was running out.

"I order you to leave at once!"

"Order?" LeRois spoke at last. "You 'order'? You do not order me."

"Very well, then, I ask that you please—"

"Sweat him."

The Vengeances were now completely encircling the man, watching LeRois, waiting for the word.

"Listen, you—" the man began again, and once more LeRois said, "Sweat him."

One of the Vengeances pulled a sword from his belt and with an ingratiating smile poked Jacob Wilkenson with the tip.

"Ow, son of a bitch, stop that!" Wilkenson shouted, and stepped away. Then the man standing beside the first poked him and made him step back farther.

All around the circle swords came out and cutlasses were raised and their dagger points reached out and jabbed at Jacob Wilkenson. He backed away and backed away, but he was surrounded and the points reached out at him from every direction.

He stepped around the winged chair, trying to escape, but they were on his every side. He moved faster, but still the blades found him. He moved faster still, around and around the chair. He began to breathe hard. He began to sweat.

Then one of the brigands grabbed him and pinned his arms, and another pulled a knife. With a motion like skinning a bird, the man with the knife cut away Wilkenson's coat and his waistcoat and shirt to reveal an obese, white midriff, already bleeding from a dozen minor wounds.

The pirate that was holding Wilkenson pushed him forward. He stumbled and then flinched as another and another sword point jabbed at him, and soon he was running around the chair again, stumbling, heaving for breath, bleeding.

"Oh God, oh God, no more," he gasped, falling to the floor. LeRois's eyes fixed on the strange patterns his blood made on the Oriental rug as the fat man rolled in agony, bleeding from dozens of cuts. They seemed to swim around, swirling and forming more patterns before his eyes. He could not understand the man's words.

One of the pirates stepped forward and with deft strokes of a dagger stripped Wilkenson of his breeches and socks so that he was lying on the rug naked, save for his shoes.

The voices were now screaming in LeRois's head, screaming to be heard over the raucous laughter of the Vengeances, the gunshots, the breaking glass, the gasping pleas of this Jacob Wilkenson.

Two of the pirates hauled the fat man to his feet again, and again he was made to stagger around the chair. His white skin was streaked with blood, which ran freely now down his sides and legs. Bottles were smashed over his head and shoulders and gouged into his flesh. He was whimpering and pleading and praying, and that made his tormentors laugh harder still.

Malachias Barrett! Malachias Barrett! The voices broke through the din, screaming their warning in LeRois's brain. The room seemed to swirl around, the faces undulating, the fat man coming in and out of focus.

He had forgotten! He had forgotten! But the voices had reminded him. To the ship! To the ship! All of this could wait, all of this would be here, but first Malachias Barrett had to die.

LeRois felt the scream rising from his bowels, and as the sound came up so his sword seemed to float out of its scabbard and rise with the sound over his head.

He charged forward. Faces floated by, surprised faces of

his own men as they stepped away, and then the great fat man on the floor, a blood-streaked, terrified face, looking up at him, and then his sword came down again and again and again and he could not stop hacking away at the man.

Malachias Barrett! the voices screamed again, and LeRois stepped back and looked around, the dead man at his feet forgotten.

"We get back to the ship. I will burn this son of a bitch *maison* now and go back to the ship."

The men stood in silence for a second, and then as if on a signal raced off to destroy and carry off all that they could before the flames drove them away. They would not question LeRois's decision. He knew that they would not. No one would, who wished to live.

Thomas Marlowe took a long pull from his rum bottle. Stared through the great cabin windows at the yellow, flickering light on the horizon. He could not move. He could not take his eyes from the sight of his colony, his adoptive home, burning in front of him.

He was alone in the great cabin. He was not drunk, despite his best efforts.

He wished the fires would stop. He wished they would just go out and LeRois would leave, but every time he thought that they had, a new fire flared and grew, one after another, following the march of destruction up the banks of the James River.

How many had LeRois killed thus far? There was no way to know. Perhaps no one. Perhaps they had all fled before him. Marlowe could picture the gentry of Virginia, in all their finery, fleeing like rats before the pirate's filthy, drunken tribe. Perhaps he had killed them all. And still he, Marlowe, sat there, immobile.

LeRois was working his way toward the Wilkenson home. Perhaps he would sack that as well, kill all of those bastards, save him the trouble. Wouldn't that be a fine thing?

The *Plymouth Prize* was safe, and her people were safe, and that was his primary concern, his first obligation. He had tried to stop the pirates, but he could not, not without killing all of his people in the process, and Elizabeth and Lucy as well. He had done what he could.

He took another drink from the bottle. He did not really believe any of that.

"Thomas Marlowe," he muttered to himself, speaking the words slowly, disdainfully. They tasted bad in his mouth. That was over now. He was no longer Thomas Marlowe. It had been a good run, two years as a member of the tidewater's elite, but it was over now. He was Malachias Barrett once again.

He supposed that once LeRois had cleared out he would take the *Plymouth Prize* to the Caribbean. His men would go with him, he was certain of that. Most men who sailed before the mast were only a few places removed from piracy, and the Prizes were even closer than that, thanks to his guiding influence. It was a short step now to the sweet trade. Bickerstaff would not go with them, of course, and Rakestraw probably would decline. He wondered about Elizabeth.

And then, as if summoned by his thoughts, he heard the sound of her light footfalls in the alleyway, her soft knock on the door. "Thomas?"

He turned in his chair, smiled as best he could. "Pray, come in."

She closed the door behind her, crossed the cabin, sat on the settee facing him. "I'm sorry for walking out as I did."

Marlowe took her hand. As if she had anything to be sorry for. "I am sorry for being such an ass. I am pleased you are safe. I am pleased that the ship and her people are safe."

"Are you?"

"I beg your pardon?"

"Are you really pleased with your safety?" she asked, and when he did not respond she continued. "You men have a great advantage over us women. When we are humiliated beyond tolerance we can do no more than cut our wrists. You can die in battle and have it said that such was a noble death."

"And you think that an advantage?"

"Having the means to preserve one's honor is always an advantage. That is why I came to this place."

"Me as well. But even here I find honor is like good family: You are either born into it or you can despair of it ever being yours."

"I do not believe that. I will not believe that. That may be true for what these arrogant bastards, the Wilkensons and the Tinlings, call honor, but it is not true of real honor."

"Real honor? Real honor is no more than what these arrogant bastards, as you style them, say is real honor. Is there such a thing as honor in an objective sense?"

They paused, Marlowe with the bottle halfway to his lips, and listened to a sudden commotion on deck. It had been going on all night, something or other causing the men to hoot and howl. They were all drunk, celebrating their escape. But this time it was louder, more sustained. He put the bottle down, looked questioning at Elizabeth, and she shrugged in reply.

He heard footsteps outside the cabin door, loud, rude voices, a gang of men pushing toward the captain's sanctuary. Perhaps it was a mutiny, Marlowe speculated. He hoped it was. He hoped they would hang him.

But rather than a foot kicking in the door there came a polite knock. Marlowe sat for a second more, then stood and tugged his waistcoat into place. "Come," he called.

The door opened and Bickerstaff stepped in. "Captain, a gentleman has come out to see you," he said stiffly.

A gentleman? The governor, perhaps, or Finch or one of the burgesses. Marlowe could well imagine what they would have to say.

"Very good, show him in." There was a pushing and wrestling in the alleyway. Whoever the visitor was, he was getting rough treatment from the men. If it was the governor, this would go even harder on them.

The gang of men parted like tearing cloth and the gentleman stepped forward. Marlowe's eyes went wide, his mouth dropped open. He took an involuntary step back, so shocked was he, for the visitor was George Wilkenson, hat and wig gone, clothes twisted, sweating with fear, standing there in the door of the guardship's great cabin.

The questions swirled around in his head. His eyes narrowed. He glared at Wilkenson.

It occurred to him that he could hang the bastard then and there. If he just said the word he felt confident his men would put a halter around Wilkenson's neck and run him up to a yardarm. At the very least, they would not try to interfere if he did it himself. From the look in Wilkenson's eyes Thomas guessed it had occurred to him as well.

"Come in," Marlowe said, and Wilkenson stumbled into the cabin, pushed from behind. "Get back on deck, you men!" Marlowe shouted, and the men dispersed, laughing, howling. Bickerstaff shut the door.

They stood there, the three men and Elizabeth, silent, staring at one another. Finally, Marlowe spoke.

"This is most unexpected."

"I would imagine so."

"What do you want?"

"I have come to beg you, with all humility, to come to the aid of this colony. You—you and your men—are the only force in the tidewater that can stand up to these animals."

Marlowe stared hard at him. He was telling the truth. This was no trick. "Indeed. You have come to ask that I lay down my life, and the lives of my men, to save the great Wilkenson estate? Is that it?"

George took a step aft and peered out of the big stern window of the great cabin. "That fire, the closest one, that is the Wilkenson estate. It is quite beyond saving. It is the rest of the colony that concerns me now."

"And do you know who these 'animals' are? Who their captain is?"

"He is some pirate named LeRois, that is all I know. And he is here in part because of my father. I am utterly ashamed of my family's role in this. Had I even an ounce of pride left I could not have come to you, but I do not, and so I am willing to admit here and now that you, and you," he nodded to Elizabeth, "have been horribly used by me and my family."

Marlowe just stared at him, then sat down behind his desk and continued to stare. He did not understand how Jacob Wilkenson was responsible for LeRois's presence on the bay. That was an intriguing bit of news. He did not know what to say.

"My father is dead by now, I should think," Wilkenson continued, "and if you do this, if you stop them from killing anyone else, then you shall never have any trouble from my family again, I swear to that."

Marlowe swiveled around and stared out the window, at the flames reaching up over the trees that surrounded the Wilkenson home. The only thing more pathetic than Wilkenson's pleading was the fact that it was necessary for him to plead at all, to plead with Marlowe to do what he had sworn he would do. If the Wilkensons had used Marlowe poorly, then they, too, had been poorly used by him. They were all of a kind: Wilkenson, Marlowe, LeRois. Pathetic.

He turned back to the men in his cabin, and his eyes met Elizabeth's. "What think you of all this?" he asked, as if Wilkenson were not there.

"I think George Wilkenson is vermin, but what he has done, coming here, asking this of you, is the bravest act I have ever seen from any man."

"Hmmph. Well, you may be right. But he asks something that I cannot do. I cannot beat LeRois. Nor do I feel much compelled to see all my men die to defend people who have behaved with so little honor."

Bickerstaff spoke for the first time. "You asked me once, you may recall, what I thought was the difference between a commoner and a person of gentle birth."

"I do recall. You said that the one had more money than the other, and the one with more money made a greater pretense at honor, though in fact he had it in no greater measure."

"That is what I said, and I should think all that we have seen this past year would bear that out. But that does not mean that honor is not worth striving for, even if you are the only one in the land doing so."

Marlowe leaned back in his chair. His eyes moved from Bickerstaff to Wilkenson to Elizabeth, and then back to Bickerstaff.

"I cannot beat him," he said again.

"That is unfortunate," said Bickerstaff, "but it is not important. It is only important that you try."

Marlowe looked down at his desk and rubbed his temples. What Bickerstaff was saying, what Elizabeth had been saying, was right. He knew it. And he was afraid. That was the truth, distilled to its purest essence. He was afraid of LeRois because he knew all that LeRois was capable of doing. His head was starting to ache. He was sick of being afraid.

"Very well," he said at last. He put his hands down flat on his desk, pushed himself to his feet. "We are all to die eventually." He looked at Elizabeth, held her eyes. "Let us take the advantage given us by our sex. Let us have it said that we died with honor."

Chapter 33

THEY WALKED back the way they had come, across the fields and along the dirt paths running beside the wide James River and down the smooth rolling roads. Pockets chinked with coins and silverware and other trinkets stuffed hurriedly into them. Pirates labored under bags filled with the bounty of their raid.

It was a dark night, but they had little difficulty in seeing their path. The flames from the last house they had set off reached far into the sky and danced and leaped across the ripples on the river's surface in bright flashing patterns, just as LeRois had hoped.

And when the light from that conflagration grew too distant to do them any good they came to the mill, which was still burning well, and then to the other house, and then the house before that, their own destruction lighting their way back.

They returned at last to the first house they had torched that night. It was no more than a heap of glowing embers, but there were embers enough to light the bank of the river where their boats remained fast in the mud.

"*Vite, vite*, come along, hurry," LeRois prompted the men. They had covered in their round trip perhaps six miles, and the Vengeances were dragging along, shuffling. The fire had gone out of them. It had been a long night, even for men well used to demanding physical activity, a long night of constant motion, screaming, drinking, destruction.

But it was not yet over, at least not as far as LeRois was concerned. There still remained the most important job, that of ushering Malachias Barrett through the gates of hell.

The heap of debris that earlier that evening had been a plantation house glowed red and orange, and the river picked up the muted colors and threw them back. Any light that might have come from the stars or the new moon was largely blotted out by the haze of smoke that hung over the countryside, a bitter, stinging smoke, smelling of charred wood and burnt paint and the ashes of three generations of tidewater wealth.

They stumbled down the long field, filing past the hillocks with their tobacco plants, and loaded their sacks into the boats. Then one by one they pushed the boats out into the stream and pulled themselves aboard and took their places on the thwarts.

LeRois went last, climbing into the longboat before it was pushed off. He did not want to get his shoes wet. It was not fitting for the *capitain* to walk through the mud like a pig.

The small crew aboard the old *Vengeance* had managed to work the decrepit ship upriver and drop anchor just below Hog Island. The *Nouvelle Vengeance* was at anchor as well, having floated free once the tide had lifted her off the sand.

LeRois grabbed hold of the cleats on the side of the *Nouvelle Vengeance* and pulled himself up onto her deck. There was no one there to greet him, no one conscious, in any event. Bodies were sprawled here and there, passed out in the warm night air, some still gripping the bottles they had drained.

"Uhh," LeRois grunted. Let them sleep. Let them all sleep. He would remain awake and vigilant. He would watch, because he knew that Malachias Barrett would come to him once again, and he would send his old quartermaster on that long voyage of the damned. They would all go, if it came to that.

George Wilkenson was surprised at the quality of the horse he was riding, the steady planter's pace it was able to maintain, the good manners it displayed. He was surprised because it was

Marlowe's horse, taken right from his stable, the old Tinling stable. George had thought Marlowe knew nothing about horses.

Perhaps he did not. Perhaps it was his Negroes who had trained the beast, just as his Negroes had been responsible for that fine crop of tobacco that he and his father had burned. Free Negroes, who stayed and worked of their own volition. George shook his head at the very thought of it. Marlowe was an enigma, and George was almost sorry that he would never have the chance to fathom him.

He had left the *Plymouth Prize* shortly after his meeting with Marlowe. Marlowe had actually asked him to stay, suggesting that it would be safer for him to remain aboard the guardship, but that was too much. Coming to Marlowe, begging for his help, was all the humiliation he could endure. Remaining in the man's protective care was beyond the pale.

Instead, he had done Marlowe a favor by escorting Elizabeth Tinling and Lucy to the Tinling—the Marlowe—house in Marlowe's coach, which had been sent down for that purpose. He was well armed, Marlowe had seen to that, with a brace of fine pistols and a musket, and he sat in silence on the seat across from the women. No one said a word. They were careful not to meet one another's eyes. It was not a comfortable trip.

When at last they arrived at Marlowe's home, having encountered no one on the road, George spoke.

"Might I have a horse? Any will do. I do not know when I will be able to return it."

Elizabeth glared at him, made no effort to conceal her dislike. "The horses here are not mine to let out, but under the circumstances I think Captain Marlowe would not mind."

"Thank you." He turned to go, then paused and turned back. He had the urge to reach out and hug her, an all-but-irrepressible need for some human contact, a touch, an embrace. But he knew the kind of rebuff he would suffer if he tried.

"Elizabeth . . . I am sorry. I can say no more than that."

She had looked at him for a long and awkward moment. "I am sorry too," she had said, then turned and disappeared into the house.

He slowed the horse to a walk as the loom of the fire from the Wilkenson house became visible over the trees. The road he had taken ran roughly parallel to the river, an almost direct route from Marlowe's home to the Wilkensons'. The last time he had ridden that way was when they had returned from burning Marlowe's tobacco. Now it was his own family suffering the ravages of the flame.

He turned the horse down the long road, past the oaks, to the front of the house. The second floor had collapsed. The entire place looked more like a giant bonfire than a home, and even from one hundred feet away he could feel the blast of the heat.

He stopped and watched as the fire consumed the only home he had ever known. He imagined his father was in there somewhere. His funereal pyre was made up of all the things that three generations of Wilkensons had struggled to accumulate in that new world, all the dreams of wealth that had first brought them over the wide ocean.

George shielded his eyes from the blaze and looked off to the side of the house. The stable was still intact. The fire had not managed to jump across the fifty feet of close-cropped grass that separated it from the main house. That much at least was a relief, for the Wilkensons' horses were the only thing left on earth that George cared about.

He flicked the reins against his horse's neck and the animal headed off toward the stable, taking skittish steps away from the burning house and looking at the fire in wide-eyed fear. Under a less-skilled rider the horse would have bolted already, but George Wilkenson had a certain authority with the beasts. It had always been a source of pride for him, one of the few.

Around the far side of the burning building he caught a movement, a flickering shadow against the yellow and red flames. He pulled the horse to a stop. There was someone there, a figure darting away from the house. He watched the man, black against the background of the fire. He moved with rapid, jerky movements. It had to be terribly hot so close to the flames.

And then the figure abandoned whatever he was trying to do and raced away from the flames, toward the stable, but George's vision was damaged from looking into the fire and he lost sight of him.

He swung the horse over to the nearest stand of trees, slid off, looped the reins around a sapling. He stepped across the lawn, toward where the man had disappeared, his footfalls on the grass nearly silent and masked by the crackling fire.

He saw the person at last, just outside the door to the stable, hunched over, his attention on whatever he was doing. George pulled one of the pistols from his belt, one of Marlowe's pistols, a beautiful weapon, light and balanced in the hand, and stepped closer.

He was five feet away before the man sensed that he was not alone. He turned, his face illuminated by the burning house.

"What the devil . . ." George could think of nothing else to say. It was the shifty little man whom Matthew had hired to run the river sloop. "Ripley . . . ?"

"Oh, Mr. Wilkenson . . ." Ripley's rat eyes darted to the pistol and then to George's face. His tongue flicked out and licked his lips.

"God, but ain't it horrible, what they done?" Ripley continued, nodding toward the burning house, his eyes never leaving George's. "I told your father, 'You don't want to have no business with them pirates,' but your father, he wouldn't listen, not to no one."

"Where are they? The pirates?"

"They gone back to their ship, I reckon. Anchored just off the Finch place, down by Hog Island." Ripley half turned and pointed across the field. He was being very helpful.

"What are you doing here?"

"Oh, well, when I heard, I come to see if I could help, maybe defend the place. I didn't reckon it would just be aban-

doned, but I was too late. I . . . ah . . . I tried to save what I
could, I got some of it, tried to save it for you and Mrs. Wilkenson and the others, so's you don't lose everything. . . ."

George's eyes moved down to Ripley's feet. There was a
horse blanket lying on the grass, half tied in a bundle. Spilling
out of it were various bits of silver service, an old clock with
gold inlay, a couple of china cups.

George looked up at Ripley, astounded at the depths of
the man's depravity. "You were looting. You were looting my
home."

"No, no, I was trying to save a few things from them fucking pirates, beg your pardon. . . ."

George raised the pistol up until it was pointing at Ripley's
forehead, just three feet away. Ripley took a tentative step back,
and George cocked the lock.

"No, Mr. Wilkenson, I was—"

Those words, that pathetic, lying protest, were the last
words that former pirate quartermaster Ezekiel Ripley ever uttered. George pulled the trigger. The gun jolted in his hand,
and he had a vague image through the smoke of Ripley blown
backward, arms flung out, onto the grass.

The gun dropped to George's side. He took a few steps
forward and looked down at Ripley's earthly remains, sprawled
out flat, dead eyes staring at the sky. Much as Matthew had
been.

He had thought about this moment many times, what it
would be like to kill a human being. He had always imagined
terror, revulsion, guilt. But he felt none of that. Just a vague
curiosity, no more. He wondered if this was how Marlowe had
felt after putting a bullet in Matthew. He never seemed to have
been stricken with guilt or any form of remorse.

George stood over the body and reloaded the pistol. It
seemed likely that he would need it again before the night was
through. He went into the stable, pushed the stable doors open
wide, and opened all of the stall doors as well. If the stables
did catch fire, the horses would be able to get out.

He found Marlowe's horse, mounted it, and rode toward

the fields. He paused to look down on Ripley's body one last time. He still felt nothing. He touched the horse's flanks with his heels and headed off in the wake of the pirate horde.

It was easy enough to follow them. The trail was blazed with burning buildings and markers in the form of discarded bottles and loot dropped or tossed aside along the road that ran beside the river. The mill was all but gone, as was the Page house and the Nelson house. The fires were burning down at last, the flames having sucked all of the life they could from the wood and plaster and cloth until there was no more left to consume.

The Finch house was nearly dark, with only an orange ember here or there, a punctuation of light in that dark, charred heap. There was nothing left to indicate that the huge, smoldering fire pit on top of the small rise had once been a house.

George could smell the now familiar odor of a burnt house, could hear the crackling of the burning timber, but here the crickets were chirping again, and he could smell the woods and the mud near the river as well. Things were already returning to their natural state.

He paused and looked at the remains of the Finch home. He thought of all the times he had danced in those rooms, or played piquet or whist, or sat down to dinner with his neighbors. What would they do now? What would any of them do?

He pulled the head of his horse around and rode off toward the water. He had no plan, did not even know why he had followed the pirates. It seemed a long time since he had had a rational thought; the night had been made up of feelings, instincts, impressions, pushing him along through no conscious decision of his own.

He came at last to the edge of the water. He could see where the pirates had come ashore, the mud and plants trampled by the many, many feet, the long grooves cut in the bank where the boats had been pulled up.

The James River was nearly a mile wide at that point. George could just make out the masts of the ships—it seemed there were more than one—against the night sky, but their hulls were lost in the darkness.

For a long time he just sat, staring at the dark, skeletal masts with the same morbid disinterest with which he had looked at Ripley's dead body, the round hole in his forehead. Anyone who heard the tale of his going to plead with Marlowe would think it an act of altruistic humility, but that was not all of it. His family had nothing now, nothing but their good name, and if LeRois lived to tell of his father's entanglements with the pirates, then that too would be gone. He needed Le-Rois destroyed, and he hoped and prayed Marlowe could do it.

His eyes moved over to a clump of bushes on the bank twenty feet away. Behind the bushes he knew he would find a canoe. The Finches had kept one there for years, to use for fishing or other recreation. He looked out at the pirates again, then back toward the canoe. Was there anything he could do to hurry the pirates' destruction along?

The instinct that had been driving him that night forced him to ride down to the bushes, to dismount, to see that the boat was still there and the paddles still lying on the thwarts. He looked out toward the pirate ships. He had no idea of what he might do.

He felt a spark of fear and panic flash through him, but there was something delicious about it, something thrilling and redemptive. He had no thought of dying, because he no longer had any thought of living. He was ruined, he was humiliated, he was a part of the clan that had unleashed the terror on the colony. He was as much a burnt-out shell as his family's home.

He pushed the canoe into the water, just as he and the Finch boys had done so many times in the past. He climbed in, carefully, and found his balance, then dipped the paddle into the river and started for the other side.

Chapter 34

THEY WERE feeling their way down the James River under fore and main topsail alone, a blind man with arms outstretched trying to keep to the center of a bridge. In the fore chains, larboard and starboard, experienced hands swung lead lines, their soft chants relayed aft down the length of the deck by the men stationed at the guns.

Marlowe stood by the break of the quarterdeck. He could just see the face of the man below him, calling up, "And a half four, and five, and a half four . . ." A smoky haze hung over the trees and the river and carried the sharp smell of wanton destruction. It blotted out most of the natural light from the moon and stars, making it that much more difficult for Marlowe to get his ship and men into battle.

He looked to either side. He could not see the distant shores. But he knew that stretch of water well enough to know from the depths alone that they were running down the center of the stream. That and the glow of the burnt and burning houses, standing like lighthouses on the north shore, told him that they were closing with the enemy.

He stared blankly at the flames half a mile away. The Wilkenson home. He considered all the things that he should be feeling—elation, pleasure, the glow of vengeance reaped—

and he wondered why he was not. He was too tired, he concluded, too tired of it all, and too frightened of what was to come.

"And three, and three . . . ," the man below him said.

The water was shoaling, which meant they were nearing Hog Island. Marlowe turned to Rakestraw, who was standing ten feet away. "We shall bear up a bit, pray see to the braces," and when the first officer had done that he said to the helmsmen, "Bear up, three points."

The *Plymouth Prize* turned to larboard, the change, of course, imperceptible save for change in the bearing of the fires on the shore.

"And four and a half, and four and a half . . ."

Marlowe turned to say something to Bickerstaff, but Bickerstaff was not there. He was off on the *Northumberland* with King James and a dozen other of the Plymouth Prizes, somewhere ahead in the dark.

They were employing their old tactic, the one that had worked so well on Smith Island. Once the *Plymouth Prize* was alongside and fully engaged, then those aboard the *Northumberland* would swarm up the other side and come at them from behind. It was not much of a plan, but any edge was better than none, particularly as they were outnumbered two to one in ships and men, and the men they were facing were very experienced killers indeed, with no reason at all to surrender and every reason to fight to the death.

Marlowe took some comfort from the plan, from the thought that they were not just going right at the pirates but instead were using some of their God-given cunning. He took comfort from the thought that the pirates had been on a rampage for some time now, were probably drunk and collapsed on the deck of the *Vengeance*, near comatose. He was comforted by the thought that the Plymouth Prizes were drunk as well, not blind drunk but fighting drunk, and he was keeping them that way. He took comfort from the fact that Francis Bickerstaff and King James would be with him on the killing ground.

But for all the comfort that he gleaned from those thoughts, he was not optimistic about their chances. He of all of them knew what they were up against. The Vengeances under LeRois had never been bested in all the time he sailed with them.

Of course, these were not the same men. Most of the men aboard now would have signed the articles after Marlowe had given up the life on the account. But he did not think that they would be any less capable than the others who had sailed under LeRois.

He turned and glanced at the place where Bickerstaff would have been standing had he been aboard. He missed his friend's steadying presence. They had been through so much together: bloody fights, and lessons in Latin and history, and two years as landed gentlemen. He owed his brief but glorious career as a member of the tidewater gentry, and his brilliant flash of passion with Elizabeth, to his friend and teacher. He would miss him.

And he would miss King James as well, belligerent, surly King James. Marlowe understood the man perfectly, understood what drove him, and he had used that knowledge shamelessly to manipulate James into doing him great service. But he liked James, respected him.

And he had given back to James as much as he had taken. Pride, honor, those things that most of the first men of Virginia did not think a black man capable of having. James, he knew, would not mind dying, as long as he died with a blooded sword in his hand.

But at least he would see them one more time, albeit across a smoke-filled deck as they fought their last in defense of their adopted colony and in defense of their own honor, their own genuine, unvarnished honor. He could not say the same for Elizabeth. He did not think that he would ever see Elizabeth again.

He had found the time to scribble out a will, leaving to her everything that was his—the house, the land, the specie— a brief document that unbeknownst to Elizabeth was included in the packet he had sent back with her and Lucy. It was something.

He thought of her smile, her smooth and perfect skin, the way her long yellow hair had a habit of falling across her face, the way she would whisk it away. He would never see her again, and for that, and that alone, he was truly sorry.

George Wilkenson swallowed hard, made a bold stroke with the paddle. The hulls of the pirate ships seemed to materialize out of the night, the formless dark suddenly coalescing into solid and unyielding shapes not forty feet ahead. From the low vantage of the canoe they seemed to loom overhead, forbidding black cliffs, and rising above the cliffs the dead forest of masts, the spiderwebs of rigging.

George gave another stroke and pulled the paddle from the water, letting the nimble, silent boat glide along. The farther ship was the bigger of the two, and even in the dark night he could see that she was the *Wilkenson Brothers*. The pirates had altered her in some way—the line of her deck did not look the same—but still George knew the family ship well enough that he could never mistake her for another.

The closer ship, the small one, he did not recognize, and he assumed it was the vessel that had brought the pirates to the Chesapeake Bay. He stared as he drifted closer. He began to see a few dim, square patches along her side, aft, some muted light from within gently illuminating the open gunports.

It was fantastic to be that close to so frightening, mysterious, and alien a world.

Once when he had found himself alone in Norfolk he had ventured into a whorehouse, stayed long enough to have two glasses of ale. He had not managed the courage to indulge in the main attraction of the place, but still it had been thrilling to be in the presence of such debauchery and danger. And this was the same, only many times more.

He dipped the paddle carefully back into the river and gave another stroke, and the canoe surged ahead again. He was still more curious than afraid, which surprised him and pleased him as well. Of course, he had seen no one moving on either ship, had heard no voices, seen no lights. He was perfectly aware that he might lose all of his courage, might even soil his breeches, if even one voice called out a challenge. But the smaller ship was only fifteen feet away, and he was closing with it, and as yet it seemed that no one had noticed him.

The canoe was still making good way through the water when he came alongside. He put the paddle in the water and with an experienced twist of the blade brought the boat to a stop right against the pirate's hull.

He hit with just the tiniest of thumps, but it sounded like a thunderclap to Wilkenson. He reached up and grabbed on to the main chains and sat, absolutely silent, waiting for the shouts of alarm, the blasphemous curses of the pirates, the musket shots that would end his life. But there was only quiet, the seamless quiet that he had heard since leaving the shore.

Then he heard a snort, like a wild pig, just a few feet away, and he almost leapt off the thwart. Felt the fear ripple through him. He sat entirely still and listened, and the snort became a more rhythmic breathing, someone snoring on the other side of the bulwark.

He sat for what seemed a very long time, but nothing more happened, so he put his hands flat against the side of the ship and slowly worked the canoe aft. The main channel jutted out over his head like a roof, blocking his view of the ship. And then he was past it and directly under one of the open gun-ports, the black muzzle of the gun thrust out above him.

He reached up and grabbed the edge of the port and checked the canoe's sternway. Slowly, silently, taking great pains not to breathe out loud, he stretched his back and craned his neck upward.

He could just see over the port sill, with the top of his head brushing the underside of the gun, and in that awkward position he took his first look at the terrible and forbidden world of the pirates.

The man who was snoring was no more than four feet from Wilkenson's face. George could smell the stale sweat from his body, the foul drunken breath that came in puffs with every porcine sound. He toyed with the thought that he could draw one of his pistols and shoot the man right through the head. One second he would be sleeping, the next he would be dead, and he would never know what had killed him. Here was a man over whom he had the power of life or death, a soul that he, George Wilkenson, could send hurtling down to hell.

That thought thrilled him, and he stared at the sleeping pirate for some time before running his eyes over the rest of the ship. The gunport opened onto the waist. He could see a few dim stars overhead, but where he would have expected to see the break of a forecastle there was only empty space. The pirates must have ripped that structure down, for what purpose Wilkenson could not imagine.

He could see a few heaps of stuff lying about the deck. They might have been sleeping men or discarded gear—he could not tell in the dark. In any event, there did not seem to be many men aboard, at least not topside, and those that were there did not seem to be awake. It was no wonder that his approach had gone unchallenged. He settled back down on the thwart and began to work the canoe aft once more.

He came at last to the aftermost gunport, save one. It was that one and its neighbor that he had seen softly outlined by some light aboard the ship. There could well be men within, men who were awake, who would see him. He stopped, gripping the bottom of the port with sweating palms, and let the rush of fear and exhilaration pass.

He sat still for a moment more, feeling the canoe's gentle motion in the river, and wondered who he was, who he had become, taking such risks for no purpose.

He had tried to court danger before, but the experience in the whorehouse was the closest he had ever come, until now.

Until now. Now that his father had killed off the last of the family's honor, what little real honor it ever had. Now that his father was dead, and his more beloved younger brother was dead as well. Now that he had been made to participate in the humiliating spectacle of failed vengeance.

The sun would come up in the morning and put an end to that terrible night, and it would find him alive or dead, and he was surprised to find how little he cared which it would be. Any fear he felt now was animal instinct, not a rational desire to preserve his life and position.

With that thought he looped the canoe's stern painter around the mizzen chains and made it fast. He craned up again and peered through the gunport and found himself looking into a great cabin of sorts. There was a single lantern hanging from a beam amidships. It was entirely shuttered up, but enough light was leaking out to vaguely illuminate the space, and Wilkenson's eyes, not quite acclimated to the dark, were able to pick out details.

His idea of a great cabin was based on that of the *Wilkenson Brothers*, with its fine furnishings and appointments, its oak and gilded trim, a luxurious apartment afloat. The cabin he was looking at now might have been that way once—he could see the remnants of paneling in a few places, and other hints of past glory—but for the most part it looked as if it had been sacked and sacked again.

Most of the space was taken up by the four long guns, two starboard and two larboard. The aftermost gunports, crudely hacked through the sides, suggested that those two cannon had been moved in after the pirates had taken the ship.

There was a big table amidships, lashed to ringbolts in the deck. The varnish on the legs glowed in the faint light and bespoke a once-fine piece. Wilkenson could picture an elegant dinner laid out there for the master and his guests. But now there were piles of debris scattered over the top, piled so high that even from his low angle Wilkenson could see clothing and bottles and discarded food.

There was not much else, no carpet, no wine cabinet, no sideboard. Most of the paneling was gone, perhaps ripped down for firewood. It looked more like a cabin for a gang of woodcutters than a refuge for a ship's master.

There was no one in the cabin, of that he was quite certain, for he could see nearly all of the space. Still, it smelled as if there were a hundred unwashed bodies there, like the hold of a slave ship. Well, perhaps not that bad, but bad enough. He could smell sweat and rotting food and a vague trace of feces and urine. He was accustomed to the unpleasant smell that ships developed, but he had never experienced anything like that outside a blackbirder.

He had no idea how long he had been staring into that dim cabin, but it seemed a long time, and in that time there had been no more noise than he had heard while paddling out to the ships. Even the snoring had stopped. The night was devoid of human sounds. And in the quiet, clinging to the side of the brigands' ship, Wilkenson's thoughts turned to Marlowe.

Marlowe had been one of these men. That was what Ripley had said. He had lived this life, a life that he, George Wilkenson, could only peer at from a canoe. Marauding, looting, raping, Marlowe had done it all. Was it any wonder that Elizabeth was so eager to fuck him? And now he was sailing downriver to fight it out with these pirates, to plunge right into battle with men the very thought of whom made Wilkenson sick with fear.

He had seen the pirates coming up the hill. There were hundreds of them, many more than the Plymouth Prizes, vicious killers all. Two ships against the one. And Marlowe was coming to do combat with them, while all he could do was float alongside in a canoe, peering in the gunport like some kind of peeper. That was all he had ever been, a peeper.

Then the next thing he knew he was standing in the canoe and half thrust through the gunport, squeezing with some difficulty around the barrel of the gun that was run out. He paused as his pistol caught on the sill, twisted around until it was free, and then slid in the rest of the way. He picked up his musket, which he had thrust in before him, and, half crouching, looked around.

He was aboard the pirate ship. That very realization surprised him, as he had never intended to do anything of that kind. He was thrilled at the thought. He was aboard a pirate ship, the only conscious man, as far as he could tell. He held their lives in his hand. He could kill them all, just as he had killed Ripley.

But that was not entirely true, he reminded himself. He could kill three of them, for he had two pistols and a musket, and then they would kill him.

But he had not come aboard just to look around, he had come to do something, to make himself a part of Marlowe's world, if even for a moment, even if he was the only one who would ever know it. These were the men who had burned his home, and he wanted vengeance on them, real vengeance, vengeance the way Marlowe would have it. These men had to be eradicated, any suggestion of a link between them and the Wilkenson family had to be wiped out. But he did not know how.

And suddenly the answer was obvious, as obvious as the glowing lantern and the pile of flammable debris and the wooden beams that smelled of linseed oil and tar.

He picked up his musket and stepped softly to the forward end of the cabin. There was a rack for cutlasses against the bulkhead, with two of the weapons still in place. There was also a portrait of a woman, probably the former master's wife. Her image had suffered great insult in the hands of the pirates. There was a slash across her face and various stains on the canvas where something—food, it looked like—had been hurled at the painting.

George took those things in as he stepped cautiously toward the door that communicated with the waist. He paused just inside the frame. The door opened outward, onto the deck, and it was half open. He leaned forward and slowly, very slowly, peered out.

There was still no movement, though he could tell that the heaps he had seen from the canoe were indeed men, deep in drunken sleep, judging from the many bottles scattered around. He could hear snoring once more. There were not many men aboard, as far as he could tell, though there may have been more below. Still, it occurred to him that most of the pirates were more likely to be aboard the relatively new and luxurious *Wilkenson Brothers* than that fetid tub.

He waited for a minute, and then another, and still there was no sound. He felt himself being taken by a recklessness that he had never known. He took another step. He was standing in the doorway, in full sight of anyone who might look up. He reached over and pulled the door shut.

The door swung in, smooth and silent on iron hinges, and then George felt some resistance and the lower hinge gave off a loud squeak that seemed to run through his body like a metal shaft. He froze where he stood, and it was only with some effort that he did not wet himself. His courage was not as great as he had thought.

He remained perfectly still, listening, but there was no sound, no alarm. The door was all but closed, save for two inches. It would have to remain as it was. He stepped back across the cabin and surveyed the detritus on the surface of the table. Clothing, bottles, food scraps. They would burn, as would the table itself and the few bits of upholstery remaining, and the thinner bits of wood making up the window frames.

All of it would burn, and it would set the larger beams ablaze and in no time at all the entire ship would be involved, and then Marlowe would have one, not two, ships to fight. And he, George Wilkenson, would have helped to rid the Chesapeake of the plague that his own father had brought. And then, perhaps, he could endure being himself. George Wilkenson.

He grabbed an armful of the stuff on the table and deposited it on the settee, frowning and turning his head away from the foul odor it gave off once disturbed. He opened his powder horn and spilled its contents onto the cloth. He pulled the lantern down and opened it up and reached gingerly inside for the candle. The flame fluttered, and he paused, waiting for it to regain its strength, and then carried it over to the settee and set the whole thing on fire.

The flame raced through the sprinkling of gunpowder and grabbed on to the cloth, flaring and growing with each second.

It greedily devoured the shirts and breeches and the old coat and then went for the settee cushions. The pirates had already managed to slash the upholstery and pull out a portion of the stuffing, and that just made it easier for the hungry fire. In less than a minute the flames were climbing up the side of the cabin, pulling at the paint and lapping over the heavy beams overhead.

George stepped back from the heat and the light. He was surprised at how quickly the fire was spreading. He stepped back again.

The fire was swirling around the after windows. It snatched up the old torn curtains, and in a flash they were gone and the flames moved on. They crawled across the starboard ceiling and threatened to engulf the aftermost cannon on that side.

Wilkenson began to feel uneasy. He could hear no sounds from the deck, but this fire could not go undetected for long, no matter how drunk the pirates were. He stepped back again and looked toward the gunport through which he had come. His route of escape. He had to go. But he could not tear himself away.

He looked back at the fire, which now consumed a good portion of the after end of the cabin. This was destruction, this was vengeance, from his own hand. He smiled with delight. A few more seconds and he would go, because now he had redeemed himself and now he wanted to live.

He took another step toward his gunport. The heat was almost more than he could bear. The aftermost cannon on the starboard side was now all but engulfed in flame.

Then Wilkenson was struck with the sickening thought that perhaps the gun was loaded.

And no sooner did that thought occur to him than the gun went off with a sound like the ship's entire magazine exploding. The wheels leapt off the deck as the big cannon flew inboard, blowing more fire from its muzzle. The breech ropes were burned through and there was nothing to stop the gun in its recoil. It crashed through the table and upended as it slammed against its opposite number on the larboard side, turning them both over with the thunder of two tons of iron hitting the deck.

"Oh God, oh God, oh God . . . ," Wilkenson stammered with rising panic. He whirled around, ready to face the brigands storming through the door, but there were none there, not yet. He did not imagine they were many seconds away. He turned again to his gunport, but the concussion of the cannon had blown the fire down the side of the ship and now his escape route was swallowed by the flames.

He turned again, toward the larboard side. And in that second the first of the pirates pulled the door back and rushed into the burning cabin, his arm flung up to shield his eyes from the flames.

George felt his bladder go. He reached his trembling hand for his musket just as the pirate saw him, framed against the fire. The pirate shouted something and reached for a gun in his sash, but George had his musket up to his shoulder. He cocked the lock and pulled the trigger, and the pirate was blown back against the next of his comrades, coming in behind him.

George flung the musket aside and drew both his pistols. He was surrounded by flames. All of the gunports were involved, and the only way out of the cabin was the door, and he had two shots left.

More pirates were rushing the cabin, guns out, cutlasses flashing. George could see them through the open door. He felt an odd calm sweep over him. He stepped forward as the first brigand charged in, a big, bearded man, his cocked hat askew, and George shot him right in the face.

In the waist the pirates stopped their rush. A pistol was thrust in through the door and it went off with a flash, barely visible in the brilliant flames that surrounded him, and George felt the ball tear through his shoulder. The pain was incredible. He felt his arm go weak. He dropped the spent pistol in his good hand and took up the loaded one from his failing arm.

Another of the pirates pushed into the cabin, and George fired his last shot into the man's stomach. The pirate pitched facefirst with a scream, and behind him was a door full of small arms, pistols and muskets, all leveled at him. George let his arm drop to his side and waited for it. This is what a firing squad is like, he thought. This is what it is like to die.

The pirates fired all at once, and George felt himself thrown back, like getting hit with half a dozen fists all at once. He felt the hard deck under him, the burn of flames near his face, but he was not burning himself. He was warm, but he was not burning.

He heard shouting all around him and the crackling of flames, but it all melded together into one smooth noise. He felt something wet and sticky under his hand and realized with some surprise that it was blood, his own blood, running out of him and onto the deck.

I cannot live without blood, he thought, and in that moment he realized that he would not live at all, that he was about to die, and that it was not that bad.

My God, my God, into your hands . . .

He had stood up to them all, his father, the pirates. He had been as much a man as Marlowe would ever be, and with that thought, and with a thin smile on his lips, George Wilkenson died.

Chapter 35

HELL WAS ready to receive them. Jean-Pierre LeRois had made all the arrangements.

He climbed up from the hold, his shoes clumping on the ladders, the voices singing in his head. He was ready to get Barrett under way. He was ready for the voyage himself, if go he must.

And not just himself. They would all go, all of those men who lay sprawled about, snoring like swine, sleeping on the night that his enemies were coming for him. He understood that now. It gave him an overwhelming sense of peace. A moment of pure clarity. They all had to die. He knew it was right.

He made his way across the 'tween decks, automatically bending deep until he remembered that the decks of this new, finer *Vengeance* were high enough for him to stand almost entirely upright.

He strode forward more purposefully. His foot hit something soft and he stumbled, and the pile on the deck groaned and rolled over and muttered, "Here, watch it, dumb arse."

"Cochon!" LeRois shouted, and spit on the man at his feet, but the man was already asleep again. LeRois stared at the pile of human wreckage, barely visible in the gloom. They would all get their reward, each to his own. The voices told him that.

He found the ladder to the weather deck and climbed up into the waist. The night was dark, and the smoke from the destruction he had wrought still hung in the air. He moved around the many sleeping men and climbed up to the quarterdeck, where to his irritation he found even more men passed out and sprawled where they fell, some hugging bags of stolen goods like women.

He spit on the deck and looked forward, upriver. Barrett was coming for him, he knew it. The voices were singing the songs of his enemies' destruction. He could not see him yet, could not see any sign of dark sails against the dark sky, but still he knew he was there.

His eyes moved from the blackness of the river to the distant shore. The evidence of his wrath and power still burned and glowed in places miles apart. He looked from one to the next to the next, turning aft as he looked upon his works.

And then something caught his eye, something bright. There was one hundred feet of water separating the *Vengeance* from the old, wasted ship that last bore that name. Light was pouring from the old *Vengeance's* aftermost gunports, those that opened onto the great cabin. He took a step forward, rested his hands on the rail, squinted at his former command.

Perhaps there was someone in the cabin, someone with a lantern. But the light was terribly bright, brighter than any dozen lanterns. And just as the terrible thought struck him that the ship might be on fire, one of the great guns went off, a thunderous sound that split the night. The old *Vengeance* shook with the impact of the recoil.

"Merde!" LeRois shouted, and pounded the rail with his fist. Now he could see flames licking out of the gunports, could hear the crackling of the fire consuming the fabric of the ship. Some idiot had started a fire and now the whole great cabin was blazing. It was already too far gone to stop.

The humps of cloth and hair that had been pirates sleeping on the weather deck of the new *Vengeance* came to life, leaping to their feet, cutlasses and pistols drawn and ready. They were well used to coming instantly awake and straight into a fight, and the sound of a great gun was their clarion. They crowded along the rail, shouting obscenities, voicing loud speculations as they watched their old ship being overwhelmed by flames.

"*Merde!*" LeRois shouted again. He did not care so much about the old ship, but there was the danger that the fire would be blown across onto the new *Vengeance*. And even that did not worry him so much, as long as it did not happen before Barrett was aboard.

And then from somewhere within the flames he heard the sound of a gun go off. Not a cannon, but something much smaller, a musket or a pistol. He cocked his head toward the flames. More small arms, two shots in rapid succession, and then another, and then a whole volley.

Men were shouting, running about the old *Vengeance's* deck. He could not see them—it was too dark and the bright flames had hurt his eyes—but he could hear the commotion clearly enough.

Another of the great guns went off, on the starboard side, like the first, firing its load toward the north shore. LeRois stared at the growing flames, considered helping the men on the burning ship.

No, he decided. To hell with them. They had a boat. If they were too drunk and stupid to get in it and row to safety, then they should burn. They should burn in any event, for being so drunk and stupid as to let their ship catch fire. They should burn, and they would, all of them.

The guns on the old *Vengeance's* larboard side went off as the flames consumed them as well, one right after the other with less than a second between. One of them fired straight across the water, slamming its load into the new ship's side, though LeRois did not reckon it would do much damage. The other must have been upended, for rather than firing out of its gunport it blew a hole in the side of the ship and showered the *Nouvelle Vengeance* with canister and grape and bits of burning debris.

Someone forward was cursing, loud and vehement,

wounded by the old *Vengeance*'s inadvertent broadside. LeRois did not care about that, but he was concerned about those bits of flaming material that had landed on the deck.

"*Allez, allez!* The flames! Get them out!"

In the waist the men pulled themselves from the spectacle and stamped the flaming bits that threatened the deck, and one by one the glowing embers flared and died.

When he was satisfied that he would not lose his new ship to the flames, LeRois turned back to the old *Vengeance*. The long tentacles of the fire were reaching out of the gunports and the hole that the gun had blown in the side, reaching up and grabbing on to the mizzen shrouds and the quarterdeck rail, pulling itself up and out of the great cabin, taking command of the vessel. They were brothers, he and the fire. Together they ruled the night.

And then something else caught his eye, something beyond the burning ship that was throwing back the light of the fire.

"Eh? *Qu'est-ce que c'est?*" He pushed forward along the rail, shoving those Vengeances out of the way that were standing there stupidly watching the ship burn. He got to the break of the quarterdeck and stared out into the dark.

It was like a ghost, wavering before his eyes, dimly seen, and LeRois felt the panic rising. And then suddenly it seemed to materialize and take form, and he realized that it was not a ghost but a sail, the gaff-headed mainsail of a sloop, coming downriver. He would never have seen it had it not been for the flames rising up from the old *Vengeance*.

He smiled, and then he laughed out loud. "The devil, he will not let you sneak up on me, eh?" he shouted at the sail, then shook his fist.

He could see the faces of his men turning toward him and then following his gaze. He could hear loud speculation through the crackling of the flames. The voices were singing their warnings, high and clear, almost shrieking, but more lovely than that. The flames danced over the quarterdeck of his old ship, and laughing faces appeared among the brilliant yellows and reds, and LeRois laughed with them.

"*Allez*, now, they are coming for us!" LeRois shouted. He drew his sword and pointed toward the sloop. "That is the first, but there are more, and last of all will come Malachias Barrett, who is the very devil himself, but I am a bigger devil than he, eh?"

His men looked confused, the stupid sheep, so he tried to make it more clear for them. "The guardship we chase here, she is coming back for us now, and soon they will be aboard us. They will try to come from two sides, the ship and the sloop, but we will be ready for them, no?"

Now heads were nodding as the men began to understand that they would soon be attacked. They scattered, some running, some limping, some walking, to see to the great guns and small arms, to load firelocks and return the edge to swords and to sharpen themselves with whiskey and rum.

They are animals, LeRois thought, they know only living and fucking and killing and dying. He alone knew better, and that was why the voices had put their lives, all of their lives—the Vengeances', Malachias Barrett's, the king's men—all of them into his hands.

"*Je suis le seul maître à bord après Dieu.*" The words came to his lips unbidden, the words the priests had taught him so many, many years before. He had not thought of them in all that time.

Thou shalt have no other Gods before me.

The sound of the great gun blasted Marlowe from his self-indulgent reverie. Brought him up all standing. His first thought was for the *Northumberland*. She was downriver somewhere, probably right up with the pirate ships. If she had been discovered, the pirate's heavy guns would rip her apart before she got within two cable lengths of the enemy's side.

He swung himself up into the mizzen shrouds and scampered up until he was ten feet above the deck and peered forward. He could see nothing beyond the darkness and the few burning buildings ashore. His shoulder ached from the tension. He flexed it, waited for more cannon to fire. Waited for the river to be illuminated by the pirate's broadside. Waited to see his sloop die in the muzzle flashes of the big guns.

But there was nothing, nothing more, no more heavy guns. Perhaps it was some of the drunken brigands making fireworks to amuse themselves. He closed his eyes, breathed deeply, forced himself to relax, hoping that the exercise would help him to see in the dark. He opened his eyes again, avoiding those lights on the north shore, and looked over the starboard side.

Now he could just make out the pale outline of sandy beach that ringed the northern banks of Hog Island. It was just abeam. He moved his eyes forward, scanning along what he reckoned were the tops of the trees, and there, just beyond the island, he saw the masts.

They thrust above the denser foliage, just visible where the dark sky met the darker horizon, skeletal limbs reaching up to heaven. Both ships were there, *Vengeances* old and new. He did not know which the pirates would be aboard. He did not know if he would be able to see well enough in the dark night even to maneuver the *Plymouth Prize* alongside.

There was another sound now, a popping like a rope under a heavy strain. Small-arms fire? Marlowe turned his ear toward the noise. Yes, that was what it was. Was it possible that the *Northumberland* was engaged? Marlowe had felt unwell for the past hour, as his meeting with LeRois drew closer, but the thought of Bickerstaff and James embroiled in a fight, and he himself unable to join in, made him positively sick to his stomach. He grabbed tighter onto the shroud.

And then another big gun went off and Marlowe nearly tumbled out of the rigging. He could see the muzzle flash this time, spewing its flame out into the night. It illuminated the side of the pirate ship, the smaller one, and the water out one hundred feet from her side. The *Northumberland* was nowhere to be seen.

Marlowe swallowed hard, forced himself to be calm. It had been years since he had felt this kind of fear. The last time, in fact, was when he had finally summoned the courage to tell

LeRois that he was leaving, and that had been the closest he had ever come to being killed.

He climbed back down and stood on the quarterdeck rail, one hand on a shroud to steady himself. The Plymouth Prizes were at their guns, craning their necks out of gunports and twisting in odd ways to see around the barrels. They had a true believer's faith in him, and that would have to sustain them now, for he could think of no inspiring words to get them riled up for the coming fight. He wished he could, but he could not, and he did not trust himself to speak.

Just as he was wondering how in all hell he was going to negotiate the shallows around the island, two more guns went off in rapid succession, one, two, and this time they fired south, straight into the *Wilkenson Brothers*.

"Good Lord!" Marlowe cried, despite himself. The blast from the guns lit the big pirate ship up in two quick flashes, like shuttering and unshuttering a lantern.

The after end of the old *Vengeance* seemed to glow with a light from within, and that light was reflected on the water around her stern section. Marlowe squinted, shook his head. Then the flames burst up around the quarterdeck and up the mizzen rigging. The ship was on fire. And the fire, no doubt, had set off the guns.

Marlowe watched the flames running over the quarterdeck and up the mizzen yard as the dry canvas of the mizzen sail was consumed.

The burning ship was a threat to them. If the *Plymouth Prize* caught fire, with her hold full of powder, the resultant explosion would rock the colony, would kill every man on the water, pirate and Prize alike.

The fire was throwing off an ever-widening circle of light. It crept out over the water, fell across the *Northumberland*, which was attempting to circle around the pirate ships undetected and come up on their far side.

So much for that idea, Marlowe thought. It was the only trick he had in his bag.

"Damn me," he said out loud, though he always figured

that God would grant that request unbidden. The *Wilkenson Brothers* was two hundred yards away. He could hear the chaos of the pirates getting ready for a fight, the rumble of big guns running out, the clash of small arms made ready.

"Damn." He glanced around, fidgeted with the hilt of his sword, opened his mouth to give an order, closed it again. His trap had been found out before it had sprung. Every one of his tingling nerves told him to put the ship about and retreat upriver, to abandon the fight until another day.

That thought gave him a great sense of relief. It was the only reasonable thing to do. He grasped at that excuse like a drowning man grasps at his rescuer, pulling them both down.

But it was nonsense. If he was to have this elusive thing called honor, this thing that somehow had become so important to his life—real honor—then he could not lie to himself. If he were to retreat, it would be because he was afraid.

What was more, explaining to Nicholson et al. why he had broken off the attack, mounting this attack again, going again through the awful hours leading up to his meeting with LeRois, it would all be more terrible than just doing it now.

"In the waist!" he shouted. "Mr. Rakestraw, we shall be falling off a bit, make ready at the braces. Gunners, you know your duty! Two broadsides, small arms, then over the sides! Listen for my orders, or Mr. Rakestraw's, if I should fall!"

If I should fall. He felt no twinge at all when he said those words. LeRois could do no more than kill him. He took a deep breath and turned to the helmsmen and said, "Fall off, two points."

The bow of the *Plymouth Prize* came around, aiming for that stretch of water between the two pirate ships. There was no question of being able to see now; the fire aboard the former *Vengeance* had broken clear of her great cabin and filled the quarterdeck. It ran halfway up the mizzenmast and was spilling down onto the waist. All of the water one hundred yards around the ship was brightly lit; it reminded Marlowe of the great bonfires they used to build on the beaches around which they would have their drunken, frenzied orgies back in his days in the sweet trade.

The side of the *Wilkenson Brothers* looked like burnished gold as the fire washed the new black paint with yellow light and cast deep shadows along the side. The light from the flames spilled over her sails in their loose bundles, the black standing rigging, the muzzles of the guns, even the steel of the weapons that flashed in the hands of men along her rails, and made it all that much more frightening.

The pirates were starting to vapor, to chant and bang on the sides and the rails, clashing cutlasses together. Marlowe felt the sweat crawling down his back and his palm slick on the hilt of his sword. They were one hundred yards away and closing quickly.

Someone was beating bones together with that distinctive hollow clunk clunk clunk. And then someone was chanting "Death, death, death," and Marlowe realized that this was his own men.

He pulled his eyes from the flickering ghostly enemy and looked down into the waist of the *Plymouth Prize*, now as clearly illuminated as if they had a fire going on the main hatch. It was Middleton, standing on the rail by the foreshrouds and chanting "Death, death, death," and beside him another man had two beef bones and he was banging them together. Marlowe saw smiles flashing in the firelight, and more and more of the guardship's men began, "Death, death, death . . ."

The Plymouth Prizes swarmed up into the rigging and along the rail, and they, too, were banging their swords on the sides, chanting and screaming. Someone on the pirate ship fired a pistol into the air, and it was met with three from the *Plymouth Prize*. Marlowe wanted to order them to stop, to save their fire, but the vaporing was doing more for his men's state of mind than any amount of preparation could accomplish.

They were fifty yards from the *Wilkenson Brothers*, and the cumulative force of the men's voices—king's men and pirates—seemed to be drawing the ships together, seemed to suck all of the air out of the space between the two vessels. Every chant, every shout, every pistol shot on either side drove all of them to

great heights of frenzy. They waved swords and beat swords and
fired pistols and shrieked with the urgent lust to kill one another.

Marlowe's carefully issued orders, repeated many times,
had been entirely forgotten. There was no thought of broadsides, no thought of small arms. The men lining the rails and
the channels and screaming and vaporing and flashing their
swords in the weird flickering light of the burning ship did not
want to think. They wanted only to kill.

The pirates were lining the rail as well, screaming back,
dancing men and dancing shadows, and there were far more
of them than there were Plymouth Prizes. Had the Prizes any
grasp of reality left they would realize how perilous their situation was, but they were swept up in the frenzy, they were
berserk, and they thought they were invincible.

Twenty yards, and the *Plymouth Prize* was in a perfect position to use her cannon to great effect, with the pirates standing as
they were on the rails, having forgotten the punishment the *Prize*
had doled out weeks earlier. But the men of the *Plymouth Prize*
were also on the rails, their big guns abandoned.

"Lay us alongside!" Marlowe shouted to the helmsmen.
"Right alongside, bow to bow!"

The helmsmen nodded, pushed the tiller over a foot. Marlowe dashed down into the waist. Found the linstock at the first
gun he came to, but the match was out, raced to the next tub.
The match on that linstock was still glowing, but barely. Marlowe
blew on it, blew again. It flared to life, glowing a dull orange. He
twirled the linstock in his hand and ran back to the first gun.

Through the gunport he could see the *Wilkenson Brothers'*
mizzen chains, crowded with howling men, her quarterdeck
rails lined as well. He did not see LeRois, but he hoped a
desperate hope that the man was there, right in line with the
muzzle, as he pushed the glowing match down into the powder train.

He leapt back as the train sputtered to life, was halfway to
the next gun when the first fired off, slamming inboard. He
could hear crushing wood and howls of outrage and agony,
and he touched off the next gun and then ran to the next.

Each blast seemed to momentarily kill the vaporing, and then it was back again, louder, more confused, more vehement. Marlowe ran down the line, firing each gun, never pausing to see what destruction he was doing. He put the match to the penultimate gun, prayed again that one of those killed would be LeRois.

Marlowe was reaching the match to the forwardmost gun when the two ships hit. The *Plymouth Prize* shuddered to a stop, throwing him off balance. The glowing match missed the trail of powder as Marlowe struggled to keep on his feet. From over the side came the wrenching, shattering sound of the two ships grinding against each other.

Thomas regained his balance, shoved the glowing match in the train of powder. The gun was actually touching the side of the *Wilkenson Brothers* when it smashed its load into the merchantman's frail bulwark and blew it clean away.

He looked up at his own men standing on the rail. Middleton was there, his sword raised over his head, his face twisted into the most insane mask of rage and bloodlust as he rallied the Prizes to leap across. The fire from the old *Vengeance* illuminated him as if he were an actor on stage or some savage before a pagan ceremonial fire.

And then there was a smattering of small-arms fire and a pistol ball smashed into the back of Middleton's skull, blew his forehead apart. The fine mist of blood and bone was perfectly illuminated by the light of the fire. The lieutenant began to topple forward, but before he could hit the deck he was pushed back by the frenzied men of the *Plymouth Prize* as they stormed over the rail and down onto the pirate's deck.

Middleton's body fell from sight. Marlowe hopped up onto the carriage of the number one gun and then stepped up onto the rail, his left hand on the backstay for balance. He was looking down at the deck of the pirate ship, where his wild outnumbered men were surging forward, pushing the pirates back.

A pistol ball struck the backstay. Marlowe felt it quiver in his grip. He drew his sword, picked his spot, and leapt down into the fight.

Chapter 36

THE WAIST of the *Wilkenson Brothers* was in deep shadow, with the bulwarks shielding the deck from the light of the burning ship. Men moved in and out of the night. Swords raised overhead gleamed as they reflected the fire. The flash of pistols, pan and muzzle, lit those dark places for a brilliant second and then the shadows closed in again.

Marlowe felt the burn of a cutlass cutting across his arm even as he tried to recover from his leap to the deck. He twisted instinctively, swung his big sword around, reached for a pistol as he fell. Felt the jar of the blade making contact, but he heard no scream and did not know if he had even struck his attacker.

He hit the deck flat on his back, his sword in his hand. The pirate was standing above him, leering, cutlass raised, ready to deliver the coup de grâce. Marlowe brought the pistol up, pulled the lock back with his thumb. The pirate bellowed outrage as he tried to bring his cutlass down before Marlowe fired the gun.

He did not succeed. Marlowe pulled the trigger, tossed the gun aside, giving no more thought to the big man he had just blown to the deck. He scrambled to his feet, his back to the bulwark. In a half-crouch, sword gripped in both hands, he got his bearings.

The Plymouth Prizes and the pirates had smashed into each other like surf across a bar of sand, and now they were fighting it out where they stood. Most of those who were wounded or dead had been shot down by the *Plymouth Prize's* great guns or by pistols in that first wave, but once those guns had been fired there was no time to reload, and now it was steel against steel.

Marlowe looked aft. More dead men there, more wounded crawling away or curled up in the shadows. His firing the great guns had had some effect, made the numbers a little more even, and now the Plymouth Prizes were plunging in with a fury to match the pirate defenders.

If I've turned them all into brigands, at least I've taught them more than just greed, Thomas thought as he stepped into an open place in the line and matched swords with a wiry, bearded little man with a scarred face and black teeth.

The little man was fast, trying to cut Marlowe down with a quick, darting attack, while Marlowe attempted to overwhelm him with his strength and the weight of his sword. It was an interesting match, and one that might have been more difficult for Marlowe to win just a few years before, before he had learned under Bickerstaff's careful tutelage the more subtle aspects of fighting with a blade.

He wielded his big sword with two hands, as was his custom, beating back the attack with twice the force needed, throwing the little man off with the sheer momentum of his parry. His left arm was starting to ache where it had been cut; he could feel the blood, warm and liquid, under his shirt. He considered pulling his second pistol and just shooting the man, but he needed that bullet to kill LeRois. He had a higher duty here, and he was just wasting his time with this ugly opponent.

The pirate darted forward, lunged, as Marlowe leaned back. The tip of his blade pierced Marlowe's coat, and Marlowe brought his own sword straight down on the man's outstretched hand. The pirate screamed, the sword fell to the deck, and Marlowe lunged himself, running the man through, then pulled the blade clean, turning to face any new threat on his flank even as he heard the man's body hit the deck.

LeRois. He could avoid it no longer. He could not continue to pretend that the Prizes needed him here in the waist.

Rakestraw was ten feet away, fighting like an ancient Norseman, rallying the men. At any moment Bickerstaff and his men would come swarming up the other side and fall on the Vengeances from behind. Ten minutes before, there would have been enough pirates to fight both sides of the deck, but that was before he had delivered the blasts of case shot right into the vaporing tribe.

LeRois was not among the men fighting in the waist, which meant either he was among the dead or wounded or that he was holding back, perhaps waiting for Marlowe to come to him.

There were no more excuses. He had to hunt the man down. As much as he did not wish to, he knew that he had to go.

"Oh, Lord, please let him be dead," Marlowe muttered. He imagined LeRois's scarred and battered body tossed up against the bulwark, half torn apart after taking a blast of canister right in the chest, those mad eyes open and dead, staring sightless up at the sky. He felt as hypocritical as a man can feel, calling on God at that juncture.

He stepped back from the fight, pressed himself against the bulwark, worked his way aft, toward the quarterdeck. It was the body of the serpent that his men were fighting. It was his job to cut off the head.

A fire was flicking, burning aft. Marlowe thought perhaps the flames from the other ship had blown across and caught in the rig. But it was not the ship that was burning. It was a torch, held aloft, and holding that torch was Jean-Pierre LeRois.

He stood on the quarterdeck ladder, on the other side of the deck. The undulating light illuminated the dirty, powder-burned face, the matted beard, the dark, wild eyes, the red sash under a once-fine coat. Jean-Pierre LeRois. Older than Marlowe had last seen him, dirtier, meaner looking, but there he was.

The pirate was squinting, searching through the crowd, and it was no great difficulty to guess for whom he was looking.

And then their eyes met. LeRois paused, leaned back, leaned forward, glaring, and then he smiled, his big filthy teeth gleaming in the light of the torch.

Marlowe took a step aft. They would meet on the quarter-deck, fight it out in that land of the dead, among the bodies of the men Marlowe had swept away with his broadside.

But LeRois did not go aft. Rather, he stepped down into the waist, standing head and shoulders above the others, and with his eyes still holding Marlowe's he stepped over to the doorway leading to the aft cabins, pulled it open, stepped through, and shut it behind.

"Goddamn it!" Marlowe shouted. LeRois had gone below. With every last bit of body and soul he wanted to let the pirate go, did not want to follow the snake down its hole. But he could not let LeRois get away, and there was no knowing what he was about. He had to go.

He pushed past the struggling, shouting men, edged around the break of the quarterdeck, worked his way to the door that LeRois had shut behind him. Felt the sting of sweat running into his eyes. He blinked it away and shifted his sword to his left hand and took hold of the handle of the door with his right.

He pulled the door open, quickly, and leapt aside before LeRois could put a bullet into him. But there were no shots fired, no noise of any kind from within.

He stepped forward, peered through the door and down the alleyway. There was a short hall, lined with small cabins, that terminated at the far end with the master's great cabin, all in darkness save for a single lantern burning in the aft cabin. It was just as he remembered it from the time that he and Bickerstaff had come aboard to enforce the king's rules governing trade. It seemed years before.

Marlowe wiped his slick palm on his coat, pulled his remaining pistol from his cross-belt, cocked the lock with his thumb. He breathed deeply, again and again, as if relishing the very act of breathing, as a man might relish a last meal, then he stepped into the dark alleyway.

He put a foot down on the deck, carefully, let his weight come on it slowly, and listened. The fighting on the deck had swelled in pitch, and Marlowe guessed that Bickerstaff and his men had come over the side, but he pushed those sounds aside and concentrated on the space around him.

There was nothing, no sound at all, save for the faint protest of the deck under his foot. He took another step inboard. Nothing. Perhaps LeRois was waiting aft in the great cabin. He ran his eyes over what little part of the place was visible to him, readjusted his grip on the pistol, and stepped forward again.

Then the door to the small cabin behind him seemed to explode outward, shards of wood showering the deck and light bursting into the dark confines. Marlowe twisted around as the great cudgel of a torch swung in an arc toward his head, behind it the big, grinning face of Jean-Pierre LeRois. He raised the pistol, and his finger squeezed the trigger as the torch slammed into the side of his head, knocking him against the bulkhead. The alleyway and the flames and the pirate swam in front of him, and his knees buckled from under him.

LeRois's laugh filled the space, as loud and sudden as the pistol shot. "Quartermaster, I am the devil himself, your bullets do not harm me! I have waited for you all night and you try to shoot me? No, no, we must go down to hell together!"

Marlowe slumped to the deck. His right hand grabbed up his sword, moving by instinct alone, but he did not have the strength to raise the blade in his defense. He felt LeRois's hand on his collar, felt the massive strength of the man's arm, felt himself being dragged aft along the deck. He clung to his sword as if it alone were keeping him alive.

His shoulder slammed into the door frame as LeRois pulled him into the great cabin. He was pulling Marlowe as if he were a child, pulling him into the aft cabin with one hand while he held the torch aloft with the other.

Marlowe tried again to raise the sword, tried to drive it

through the pirate, and he managed to get his arm to move when he felt the deck disappear beneath him. He was falling, plunging down into the dark, and before he even realized that he was falling he stopped, slamming into the deck below.

His sword wrenched from his hand. He heard it clatter away in the dark. He rolled over. Above him was the square hatch through which he had been dropped, and beyond that the white painted deckhead in the great cabin.

Then the hatch was filled with LeRois's huge frame. Marlowe rolled out of the way, and the pirate jumped down after him. He heard the man's boots hit the deck a foot away, and his only thought was to get his sword.

He rolled again, onto his stomach, and looked up, waiting for LeRois to run him through. They were in the hold, the lowest part of the *Wilkenson Brothers,* and the black space was now lit with the flames from LeRois's torch. The pirate was stamping off forward as if he did not know Marlowe was there.

Thomas pushed himself to his knees. His head was still spinning from the blow, his shoulders and one knee ached from the impact with the deck. The wound he had received when he first leapt aboard was bleeding again, but his thoughts were on nothing but his sword and LeRois's back.

He could just see his sword, all but lost in shadow. He clenched his teeth, shuffled over and picked it up, then painfully stood.

LeRois was at the far end of the hold. He was bending over, holding the torch to a black pot on the deck. It sputtered and lit, like a little bonfire. He turned and lit another and another. Smoke poured from each as it took flame.

LeRois straightened and turned, squinting into the shadows. Thomas did not move.

"Barrett? Are you here, Barrett?" LeRois's voice was pleasant, as if welcoming a guest into his home. "We are in hell now, *mon ami,* and we will see which of us can last the longer. We will fight to see who rules here, eh?"

Marlowe crouched, held his sword in front of him. LeRois was a mad dog; he had to be killed. He took a step forward.

The hold was filling with smoke, yellow smoke, that made a halo around the pirate's torch. Thomas's eyes were burning and watering, his lungs ached. It was brimstone burning in those pots. LeRois had set brimstone on fire, and now the hold was filling with the sulfur smoke. He had indeed created his own hell, and now they would do battle to see who was prince of the underworld.

Marlowe knew he could not last long in that yellow fog, but neither could he leave LeRois to his own devices. He had to finish the pirate and go.

He made his way along the hold, his various aches and wounds all but forgotten in the energy gleaned from the pending battle. He moved toward the flaring light of the torch. He could no longer see LeRois through the smoke, but perhaps the bastard was still holding the thing. He held his hand out, feeling his way, unable to see more than a few feet in any direction.

"You have been haunting me, Malachias Barrett," the pirate called out from the fog. "Your spirit has been haunting me, but now the devil has made you flesh so that we can see who is to be *capitain,* eh? *Capitain* in hell."

The voice seemed to come from the direction of the flames, but Marlowe could not tell for certain. Still he kept moving toward the burning torch, the only reference in the dark and smoke-filled hold. Ten feet away. He paused and listened. He could not see LeRois. The torch did not move; it looked as if it might have been jammed in place. Perhaps LeRois was not there at all.

And then he heard a flurry behind him, a rustle, sensed a motion at his back. He spun around, sword up, horizontal, and out of the yellow smoke LeRois's weapon came down with the familiar shock and ring of steel on steel.

Marlowe twisted his blade aside, knocking LeRois's sword away, then stepped forward on the attack. He could just see the man now, shadows of a black beard and a swirling coat, the suggestion of wild eyes through the sulfur smoke.

Marlowe slashed away, but LeRois's blade was back, fend-ing him off. Marlowe swung again and again, wielding the sword like an ax, driving LeRois back. He could hear the old pirate's breath coming harder, realized that he was gasping as well, forced to take shallow breaths to avoid choking in that lethal atmosphere.

Here we are again, Barrett and LeRois, he thought. Both a little older and a little slower, and the *Vengeance* beneath them might not be the same as that of years before, but it was the same fight.

He had to kill LeRois and get out. He lunged, but his sword found only air. LeRois was gone.

Thomas stopped, crouched low, listened. He closed his eyes and was rewarded with a wave of relief from the burning sulfur. Overhead he could hear the muffled sounds of the men still locked in battle. He took a step back and felt his shoulder press against something. It felt like a cask. He could hear LeRois breathing, somewhere off in the smoke.

"Eh, quartermaster, you are still the devil with a sword, but can you live in hell as I can? Eh? Can you breathe, quartermaster? Can you see?"

"I can breathe, LeRois," Marlowe said, which was just barely true. "But you do not sound so good yourself. Perhaps you are not the devil you think you are. Perhaps you are just a drunk old man who is too weak to be a *capitain.*"

"*Merde!*" LeRois roared, and suddenly he emerged from the smoke, sword swinging as if he were trying to cut a swath through the fog, hoping that Marlowe was in the arc of his blade. Marlowe dodged the weapon, leaped across the deck, and this time it was he who lost himself in the smoke.

He heard LeRois coughing, gasping, and wanted desperately to cough himself, but he held back as long as he could. He shuffled forward, and when he could hold it no longer he doubled over, coughing and gasping and retching.

"I am coming for you now, quartermaster," LeRois shouted, croaking the words through his damaged throat. The hold was entirely engulfed. Marlowe could no longer see the burning pots of brimstone, and the torch fire was just a dull yellow light illuminating the thick gloom. He coughed again and held his sword up, and LeRois was on him once more.

There was less power in the pirate's strokes, and that was the only thing that saved Thomas's life, for he barely possessed the breath to defend himself. Thrust and parry, attack and fend off, the two men went back and forth, emerging and disappearing in the yellow smoke, coughing, wheezing.

Marlowe could hardly see through his watery eyes. He had no sense for what was forward and what was aft. He stumbled on something and almost fell, and as he recovered he waited for LeRois's blade to come through the smoke and finish him off, but it did not, and Marlowe was alone again in the yellow acrid hell.

"LeRois!" he croaked, then gagged. "LeRois, you stupid son of a whore, you drunken useless madman! You pathetic wretch!" If he could make him mad, furious, he might make a mistake, and then he could kill him and get back on deck before he passed out. "LeRois!"

Coughing from somewhere in the smoke, retching, and then LeRois's voice, slurred, faltering, "The devil, he has brought us here, and he will kill us both."

Marlowe blinked hard, looked in the direction from which the voice had seemed to come. There was a dancing light, like a ghost, like a spirit moving through the smoke-filled space. He blinked again. He could no longer tell if he was conscious or not, dead or alive. Perhaps he was already in hell. He was no longer afraid. He did not care.

And then from some back corner of his mind came the realization that the moving ghost was the torch. LeRois must have picked up the torch. He must be carrying it, and that meant that where the light was, so was LeRois.

Marlowe panted, coughed, and held his sword in front of him like a lance. He took a faltering step forward, and his foot came down on something soft. He bent at the knee and touched it. It was a hat. LeRois's hat. He picked it up and took a step toward the bobbing light, then another, stumbling toward the torch, trying to reach it before he passed out, before he fell for the last time.

The fire burned brighter as he ran, and suddenly he could see flames, actual flames, but LeRois was just a shadow, a dark outline in the yellow smoke. He paused, tensed, and then threw the hat at LeRois.

"*Merde!*" the dark shadow screamed, then twisted, and a blade cut through the smoke, the shadow slashing at whatever had hit it.

Marlowe charged. Two steps, and in the diffused light of the torch he could see the dark face of Jean-Pierre LeRois, his filthy cheeks streaked where the tears ran down. He saw LeRois blink and look up from the hat, confused by what was coming out of the smoke, and then Marlowe felt the point of his sword make contact with flesh and with all the strength remaining in his arms he shoved the blade in.

LeRois's eyes shot open, his mouth gaped wide, and he screamed, a long, prolonged howl. The torch fell from his grip, and he staggered back as Marlowe twisted the blade and dragged it free.

They were so close that Marlowe could smell LeRois, even through the sulfur, smell the sweat and the rum and the foul breath and corruption. He could see the dark blood erupting from his mouth as he fell. He watched, unable to move, unable to breathe as the man he feared most in the world collapsed onto the deck.

He took a step forward, leaned over, unable to believe what he was seeing. It was not possible that LeRois was dead, yet here was his sword, Thomas Marlowe's sword, dripping with the pirate's blood.

And then suddenly LeRois gasped and choked and coughed up more blood that ran black down his cheeks and into his beard. He blinked and looked up at Marlowe with wide eyes, and then with a sound that was equal parts retching and coughing and screaming he rolled over and grabbed the torch and flung it away.

They were swallowed by the darkness again, the darkness

and the diffused yellow smoke from the sulfur pots, and out of the dark came the retching and the coughing as LeRois fought his last battle.

And then the torch flared and the light grew many times brighter. The yellow smoke was lit up from within, and Marlowe could see the wild death grin on LeRois's face, but there was still life in his eyes. He coughed and in a weak voice said, *"Cochon."*

From the center of the light Marlowe heard a crackling and a popping and hissing, the unmistakable sound of gunpowder burning. He felt his eyes go wide, despite the pain from the sulfur smoke. LeRois must have laid a powder train to the magazine. Of course he would. He would not have created his own hell without thinking of that.

"Oh, damn you!" he heard himself say, and at his feet the pirate laughed until he started to choke. Marlowe rammed his sword into the sling at his side and crouched low and raced back in the direction he had come. The ship was going to blow up. He had to get his men off. Did not know how long he had.

He plunged through the smoke, coughing, gasping, wasting his precious breath cursing LeRois. He stumbled on something and began to fall, arms flung out in front of him, hit something solid and caught himself. He was inches from whatever it was he had run into, but he could not see what it was. He ran his fingers over it. A stack of barrels. There had been no barrels aft that he could recall. He must have run in the wrong direction.

He felt his head spinning, felt his legs grow weak as the smoke overwhelmed him. He tried to stand, but he could not. His knees buckled, and he fell. He grabbed at the barrels for support, but they slipped from his weak hands and the next thing he knew his face was pressed against the deck and he was gasping and coughing.

But he was breathing. He was breathing clean air, or at least cleaner air than he had had in some time. Down next to the deck the smoke was not so thick. He felt himself revive, and he breathed deeply until he began to gag again. He crawled away, prayed it was the right direction.

Off to his right the fire flared and began to race along, illuminating the yellow fog. Marlowe got on his hands and knees and crawled faster. Could hear the hissing sound of burning powder.

As long as the fire was just consuming loose grains the powder would only burn. It was when it hit the tight-packed barrels that it would explode. He had until then to get his men off, and he did not know how long that would be. Minutes, if he was lucky, but it could just as easily be seconds.

He scrambled along, and now he could see LeRois's lifeless body illuminated by the fire he had started as his last act on earth. Surrounded by the glowing light, he looked as if he was being lifted up into heaven, which Marlowe very much doubted. It was a reference point, a landmark in the fog, and Marlowe scurried past.

The fire flared again, igniting something, and Marlowe leapt to his feet. He had to risk passing out. He had to get on deck fast.

He careened off a post, stumbled, kept running. He could see a motion in the smoke, a swirl of gray and yellow as the sulfur was sucked up overhead, and he knew that he had found the hatch. He leapt for the space, and his hand found the combing and he pulled himself up.

"Oh, Lord, help me!" he cried, trying to find the strength in his tired arms and aching lungs to pull himself up through the hatch. His hand touched something—the leg of the cabin table—and his fingers wrapped around it and he pulled himself out of the smoke-filled hold, out of that special hell that LeRois had laid along for them, and up into the great cabin.

The cabin was filled with smoke as well, but after the hold it seemed like the freshest of air, and Marlowe wanted to just collapse on the settee and breathe, just breathe. He took a staggering step aft, recalled that the ship was about to explode. How had his mind become so addled?

He turned and lurched out of the great cabin and down

the alleyway, careening off the cabin doors as he struggled to get to the waist. The door was open, and he stumbled out into the open space.

The old pirate ship was still burning, though not as bright now, and Marlowe's damaged eyes could see nothing but a few shapes moving about. The fight was over, apparently, but he did not know who had won. He tried to shout a warning, but all that came was coughing and retching.

"Marlowe! Marlowe, dear God!" It was Bickerstaff, standing in front of him. His face came in and out of focus, and he looked so very concerned.

"Bickerstaff . . . ," Marlowe managed to get out, and then broke into a coughing fit again.

"Marlowe, pray, sit! We have won the day!" Bickerstaff said, but Marlowe just shook his head and pointed feebly down. "Magazine . . . ," he said, ". . . fire . . ."

Bickerstaff stared at him as if not comprehending. Marlowe tried to summon the power to explain further, but Bickerstaff said, "The magazine is on fire?"

Marlowe nodded. It was all he could do.

"Shall we get the *Plymouth Prize* under way?"

Marlowe shook his head. No time for that, not by half. He glanced over at the guardship, still riding against the pirate's side. They would never save her. He pointed toward the other bulwark, the one closest to shore, and staggered toward it, hoping Bickerstaff would understand.

And he did. The teacher let go of Marlowe's arm and turned to the dark shapes in the waist that Marlowe guessed were his men. "The magazine is on fire!" he heard Bickerstaff shout. "Over the side! Everyone over the side! Throw the wounded over, we shall get them to shore! If you cannot swim, grab something that will float!"

Marlowe sensed the stampede to the side but could see no more than dark shapes rushing past, men carrying other men. He heard the pounding of bare feet and shoes on the deck, voices full of fear and pain, the cries of the wounded. He could still smell the sulfur, but mostly it was sweet night air, the most delicious sensation he had ever had. He paused by the main hatch and closed his eyes and just breathed.

And then he felt rough hands on his arms. He opened his aching eyes to see King James and Bickerstaff on either side of him, hustling him to the side of the ship. Men were leaping over the rail. He could hear splashing and shouting in the river below.

They reached the bulwark, and he heard Bickerstaff say, "Marlowe, can you swim? Isn't it odd that I don't know?"

But Marlowe did not know either. Can I swim? He could not recall.

He felt the deck heave under his feet, thought that he was going to pass out again. It was the strangest sensation, the solid deck moving thus. Wanted to comment on it, felt hands lift him up. Realized that the ship was about to explode.

"Dear God!" he shouted, regaining some of his senses. He put a foot on the pin rail and stood up, and on either side James and Bickerstaff did the same, then he launched himself out into the air.

He felt himself plunging down through the dark, and then the warm water was all around him, covering him, smothering him with its blackness.

And then the water was lit up like it was daytime, only much brighter than that, and the colors were brilliant reds and oranges, not the pale yellow of sunlight. He felt himself shoved through the water as if pushed by a giant hand.

He kicked and kicked again, and his head broke the surface and he gasped for air, that precious element. Flaming bits of the *Wilkenson Brothers* were falling all around him, splashing and sizzling in the water.

He could see things—people, wreckage, he could not tell—bobbing in the water, lit up by the great flames that were consuming the merchantman turned pirate. A night of fire, a night of death.

There was something beside him, floating, and he grabbed it. It was a section of a yard. The main topsail yard, he thought. He could see the footropes trailing off of it, a charred section of the sail still made fast by its robands. He held on as a child clings to its mother. Drifted until he felt sand scraping the bottom of his feet.

He drifted a few more feet and then realized that he could stand, so he began to walk for shore, pushing through the water, dragging the section of the yard behind him, because suddenly it was very important for him to save it from the flames.

At last he was in only a few inches of water and he could not pull the yard any farther, so he decided that it would be all right where it was. He just wanted to sit down for a moment, and then he would find Bickerstaff and King James and they could start cleaning all this up.

And then he was sitting. And then he was lying with his cheek pressed against the rough sand of the beach. He was very warm and comfortable. He felt himself sinking into the earth, and the darkness enveloped him like a blanket and then all thought just floated away.

It took him some time to realize that the voices were not in his head, that what he was hearing was not a dream. When he finally realized that he was indeed awake, he lay very still and listened and tried to reckon what was going on. He did not open his eyes.

His body ached as if he had not moved for some time. Where he was pressed into the sand he was still damp, but his face was warm and the parts of him exposed to the air were dry, and he guessed that it was daytime, a warm, sunny day. What day, he could not begin to imagine.

Then memories began to filter back of the last night that he could recall. He could still taste the sulfur in the back of his throat. He remembered the fight on the deck, the brimstone-filled hold, LeRois.

He opened his eyes and was greeted with a face full of sunshine that made him blink and turn away. He could feel the tears rolling down his cheeks, and he groaned out loud. He put a hand down in the warm sand and began to push himself up, and that made him groan even louder with the pain and the effort. At last he sat up and held his face in his hands.

"Here, sir!" he heard a voice call out, a voice that he did not recognize, so he ignored it. "Here's one still alive!"

He heard the soft sound of footsteps in the sand, getting closer. Guessed that he was the one they meant. He opened his eyes again and blinked, easing them into the full brunt of daylight. He let the tears run unimpeded down his cheeks.

At last he looked up. He was on the edge of the James River. It was a fine day, the sky blue and the sun warm, the few clouds overhead white and pleasing to the eye. It was all quite at odds with the way he felt.

Forty feet off the beach the charred bones of the former *Wilkenson Brothers* and the *Plymouth Prize* reached up from the brown water, skeletal hands from the grave, two enemies locked together in death. Wisps of smoke still rose from the black timbers. He could not see the *Northumberland* but guessed she was down there too. Half a cable length beyond that the burned stumps of the other pirate vessel's masts stuck up from the river like old pilings.

None of those things were a surprise, of course, now that he had pieced together his memories of the night.

What was a surprise was the man-of-war, anchored just beyond the farthest wreck, her lofty rig towering over the river, sails furled to perfection, her many gunports open, great guns run out. Colorful bunting flew from all her masts and yards. She did not look real.

He closed his eyes and then opened them again. The ship was still there.

He looked to his left. The beach was scattered with blackened pieces of hull and rigging. Men lay in clumps, some in the surf, some well up in the sand. It would take a closer inspection to see if they were alive or dead.

"You, there!" a voice called, and he looked to his right. A sailor was approaching him, pointing at him, and behind him came a gentleman with a long white wig and a walking stick and a sword at his side. Wearing a uniform of sorts.

"You there," the gentleman said again. "I am Captain Carlson of yon man-of-war, HMS *Southampton*. I am looking for the captain of HMS *Plymouth Prize*. The guardship."

"There is no more guardship."

The gentleman sighed, an exasperated sound. "Well, the captain of the former guardship, then."

"I am he."

"You are Captain Allair?"

"No."

"Well, then, sir, who are you?"

That was an interesting question. He almost said Malachias Barrett, but he did not. There was still the hope that Malachias Barrett was dead. Was he Thomas Marlowe? Would Governor Nicholson still call him that? He did not know if Wilkenson had told the governor the truth of his past. He did not know, after all that had happened, if he would be called a hero and praised for defeating LeRois, or called a pirate and hanged.

He answered the question truthfully.

"I have no idea."

Epilogue

As it turned out, he was Thomas Marlowe.

That at least was what Governor Nicholson called him, as did the burgesses who turned out in welcome when he and the remainder of the Plymouth Prizes were brought ashore at Jamestown. That, their second hero's welcome, far outstripped even their arrival back from Smith Island.

The praise was much thicker, of course, because it was spread over so many fewer men. Marlowe and Bickerstaff and King James were all there, and all were relatively unscathed due to the simple good fortune of their having been under water at the exact moment that the *Wilkenson Brothers* exploded.

Rakestraw was there too, though the better part of his right arm was not, having been hacked off by a cutlass in the last minutes of the fight. Only Bickerstaff's quick work with a tourniquet saved him from bleeding to death.

In addition to them, there were nineteen of the Plymouth Prizes remaining. Of the rest, only ten actual bodies were found. The rest, as well as those pirates who had remained aboard the new *Vengeance*, were at the bottom of the James or scattered around the shore of Hog Island. No parts large enough to warrant burial were ever found.

And they were all heroes, the survivors and the honored dead, the saviors of the tidewater. Those who came back were paraded through the countryside to Williamsburg, where they were each given a handsome reward, voted them by the Burgesses the day after the fight, and then toasted in the taverns up and down Duke of Gloucester Street.

No one ever asked Marlowe why he had abandoned the fight that first day, and Marlowe satisfied himself with the thought that if he had not, then they surely would have been defeated, having been tricked by LeRois into fighting him on his own terms. The beauty of that excuse was that it was genuinely true, even if it was not the real reason he had run away.

But no one ever asked, and Marlowe was smart enough not to offer an explanation unbidden.

He also learned, after his return to the world, another of the factors that had contributed to the Plymouth Prizes' victory over the pirates. Those men aboard the old *Vengeance*, after abandoning her to the flames, had not returned to the *Wilkenson Brothers* at all, but instead had gone ashore in an apparent attempt to find yet another home to sack. They had stepped right into the arms of Sheriff Witsen and Lieutenant Burnaby and the militia who had finally assembled and who were watching from the shore, trying to find a way to join in the fight.

The pirates surrendered with never a weapon raised, leaving those aboard the new *Vengeance* with fewer men to fight the Plymouth Prizes and providing the people of the tidewater with the kind of tangible end to the threat that only a good mass public hanging can provide.

Two weeks of celebration and sensational trials culminated in the largest crowd ever to gather for an execution in Virginia, where that sort of thing generally lacked the popularity it enjoyed in London. It was like Publick Times all over again, and Thomas Marlowe was very, very eager for it to end.

He knew that the questions would come sooner or later, the accusations would fly, and he wanted it to be sooner. He did not care to loiter around, letting his worries fester. If there was one thing that he had learned from LeRois, it was that the anticipation of the fight was at least as bad as the actual event.

But the questions did not come. The questions about his personal history, the questions about Elizabeth's background, the accusations concerning the death of Joseph Tinling. They were never asked.

Jacob Wilkenson was presumed to have been killed by the pirates, his body burned with the Wilkenson home. George Wilkenson had disappeared, the horse that he had been riding found near where the pirate ships had been anchored. As far as the governor knew or cared, Joseph Tinling had been murdered by a now dead slave, acting alone. A dead man, later identified as one Ripley, captain of the Wilkensons' river sloop, had been found beside a sack of items he had looted from the Wilkenson home.

There was no one else in Virginia who knew or cared about the history of Elizabeth Tinling, no one who would question the pedigree of so heroic and dangerous a man as Thomas Marlowe.

It was months after the fight, after the adulation had subsided and Marlowe was again just another wealthy planter going unmolested about his business, that he would finally admit to himself that Malachias Barrett was dead, that the man the tidewater recognized as Thomas Marlowe had risen pure from his ashes.

And when he was certain that that was true, he asked Elizabeth Tinling to marry him.

And Elizabeth Tinling said yes.

The wedding ceremony and subsequent supper at the Marlowe plantation was well attended, with the governor and the House of Burgesses there, as well as every other person of note in the tidewater, and their families.

The celebration went on for two days, which was a day and a half longer than Marlowe or Elizabeth would have preferred, but they did not think it would be neighborly to ask the people to leave, so they did not. Instead, King James, whose own marriage to Lucy a week before had caused considerably less fervor, sent Caesar and his assistants back to the wine cellar again and again to make certain that none of the guests ran dry.

It was some weeks after that that Thomas found himself alone with Francis Bickerstaff on the wide front porch of the plantation house. The evening was cool, the first signs of summer stepping aside, yielding to autumn its rightful place. Little bursts of red highlighted the green oaks, and the fields behind the house were studded with the short brown stalks of cut tobacco. From the big tobacco barn they could smell the rich aroma of the curing leaves.

"Well, Thomas," Bickerstaff said at last, "it would seem that your metamorphosis is complete."

Marlowe turned and smiled at him. It was the first that his friend had said on the subject, and he knew it would be the last. "So it would seem. When LeRois died, and Ripley and the Wilkensons, I reckon they took Malachias Barrett down with them."

"And I think it safe to say, between us two, that Master Barrett died an honorable death. A death in defense of true honor." Bickerstaff raised his glass.

"True honor. And an end to Master Barrett."

He had come to this place and he had re-created himself, taken his old self from the woods, planted it in the rich earth of Virginia, and raised himself up from the dirt into something new.

After all, he thought, what is this place, this New World, this America, if it is not a place of redemption?